the Pleasure Protocol

DARCY ROMAINE
KAT ALEXANDER

To those photos of a lingerie-clad Evan Rachel Wood perched on Mads Mikkelsen's lap, thanks for launching a thousand kinks and inspiring our dirty little minds to write this.

The Pleasure Protocol was originally available on Kindle Vella and has received minor updates to be published in novel format.

This book is for mature audiences. It contains <u>explicit</u> sexual content between consenting adults, including consensual non-consent, teacher/student roleplay, and intense objectification (specifically, being treated and referred to as an actual object). There are mentions of parent death, a mention of domestic violence, and a mention of anti-sex-work language.

Take care and enjoy!

sir meets pet

NIKOLAI ZAITSEV HAS BEEN USING the Calypso Escorts service for years.

As the CEO of Zaitsev Security, the largest cybersecurity company in the world, he doesn't have time or energy for dating or relationships. He finds paying for companionship easier than trying to keep a partner happy or pawing off suitors who are more interested in the money than him. It's a transaction, a finite moment of intimacy. No strings, no worries, and no heartbreak on either end.

That's appealing to a businessman such as himself.

He will admit he's a man of habit, which is why Elijah has been his only escort for several years. Elijah is a brat of the highest order, but he knows Nikolai, knows what he likes in a date, and knows what he likes in the bedroom.

Their arrangement has worked fine until Nikolai texts him one Monday afternoon to ask what Elijah will wear to the charity function they're attending in five hours.

He sets his phone down to get back to work, but not even a minute later, it lights up with an incoming call from Elijah.

He furrows his brow, alarm bells going off in his head at the immediate phone call in response to a routine text. "Elijah. Fashion trouble?"

Elijah's laugh is a higher pitch than usual. "Nikolai, darling, how are you?"

His eyes narrow as the bells get louder. "I was fine until you called me sounding like that."

"Well. What if I told you a very handsome gentleman has swept me off my feet, and I'm quitting the business? And also, we're in Vegas until tomorrow, and"—the rest rushes out so quickly Nikolai barely catches it all—"I couldn't possibly make it back to Chicago tonight to be your date?"

Irritation flashes through him. He swivels in his chair and rests his elbows on his knees. "Elijah. You're not serious right now." He can't be. He *can't* be. Tonight is too damn important.

"Darling, I got so caught up in the beauties of love and Las Vegas that I completely lost track of, well, everything." Elijah makes that same little whine as when he's been bad and his ass is about to face the consequences of Nikolai's hand. "I really am sorry."

Fuck. Nikolai rubs his forehead, a headache building in his temples. Another reason he hires from Calypso is to guarantee dates to functions where the lack of one would raise irksome eyebrows. Now he's stuck.

"I'm happy you're happy, Elijah, but this is shitty to do to a long-standing client. It's not professional. Though, it sounds like you don't need to worry about that anymore." He groans. "What the fuck am I supposed to do now?"

"I promise I'll make it up to you. You could... hmm, let's see." Elijah snaps his fingers. "I could ask my best friend, Corinne. She's worked at Calypso for years. She's charming and gorgeous, and you will love her."

Nikolai closes his eyes, his head falling to rest on the back of his chair. "You know how important this event is, Elijah." He likes to ease into a new companionship with a lower-stakes event, until he's confident they're a proper fit. "Are you sure she's the one for it?"

"She's the best in the business. She'll dazzle all the suck-ups you hate, and"—a smile lights up his voice—"she's great in bed. I brought her in for a threesome with a female client who'd never been with a woman, so I've got firsthand experience. I promise you, Nikolai! You will not be disappointed!"

He doesn't have much of a choice, does he? He could call Calypso's owner, his long-time friend, Margot, but he can't afford to wait to be matched with whoever might be available on such short notice.

"Alright," he sighs. "You're sure she can make it? We're down to the wire here."

"I know, but what are best friends for?"

Elijah gives Nikolai her number and another apology before leaving him to his own devices.

Nikolai stares out his office windows, the view of Lake Michigan and the other high-rises in the Loop as good as invisible as his brain works through the logistics of switching companions for tonight—and for every other event Nikolai has on the books.

He looks at the number he hastily scribbled on his desk notepad and takes a deep breath before picking up the phone again.

It rings so many times he's preparing to leave a voicemail when she finally answers. "Hello, this is Corinne." Her voice is pleasant but a bit breathless, no doubt from her racing to the phone.

"Hello, my name is Nikolai Zaitsev. Elijah gave me your number. He was supposed to accompany me to an event this evening but has canceled last minute. He provided your information as an alternative."

"Oh, Elijah," she sighs. "I guess he didn't fly back from Vegas last night after all. I'm sorry, Mr. Zaitsev, but I have plans this evening, and I don't take last-minute clients. I need at least forty-eight hours' notice."

Fucking hell, Elijah. "Which I would have been happy to provide, had it been provided to me." Deliberating his options, he stands and crosses to the window, traffic crawling along forty stories below him. He sighs. He doesn't love this move or being that guy, but it's a tactic that works.

When in doubt, throw money at the problem.

"Whatever your regular rate is, I'll triple it."

"Triple? My fee is higher than Elijah's. That's a lot of money for one night."

She's damn right, but it's not like he can't afford it. "Which should express that while I'm happy Elijah is happy, I am also very inconvenienced."

"I'm going to a concert tonight. So you see, it's not something I can cancel."

Fuck. "Pick any other night of the tour in any location of your choice, and you will be there with the full VIP experience: front-row seats, backstage passes, hotel, and flight."

"But—"

"Including your friend or date."

It takes her a moment to respond. "What's so important that you're willing to spend that much money for a date with a woman you've never even seen, let alone met?"

He pinches the bridge of his nose, that headache getting worse. "I am the guest of honor at a charity function tonight, and there will be... attention on me. Some of the attendees are people I deal with in business but generally do not like, and if I go alone, I will almost certainly insult someone because..." He clears his throat. Is he about to share something this personal with a complete stranger? What do they say about desperate times?

"That sort of attention makes me uncomfortable," he continues. "And when I get uncomfortable, I am less tactful than my position demands. I don't want to ruin the night for the charity, so I need a buffer, badly. And, on top of all that, Elijah says you're the best in the business."

"A buffer," she repeats. "That *is* a role I play sometimes." She pauses. "Is your profile with Calypso up to date?" The service keeps a profile on every client—complete with photos, their preferences, dislikes, limits, and sexual health results. It's a beast to fill out, but an escort will have access to everything, from a client's favorite food to their favorite position.

He tries not to let himself hope this could work out. "Yes, it's all up to date. I made sure of it at the new year."

"I'm sending mine to you now." His phone buzzes with a link from her number. "Oh, look, the devil himself is calling me. Glance over that while I deal with him for a minute, hm? You should at least know who you're asking out on a date."

"Thank you, I'll do that." When the line clicks over, he pulls the phone away from his ear, putting it on speaker so he can look at her profile but hear when she comes back on.

Her photo appears first, and Elijah was right. With dark hair, full lips, and a heart-shaped face, she's beautiful. His eyes quickly scan the page: she's twenty-nine years old, a trained artist, and has lived in Chicago her whole life, just like him. She's open to most sexual activities and has experience as both a dominant and submissive—his eyebrows arch—though it says her complete kink limit list is available upon request.

He's scanning over her limits—no lasting marks, amongst a few others—when she switches over.

"Elijah's always been flighty, but even this takes the cake for him."

He laughs, a tiny breathy thing, more a release of tension than amusement. "You see my dilemma, then. I wouldn't have predicted this from him at all."

"Yes, and I'm sorry he left you in a lurch. Since this is so last minute, do you just want a date for the event? Or do you want private time afterward? Companionship? Sex?"

He takes his phone off speaker mode.

"The event is my priority, but I'd like everything if you're amenable." She's gorgeous; he won't give up the chance to take her to bed. "I can have one of the standard Calypso contracts adjusted with my proposed rates and sent to you in the next half hour. If you choose to agree, of course."

Corinne hums. "You're lucky Billie Eilish is playing in LA next month, where it's nice and warm."

Nikolai both laughs and breathes a sigh of relief.

Then she adds, "And that your profile photo is quite dashing."

He leans back with a lazy smile. Maybe Elijah's faux pas won't be such a disaster after all.

* * *

A few hours later, Nikolai is standing in his foyer, waiting for his new companion's text. He's making last-minute adjustments to himself—retying the silk bow tie, straightening the shawl collar of his oxblood velvet tuxedo, smoothing his black hair one final time—when Corinne lets him know she's downstairs. He shoots off a reply and heads out of the apartment with his coat in hand. A private elevator runs exclusively to his floor, but meeting guests in the lobby is easier.

And when he steps out of the elevator, she's difficult to miss.

The picture on her profile was nothing compared to the

vision before him: deep brown eyes and full red lips. She's in a cream halter dress with a cinched waist and a dramatic slit at the thigh. The collar is secured by a cape split down the back and draped over her shoulders. Her dark hair, styled loose and wavy like a starlet of old, brushes down her back. And there's the barest peek of thigh-high stocking covering pale skin as she steps up to meet him.

She immediately puts her hand on his arm and kisses his cheek like they've done this a hundred times before. "Hello, Nikolai."

He returns the kiss, pulling back with a smile. Even in heels, she only comes up to his chin. "Corinne," he says, unable to stop himself from giving the curves of her body another once-over. "You look beautiful."

"Thank you. I have a very important date tonight." She gives him a secret smile. "Who apparently cleans up very handsomely."

He nods his thanks. "If you're ready, I'll help you with your coat."

It's pale gray and fitted with a fur collar and cuffs. After he assists her, he shrugs on his own and offers his arm, then leads her outside to the black Range Rover waiting at the curb. It's January in Chicago, frigid and unforgiving. But he's never minded it; even if he's spent all forty-one years of his life here, he's still Russian. He'd be disappointed in himself if it *did* bother him.

He opens the door for her, and when he joins her on the heated leather seats on the other side, his driver, Adrian, takes off.

"If you don't mind, I'd like to set my expectations for tonight."

"Of course. That's exactly what you should be doing."

He settles himself, one ankle propped on the opposite knee.

"I need someone good with small talk and can navigate the brown-nosers and rich investors who think they know what they're talking about but do not. Witty and likable, but also knows how to exit a conversation gracefully." He smiles ruefully to himself. "I would prefer you to be slightly less of a flirt than Elijah always was, though I knew him long enough to know that was just his nature."

Corinne laughs. "There's no controlling that man, and I'm sure you know that even more intimately than I do. Alright, small talk, wrangling incompetent suck-ups, and no flirting. The last one is easy when my date looks the way he does." She looks him up and down quickly, but obviously, so there is no mistaking her intent.

But then she's right back to business. "Anything else? Anyone I should know so I can say, 'Oh, Mrs. Packard, I've heard so much about you!' and win you brownie points?"

He taps his fingers on his knee. "I make it a point not to know any of the guests too personally. Most hope to talk business, and anything seen as special treatment encourages them. But playing up the devoted-date aspect can't be bad. Make me look good to the old ladies, at the very least."

Nikolai pauses for a moment before continuing. "To be frank, Corinne, I donate to this charity because they help first-generation kids of immigrants, and that's important to me. But it also means I receive a lot of attention as a thank you." He clears his throat. "Which I do not care for."

Her brows pinch together, and she nods. "That makes sense. I'm sure they appreciate your generosity, but I understand how that might feel overwhelming."

He shakes his head. "It's not generosity. It's an obligation." His tone is sharp. Fulfilling that obligation is the least he can do, but it's not generosity.

"Oh," she says softly. "Alright. Well then, we'll try to steer clear of that attention, hm?"

"Thank you," he says, appreciating that she doesn't object like many others when he mentions obligations.

"Now, for tonight," he continues, "I typically enjoy PDA with my partners. Nothing grotesque, but physical affection is the norm. Circumspect but also obvious."

He slides a little closer, draping his arm over the seat, enough to play with the shoulders of her coat. Part of him wishes she'd taken it off for the drive. Her skin looked so tempting in the lobby, and he'd like to feel it beneath his fingers. "I tend to use pet names," he says, "so is there anything you'd rather not be called? Any areas you don't want to be touched, anything off-limits?"

She leans toward him, allowing his fingertips to brush against her throat. It's just as soft as he imagined. "Any pet name is fine. I don't like sexual groping in public unless the particular event calls for it, but I'm open besides that."

"Excellent. Sounds like we'll do well."

"Elijah assured me we would."

He huffs a laugh. "He was never overmuch one for rules." He looks her over, his perusal frank and assessing. "He recommended you so highly, I have to wonder if you're the same."

"We'll have to find out, won't we?" She smirks before sliding a manicured hand over his thigh.

It's been weeks since he's had anything more than his own hand to keep him company, but one touch from Corinne is enough to make his breath stutter and his cock twitch. He'd like nothing more than to sample what's in store later tonight, but then the car smoothly pulls to a stop.

Damn.

Straightening, he looks out the window and takes a deep breath to calm the fire in his blood. They've arrived at the

Waldorf Astoria, and he needs to keep his wits about him if he's going to survive the night.

She grabs his arm and turns that gorgeous smile his way. "Hey," she says softly. "We've got this. We'll charm their pants off, hm?"

He chuckles and tucks his finger under her chin. "Just *my* pants, Corinne."

"Of course." Her gaze slips to his mouth. "Just as soon as this gala is over." She kisses his jaw before whispering in his ear. "That's a promise, Nikolai."

For the first time he can remember, he can't wait to head inside. If only so they can leave, and he can properly get his hands on this exquisite woman.

a formidable companion

NIKOLAI

NIKOLAI HELPS Corinne out of the car and takes her inside, where they're ushered into a sizable gilded ballroom. And it's already crowded.

He rests his hand at the small of her back, a thrill from the touch zipping up his spine. The placement tells everyone in this room that this stunning woman is his. At least for tonight. "Can I get you a drink, Corinne?"

"Oh, a glass of champagne would be great."

Nikolai nods and heads toward the bar to order her drink and a scotch, neat, for himself. He finds her just where he left her, but already chatting with Simon McHoy, who no doubt swooped down upon the first beautiful woman he found alone. Of all the people Nikolai hates running into at these things, McHoy is in the top five—a slimy, disingenuous snake of a man, who has never heard the word 'no' and believed it.

"Nikolai," Corinne says when she sees him, reaching for him and her drink. She wraps her arm around his waist and turns back to McHoy. "I've just met Mr. McHoy—"

"I told you you can call me Simon, sweetie," McHoy replies. Although Corinne's smile doesn't falter one bit, the muscles of her back tighten at the pet name. Nikolai pulls her closer. "Didn't realize this gal had a lucky gentleman with her, Zaitsev." McHoy extends his hand. "And it's the man of the hour himself."

Nikolai begrudgingly disentangles himself from Corinne to shake it. "Not every woman standing alone is there for the taking, McHoy." The urge to wipe his hand on his trousers is strong, and only many years of practice keep him from giving in to the impulse.

Corinne laughs softly, wrapping her arm around him again. "Nikolai was just being sweet like always and getting me a drink. Thank you, darling." There's adoration in her eyes when she looks up at him, and if he didn't know the truth, he would believe it was genuine.

Before he can even respond, McHoy is already butting in. "You know he's the richest man in Chicago?" He elbows Nikolai. "Or maybe she's well aware, eh, Zaitsev?" He leans in and whispers, "The gold diggers are always the prettiest."

Irritation flares within him. Even with Nikolai's own history with 'gold diggers,' Corinne shouldn't be subjected to this. Not when she's here because of him. He tucks her behind his body, putting space between her and McHoy before telling him precisely what he can do with his unwanted opinions. "I would—"

"Do I look like the kind of *gal* who needs a man's money, Simon?" Corinne asks, stopping Nikolai in his tracks.

Nikolai looks back. She is the very picture of self-assurance and confidence, perfectly poised with one brow raised in question. Her smile is amused, but her eyes scream murder. He doesn't know how he expects McHoy to react, but the son of a bitch surprises him by barking in laughter.

"No, I suppose not!" He's still chuckling as he pats Nikolai's elbow. "Your girl is a trip. You know, I would love to get together some—"

"Oh, Nikolai, darling," Corinne says, pointing toward the front of the room. "There's my friend Samantha; we should go say hello." She nods to their companion. "It was such a pleasure to meet you, Simon. I hope to see you again soon." And then she's steering him away before McHoy even has a chance to respond.

"What a fucking asshole," Nikolai murmurs and Corinne relaxes against him. He stops her once he's confident they're far enough that McHoy won't follow them. Turning her to face him, he places a knuckle under her chin and directs her gaze to his own. "Are you alright?"

She smiles wryly. "If I wilted every time a man was gross toward me, Nikolai, I wouldn't have lasted a day in this business." She brushes a piece of lint from his lapel. "But I appreciate you asking."

He scoffs, eyebrows drawing together. She's a saint, putting up with this kind of boorish behavior on a regular basis. "I know I asked for charm, but never feel like you have to be charming to assholes for my sake, Corinne. That's not fair to you."

Tilting her head, Corinne regards him for a moment before responding. "Alright." Her face grows serious. "Though sometimes as a woman it's easier to deflect and distract than to take them head-on." Then she taps her finger against his chest. "And I appreciate when a handsome gentleman steps in to help."

He smiles. "I tried my best, but you beat me to it. As for what he said—"

She shakes her head with a smile. "I already knew about the extent of your wealth, Nikolai. I make it a habit to learn about my clients so I know how to meet their needs, even when they book last minute." She winks. "Funny that he had snide things to say about gold-digging women when he practically vibrated at being in your presence. Seemed like quite a bit of projection, if you ask me. Now…" She grabs his arm and pulls him toward the left side of the room, "who shall we say hello to next?"

Well, isn't his date astute? And, as it turns out, exceptionally good at her job.

She's attentive in a different way than Elijah was, less concerned with making a joke or slipping in a flirty comment than with turning on the charm. As soon as Nikolai makes his introductions, she steps in, making the small talk he's always hated, steering conversations as necessary. He can't help but find himself as charmed by her as the other party guests, which is unexpected.

She leans against him as they mingle, brushing her fingers along his arm, holding his hand, whispering in his ear before pressing a kiss right below it. And it's easy to reciprocate, keeping his hand on her waist, kissing her temple, or lightly dragging his fingers up and down her arm at dinner.

She's perfect. It's never gone so smoothly with one of his 'dates.' He dislikes unfavorable comparisons between partners as a general rule, but he can't stop thinking about how different this evening is with her on his arm instead of Elijah. She's the perfect mix of sweet and charming without ever crossing a line.

A good girl, he thinks, smirking into the dregs of his scotch.

Once dinner and dessert are finished and most of the speeches are out of the way, the president of the organization is introduced to close.

"Thank you to everyone who has attended tonight. We would not be able to continue our work without your help. Our tenth anniversary marks our biggest drive yet, and I am honored by your amazing generosity. I would, of course, be remiss not to thank one donor in particular."

Nikolai's gut suddenly churns in discomfort. It's not that

he's uncomfortable in the spotlight; he's a renowned business-man, for God's sake.

"Ten years ago, we were working out of my apartment and scraping by to help kids here in our city. Then one day, we received a call from an angel who wanted to donate *fifty million dollars*. Now, we are a nationwide organization and help hundreds of thousands of first-generation kids each year. And our numbers continue to grow. We couldn't have gotten this far this quickly without the help of Nikolai Zaitsev, our biggest donor and advocate year after year and tonight's guest of honor. He politely begged off an award or speech, but please stand, Nikolai, so we can properly thank you."

Corinne squeezes his hand and brings her mouth to his ear. "You've got this. Imagine they're applauding you for being a cybersecurity genius instead of a philanthropist."

It's such a surprising suggestion that he huffs in laughter, meaning he's already smiling as he stands. Corinne is still holding his hand as the applause starts, and because he has nothing to lose, he does exactly as she suggests. He'd never say he's a self-made man—his family had money, after all—but he is proud of his business and the work he's accomplished. People acknowledging that instead of a donation when fifty million dollars is pennies to him is much easier to swallow.

He gives a quick wave, nods to the president in thanks, and sits down to listen to the closing statement.

"You killed it," Corinne whispers. "You looked like a natural."

Did he? Huh. Elijah *was* right about her.

"Thank you, Corinne."

When the speech is finished, she asks, "Now that all that is over, do you want to head out?"

He thinks about what leaving means: escaping the crowd, yes, but also taking her back to his apartment, getting to know her in a completely different way. A welcome distraction if he's ever heard one.

"Yes," he whispers, trailing his fingers along the back of her neck, delighting in her resulting shiver.

Corinne yawns, hiding it behind her hand. "Hmm, are you almost ready?" she asks, just loudly enough for their half of the table to hear. She rubs his knee under the table. "I don't want to cut the guest of honor's night short, but I've had such a long day."

He kisses her cheek. "No, darling. You're tired; let's go home."

She sags slightly, playing off her relief, and damn, she's good at this. "You're the absolute best."

He kisses her cheek again. "Anything for you."

They say their goodbyes and grab their coats, and she takes his hand in hers. It takes a while to make it outside with people stopping them to say goodbye, but she does a damn good job of keeping things short and moving them toward the door. When they finally climb inside his waiting vehicle, she releases a deep exhale, her hand finding his again immediately. "How are you feeling? How did it go?"

"I'm surprisingly great, Corinne. Thank you. And you were... perfect." It's an understatement, truly. The night was a triumph, and she certainly got him through the worst of it. He kisses her hand. "If I had a list of events for the next few months, how likely would you be available? I'd like to make this recurring."

"I do have other regular appointments, but I can usually move things around with enough notice." She smiles. "You know, triple rate and concert getaway aside, I really did enjoy being your date tonight. I'd be happy to come with you when-ever I can." She looks down, then back up, gazing at him through her lashes. "Would you still like me to come over?"

He hums deep in his chest and smooths his hand over her hair, contenting himself with this slight touch until he can get his hands all over her properly. "I'd like that very much, Corinne." He relaxes the farther they get from the gala, his focus shifting to this lovely woman before him. "You are beautiful in that gown, but..." He trails off, looking her up and down. "I'm sure you'll be stunning out of it."

She raises her brows, a pleased little grin curling up the corners of her lips. She slides her other hand along his thigh, up and down, a bit higher each time. "I promise you won't be disappointed." She gets his earlobe between her teeth and tugs it gently.

Nikolai grips the back of her neck, squeezes tenderly, and pulls her back. "Whereas I," he tells her, nipping at her bottom lip, "can guarantee *you* won't be disappointed."

She kisses him, a hot, fierce press of lips as she cradles his face with her hands. And damn, it's good. Her mouth, her tongue. The way she moans so softly. She hooks her leg over his lap and straddles him, grabbing his hands and sliding them up her thighs where her dress is split. "You remember our discussion over email?" she asks. "My limits. Rough is okay, but no marks."

"I remember," he breathes, rubbing his hands along her inner thighs, making her sigh.

"Thought about these hands all night." She grinds against his lap. "Every time you touched me."

He snaps her garter against her leg, tracing the edges of her stockings where they meet her thighs. He wants his mouth on them, wants to make the silk damp and clingy. "Is that so, darling? And what else did you think about?"

"How big they are." She rubs her hand over his. "How long your fingers are." She meets his eyes. "How good they'll feel inside me."

He smirks, trailing his hands up to the crease of her thighs. "I am *very* good with my fingers, sweet thing. They're very dexterous."

She lets out a whimper, her hips rolling upward, like she's trying to coax his hand to her center. Mouthing at his throat, she tugs at the corner of his bow tie to untie it. "I heard you like pretty underthings."

Like is an understatement. Nothing does it for him more than a beautiful person in beautiful lingerie. "I do," he says, trailing his fingertips back to the edge of her stockings.

"And naughty little things." She gently scrapes her teeth against his throat before pulling back and looking at him with big, wide eyes. "Is that what you want from me, Nikolai?"

"Oh, I like every kind of pretty thing. Elijah is naughty and can't change it. I'd like you however you prefer, though I understand that is... an interesting desire in this situation." He arches an eyebrow at her, tracing circles on her inner thighs. "What do you prefer to be?"

Corinne widens her legs, inviting his touch. "I'm a switch, so I like lots of different things. Given the chance, I like to see what dynamics happen naturally. But if I can tell you a secret," she says with a sly grin before leaning toward his ear. "I've wanted to call you 'sir' twice in the last five minutes."

He meets her confession with a feral smirk, just this side of possessive, thrilled with this new knowledge and eager to hear her say it in pleasure. His hand slides around her hip and grabs a handful of her ass. "Then it sounds like we've figured out how to begin."

The car pulls to a stop, and he slides her carefully off his lap before offering his hand to help her out of the vehicle. "Shall we, pet?"

desperate little thing

NIKOLAI

NIKOLAI LEADS Corinne into his private elevator, and she is *on* him as soon as the doors are closed. Kissing him, grabbing his ass, pressing herself against him. He seizes her wrists and backs her against the wall.

"Desperate little thing, aren't you? So eager. Like you haven't been fucked properly in ages." He leans in, biting at her ear. "Don't worry," he whispers. "I'll fix that for you."

She moans. "Yes, I want it. Want you, sir."

A shiver washes over him, and he immediately wants to hear that word on her lips again. His attention settles on the lovely woman before him, and he smiles wickedly. "Of course you do, pet. You're a smart girl. You know I'll take care of you, don't you?"

She nods, still locked in his hold on her wrists. "Yes, sir, I do know."

He lets her go when the elevator doors open, standing back just enough that she can slide out from between him and the wall. "After you."

She glides into the small hallway between the elevator and

the door to his apartment, an extra level of security just in case someone unapproved makes it this far.

"Keep going, right up to the door," he says. Her hips sway enticingly before she stops at the threshold, whirling to face him as he comes up behind her. "Did I say turn around?" He puts his hands on her hips and spins her, pressing her against the door and pinning her with his hips.

She gasps, and he's so close he can feel her lungs expand. "No, sir. I'm sorry."

"Hmm." Boxing her in with his arms, he opens his door, then nudges her forward. He unties the sash of her coat and slips it off her shoulders. "Living room's straight ahead." Then he takes his off as well. "Bedroom's the open door down the hall. Would you like a drink?"

"A drink would be nice, thanks. I'll take whatever you're making for yourself."

He pours them both a glass of pinot grigio and stops in the bedroom doorway. She's slipped her heels off, her dress pooling at her feet as she takes in the space. His tastes run modern, creams and tans and sharp lines. But what does she like?

He hands her a glass before walking toward the dresser to remove his cufflinks. "Up to your standards?"

Her eyebrows lift, and she takes a sip of wine. "I need the full experience before I can give my final review."

Nikolai hums again, removing his tie and jacket before rolling up his sleeves. When he returns, he drags a finger across her shoulder and circles her once before putting his finger under her chin and raising it. "And what does the full experience consist of, I wonder?"

She looks up at him. "Hopefully sucking you off and then getting fucked out of my mind, sir." She angles her head with a grin. "But you're in charge."

He has to give it to her. She knows what she wants. He likes that she's telling him, that she isn't playing too much of a role with him. She still is; it's the nature of their situation, and he doesn't mind. But he likes that she's taken him at his word.

He smirks at her, devilish and calculating. "Oh, is that all?" He plucks lightly at her dress and sets her glass aside. "Then you'd best lose this lovely gown, pet. We don't need to ruin it."

Corinne turns, scooping her hair up and over one shoulder. "Unzip me, please?"

He trails his fingers along her back before he pulls down the zipper.

Facing him again, she slips the dress off her shoulders and lets it fall to the floor, revealing her beautiful lingerie—stockings and a matching garter belt and underwear set.

She cocks her hip to the side. "Like this, sir?"

Fucking hell, but she's stunning. It takes everything in him to step away and lay her gown over the chair, to come back and take his time to circle her. To just enjoy the beauty before him and not rush it. He keeps his hands in his pockets to hide their shaking.

The smooth cream of her skin is highlighted beautifully by the blush and champagne of her lingerie, the pink just a shade or two lighter than the dusty pink of her—*God*—pierced nipples. He hasn't even gotten his hands on her yet, and he's already salivating for a taste of her. He wants to lick along the line of her stockings, feel her soft breasts in his hands, run his fingers under the delicate lace resting against her ass.

A pretty thing all wrapped up in pretty things, just for him. Delightful.

He waits until she starts to fidget, a minor twitch of her fingers, before he finally speaks. "Yes, that'll do, sweet thing." He spreads his feet and removes his hands from his pockets to slowly undo his belt. "Now, why don't you come over here and cross item number one off that wishlist of yours?"

She drops to her hands and knees and crawls across the few feet between them, her eyes on him the whole time. It shocks the hell out of him, but he can't say he minds the initiative. He keeps his face impassive, trying to gauge her reactions, but she's too good. Of course she is. It's her job to keep her visible feelings in line with her clients' wishes.

As Elijah learned, Nikolai wants to know if someone is really enjoying something. So maybe he's a little heavier on the feigned disinterest than usual right now. But he has to be because otherwise, he would lose his mind over this gorgeous woman.

She rises onto her knees and unbuttons and unzips his pants. His cock is a hard line against his underwear, and she rubs him slowly through the fabric.

Corinne hesitates for a moment, her hand still rubbing him, and a little wrinkle forms between her brows like she's considering something. "I always use condoms for penetration," she finally says, her gaze finding his, "but do you want me to use one for oral?"

He tips her chin up gently with one finger. "Whatever makes you feel most comfortable, Corinne. I won't object."

"I just..." She leans into his finger until he catches on and opens his palm, and she nuzzles against it. "... want to taste you."

He pets her and watches with rapt attention as she closes her eyes against his touch. As she luxuriates in it, basks in it, as she takes a moment for herself in the midst of bringing him pleasure. Her eyes flit open, and she kisses his palm before returning to the task at hand.

"God, look at you," she breathes as she pulls out his cock. She wraps her fist around him and strokes up his length. "Had me focused on your hands all night when this was hiding in your trousers." She looks up at him with raised brows and a barely concealed smirk.

His hands clench at the feel of her skin on him, and he lets out a shaky breath. "My hands are far more dexterous. Good for more than just a couple of things." He tangles those hands in her hair, tugging ever so slightly. "Go on, then," he says, voice deeper than before. "Show me how impressed you are."

She keeps her eyes on his as she mouths at the head of his cock, slowly laving it with her tongue before licking up the entire length. It's torturous how unhurried she is, taking her pretty time as he aches with need. It's been a long time since Elijah last did this, and he hasn't been with anyone else since.

By the time she finally slips his dick into her mouth, letting out a little hum as she does, he groans, unable to help the push of his hips.

He runs his hands through her hair. "You look good like this, pet," he croons, slowly dropping the indifferent front. He believes in giving credit where credit is due, after all. "Your mouth is heavenly. Or maybe sinful? Are you an angel or a devil, I wonder?" He strokes her face, tracing her lips where they're stretched wide around his cock. "Are you a good girl? Or are you bad, hm?"

Pulling off, she chases after his thumb, biting it before glancing up. "A little bit of both, sir, if I'm being honest." She smiles at him before slipping her mouth over his cock again.

"A little of both, huh? Well, it is fun to be bad sometimes, isn't it? And you may be a good girl, but you're not a *nice* girl, are you?"

Corinne moans at that, relaxing her throat and taking him down to the hilt, until her nose is pressed against his groin. She swallows around him, letting out a muffled moan, and he swears softly under his breath. Then she raises his free hand to her hair, tightening it into a fist around her locks.

"Yeah?" he asks with a tug. "You want me to pull you onto my cock and fuck your pretty face?"

She nods vigorously before slowly bobbing her head up and down along the length of his cock. He gently matches her rhythm, watching as she sucks him off, then he speeds her up slightly, pulling just a bit more forcefully.

Her arm shifts, and his gaze follows it down—she's reaching into her underwear and touching herself, whimpering around his length. He cocks an eyebrow, smirking. "Bad girl, indeed. You need to touch yourself that desperately? Couldn't even ask first?"

She sits back. "I'm sorry, sir. May I touch myself?"

"You wanna touch yourself, pet?" He takes a hand from her hair to thumb her bottom lip, spreading the spit he finds there until she's messy. "Alright then. You can touch yourself." He grabs her by the hair again and shakes her head gently. "But *I* make you come. Understood?"

She groans, nodding. "Yes, sir." He watches, enraptured, as her hips buck against her hand, as her brow furrows and her body tenses. She brings her mouth back to his cock with a moan, letting him hear and feel her pleasure as she sucks him again.

"Good girl," he says, thrusting lazily, taking his time. He could come like this, spill down her throat, make her choke on it. But he wants inside her too severely. Wants to find out how good her cunt feels, and he can't wait anymore.

He yanks her up by her hair and kisses her roughly as he walks her backward.

"On the bed," he growls, ready to sink inside his new pet.

indulge me?

CORINNE GRABS A CONDOM from her purse and hands it to him before following his order and lying back against the pillows. He strips, then stalks toward the bed, eyes hot as they rake over her in all that beautiful lingerie.

"God, you're stunning. Spread your legs for me, sweet thing. Let me see how wet you got for me." He's got a hand wrapped around his cock, stroking it as he kneels on the bed.

Her heavy-lidded gaze drinks him in, and she pulls her panties to the side, spreading the lips of her cunt open for him to look his fill. "Do you see what you do to me, sir?"

Damn, she's got his number already. The lingerie next to her slick cunt is almost too much to bear. "I do, pet," he manages to choke out. "All from sucking my cock. What a good girl you are for me." He tears open the condom with his teeth and rolls it on. Shuffling forward, he slips off her underwear and tosses it behind him. He leans in, kissing and nibbling her ankles as he gets closer, licking along the silk of her stocking, now ruined from when she crawled to him.

Fuck.

He puts her leg over his shoulder and lines himself up, rubbing his cock over her slick cunt. "Ready?"

She gasps and nods. "Yes."

Nikolai grabs her hip as he pushes forward. "God, you're so tight." He keeps his thrusts steady, long and slow as he adjusts to her grip, and she rolls her hips against his, meeting each of his movements. "So perfect, you feel so good."

One of her hands curls around his shoulder, and the other threads through his hair, dragging him down for a kiss. She moans against his mouth and scratches her nails down his shoulder and back. "Fuck, Nikolai," she breathes, and trails her mouth down his throat, kissing and nipping along the way.

Picking up the pace, he growls as he drives in harder, hips slapping against her ass. He spreads his knees a bit, bracing himself to sit up, draping her legs over his hips before he presses his thumb against her clit. "What pretty sounds you make. The way you feel, fucking hell." He angles his hips, thrusting up and in, trying to get her to make more of those sweet sounds.

Corinne whimpers, moaning with every push of his hips and swipe of his thumb. "Yeah?" She clenches around his cock, tightening the walls of her cunt. "I'll be really sweet for you, sir. You make it so easy." She presses herself more fully against him and grinds down against his hips. "Fuck, I'm close."

"Go ahead. I want to feel you, sweet little thing. Let me hear you." Nikolai is holding on by a thread, sweat dripping down the groove of his spine. He licks along her throat, tasting the salt from her skin, nipping at her collarbones. "Beautiful," he whispers, suddenly overwhelmed by just how stunning she is, "you're so fucking beautiful, Corinne."

Closing her eyes, she uses his body as leverage to move against him, the rhythm of her hips increasing until she finally comes with his name on her lips, shuddering in his arms.

She's fucking lovely, coming on his cock, gasping as she grinds against him, and he fucks her through it, making it good for her before he speeds up, chasing his own release. He's chanting her name at the end, *Corinne* falling from his mouth like a prayer. He jerks forward twice more before he stills, pressed tightly to her as he comes.

He's still for a moment, panting, shivering with aftershocks before he finally pulls out and rolls off the side of the bed. He crosses to the bathroom to dispose of the condom and dampen a washcloth with warm water.

When he comes back, his gaze trails over her tangled hair, her gorgeous breasts, the runs in her stockings, made worse by his rough hands. He'd ruin them even further if they had time. Instead, he presses a kiss to Corinne's lips as he begins to clean her up.

"Oh," she says, smiling up at him. "That's sweet, thank you." She drags him down for another kiss and nips his lip gently. "Do you like touch after or"—she eyes her dress across the room—"would you like me to leave now?"

"Oh, touch, absolutely. I believe in the afterglow," he says, tossing the cloth toward the bathroom and flopping on the bed. He snakes his arms around her and draws her close, then suddenly stops and leans back to look at her. "Unless you'd rather not?"

"I prefer enjoying the shared afterglow as long as I like the person." She nestles closer to him and taps her index finger against his chest. "And I like you, so yes. But you know... we can also do things just because you want to. That's what I'm here for."

He hums, stroking his fingers along her arm. "I know that." He pauses while he arranges his thoughts. He had the same conversation with Elijah years ago, and he should have been expecting it, but frankly, his mind is still scattered after his orgasm.

She shivers under his touch, and he smiles as he continues. "I understand I'm paying for your time, and ordinarily that would entitle me to certain things, but for me..." He trails off, breathing deeply.

"For you?"

"I like knowing the person I'm with is enjoying themselves. You're going to be good for me. And at the very least, you deserve to enjoy the time we spend together. You enjoying yourself won't..." He waves his other hand around, searching for the word he wants. "It won't detract from me enjoying myself. If anything, it makes it better."

"That makes sense. And it's very nice for me, so I appreciate it. But..." She tilts her head and looks toward the ceiling. "How about this?" Her gaze finds his again. "I won't offer to do something I don't want to do. And if you want to do something I don't like, I promise to be honest about it, and we won't do it. That way, we're not worrying too much about each other and second-guessing ourselves."

"Sounds good to me." He presses a kiss to her forehead.

"We should probably debrief a little on what we just did. What did you like or not like? Are there things you'd like to do next time?"

"There's nothing I didn't like. I enjoyed everything we did. The crawling was a surprise," he admits with a chuckle. "Usually it takes more negotiation, but I admire your initiative, pet." He waits for a beat. "What about you? Anything you didn't like? Anything you were waiting for me to do that I didn't, and you wish I had?"

"Well." She pauses. "The... disinterest? I'm not used to that, in all honesty, and since it was our first time, I was a little worried you were disappointed. I am very much not Elijah, after all. But, ah, I'm not worried about that anymore."

She smiles softly as she continues. "Everything else... was *wonderful*. You're an excellent kisser, you know? The crawling... Well, you'd been calling me 'pet,' and it felt right in the moment. It was why I wanted you to pet me, too. I guess I just got in the headspace. But even if I like to think I'm good at reading people, I'm not always perfect."

She hooks her leg over his and rubs them together. "As for what I was waiting for," she continues, "I heard all this talk about dexterous fingers and barely got to experience them." She gives him a little pout.

"I asked what you wanted," he says, teasingly tugging her hair. "You asked me to fuck you, so that's what I did." He holds his hands up. "Next time. They're all yours."

He ponders what else she said before responding. "The disinterest... I'll admit, I was testing the waters. Trying to figure out which path to take. It didn't feel right, in the end. You're a good girl at heart, I think." He winks at her. "You're always welcome to be my pet and crawl for me or be my pet and let me take care of you. Or even be something or someone else entirely. Whatever you want."

"Nikolai." She cups his face and brushes his cheek with her thumb. "Is that all you want from this? Just to please me? That's perfectly fine if that's the case; I can work with that. But I also enjoy pleasing, you know. I want you to tell me what you want and like, too."

He takes a deep breath. "When you're in the position I am" —he leaves *billionaire* unsaid, as he's never felt comfortable saying it and likes complaining about it even less—"you find yourself second-guessing everyone. Who can you trust? Who actually wants you in their life versus just wanting something from you? But here..." he stops and reaches for her hand, "...we have an agreement. An exchange. There are protocols and parameters. It's the one place I can give as much as I want and not worry about ulterior motives." He smiles, but it's sadder than he'd like it to be, and he clears his throat. "Indulge me?"

Corinne kisses him, and it's a tender thing. Gentle. *Understanding.* More so than he'd expect on their first night together. "I know exactly what you mean." She laughs softly. "In my own way. It's all on the table here, right?"

He nods. "Right."

"Well, then," she says before getting up and straddling his hips. "Nikolai, sir. I want you to imagine that a few nights from now, you can't stop thinking about what a lovely time we had here tonight. And you want to fuck me so bad, and you get so turned on that you have to do something about it. So you lie in this bed and wrap your hand around that gorgeous cock of yours, and you imagine what you'd do to me next time you had the chance. There's no one there; it's just you and your dick and a limitless imagination where you can do anything to me or make me do anything to you."

Grinding against him, she takes his hands and slides them over her ass. "What are we doing, sir?"

His hand snaps up and grips her chin as he stares directly into her eyes. "You're on your knees for me, pet. So pretty and sweet, wrapped in lovely deep red lingerie I've bought you." His thumb tugs at her lower lip. "Sitting up straight and tall, hands on your knees. Just waiting. Waiting for whatever it is I want from you." He trails off, watching her face, taking everything in as her eyes flutter shut.

"I would love that, sir." Her eyes open. "I want to be good for you. And sweet to you."

"I know you do. You're such a good girl, aren't you?" He dips his thumb into her mouth and squeezes her ass with his other hand. "Would you be still for me? If I asked you to open your mouth and not move while I slipped my cock inside, used your pretty mouth for myself?"

Corinne licks the pad of his thumb and nods, keeping that mouth open for him, staying still above him just like he requested.

"So good, look at you," Nikolai breathes. He pulls his thumb from her mouth, stroking it along her cheek. "That's what I want, Corinne. I want a very pretty pet who's very good for me. Who lets me dress her in pretty lingerie, all silk and lace, who likes when I buy her presents and enjoys when I take control. So when I think about you, that's what I'll imagine. My perfect pet doing exactly what I want."

She smiles and turns into his palm, kissing it. "I like presents, sir. And I like pretty things. And I will very much enjoy being your pet." She brushes his hair from his forehead. "I had so much fun tonight."

He likes to think she's sincere when she says it. "Darling, tonight was wonderful. We're going to enjoy each other very much."

Corinne trails her index finger down the bridge of his nose. "I think so, too." She gives him a final kiss and gets out of bed, searching briefly for her underwear before finding it on the floor and shimmying back into it. He helps her into her dress and presses a kiss to the nape of her neck when he's finished.

"Have you sent gifts to Elijah before?" she asks. "Do you know how it works through the agency?"

"Yes, I'm familiar." All gifts are sent to the service, who then delivers them to the escorts, keeping addresses out of the clients' hands. "Elijah got more presents than such a bratty boy deserved, but I do have a habit of spoiling." He chuckles as he says it, all affection for Elijah even through the admonishment. "If it's too much, please let me know. It's not something everyone is comfortable with."

She wraps her arms around his waist. "I doubt it will be too much. I told you I like pretty things, sir. Let me know next time you'd like to get together. You can do it through the service if you'd like, but I honestly just prefer it if you text me."

He hums deep in his chest, content and sated. "Whatever you'd like. I'll text you my upcoming events, but would you be open to making this regular? Outside of those evenings where I need a date."

"Of course. What were you thinking?"

"Ah." He pauses, thinking about the ebbs and flows of his schedule, considering when would be best. "What about Sundays?"

"I might have a couple of one-offs on the calendar right now, but I don't have any regular appointments that day. I can text you to let you know for sure?"

"Yes, that would be fine."

"Wonderful." Her gaze darts to his mouth before she gives him a languid kiss that has his cock stirring all over again. When he groans against her mouth, she pulls back and winks. "See you Sunday."

to sundays

"OKAY, SO TELL ME EVERYTHING!" Elijah hands Corinne a glass of rosé and curls up beside her on the sofa. "I'm so bored with Rick out of town again—I need every dirty detail!" His pajamas have rubber ducks all over them, and she can't help but grin every time she looks at them.

"It was…" Corinne answers, blowing out a breath. "Really good."

"Right? Fuck, he's so hot. I will miss him forever," he says, dreamily looking into the distance. Elijah is tall and slender, with blond hair, green eyes, and a smile so charming it could thaw even the coldest of hearts. It's no wonder Nikolai likes him.

"Oh, like it's not your fault you're not seeing him anymore."

"And? I can still miss his entire sexy self, Corinne. I'm in a relationship, not dead." She kicks him lightly with her socked foot, and he grabs her ankle and holds it in his lap. "Tell me the juicy bits."

"Well, thankfully you told me he's safe, so when he did things like pushing me against the door, I didn't have to worry about whether he was going to do something dangerous, and I could just enjoy how fucking hot it was."

Elijah groans. "Ugh, delicious."

Corinne smirks; he'll enjoy this next bit. "He said something about me being a desperate little thing who hadn't been fucked properly in ages, but he'd fix that for me."

"*Fuck.* The BDE of a man saying that to a woman who has sex for a living."

She takes a drink of her wine. "BDE or arrogance, but he does have a big dick and did fuck me properly, so we'll give him that." She regales him with the rest: the crawling, *sir* and *pet*, the face fucking... with no condom.

He gasps and slaps her leg. "Corinne Ryan! You naughty minx."

Groaning, Corinne covers her face with her hand. "I know. I don't know what came over me. He had recent test results in his file, and I just really, really, really wanted his cock in my mouth."

"I know that feeling too well." He finishes his wine in one gulp and sets the glass beside the sofa. "Anything else new? Still seeing that one guy? Sam?"

She huffs. "No. I told you it wasn't going to work out."

He pinches her shin. "Why do you refuse to believe you can find love?"

"Because the work always seems to get in the way of things! The hours, the sharing. Sex work has been legal for twenty years, and there's still a stigma. One way or another, we go our separate ways." She dated Natalie for a couple of years, but Natalie was also a sex worker. That's the only way Corinne could ever imagine it working. Maybe her first relationship had scarred her for life, but Will had been the first in a long line of partners who became unhappy because of her career.

"It worked for me," Elijah says, placing his palm on his chest.

"Yeah, and you're no longer an escort. No offense, Elijah, but if I leave this line of work, it will be because of a better opportunity, not a relationship."

Just then, her buzzer rings. She sets her wine glass on the coffee table and gets up to answer it. "You can bring it up," she says over the intercom, pressing the button to unlock the main entrance. She received a text about a package, so she's assuming it will be the courier. Instead, Margot Malone, the owner of Calypso Escorts, walks up the stairs, her waist-length box braids swinging with each step. Her kelly green sheath dress highlights her generous curves and sets off her dark skin perfectly. With the addition of heeled boots and a knee-length black coat, she's impeccably dressed—as always.

Corinne frowns at the stack of slim white boxes Margot's carrying, all tied together with a deep red silk bow. "What are you doing here? Did you give Josiah the day off?" Josiah is Calypso's courier, who delivers gifts or packages from clients to the escorts.

"He went home sick. These came in right before I was heading out, and considering who they're from, I figured I'd make the trip to Wicker Park and drop them off right away."

"And who *are* they from?" Elijah calls from the couch.

Corinne rolls her eyes and takes the stack of boxes. "Elijah is here if you want to say hi."

"I still haven't forgiven the mayor's son for leaving," Margot says, but she steps into the apartment.

"Margot, darling. How I've missed you, even if you insist on bringing up my father." Elijah jumps up and hugs her.

She allows the hug but retorts, "It's payback for abandoning us."

Corinne grabs the card tucked under the bow, and Elijah

crosses the few feet between them, nosily peering over her shoulder as she opens the envelope. Inside is thick cream paper, embossed with a *Z* at the top, and he's scrawled a note in spiky handwriting.

> *Pet,*
>
> *Here are your pretty things, as promised. I look forward to seeing you in my favorite color on Sunday.*
> *Thank you, again, for a perfect evening.*
> *N*

Elijah grins. "Well, well, well. Let's see what you've got, Miss Corinne."

Corinne glances at Margot, who is looking out the floor-to-ceiling windows. "You're welcome to stay for sushi when it arrives, but no pressure. I'm sure your husband would love to see you."

Elijah clasps a hand to his chest. "And deprive me of the opportunity of drinking and revelry with the Malones? Absolutely not. Margot, take your coat off, call Tobias over, and come sit next to me. We'll order more sushi, too."

Margot purses her lips for a moment and then sighs. "Oh, alright."

While Elijah is completely preoccupied flirting with Margot's husband on speakerphone, Corinne carries the boxes past her studio space, crammed with canvases and art supplies, and up to the loft bedroom above the kitchen. She unties the ribbon and opens each box, smiling down at three sets of lingerie in the now familiar dark red, and three in teal, her favorite color.

He must've studied her profile.

She takes a photo with her work phone and sends it to him.

> Thank you, sir. These are lovely.

It's only a minute until she receives a reply.

> Glad you like them, pet. I can't wait to see you in them.

She responds with a kiss emoji before joining her friends for an evening of too much food and drink.

* * *

On Sunday, Corinne arrives at the restaurant in West Loop right on time. She had an appointment in the afternoon, and while Nikolai offered for his driver to pick her up, it was logistically easier to meet him here instead.

Under a knee-length cherry-red coat, she's wearing a black leather skirt and a soft black sweater, her hair in loose waves over one shoulder. Day-old snow is piled high at the sidewalk's edge, already dull and gray from passing vehicles. When she steps out of the car, only years of maneuvering around Chicago in the winter keep her from slipping in her heeled, over-the-knee boots.

Nikolai is already waiting for her out front. His face is steely under the sharpness of his dark stubble, his hair swept back and eyes narrowed against the wind. He's dressed for the weather in a heavy black overcoat, boots and leather gloves to match, and a thick gray scarf draped around his neck.

She smiles as his eyes catch hers, his face shifting when he sees her. Her heartbeat jumps as she remembers everything they did together last time. She walks up and kisses him gently. "Hello, sir."

"Hello, pet," he says as he clasps her hand. "Did you have any trouble finding the place?"

She squeezes his hand and lets him bring her inside. "Not at all. I've never been here before, but I know the neighborhood. Have you eaten here?"

"I haven't." He helps her with her coat. "A friend of mine recommended it to me. She says it's the best meal she's had in ages."

"How sweet of you to bring me, then."

He removes his coat, revealing a gray cashmere sweater beneath, showing off his defined arms and chest. He's... certainly her most attractive client.

Nikolai leans in and presses a delicate kiss to her cheek. "I believe I told you I enjoy spoiling you." He pulls back with a wink before stepping away to check their coats. She spends a moment taking in the restaurant; it's sleek and dark with clean, stark lines softened by velvet-upholstered seating in various jewel tones.

Nikolai catches her attention by grabbing her hand and kissing the inside of her wrist. He tucks her hand into his elbow and guides her to the host stand. "It's under Zaitsev," he says to the host.

The woman leads them to a table for two, and Nikolai pulls Corinne's chair out for her, then tucks it back in after she sits. Corinne smiles up in thanks as he rounds the table to join her.

"I wasn't sure if spoiling just meant lingerie," she says, glancing up with a knowing grin, hinting that she's wearing one of the sets he sent her. She doesn't count her upcoming concert as spoiling since that was negotiated before they even met.

He looks her over slowly, gaze dark and heavy. "You'll come to learn that's the least of it."

"Oh?" Her boot rubs against his ankle under the table.

With an easy smirk, his posture slips into something predatory and languid; he reclines in the chair but broadens his shoulders. There's a taut, anticipatory stillness about him as his dark eyes study her. "Didn't Elijah show you any of his pretty jewels?"

"There was some gloating when he saw what you sent me, since he happened to be over at my place. But... you saw him for several years, and we've only just started." She laughs, just this side of nervous. "I didn't want to make any assumptions, sir."

"Oh, when it comes to spoiling my pretty pet, always assume there is no limit."

She bites her lip and grins. "Alright." It's not the first time a client has wanted to spoil her, but it usually takes a few sessions together before they start up.

Their waiter comes, and they order drinks: a gin cocktail for Nikolai and a sweet bourbon drink for Corinne.

"I looked up the restaurant when you sent it to me," she says. "Apparently, their burger was rated the best in the country last year. I feel we'd be dishonoring them not to order it."

He glances at the waiter and passes over their menus. "Two of your best burgers, as well, please." When the waiter leaves, he reaches across the table for her hand and plays with her fingers. "And how was your day?"

"Well, I was out pretty late last night, so I slept in, had brunch with a friend, ran some errands, and now I'm here." She grins warmly. "So all in all, pretty good, sir. How about you?"

"Far less nice than yours sounds, that's certain." A rueful smile crosses his lips. "Lots of fires to put out today and several phone calls that could have been emails." He picks up her hand and kisses her fingertips. "It has greatly improved with your presence, though."

Damn, he's smooth, and she'd be lying if she said she wasn't charmed by him. She knows how to read people, and his appreciation seems genuine. Plus, in this business, there's no need to lie about it. If he didn't like her, he wouldn't pay her. As simple as that.

She closes the space between them as much as the table will allow. "Phone calls on a Sunday should be illegal. But if I can make your Sunday tolerable, then I'm glad we're here together."

"Sweet pet, you make it far more than tolerable." He sits back, holding her gaze, when their waiter approaches with their drinks. He thanks the waiter and then raises his glass. "To Sundays."

Corinne clinks her glass against his. "To Sundays," she says, genuinely looking forward to what their Sundays, and especially tonight, may have in store.

delayed gratification

CORINNE

CORINNE SIPS HER COCKTAIL, her eyes closing as she savors it. "Oh, that's good." She sets down her drink. "You know, Elijah *was* rather pouty that I'm seeing you every week now, though. He said he didn't see you as often."

Nikolai chuckles. "Elijah was a very popular young man, if I remember correctly. I was traveling more for business than I do now, and he wasn't always available for business trips." He takes a drink, watching her over the rim of his glass. "His loss."

She barks out a laugh. "He would be so offended if he knew you said that, which is exactly why I will tell him." She winks. "And yes, he did work all the time, which never made sense to me when he would've lived quite comfortably never working a day in his life. Though, I suppose that wouldn't anger Mayor Merrick quite so much."

Nikolai tips his glass to her. "You're right there. Elijah loves nothing more than pissing off his father." He tilts his head. "Have you known Elijah long?"

"As long as he was working for the agency. So... four years? I'd already been there about five years by that time. He was the biggest flirt I'd ever met, but we still clicked right away." She takes another sip of her cocktail. "What about you? Did you know him first, or did the agency pair you with him?"

"I met him briefly at a charity event years ago, but I didn't meet him properly until the agency paired us. Bratty little thing," he says fondly, his displeasure from last week missing from his voice.

Does he forgive quickly, or does he like how Elijah's blunder turned out for him in the end?

"He is truly the worst." She rests her elbow on the table and presses her chin against the palm of her hand. "I'm always curious as to how my clients find the agency. The owner, Margot, is so particular about not advertising because she doesn't want to *ruin the mystery of the Calypso experience*," she says, doing her best imitation with a flip of her hand. "I always wonder how it survives on word of mouth, but it somehow does."

Both his eyebrows arch, and he chuckles. "Well, I'm a bit of a special case. I've known Margot longer than Calypso has existed. We go back a very, very long way."

Corinne's mouth falls open. "Nikolai, are you telling me you were one of her *clients*?"

He laughs, then reaches across the table and places one finger under her chin. "Close your mouth unless you plan on doing something with it, pet." He sits back. "And I wasn't just *one* of them. I was one of the first."

"Oh my god," she says, her hand against her chest. "Please tell me what she was like."

Amusement dances in his eyes. "She was a menace. We met at a party one summer when I was back home from university. So, you know, twenty years ago, at least. She used to drink everyone under the table." He smirks. "I helped her write her business plan, actually."

"Wow." She shakes her head. "I can't believe it. And now

here you are"—she grins with a flirty shrug—"reaping the benefits of that very plan."

"What can I say," he drawls before tipping his head back and finishing his drink. "It was an *excellent* plan."

She gives him an exasperated, but fond, look. "I admire her, you know. Making a successful business out of the work we do." She trails her finger through the condensation on her tumbler. "I would love to start my own business, but I don't want to compete with her. She's been so good to me, and I care for her too much to do that."

His eyes roam across her face before he speaks. "I think, pet, if you really wanted to do something like our dear Ms. Margot, you absolutely could. It doesn't have to be an escort service. There are many similar markets out there ripe for the picking." He grabs her hand. "And I have no doubt you'd be successful."

"Oh." Her cheeks heat. "That's sweet of you to say, sir. Especially when we haven't known each other long."

"I'm a businessman, Corinne. I know talent and drive when I see it."

Their waiter politely interrupts with their food and places two messy heaps of burgers in front of them. Corinne's stomach grumbles at the sight; brunch was quite a long time ago. She cuts her burger in half and takes a bite, a little moan escaping her mouth. "Damn, they weren't kidding."

Nikolai smiles as though her reaction amuses him before he picks up his burger. As soon as he takes his own bite, however, he's making a similar noise. "Okay, that *is* fucking good."

"Tell your friend she has excellent taste."

He snorts into his next bite. "I absolutely will not. She'll gloat for ages over it. But the sentiment is appreciated."

"Oh, one of *those* friends!" She eats a couple of fries. "Imagine her and Elijah together. Insufferable."

"I've had the thought." He reaches for a napkin and wipes

his mouth. "She proclaims she'd never have the patience to properly deal with a brat, but I think she'd enjoy the challenge." He takes another bite, groaning and looking at the burger in disbelief. "But as much as I think Indali could tame a brat, dear Elijah might be the brat that broke the tamer's back, so to speak."

"Well," she says coyly, "he's very good with his mouth when it's not spouting off nonsense." She and Elijah have never dated, but they did work together once. "Maybe it'd be worth her while."

He arches a brow at her, a smirk playing at the corners of his mouth. "You don't have to tell me how good Elijah's mouth is. I put it to good use. Though..." He drags a finger along her forearm. "*Your* mouth was a true delight, pet."

"Yeah? I'm glad you thought so." She turns her arm slightly so she can caress his arm in return. "What about your mouth, sir?"

He licks his lips slowly, then raises one of her fingers to his mouth and nibbles at the tip. "My mouth is excellent, too. Would you like me to show you later?"

She nods, her lips parting, heat pooling in her belly from the scrape of his teeth against her skin. "Yes, sir. I was also promised a show of your talented hands."

He hums against her fingertip before returning her hand to the table. He sits back in his chair as though lazily watching his prey. "Eat your dinner, sweet pet, and I'll take you home and show you just how talented they can be when used together."

She bites her lip and nods, reaching for her fries while she works to ignore the pulsing heat between her thighs. Thankfully, it eases as they finish their dinner. Corinne is generally good at pulling clients out of their shells and asking the right questions to avoid awkward silences, but it doesn't take much work at all with him. There's a natural chemistry between them, an easy give-and-take, and it's not difficult to talk and share and spend an effortless dinner with him.

Once they're finished, the waiter clears their plates and asks if they want dessert. Corinne looks at Nikolai expectantly.

"We'll have dessert at home," he says, holding her gaze before glancing at the waiter. "Just the check, please."

When the waiter returns, Nikolai pulls several bills from his wallet and places them in the leather folio with the check before handing it back, not even looking at the bill. He stands, rounds the table, and pulls out Corinne's chair.

"Thank you so much for bringing me," Corinne says, and means it. She had a great time.

Walking them toward the coat check, Nikolai leans in and kisses her cheek. "You're very welcome. The food may have been exceptional, but the company was divine."

"You know, you are very charming. I can't imagine why you'd need any help at parties."

"It's easy to be charming when it's someone I like so much, pet." He gets her coat and helps her into it, coming around to button her in securely with a kiss. "Less easy when they're people like Simon McHoy."

Her mouth curls in disgust. "Let's not talk about him tonight."

He laughs as he slips on his own coat, retrieving his scarf and gloves from a pocket. "Let's not." He offers his elbow once he's bundled himself up. "Ready?"

"Mhmm!"

She accepts his arm, tucking in close to brace herself against the chill as they walk into the cold night air. His driver swings in front a moment later, and Nikolai hands her into the car before coming around the other side. She crosses her legs, the bottom of her coat parting to show the sliver of thigh between her skirt and boots. "Sometimes I wonder why I don't move to a warmer climate," she says, righting her coat.

He looks at her sharply and then adjusts the heat. He unwinds the scarf from his neck and drapes it over her legs, scooting closer. "I ask myself the same sometimes, and I don't even have the social pressure to dress fashionably instead of seasonally appropriate."

She leans into him, happy to accept the warmth and closeness. "Yes, well, my service is providing an experience, which usually involves unwrapping a pretty present. I don't know if showing up in snow boots and wool-lined leggings would be welcome."

"Consider this my full approval to wear something warmer next time." He drags his fingers along her shin, which is covered by her boot, his gaze lingering there. "I don't mind taking my time unwrapping something as lovely as you."

"No?" She uncrosses her legs, letting them fall open just a little.

He slides his hand higher, teasingly caressing the back of her knee. "Not at all. You'll find patience is one of the only virtues I subscribe to." He traces the contours of her knee through her boot, slipping his finger just under the edge. "It's important that one learns how to wait. Delayed gratification can be immensely satisfying, don't you think?"

She hums, parting her thighs another inch, her belly quivering. "Sometimes, sir."

"Only sometimes?" He trails one finger in the slowest of circles on the inside of her thigh, barely touching her, eyes locked on hers the entire time.

She whimpers and bites her lip. "Sometimes I don't want to wait."

He clicks his tongue and moves his finger infinitesimally higher, still barely above her knee. "You know, that's unfortunate, pet, because I quite enjoy making people wait. It adds to the experience, don't you agree?"

"But..." She lets him hear the heaviness of her breath, lets her legs fall open further. "What if I want you really badly?"

"Poor little pet." His fingers walk up to midthigh and stop. "I guess you'll just want me even more by the time I let you have me."

"Sir," Corinne whines, pressing closer against him. "Please."

He splays his hand on her thigh. Leaning in, he nibbles her ear before saying, "You sound so pretty when you beg, Corinne. I think I'd like to hear it some more."

devoured

THE ELEVATOR RIDE UP to Nikolai's apartment is full of heat and tension, and Corinne tries to pretend he hasn't gotten her so desperately worked up from one little car ride.

"You alright?"

Well, he must've noticed her act.

She finally gives in and slips her hands under his coat to wrap her arms around his waist. "Want you," she sighs, looking up at him coyly. She's well aware he's going to toy with her all night at this rate, leave her a shivering, desperate mess by the end. But that doesn't mean she can't make him want her just as badly.

"Hmmm. Patience, pretty pet. I'll give you what you need." He thumbs her bottom lip. "No pouting or you'll have to wait even longer, understood?"

Ugh. Corinne sobers and nods. "Yes, sir."

He kisses her fiercely, coaxing a moan as she clings to him, not stopping until the elevator dings and the doors slide open. He laces their fingers together, tugging her out after him. "Come along. Time to test that patience."

She takes a deep breath, steeling herself as she follows him.

The apartment is spacious, with the primary suite running along the right-hand side, the kitchen, living room, and extra bedrooms toward the back. The back wall of the living room is all windows, and Lake Michigan sparkles with the city lights below. The apartment itself is all tans and creams and browns, with heavy, well-made furniture and luxurious fabrics, from the leather of the chairs and couches to the plush carpets over the hardwood. And while she herself likes things a little more colorful, she can still appreciate its elegance. Even if it's more understated than she'd expect from a billionaire.

Corinne remembers what he told her last time, and, after he removes their coats, she gets on her knees and looks up at him, waiting. He turns, gaze sinking to hers, and smiles.

"What a perfect little thing you are, pet." He crouches and tugs at the collar of her sweater. "What say we leave these clothes here? You won't need them, after all." He holds out his hand and helps her to her feet.

Slowly, she undresses. It's a sensual tease, taking her time to reveal which gift she picked to wear tonight. She uncovers the pretty oxblood lace at her hips and the matching bustier lined in boning and trimmed in sheer, delicate lace. Stepping back, she lets him see all of her: the lingerie, the boots, the anticipation in her gaze, the parting of her lips.

He trails a finger down the column of her throat, over her collarbones, down to the edge of the lace covering the curve of her breast. "Beautiful," he breathes, eyes heavy. "Absolutely stunning. I could eat you right up."

Her breath trembles as he touches her, and she wraps her hands around his biceps. "I wouldn't stop you."

Nikolai drags his gaze upward and meets her eyes with a dark smile. "I know you wouldn't. You want it too much." Walking her backward toward the living room, he shifts to stand behind her and nuzzles at her throat. "You've just been waiting, haven't you?" It's a whisper, an exhalation, soft in the quiet of the apartment. He rests his hands on her hips and guides her toward the overstuffed club chair. "Just waiting for someone to come along and devour you."

Playing up the fear just a little, she moans shakily, her lip quivering. "Please, sir."

"Mmm, I do love to hear you beg, pet. So very pretty, your pleas." He moves her hair to the side and kisses the back of her neck. "Sit down, lovely thing. Let me show you what it's like to be properly devoured."

For a brief moment, she hears Elijah yelling *big dick energy* in her head. A part of her hates that he's right, and the other part is ready to be shown just how right he is. Corinne sits and spreads her legs, resting her forearms on the arms of the chair. She looks up at him. Heat stirs in his gaze, and she smiles sweetly. It's nice to know how badly he wants her, too.

"Lean back. Get comfortable," he says, kneeling. He wraps his hands around her thighs and drags her to the edge of the chair, kissing and nibbling his way up one leg and then the other before draping them over his shoulders. He stops at her center, inhaling deeply and licking his lips. He's so close that she's aching, and she whimpers from anticipation alone. "Your safewords. What are they?"

"Red to stop, yellow to pause."

He smirks, hungry and feral, and noses at the lace so gently she can barely feel it. "Three rules tonight." His eyes meet hers. "You're to tell me when you're close, you're to ask permission before you come, and you're not to come without permission. Understood?"

She bites her lip, her body already taut from his nearness. "Yes, sir."

He doesn't hesitate after that, rubbing his lips, his cheeks, his jaw all over her lace-covered cunt. He mouths at her, licking at her center until the lace is soaked. It's the biggest fucking tease, and she's already so keyed up; she doesn't know how she'll take a whole night of this.

"Nikolai," she sighs, wanting nothing more than to slip her underwear to the side and press herself against his mouth.

He chuckles and looks up at her. "That's not my name, pet," he says, just loud enough to be heard.

She whimpers, holding his gaze as she speaks. "Sir. Please."

With a smirk, he slides his hands over the tops of her thighs. He noses at the lace, then uses his fingers to pull it out of the way. Each movement is so slow and deliberate and light that she wants to sob.

When he finally gets his mouth properly on her, it's only with delicate little kitten licks to her clit. She still comes unglued from just those alone, a gasp falling from her mouth, but it's not enough. Frustration bubbles within her, and she presses her lips together to keep from whining. He continues licking softly, all over her lips, the crease of her thighs, and finally, her entrance. Groaning, he digs his fingers into her thighs, flattening his tongue and dragging it over her entrance.

"Oh my god." She grips the armchair tightly as he hums against her with a deep rumble. It's so much and not enough all at once. She rests the edge of her boot lightly against his shoulder as leverage to push herself into his mouth. "I need more. Please, sir."

He slowly shakes his head, never stopping his tongue, his jaw. His nose presses against her clit, and she whines—it's something, but it's not enough. "*Please,*" she begs, writhing under his mouth. "Please lick my clit."

He eases back, stubble glistening. "Begging already?" He turns his head and nibbles her thigh. "We've only just begun."

"I've been thinking about you all day. Just seeing you and

remembering last time turned me on so much." She pleads with her eyes. "Don't you want me, sir?"

"Of course I want you, sweet thing." He sits up and moves both her legs to one shoulder, then reaches for her underwear. He slides it off and winks at her as he tucks it in his pocket. "I just want to make you a shaking, begging, wrecked little mess first."

Her lip quivers, desperate to fall into a pout, but she *can't*. Instead, she takes a deep breath, looks up at the ceiling, and waits.

"Oh, very good. See?" He drags a finger over to her clit and just rests it there. "See what a little patience can get you?"

Corinne whimpers and squeezes her eyes shut. His finger dips down and traces circles around her entrance, then he does the same with his tongue. His mouth latches on with a strong pull as he slips his finger inside.

"Oh, god!" she gasps, back arching off the chair. It's ridiculous how easily he's turned her into this, that one finger and one press of his mouth can completely unravel her. She's already shaking and desperate, and she knows what's in store —drawn-out glimpses of pleasure, long stretches of denial. She doesn't know how she's going to handle it.

He crooks his finger, slides out slowly, and pauses just a second before slipping back in. Then he speeds up, fucking her with his fingers while he looks at her expectantly, waiting for what's next.

"Sir," she breathes because it's already building inside her, already rushing at her as soon as he's moving faster. "I'm close."

He removes his fingers and mouth and smiles at her. "Very well done, pet. You're doing so well." After a brief moment, he asks, "Ready?"

Corinne whines but nods reluctantly. He smiles and starts

again, this time with two fingers, eliciting a cry. He tilts his head, and she glares at his tongue licking idly against her, like he's got all the time in the world.

She's panting, bottom lip trapped between her teeth as he works to pull her climax from her, coaxing it forth with his hand and mouth. A crook of his fingers makes her gasp, and her body goes taut. "I'm close, sir. Please."

He stops again, pulling his mouth away. She wants to scream. "Wonderful." He waits again, giving her a moment. "Ready?"

"Sir, please." Her voice shakes. "Please let me come."

"Mmm, I do love how you beg, but no. Not yet." He blows a light stream of air across her clit, and she groans in frustration. "Ready?"

Her jaw tightens, and she's so on edge that she could explode. She takes several deep breaths before answering. "Yes, sir."

"What a sweet little pet you are. You're doing so well." He presses another finger against her but doesn't push inside. "Can you handle three?"

"*Please,*" she keens. "I feel so empty."

He eases forward slowly, and she's so wet that he slips right in. "You're taking them so well; look at you. So good for me." He watches a while longer before he sets his mouth back to work.

Sweat is beading on her temple, January in Chicago be damned. Her hips roll against his face, her body chasing what she so desperately needs. It's too much. It's too damn much. The edges of her mind start to soften, everything growing hazy and sluggish, like she's wading through fog. He's still there, fingers and lips taking her apart, but it's dampened now.

"Sir," she murmurs, her brow furrowing as she feels the tell-tale sign of her climax building. "I'm there. Please? Please just let me have it."

He stops, but this time, he rises on his knees and looks at her, one hand caressing her face as the other grabs a condom from the end table next to the chair. "Last one, pet. Just once more for me, okay?"

She nods, gasping in anticipation.

He undoes his trousers and shoves them down his thighs before slipping the condom on. Then he drags her right to the edge of the chair, her legs draping over his arms. "Ready?"

Her brain finally catches up to what's happening. "Oh, god. Please. Please fuck me. I need to come so bad."

"I know you do. Hold out as long as you can. Don't forget to ask." He lets go of her leg and lines himself up, spreading her open with the head of his cock. "Spectacular," he murmurs, almost to himself.

Then he pushes in oh so slowly.

f*** me boots

CORINNE CRIES OUT. Not even three fingers compare to the rightness of his cock inside her, filling her, stretching her. He pulls almost all the way out before slowly pushing forward again, and it's like she's melting. She squeezes around his cock, hoping to spur him on, even though she has to try to make herself last as long as she can.

He hitches one of her legs over his shoulder again, lowering his lips to her thigh but stopping when he finds her boot instead of skin. "These fucking *boots*." He nibbles her leg where the boot stops, increasing the pace of his hips. "Fuck."

A pleased smirk graces her face because here, with her, is where Nikolai Zaitsev lets go, where he drops his tight control on himself, even the smallest amount. His nonchalance last week had worried her. But when he'd slipped inside her and called her beautiful, it all melted away as he lost himself in her body.

Tonight he's no different—edging her until she's falling apart, acting completely unfazed by every sigh and moan and plea for pleasure. Until he's buried inside her, and then he can't help but drop the pretense.

The realization clears her head, and she meets his hips with her own, grinding against him as he fucks her. "I'll wear them anytime you like, sir," she says, her orgasm simmering as she tries to hold it at bay.

"Perfect little thing." He smiles down at her, fierce and proud. "So good for me." He places his thumb gently over her clit. "Ready?"

She gasps, arching into his hand. "Yes. Fuck. Please touch me. I'm aching."

Increasing the speed of his thrusts, he presses his thumb to her. "Come on, pet, you've been begging all night. Let me see it. Let me see you."

"Sir," Corinne sobs, accepting his permission, and she lets the current hit her, white-hot and all-encompassing. She arches against him, shaking, her nails digging into his shoulder, overcome with pleasure and relief. His cock is a steady rhythm inside her as she comes down, and when she looks up, he's staring at her—mouth parted, eyes glassy, completely enraptured. "Sir." It's a whisper this time, and he groans, head thrown back as he begins to fuck her harder, sweat dripping down his temples.

"You feel so good inside me," she says. "Stretching me full." She pulls him down for a kiss, bending her own body in half to reach him, moaning at how much deeper his cock feels like this. "Please come for me. Want to make you feel so good."

Picking up force and speed, It doesn't take much longer until Nikolai follows her, burying himself inside her as his climax overtakes him, hips twitching, his face pressed to her throat.

She holds him close, her fingers trailing along the short hairs of his undercut. "Did anyone ever tell you it's not nice to tease, sir?" she asks playfully, a smile dancing on her lips.

Nikolai hums and nuzzles against her throat, the scratch of

his stubble making her shiver as he presses kisses to her skin. "Hm, I'll take that under advisement." He pulls back and studies her face closely. "How are you, sweet thing?"

"I feel like I've been put through the wringer." She laughs. "Holy shit. That's a lot for a girl's second time."

He chuckles and kisses her. "I knew you could handle it. And you did. So very well." He strips off the condom. "Will you be alright if I step away for a moment so I can get us cleaned up?"

"Of course." She shakily pulls herself up to sit properly in the chair. Thankfully, it's leather; the evidence of her arousal would've made a proper mess of fabric.

Cradling her jaw, he tilts her face to look at him. "It's okay if you wouldn't be. I'll believe you if you say you're fine, but I also ask that you tell me if you need more contact or cuddling or just time together."

"Thank you, sir. I appreciate it. I feel fine, even if I did get a little spacey there for a minute." She doesn't usually let herself get that way with clients, doesn't let her guard down that much. Safety is one concern, but she also can't do her job if she's floating in outer space. But it was so intense that it happened all on its own.

Another rule broken for this man she's just met.

His eyes twinkle, and he smiles at her, slow and syrupy. "Good to know." He brushes a kiss to her lips and steps back, tugging his trousers up and over his hips. "Be right back."

He walks away and returns with a wet washcloth and a couple of water bottles.

Her breath hitches as he cleans her with the cloth; it's warm, but her clit is overstimulated from all the edging. She watches him, his face serious as he works on the task at hand, a little wrinkle between his brows, and it's so cute that a giggle escapes her lips. "Thank you, sir."

"Are you laughing at me?" He glances up, eyes narrowing playfully.

She gives him a bright smile. "You're cute when you're concentrating."

He leans in and kisses her clit gently, and he smirks at her sharp inhale. "You were saying?"

"Oh, is that how it is? Well then," she says with a sassy quirk of her eyebrows, "you're not cute at all. Happy now?"

His eyes narrow further. "It'll do." He opens a bottle of water and hands it to her. "Drink, pet. Then we can debrief a bit, okay?"

Corinne nods and takes a sip. She doesn't realize how thirsty she is until she starts drinking, and she finishes half the bottle before speaking. "Thank you." She pulls him onto the chair with her, maneuvering until she's sitting in his lap. "How was your evening?"

He sits back, settling her more firmly on his lap. "My evening was delightful. I especially appreciated how hard you tried to be patient for me. I know it was difficult."

"Being fingered and eaten out by a gorgeous man and not being allowed to come?" She huffs. "You have no idea."

He laughs, fingers lightly toying with the top of her boot. "Yes, I'm sure it was terrible. I won't make you wait next time, how's that?"

Her eyes narrow. "Mm, see, I don't trust that, sir. No agreements until I can read the fine print."

Nikolai tucks her hair behind her ear. "What a smart girl you are, pet." He sits quietly for a moment, eventually asking, "Any complaints? Concerns?"

She thinks for a few seconds before answering. "No, sir. I really do have a lot of fun with you." Smirking up at him, she grabs his hands and entwines them with her own. "You were right about both your hands and mouth." She kisses him, tasting herself on his lips, humming in appreciation.

"I try not to oversell my skills, as a general rule. So if I tell you I'm good at something"—he kisses her deeply and thoroughly—"I'm very, very good."

"You're getting me all worked up again, sir."

He slides his hand between her legs, fingers teasing around her clit. "One more? You were very good for me tonight."

"Please," she gasps, and arches against his hand.

It's different than before. It's slow, but not to tease and yank the pleasure away. Now it feels slow for the sake of it, and she savors it, sinking into each wave of pleasure as it builds within her. "Oh my god." Her thighs shake, the coil of her climax winding within her with each soft touch.

"That's it, pet, just like that."

"Sir." She slips her hand around the back of his neck. "I'm close. Please let me come."

"Thank you for asking. So polite." He takes a very long moment to kiss her neck, and a whine is forming in her throat when he finally whispers, "Go on, pet," right against her skin.

Corinne comes with a cry, her head falling back, her body trembling against him as pleasure washes over her. She's panting and shivering, and she curls into him as she catches her breath. "Thank you, sir."

His breath hitches so quietly that she wonders if she's imagined it in her postcoital haze. "You're welcome."

"Happy?"

He smiles back, and it lights up his whole face. "Immensely, pet. You are marvelous."

"Thank you." She gives him one final kiss and sits up. "Do you need anything else from me?"

Nikolai pauses and then smiles briefly with a shake of his

head. "No, thank you. Here." Picking her up, he stands, then deposits her back in the chair. "I'll get your clothes for you."

Watching him walk to the foyer to retrieve them, she admires the shift of his muscles under his sweater. "Should I assume I'm not getting my underwear back?"

He calls out, "You should!" and she laughs, rolling her eyes.

"Next Sunday still good?" she asks as she gets dressed.

"Next Sunday is perfect, pet."

"Wonderful. Let me just freshen up." She heads to the bathroom and cleans herself up, wiping her smudged mascara and setting herself to rights. She sends a message to the car service and finds Nikolai waiting in the foyer with her coat in hand. "Thank you, sir."

He kisses the back of her neck as he moves her hair out from under her coat. "You're very welcome. I'll see you next week."

"Good night, sir." She smiles up at him and gives him a kiss before heading out to the elevator.

A glance at her phone tells her it will be an hour until the car service can have someone get her. Hopping on the L will take a fraction of the time, so she sighs and steps out into the cold, pulling up the collar of her coat. When she puts her hands in her pockets, however, her fingers brush something unexpectedly soft. She pulls it out and there is his scarf from earlier. Warmth blooms in her chest at the thoughtfulness. She smiles to herself and wraps it around her neck before hurrying to her stop.

When Corinne gets home, she grabs her work phone to send him a thank-you text, but it's late, and he might be winding down for the night. Instead, she grabs her other phone to send a message to Elijah. She'll text Nikolai tomorrow.

> The BDE strikes again.

Elijah doesn't respond until the morning.

I TOLD YOU!

Chuckling, she leans up on her elbow and pats around for her work phone to send her thanks to Nikolai, but he's already beat her to a message, sent hours ago like he either had a late night or an early morning.

Good morning, pet. I hope you slept well and kept warm. I'd like to adjust my standing appointments to overnights. Let me know at your earliest convenience if that's possible.

She falls back to the mattress, unable to help the grin that tugs at her lips.

holy week

NIKOLAI

NIKOLAI IS HURRYING toward the elevators, lunch in hand, when his assistant flags him down.

"Sorry, boss, just a couple of things," Thomas says. He's got his planner in one hand and a pencil in the other. "First, I just wanted to confirm that you wanted to double this month's donations. The accountants called, and I know you give more during Lent, but I wanted to confirm. It's not my money, after all."

"The amount is correct," Nikolai confirms. "Thank you for checking."

He gives to charities, foundations, and museums throughout the year, but almsgiving is a large part of celebrating and observing the Triodion, the period before and during Great Lent and the Holy Week leading up to Easter. He focuses more on the places and services providing food, shelter, and healthcare to those who need it most.

"Of course. Second, that new German company just called to ask if they can move tomorrow's call to Monday in the early morning. I know it's your late day, but"—he shrugs the shrug of a man who already knows the answer—"I told them I'd ask.

They were very insistent."

Rude, then, Nikolai surmises. Thomas is too polite for his own good some days. "You're right, Monday won't work. Ask about Tuesday. I can move my lunch with Indali, if need be."

Thomas makes another note in his planner and begins to walk away before pausing and turning back. "If it's not too bold to say, Mr. Zaitsev, it's nice to see you making time for yourself. You work too much."

Nikolai heads for the elevators again. "You know, I hear that a lot lately."

"Corinne is a smart woman!" Thomas calls out as Nikolai steps onto the elevator.

Nikolai smiles and shakes his head as the doors slide shut. "He's not wrong," he murmurs to himself. "Not wrong at all."

In fact, the reason Monday mornings are now off-limits is because Corinne has been staying over on Sunday nights the last few months. Rushing out in the morning like he usually does would be rude, so he's started fixing breakfast for them both before sending her out the door with a kiss.

Breakfasts have been different these last weeks during Great Lent. With restrictions on how many meals he can eat, he's been cooking solely for Corinne. This last Monday, he whipped up some crepes since he's discovered that they're the best Lenten breakfast, and he didn't have any meat or dairy in the apartment. He made up for the lack of butter by getting the best jams and preserves money could buy. She isn't Eastern Orthodox herself, but she offered to follow the strict rules he observes to make things easier on him. He can't remember anyone ever doing that for him. His ex, Olivia, certainly didn't.

He'd just started cooking when Corinne finally walked out of the bedroom, adorably sleep-mussed and stunningly beautiful. And, well, he just couldn't help himself. He turned off the burner, picked her up, and took her back to bed to have *her* for breakfast.

Now, as he gets into the backseat of the car, a smile tugs at the corners of his mouth. His Mondays are undoubtedly different these days, and he can admit how much better he feels taking the extra time for himself.

"Good day, boss?" Adrian asks, catching him in the rearview mirror.

He schools his face and clears his throat. "Not too bad."

Adrian takes him to Grant Park, and before getting out of the car, Nikolai slips him some money to treat himself to lunch. He walks further into the park to the usual bench he shares with Indali, and sits, pulling the lunch container from his bag.

A few minutes later, his oldest and dearest friend arrives, bundled in a royal blue coat and hat. Indali Pavlovna has a small frame, light brown skin, and thick black hair that's currently pulled into a neat bun. She's beautiful and always has been, with big dark eyes under perfectly arched brows and a smile that can charm or kill depending on her mood.

The Pavlovnas and the Zaitsevs have been friends for hundreds of years, at least to hear their grandparents tell it. The story goes that one of the Pavlovna matriarchs saw the stirrings of revolution in Russia long before others and advised her dear friends, the Zaitsevs, to move their fortune and business dealings out of the country as soon as possible.

Nikolai has always thought it was mighty rich of the oligarchs to abandon the country they purportedly loved at the first sign of consequences of their own actions, but that was just him, the many-times great-grandson who benefited from generational wealth that helped him start a multibillion-dollar company.

After the families spent a few decades moving around

Europe, they immigrated to America. Nikolai's parents and Indali's father decided to go together and settle here in Chicago.

"Hi, hi," she says, kissing each of his cheeks when he stands to greet her. "Have you been here long?"

"Hello, Indali. A couple minutes, at most." He gestures for her to sit. They're only allowed one meal on weekdays, and he and Indali always eat together since she observes as strictly as he does.

She unpacks her lunch while Nikolai opens his container of stuffed tomatoes, wasting no time digging in. The tomatoes are still warm, filled to the brim with currants, toasted pine nuts, and rice. He's been looking forward to lunch all day.

"What have you got today?" Indali asks, and he tips it toward her. "Oh, that looks good." She shows him her baked chickpeas and bulgur pilaf before taking a bite with a sigh. "I'm glad it's Thursday."

"Lent'll be over soon," he says. "It's Holy Week, after all. We'll be up to our eyeballs in *pashka* and *kulich* in just a few days." Pashka and kulich, a cheese dessert and a sweet bread, are staples on Easter, and they are perfect after weeks of restrictive fasting.

A noise escapes her mouth, and if it were anyone else, he'd call it a whine. "Why are we so strict, again? Why do we do this to ourselves?"

Nikolai shoots her a look. "Because we tried giving up sex one year like we're supposed to, and we decided we'd rather just be stricter about the food than do that again."

Indali nods in concession. "You're right, you're right. That was the worst Lent ever." She takes a bite. "Plus, Papa always judges me if I cheat! He always knows. He calls me every time it happens. He doesn't give Mama any grief when she slips, so he saves it all for me."

"Well, you're not the love of his life who converted to his religion to marry him."

"But I am his lovely daughter! And that should count for something."

"Whatever you say, Indali darling."

She slaps his arm. "Enough about me, hm? It's been, what, three months since the mayor's son retired for the easy life? Still booking with what's-her-name?"

"If you mean Corinne, then yes, I'm still seeing her." He sets down his container and wipes his mouth. "Turns out, she is the sweetest little pet."

Indali raises her brows in surprise. "Kolyenka! Have you got yourself a little cat-girl?"

He laughs, shaking his head at the old childhood nickname. "No, Dali, I don't have a cat-girl."

Indali leans in conspiratorially, looking around before asking, "A horse-girl?"

"God, would you stop?" He elbows her in the side while she laughs. "Not all of us enjoy pet play as much as you."

"Quite true. Some of us are sadists with a lingerie kink. We can't all be perfect."

He rolls his eyes, letting out a long-suffering sigh. "Why am I friends with you again?"

She sips her tea and shrugs. "Familial obligation? Kink kinship? My excellent taste? Who's to say at this point."

He laughs because she's not wrong on any count. They may have started as children begrudgingly brought together at every baptism, chrismation, and holiday, but they'd formed a bond over being the only children in their families. By the time they got to high school, they'd been best friends for years.

"So," Indali says a few moments later, "I saw Olivia yesterday."

Nikolai stops midbite. It's been eight years, so he rarely

thinks of her anymore, but hearing the name still makes his stomach plummet. "Did you, now?"

"Yep. At the Federov." Indali's family owns several boutique hotels in the city, and the Federov is its grandest. "Seems she's back in Chicago. With a fat new ring on her finger from Husband Number 3. You'd think she'd have enough money by now to quit her little charade."

Olivia had been a beautiful and distracting whirlwind when she came into his life. Most people don't know him from Adam on the street, but if you're in his line of work or keep an eye on the Forbes 400, then you know Nikolai is a billionaire.

And Olivia knew that list of wealthiest people in America like the back of her hand.

He was too dazzled by her to question her sudden presence or how quickly she wormed her way into his life. She was fun and sexy and a welcome break from the stress of being the CEO of a company that had taken off faster than he ever could've imagined.

Nikolai has always been a man who calculates and plans and looks at things from every angle, but he fell for her so swiftly that he bought a ring and proposed to her four months in.

However, everything turned for the worse when he wouldn't budge on loosening the prenuptial agreement a few months before their wedding. Thank God he had the sense for that much. After a nasty fight, he came home from work the next day and found her gone. And she'd taken all her things with her.

It was like she'd never even been there.

"You alright, Kolya?" Indali asks, bumping his shoulder with her own.

He blows out a breath. "Just thinking about her. And the bullet I dodged." And has been trying to dodge ever since.

He's been successful thus far. He went back to paying for his companionship, and now he has the most delightful companion he could imagine. The sex is great, the company is even better, and he doesn't have to worry about another Olivia.

"I did try to warn you."

He sighs in exasperation. "Yes, yes, you are always right, Indali."

She cackles. "I know, but I still love to hear it."

They finish their lunch, chatting and catching up before saying their goodbyes.

Indali hugs him tightly and kisses him on both cheeks. "I'll see you at church, Kolya." She walks away before spinning back around. "Oh, and watch your mail!"

His brow furrows in confusion, but he waves all the same as she laughs and turns onto the path toward her office.

He pulls out his phone and opens his text thread with Corinne. The half-written text message started while waiting for Indali is still sitting there, unfinished. And after that conversation about Olivia, he could use the distraction until Adrian retrieves him. He types the last few words before hitting send.

> I have a request for Sunday if you're open to it.

She responds immediately.

> Ooo! Yes, spill!

schastlivoy paskhi

NIKOLAI

HE TYPES OUT A QUICK RESPONSE.

Well, it's a two-part request. The first is the part I'd like most. The second is a bonus.

Hmm, okay. Color me intrigued

Part one isn't for everyone, but it's one of my favorites. I'd love to see my pretty pet dressed in a school uniform, asking for something from her teacher.

Of course I would do that for you, sir! I'm very into it, so don't worry your gorgeous head about that

Wonderful! Would you like to hear part two? It would require a bit more prep than usual.

I'm all ears!

I'd also like her to protest being fucked because she's a virgin and wants to stay that way but would only protest a little when her teacher tells her there's a way to get fucked that works around that, and then she lets him fuck her cute little ass.

Fuck. Yes, please

Eager much, pet?

Aren't I always eager for you, sir?

You are. Do you have any requests or adjustments? Limits?

Oh boy, lots of questions. Is this a punishment scenario? If so, spanking is fine, but no belt for marking reasons. Do you want me to play up the virginal aspect? Naive and innocent? I like the idea of Mr. Zaitsev taking advantage of me if you're into that. Do you want me to dress like a good schoolgirl with an appropriate skirt length or something too short for school rules? What about underthings? Something plain or something sexy?

Perhaps you could ask me for something. The typical raised grades, or maybe an exception to a project. I very much like the idea of taking advantage of you. You're just such a good girl, aren't you? And I'll send you everything I want you to wear, don't worry.

I try to be good for you, sir. I'm at a boring art lecture right now, but now you've got me all worked up. I'm wet just thinking about it.

Poor pet. Whatever are you going to do?

Sit here squirming until I can go home and do something about it. :(

You poor neglected girl.

Do you want the scene to start when I get there? Or later in the evening?

I'd like to talk it through one last time before we start, so not right away, but not too long after. I'll send you the options I'd like you to wear this afternoon. Choose which you like best, and I'll have it sent to you tomorrow. You can change in my room while I get set up in the study. Sound good?

Sounds perfect, sir. I'll see you Sunday!

See you Sunday, pet.

* * *

Corinne arrives on Sunday afternoon, though a bit later than usual. When he answers the door, she's dressed comfortably, as she always is when they stay in: a knit dress, tights and ankle boots, hair worn loose over her shoulders. There's an overnight bag in her hand and a garment bag over her shoulder.

He smiles and pulls the door wide. "Hello, Corinne. Come in, please."

She walks in and gives him a quick kiss. "Hi, Nikolai. I'm so sorry I'm late. My driver through the service got double-booked, and they could've found me someone else, but that would've taken so long. So I just took the L, and the train got stuck for a few minutes." She blows out a breath. "But I'm here now."

"Corinne, you should use my driver." He shuts the door behind them.

"Oh. Oh, no, sir, that's not necessary."

He raises a brow. "I insist, pet," he says with finality.

She sighs but gives him a grin. "Alright." She looks him over, eyeing the three-piece suit he always wears to the office. "Did you work today?"

"Just for a few hours this afternoon. I had a meeting with an overseas client with a weird schedule, and the timing worked for both of us. I couldn't make a morning meeting, what with it being Easter. Pascha services started at midnight, and then after, it was time for a long, drawn-out brunch full of all the things we gave up for Great Lent and Holy Week. I came home full and happy and slept like a log till about two."

"Working on Easter? You officially work too much."

"Hmm, perhaps," he replies, knowing full well she's right.

"Hmm," she says pointedly. "Well, happy Easter anyway, sir."

"*Schastlivoy paskhi*, pet." He takes her bags to his room and settles them on the bed. Then, with his hand on her lower back, he guides her to the living room. "Can I get you anything to drink?"

"No, I'm alright, thank you." She waits for him to sit and then joins him, her shin pressed to his outer thigh.

"How was your week?" Nikolai asks.

"Oh, fine. I'm trying to finish up a piece I've been working on for ages." She takes his hand in hers, squeezing it gently.

"How's it coming?" He loves hearing about her art; he could listen to her talk about it for hours.

"I've bitten off more than I can chew, honestly. It's much larger than anything I've ever painted, and even with the few extra days this week, it's still not done. I want to show it at a gallery next month, so the clock is ticking."

"I'm sure you'll figure something out."

She rubs her thumb against his hand. "How about you?"

"It was Holy Week, so I fasted for most of it. It has been, as I know for certain it's meant to be, difficult." He clears his throat. "This is what I've been looking forward to all week."

"Yeah?" she asks softly. "Me too. Ever since you texted me with your proposal."

Ah. Yes, right, the scene. He'd nearly forgotten in his anticipation to merely spend more time with her.

"Got myself off that night thinking about it," Corinne continues. She gives him a sly grin, which he meets with a smirk. "Do you want to run through things again before we start, sir?"

"Yes, certainly. Is there anything you'd like to amend before we go through it?"

"Hmm. Just reiterating my safeword. I will say 'red' if I actually want you to stop. Because I don't want you to hesitate if I say no or complain about what's happening. If you're comfortable with the consensual nonconsent nature of it?"

He nods. "I'm *very* comfortable with it. Anything else, or should we talk through the basic points?"

"That's it for me."

They discuss the plan—where it will take place, what they'll say and do to set up the scene, that he'll ignore her protests unless she gives her safeword.

Afterward, he takes a deep breath, looking her over. "Anything I missed?"

She licks her lips and shakes her head. "No, sir." Arousal warms her voice, which is something he might not have picked up a few months ago. "That's everything. Shall I go get dressed now?"

"Yes, pet. I'll see you shortly in my office." He stands and kisses her before walking toward his office, then stops. "Do you have a last name I can use?" He doesn't know her full name—a security precaution of the agency. He wouldn't have known Elijah's if he hadn't already known of his family.

"Um... Russell," Corinne replies.

Nikolai nods and enters his office, closing the door behind him. After removing his jacket, he rolls up his sleeves but leaves on the vest and the tie. He also takes out his contacts and puts on his glasses.

While he waits, he tries to read a report Thomas gave him when he left the office on Friday, but he can't concentrate. Nikolai Zaitsev doesn't fidget, but it's a near thing; he's so keyed up in anticipation that he has to will himself to stay still.

When she finally knocks on the door, he walks over and opens it, taking Corinne in. She looks perfect—plaid skirt (regulation length), white shirt, tie, blazer. Knee socks and Mary Janes. The diamond stud earrings he sent along with everything else, the ones his classmates always wore when he was in school. Her hair is parted in two low pigtails secured with red ribbons. He's so used to seeing her in lipstick that her lip gloss is a surprise.

His cock twitches in his trousers.

"Good evening, Miss Russell. Come in."

"Hi, Mr. Zaitsev." Corinne's voice is soft and timid, as though she's nervous about why her teacher would want to see her so late after school. It's strange to hear when his pet is always so confident and sure of herself. She walks in hesitantly, fiddling with the hem of her skirt.

He closes the door, then rounds his desk and sits. "Please." He gestures to the chair across from him. "Have a seat."

She does as she's told and sits on the other side of his desk. Crossing her legs, she smooths her skirt over them and looks around the office like she's never been here before. Like she didn't wake up in the middle of the night last week and go searching for him when she found the bed empty. Like she didn't drag him back to his room with the promise of another round if he vowed to stay in bed.

No surprise to anyone that he agreed.

He intertwines his fingers and rests his hands on his desk. "Do you know why I've asked you here today?"

She blinks several times. "I..." She acts as though she's trying to figure out the best answer. "I didn't turn in the latest essay?"

"Hmm. Or the one before that. Quite important essays, too, Miss Russell. Worth a lot of your grade." He looks at her over the top of his glasses, eyebrow arched sternly.

Her chin juts out slightly. "I had a hard time getting through the last two books, Mr. Zaitsev."

"And yet, you didn't ask for help." He sits back, lounging in his chair.

Corinne opens her mouth as if she'll counter his response. But then she closes it and lowers her gaze. "No, sir. But..." She looks at him through her lashes. "I can ask now?"

"Oh. So *now* you want to know if there is a way to make up the points you've cost yourself."

"Yes."

He shrugs. "There might be a way." He stands and circles the desk, then sits in front of her.

Shoulders around her ears, she looks up at him with big eyes. "Will it be a lot of work? I have a zillion extracurriculars right now, on top of normal homework." Her lip trembles. "This semester is so hard."

Fuck, she's good.

Nikolai tuts at her, crossing his arms. "Oh, it won't be too much work. I'll even do most of it, how's that?"

Her brows knit. "What sort of work, then?"

"Nothing complicated. Just you doing something for me. Something to put me in an agreeable mood." He leans forward, placing his hand on the bare skin of her knee. "Something very special."

She shifts back in her chair and laughs nervously. "Mr. Zaitsev." She tries to push his hand away, but he doesn't budge.

Instead, he squeezes her knee. "What? You want something from me, right?" His hand slides up her thigh a little more. "Is it so surprising I want something in return?"

She closes her eyes, keeping her back straight against the chair. "I can't do... *that*." The last word is a whisper. "Mr. Zaitsev, please."

He clicks his tongue at her. "Why not?" A sly smile crosses his mouth. "Sure, I always figured you were a good girl, but are you really *that* good?"

"I've never..." She looks up at him and then back down. "I'm a virgin," she whispers. "My parents are strict. I can't even date." Her eyes meet his. "I'd be in so much trouble."

He flicks the edge of her skirt, flipping it back just a bit, and then whispers in her ear. "How would they know? Would you tell them, Miss Russell?"

An exhale escapes her. "I would know. I promised I would wait until I was married. Please, Mr. Zaitsev. There has to be something else."

"Such a good little girl you are." He sits back, cocking his head to study her. She looks so prim and proper, so demure. The desire to ravish her and ruin her is damn near overwhelming. "There's... an alternative. Another way you could give me what I want without spoiling yourself for your future husband."

She blinks up at him. "H-How?"

He takes her hand and gently pulls her to her feet until she's standing before him. "Well," he says, slowly running his hands up her arms and down her torso. "The same way good girls have been getting fucked without robbing their husbands of their first time for centuries." His hands slip down until he's grabbing her ass tightly over her skirt. "Let me have this sweet little ass, since I can't have your pretty cunt."

schooled

CORINNE GASPS and tries to push him away. "That's vile, stop it."

Catching her wrists, Nikolai stands and uses the advantage of his height to loom over her, to overwhelm her. "Vile? How is it vile?" he asks, brow furrowing. "Either way, I think you'd better make peace with vile, little miss. It's your only option."

Her eyes squeeze shut. "I don't…" She sighs. "If I—if I do this, you'll give me *As* on my papers?"

"Every one of them." He smirks. "Who knows? Maybe you'll even like it."

Clenching her jaw, she opens her eyes. "What do I do?"

"Such a very good girl. Always doing what she's told." He releases her and pulls back to assess her. "Take off your blazer, little miss. There's a good girl."

She takes it off shakily before folding it in half and putting it over the chair.

His eyes rake over her, taking his time as he appreciates how her shirt is snug across her chest. "Now the tie. Hand it to me."

She does so, and he runs the silk back and forth through his fingers, eyes never leaving her.

"Undo a button," he says, voice rough. "Just one." She gives him a confused look and unbuttons the top button of her shirt. "Another, Miss Russell."

"Mr. Zaitsev," she says nervously, but does as she's told, unbuttoning the next.

"Yes, Miss Russell?" His eyes are locked on her. "Did you have something to say?"

She shakes her head. "I'm just… nervous."

A condescending smile spreads across his face. "Why are you nervous? Don't you trust me to take care of you?"

She stills. "I'm your student," she whispers.

God, she'll be the death of him. Standing there dressed like his former schoolmates, the absolute picture of naive young innocence. She's being so sweet and virginal, his pet, and he's salivating for her. He wants to ruin her, to tarnish this pristine little thing. The idea that he's some older teacher, pressing his advantage? He's losing his mind trying to rein in the force with which he wants her.

"You are. So, it's my duty to take care of you. I promise you'll enjoy it." He pulls her close. "Would you like me to do the next one?"

She nods. "Okay."

Keeping eye contact, he takes care of the next button, and the barest hint of pink against her skin is unveiled. A groan escapes him. "And what do you have here, miss?" He slips a finger between the open sides of her shirt, tugging them apart, revealing one of the sets he sent her recently: soft pink lace, so delicate and pretty.

Her breath hitches. "Just my bra, sir."

He smiles gently as he flicks another button, exposing more of her beautiful skin. "This doesn't seem like something a very good girl would wear. Or, rather, it looks like what a good girl who wants to be a bad girl wears. Still so very sweet and innocent, but very sexy." He traces a finger along the edge of one cup. "So which are you, little miss?"

She whimpers. "I'm... I *am* good, Mr. Zaitsev. But... I like lingerie." She looks up at him through her lashes. "I buy it with my allowance."

"Mmmm. You like things that make you feel good, don't you?" He just barely drags his finger under the edge of the cup, slowly dipping further with each pass until he brushes the edge of her nipple. "Do you like this?"

Her breath is ragged. It takes a moment before she reacts, but then she finally and minutely nods her head.

He looks her straight in the eyes as he drags the edge of the cup down all the way, leaving it bunched under her exposed breast. "Well now," he says, eyes wide as he takes in what he's discovered. "What have we here?" He smiles, just the right side of lascivious, and tugs gently on the barbell piercing her nipple. "You are full of surprises, Miss Russell."

She gasps in pleasure. "My best friend's sister is a piercer. I never thought—" She stops as he tugs on it once more. "I never thought anyone would find out."

"Never?" He's twisting the barbell now. "You planned to keep yourself that pure, that chaste?" Watching her, he leans close enough to breathe hotly over her nipple. While she's focused on his mouth, he pulls the other cup down, too, and tugs swiftly on the barbell he finds there. He chuckles as she gasps again. "I wonder, miss..." He stands and drags his fingers over her pretty tits, never quite touching her nipples. "Are they more sensitive now?"

She arches into his touch and then pulls back, as if catching herself. "Y-Yes, Mr. Zaitsev."

He pinches one nipple between his fingers, rolling the barbell he can feel beneath her skin. "And how does that feel?"

Her face crumples in frustration. "Please. You know what

you're doing to me. Why do you want me to say it?" Her cheeks are flushed and so sweetly embarrassed.

"It's important to acknowledge the things that bring you pleasure, little miss." Whispering in her ear, he pulls on both nipples roughly. "How else will you be able to tell that future husband of yours just how you want to be fucked?"

"Fuck," she gasps, and immediately brings a hand to her mouth. She drops it with a nervous laugh. "I guess school rules don't apply right now."

He smirks. "They could, if you want. I'd be more than happy to punish you for your swearing, Miss Russell."

"I'm—" She licks her lips and reaches for his forearm as though she needs something to hold on to. "I'm not sure, Mr. Zaitsev."

"No?" He flicks her other nipple. "Would you like to know what your punishment would be? And then you can decide?"

She nods. "Okay."

He turns her toward the desk and helps her place her hands on the polished surface. "I'd have you like this. And then for every letter of that word"—he slowly runs his hand over the fabric of her skirt where it covers her ass—"I'd smack this pretty little ass."

She arches back against his touch. "Okay. It's only four. That's not so bad."

"Hm, and one for a reminder. So we'll settle at five, shall we?"

She looks back at him and pouts. "That doesn't seem fair."

Tutting, he pulls that pouty bottom lip. "We could make it six if you'd like to argue some more."

"No, sir."

He smooths his hand over her hair, her back. "Good girl." Stepping back, he tugs at the hem of her cute little skirt. "Skirt up, miss."

She remains bent over the desk and flips up her skirt, revealing her matching underwear. He sucks in a breath at the sight, so sweet and delicate. So innocent. "What a sweet girl you are in your pretty lingerie." He snaps the elastic at the waistband before he kneels and presses a kiss to each cheek. "As much as I love these," he says, nipping at her ass, "they need to go." He slides them down her legs, then stands and slides them into his pocket. "Ready?"

"Yes, sir," she mumbles against her arm.

"Good girl." He gives no warning before he draws his hand back and lands a smack against her left cheek. "Count."

She gasps. "One."

"Perfect." He smooths the sting of the hit with a caress before abruptly landing the second hit on the other cheek.

"Two." She spreads her legs the tiniest bit, and Nikolai smiles to himself. It's a readjustment, sure, but he knows she'll feel each smack reverberate through her cunt that way. He lands the third strike a little harder, a little lower, and squeezes roughly.

Corinne cries out and pushes herself back against his hand. "Three."

He laughs, just this side of mean. "Oh, is that so, little miss? You like this?"

She whines. "Yes, sir."

"Hmm," he says, almost like he doesn't believe her. Then he barely brushes one finger against her cunt. "Oh. Oh, yes, I see. You *do* like it. What a naughty girl you are, Miss Russell."

A gasp escapes her lips at the touch, and she arches back even further. "Mr. Zaitsev, *please*."

"Please, what? Please touch you here some more? Please finish spanking you?" He drags his finger up and brushes over her asshole.

She shivers, and he hears her press her forehead to the desk.

"Please, you've made me so... I'm..." He looks over. She's shaking her head like it embarrasses her. "I'm *aching*. And I *need*. So please just do what you're going to do, sir."

"Oh, well, since you insist." He slaps once more on the left cheek, hard, so hard his hand stings.

"*Fuck!*" she sobs. "Four," she quickly adds. "It's four."

"Tsk, tsk, Miss Russell. You're lucky I have other plans, or you'd get another five." He smacks her one last time, loving the way her ass bounces from the impact.

"Five. I'm sorry, Mr. Zaitsev, but it hurt."

God, but she looks good. Her pretty little cunt all wet and glistening, her ass flushed from his hand. Her knee socks are killing him, as is her sexy skirt. Fuck.

Nikolai can't wait to get inside her.

"You're forgiven." He reaches into his pocket for the little bottle of lube. "Besides..." He leans over her and places it where she can see it. "We still have our original agreement to uphold."

She glances at the bottle before looking back at him. "Right," she says softly. "What do I have to do?"

"I'll walk you through it." He rubs a hand on her back, ostensibly to help soothe her. "Just relax and do as I say, alright?"

She crosses her arms on the desk and rests her head against them. "Okay." Her voice is small when she continues. "Does it hurt?"

He shushes her gently. "I'm going to make sure it doesn't. I'm going to make it so good for you. Do you believe me?"

She nods against her arm. "Yes, sir."

"Good girl." He kneels behind her and pulls her cheeks apart, giving him a perfect view. "So pretty, even here. I cannot wait to taste you." Before she has a chance to respond, he leans forward and licks a broad stripe across her hole.

"Oh!" she squeaks. "I wasn't expecting that."

He hums, licking again before he pulls back. "I told you I'd make it good, Miss Russell. Did you think I was lying?"

"No, sir. I promise I believe you," she says earnestly, much of her earlier hesitance missing from her voice. "I just... I haven't done this, so I don't know what to expect."

Nikolai chuckles.

"You must think I'm silly because of how much I don't know," she says.

"I think it's sweet, little miss." He runs the tip of his finger around her hole, watching it twitch. Delicious. "Do you like it? Do you want me to stop?"

She whimpers. "No, sir. I don't want you to stop."

With a grin, he gets back to work.

He's sloppy about it, sucking and licking broad, flat stripes with his tongue, diving in to loosen the muscle, turning her into a gasping, groaning mess. Then he slowly pushes in his finger alongside his tongue.

"Mr. Zaitsev," she breathes.

He pulls his mouth away, now slick with saliva. "Yes?" His finger is still moving, and he takes the opportunity to gently slip just the tip of a second finger in alongside the first.

She gasps. "God." He presses a little farther. "I just... It's a lot at once, sir. Your mouth feels so good, and your fingers... I feel so full."

He chuckles and slips his fingers out just enough to stand and grab the lube. He leans in close and murmurs, "Alright still, Corinne?"

Nodding, she turns and smiles. "Perfect, sir." She kisses his cheek.

He grins back before letting the stern demeanor fall back in place. While most people only see his serious side, Corinne is one of the few who most often sees *Nikolai* and not *Mr. Zaitsev, CEO*, and he rather likes that.

Filing that away to think on later, he kneels back down and palms open Miss Russell's ass. He pops the top on the lube and drizzles some over his finger. He kisses her hole one last time. "The key thing is to relax, little miss." Then he slides his finger all the way in.

She obeys his command, letting her limbs loosen with a sigh. She moans as his finger fucks in and out of her. "That's so good."

"Why, Miss Russell," he says, faux-scandalized. "You like having your ass played with?" He slicks a second finger with lube and begins to slip it inside. "Such a tight little ass, Miss Russell, fucking hell."

"Is that good, Mr. Zaitsev?" she asks, whimpering.

"S'perfect." He scissors his fingers open, still slowly rotating them as he stretches her.

She groans, writhing against the desk. "*Please.*"

"Please what, Miss Russell? Communication is the most important thing. What do you want me to do to you?" He stretches his fingers wider. "What a pretty little hole you have. I cannot wait to be inside it."

She keens at that, fucking herself on his fingers. "Please, that's what I want, Mr. Zaitsev. Please... fuck me." The last two words are barely a whisper.

"Where, little miss?" His cock is achingly hard, and his voice is rough and raspy. "Where do you want me to fuck you?"

She tucks her face against her arm again with a groan of frustration. "I can't say that."

He slides a third finger in, slowly, so slowly, letting her get used to the stretch. "You can," he cajoles her. "Come along, Miss Russell. Where would you like me to fuck you? Is it your mouth?"

"No, sir." She whines as though she'll absolutely die from saying it. "My ass."

He presses his forehead to her ass, groaning, and turns his head so he can watch his fingers at work. "Ask me," he rasps. "Ask me for it, Miss Russell."

She's quiet for a moment, nothing in the room but her breathy whimpers, the slick sounds of him stretching her open. And then, finally, she begs.

"Please fuck my ass, Mr. Zaitsev."

thank you, mr. zaitsev

NIKOLAI

IT'S DAMN NEAR A GROWL, the sound that comes out of Nikolai when she asks him to fuck her ass. He bolts upright, removing his fingers to reach for the condom in his other pocket. Their breathing is so loud it almost drowns out the zipper when he pulls out his cock.

God, he hasn't been this fucking hard in ages. He takes a deep breath as he rolls on the condom and slicks it with lube before pressing his cock against her now pliant hole. "Alright, Miss Russell. Push out a bit and relax."

Corinne groans and takes loud, deep breaths as he begins to push inside her. "Mr. Zaitsev," she says around a hiss. "You're so big, God."

He laughs at that, choking it off as he gets deeper. "Miss Russell," he says on a sharp exhale. "Make sure you tell your future husband that. Men are fragile things. Need their egos stroked." He pushes forward, swearing at the blood-hot feel of her around him. "Fuck. You have the tightest ass. Feels so fucking good."

Pressing his hips against her ass, he waits, letting her get used to the stretch of his cock until she pushes back against him, wriggling a bit like she wants more. He swats at her ass, baring his teeth in a feral grin. "You want more already, eh, little miss?"

"Yes, *fuck*, please." Arching her back, she reaches behind herself to pull her skirt back up where it's fallen, giving him a hell of a nice view.

As he tucks in the hem of her skirt, he pulls almost all the way out, savoring how her rim stretches around him. He pushes back in with more force, hands gripping her hips tightly.

"Mr. Zaitsev," she gasps as he fucks her more deeply. "Will you... will you spank me again? Please?"

His hand snaps out immediately; he can't do it fast enough, in fact. "Looks so good, little miss." He raises his other hand to slap the other cheek, groaning at the way it makes her clench. "Look at how that pretty little ass bounces, huh? Fuck. Stretched so tight around my cock. You're taking it so well, Miss Russell. So fucking well."

A cry falls from her lips at each hit, trembling against the desk. "Will you please touch me, sir?"

"Ah ah, touch you where, little miss?" he asks, even though he knows full well what she wants. "You know I want to hear you ask."

She whines but acquiesces much more quickly than before. "Please touch my clit. Need your hand on me."

"Very good girl," he praises, his hand darting to where she wants him. "Always ask for what you want."

She mewls, arching against him as his fingers knowingly take her apart. "Oh, God. Fuck, fuck." She falls over the edge, and God, the fucking *grip* of her when she comes. She's whimpering and shuddering under him with aftershocks, and he gentles his fingers on her clit before shifting his hand back to her hip, pulling her onto him.

"So fucking tight, goddamn." He smacks her ass again, this

time with both hands, gripping tight and digging his fingers in after each hit.

She looks so fucking sexy; he cannot believe he gets to fuck her like this, acting like this. His climax is barreling toward him, getting more powerful every second. "What do you say when someone makes you feel good, little miss?" he asks. He's barely staving off his orgasm, but he wants to hear her say it. "Eh? What do you say after I've fucked this little ass of yours and played with your clit and made you come all over my cock?"

"Mmm." She looks back at him with big, wide eyes, biting her lip before she speaks. "Thank you for fucking me, Mr. Zaitsev."

It's like getting sucker punched. The second the words leave her lips, his orgasm is on him. "Oh God, *God*, ah, fuck!" His last few thrusts are brutal before he cries out, every muscle in his body freezing, clenching. It lasts forever, aftershock after aftershock rolling through his body.

At last, it finishes. Damn, his knees are going to give out. He braces his hands on the desk; they're shaking, but he can't find it in himself to care.

She reaches for his hand on the desk and twines two of her fingers with his. "Was that alright, Mr. Zaitsev?" she asks shyly.

Still lost in the haze of pleasure, he groans. "Delightful, little miss." He takes another moment before he pulls out, dealing with the condom before he stands and tucks himself away. He helps her stand and spins her around, kissing her gently. "Perfection, pet. Absolute perfection."

Her body is still quivering, and she gives him a dopey, lazy little smile. "God, that was so good. Fuck."

While he fastens his trousers, he kisses her soundly and then scoops her up in his arms. "You were..." He trails off as he walks them to the en suite off his bedroom. He sets her on the counter and kisses her sweetly. He can't seem to stop. "You were spectacular, darling pet." He turns to the sink to wash his hands.

Her cheeks flush pink, and she grins up at him again. "Thank you." Once he finishes, she widens her legs and tugs him by his belt loops to stand between them. "You were..." She sighs dreamily. "... so fucking hot. My high school experience would've been very different if you'd been my teacher, Mr. Zaitsev."

Nikolai chuckles, running his hands over her, keeping in contact. "I'm sure you were a very good girl in school, weren't you, pet?" He presses a kiss to her forehead before stepping back to turn on the tub.

"Yes, I was good. I liked my mom too much to cause her any trouble. Plus, she pretty much let me do what I wanted." He looks back. She's grinning at him. "I bet you were a force to be reckoned with."

He smirks. "I believe my teachers would have qualified me more as a pain in the ass, but you're not wrong, pet." He pours some bath oil into the water and faces her, still crouched in front of the tub. "Will you be alright here for a moment? I have a surprise for you."

She nods, her eyes getting bigger. "Another surprise?" She touches one of her new earrings, which she'd thanked him for when they'd arrived two days ago. "You've already gotten me so much for tonight. You're going to spoil me rotten."

Nikolai stands and walks toward the bedroom. "I like to spoil you." He gently tugs her pigtail as he passes her. "And I like seeing you in things I've bought you. Humor me."

"Okay, fine," she says with a sigh and a smile.

He retrieves a box, slim and pale gray, tied with a delicate ribbon, and returns to her. She's waiting for him with her hair out of her pigtails.

"For when you stay over, if you wish." He pulls on the bow,

letting it fall from the box before he opens it. Inside, wrapped in white tissue paper, is a robe and slip, both teal silk with delicate cream lace details.

"Oh," Corinne breathes. She unties the sash of the robe and lifts the slip out of the box. "Of course I wish. It's beautiful. I love it so much." She pulls him down for a soft, gentle kiss.

"I'm glad." He moves to turn off the water, steam rising from it as it waits for her. "Let's get you out of this very enticing outfit, pet." He kneels to tug off her shoes and roll down her socks, kissing each knee as it's revealed to him. Then he helps her out of the rest of her uniform. "Would you like to be alone for your bath? Or do you want company?"

"Hm, company, definitely." She picks up her hair tie from the counter and pulls her hair into a hasty bun, kissing his shoulder as she passes him. When she eases herself into the bath, she asks, "Do you want to join me? The water feels nice."

He smiles broadly and quickly undresses, leaving his clothes where they fall before stepping into the water and sinking behind her. "Hello, pet," he murmurs.

"Hi." She wraps his arms around her body as she nestles against his chest. It's... nice. He hasn't done this with anyone in a while, and he forgot how comforting it can be.

How intimate it feels.

"So," she begins, pulling him from his thoughts, "what was your favorite part?"

He idly traces his fingers along her arm. "It's hard to choose. I loved how you seemed so sad when I spanked you. The contrast of that and the way I could smell how wet you were... Delicious. How innocent you acted did even more for me than I expected."

She giggles. "I had a feeling it would. Plus, playing an inno-cent, naive little virgin is ridiculously fun." She grabs his hand and entwines their fingers. "I loved it when you made me explicitly tell you everything I wanted. And when you made me thank you for fucking me when you were taking advantage of this poor girl?" She gives a satisfied groan. "You delicious deviant. Well done."

He laughs and holds her close. "We can keep a few of those things, if you'd like. Telling me explicitly, or thanking me, maybe. Up to you, sweet pet."

"I liked you making an innocent girl tell you what she wanted, but I think we both know I'm not innocent, sir." She peeks at him over her shoulder with a mischievous grin. "But thanking you would be nice. I'd like to do that from now on." She pulls his hand up and kisses it. "Would you like me to wash you, sir?"

"You know, pet, I rather think I would, since you offered so sweetly. Thank you." He hands her the soap and the loofah. "Such a very good girl for me." His smile is wicked and fond all at once as he watches her, an idea forming slowly in the back of his mind.

She gets on her knees and faces him, water dripping down her pretty skin in rivulets, pearling at the tips of her pierced nipples. A thought crosses his mind as she soaps up the loofah and rubs it along his body.

The invitation tucked away in his kitchen drawer. What she would look like—

"What's that look for?" Corinne asks with a tilt of her head.

A smile spreads across his face. "A surprise."

persephone's choice

NIKOLAI

"A SURPRISE?" she asks.

He drags a finger across her cheekbone, along her lips. "I'll share with you later, pet. I promise."

Corinne's eyes narrow playfully before she pokes his chest. "Fine, then." She continues washing him for a moment and then looks up at him with a grin. "So, how did *you* lose your virginity?"

He barks out a laugh, thoroughly surprised by the question. "Well," he says, still chucking. "Uh, well. Hm. I was seventeen. We'd visited Rättvik in Sweden for the summer to visit some distant aunt of my mother's. It's a small seaside village, and I spent the whole trip wrapped up in a local boy. His name—" He squints over her shoulder as he tries to remember.

"His name was Mikael," he continues. "He drove an old Volvo wagon, and his family had land just outside the village. We went out to the back pasture one night after a swim." He laughs as he recalls the details. "I had mosquito bites all over that itched like the devil."

She laughs. "Sounds magical and terrible at the same time, really. Fucking in a field sounds lovely until you remember insects exist." She finishes washing him and tries to turn the loofah to herself, but he takes it and washes her in return.

"What about you, pet? Was it candlelight and roses? A hasty fuck in a basement before someone's parents came home? Or something else entirely?" Her nose crinkles, one eye closing as she tilts her head. "That bad, hm?"

"No, no. It wasn't. It's just a complicated history."

He holds out his arms, gesturing to the space around them. "We've got all night, pet."

She sighs, pressing her lips together, and it takes several moments before she speaks. "His name was Will, and he was my childhood best friend. And I loved him so much. But I was invisible to him. Like a kid sister. Until another boy asked me out at school, and he couldn't handle it."

With a shrug, she continues. "Suddenly, he did care. Suddenly, he gave me all the attention I could want. And I'd wanted him for so long, I didn't question it. I took what I had been so desperate for, even if it was..." She trails off, her eyes unfocused before she shakes her head. "Our first time... God, I loved him so much I didn't even care that it was just... fine. Not bad, not good, but fine. Things were always *fine*."

Nikolai presses a kiss to her hair, not rushing her, letting her take her time.

"We stayed together through high school and into college. When I started sex work..." She blows out a breath. "Will couldn't handle it. He was so *jealous*," she spits, like the word is bitter in her mouth. "He couldn't see it was possible for me to have sex for work and still love him and still be his." She shakes her head. "I liked what I was doing. I was good at it. And it took too long to see that what I thought had been great for so long just wasn't."

Corinne sniffles, and he tightens his arms around her. "So," she says, wiping her cheeks. She laughs shakily. "Damn, you asked about my first time, and I wrote you a whole sad novel."

Cradling her in his arms, he kisses her spine, her shoulders. "You deserved better than *fine*, pet, and I'm glad you realized that. Whoever this man was, he sounds like an insecure *zasranets*, and good riddance to him." Bending forward, he rubs his cheek against hers. "Thank you for sharing, pet." He laces their fingers together. "You know, this is the first time someone's story has made mine sound sweet and romantic instead of a quick fuck with too many insects and not enough lube."

Corinne laughs and kisses his cheek. "Well, now you have me to kiss your bites better if it ever happens again."

Warmth floods his chest at that idea, and he knows better than to look at it too closely. "Is that your way of saying you'd like to get fucked in a field?"

She looks out the window toward the city. "In the middle of Chicago?"

He quirks an eyebrow and shrugs cockily. "I know a guy. I could make it happen if you wanted. It wouldn't be *right* in the middle of Chicago, but I could make something happen."

She quirks her own eyebrow. "And what would this entail, sir?"

"Oh, whatever you wanted. I've fucked in a field before," he teases. "I have some ideas, but I'd like to hear yours."

"Remember when we said we'd be honest about what we wanted?" she asks, and he nods. "Fucking in, say, the French countryside? With wine and candles and starlight? That sounds delightful." Then she scrunches her nose. "Fucking in a cornfield in Illinois sounds terrible, sir."

"Then I'll just have to take you to France." He flips the lever for the drain and stands to get a towel.

"Really?" Corinne asks, as he offers her a hand out of the

tub. Nikolai dries himself quickly before grabbing a fresh towel for her.

"Really." He takes his time to dry her off then helps her into her new slip and robe. "I do a lot of business in Europe. If you want to go to France, we'll go to France, pet."

Taking his face in her hands, she kisses him gently. "Thank you, sir. I'd love that. Business trips with me are very fun, you know." She winks.

He laughs and slips on a pair of sweatpants. Entwining their fingers, he pulls her to the kitchen. "Of that, I have no doubt."

"Mhmm. Every meeting you go to or presentation you attend is made a little brighter knowing I'm waiting for you to come back and fuck me. I can send you naughty little messages, too, unless you find them too distracting." She stops in front of his liquor cabinet. "Would you like a drink, sir?"

"Yes, pet, thank you. Rye is fine."

Corinne told him early on that she's "worthless in the kitchen," but she makes herself useful when she can. Nikolai loves to cook. It's a calming ritual of sorts, especially after a long day. He pays someone to do most things for him these days, but this? This he does for himself.

Pulling out the ingredients he'd prepared earlier, he sets them on the counter so he can make quick work of their dinner. "Any distraction you could present would be welcome. Those business meetings are fucking tedious."

She pours him a rye whiskey and herself a glass of wine before hopping onto the counter. The marble must be cold against her legs because she shivers, and her nipples instantly harden under the silk. His eyes rake over her. She smirks.

"You're the boss; can't you make someone else attend for you?" She peers over the ingredients, and he slides her a bit of goat cheese, glad he's left the pomegranate in the fridge or she would've eaten all of it.

"I could," he agrees as he starts on the chicken. "But if it's a large enough opportunity, then it's worth my time to personally attend."

"Do you have offices in Europe too? I really don't know anything about cybersecurity." She snags another little bite of goat cheese.

"Stop stealing the cheese, pet," he reprimands, just this side of stern, and her resulting pout almost makes him grin. He slides the dish out of her reach. "I have a London office that serves as the European headquarters and a smaller one in Paris." He walks to the fridge for the pomegranate seeds and makes a show of how far away he places them from Corinne.

"Pomegranate, sir?" She bites her lip and looks at him through her lashes. "Are you trying to trap me in your Underworld?"

Arching a brow, he grabs a seed and holds it in front of him. "Hades didn't trap Persephone, pet. He offered her an equal share in his life, his kingdom, his power. He saw her for *her*, not what her mother wished her to be. And then he offered her a choice." He rests the pomegranate seed on her lips, holding her gaze. "Open, pet."

Her eyes narrow. "Before I take it, I have to know what you're offering." She blinks up at him. "That's only fair."

He smiles at her and pops the seed into his own mouth. "Smart girl," he praises before walking over to a drawer on the other side of the kitchen. He pulls something out before returning to her and handing it over.

The save-the-date is lovely, the paper heavy and thick, a dark midnight blue with gold script. The date is a month away, and while it looks for all the world like a wedding invitation, it's not.

"There's a party," he murmurs. "I used to be very involved in the High Protocol community here in Chicago. When the company took off, I didn't have time to be as involved, but I still get invited to parties throughout the year. It's been a long time since I attended. There are a lot of rules, and we'd need to start incorporating more aspects of it here at home to get you comfortable, but I'd like to know if you'd be interested."

Her thumb idly brushes the gold lettering, and his eyes never leave her as she reads over it. He's holding his breath, butterflies suddenly taking up residence in the very pit of his stomach. He wants her to *want* to go, to want to try this together as much as he does, and the wait has his heart rate kicking up even as he tells himself he's being ridiculous.

She's quiet for a long moment, the silence stretching between them until it's almost unbearable. And then, finally, she murmurs, "Yes, I'd like that." She smiles at him, a surprised, breathy laugh escaping her lips. "I'd like that very much, Nikolai."

He schools the excited relief that floods him and picks another pomegranate seed to press to her mouth. When her tongue slips out to catch it, his eyes darken. "Well then, Persephone," he says, his voice deep. "Seems you've made your choice."

rules and propositions

CORINNE

THE FOLLOWING MORNING, Corinne is finishing up her breakfast when Nikolai walks into the kitchen, fully dressed with his jacket hooked on his index finger. She's still wearing the new slip and robe he gave her last night; she wasn't expecting him to be fully dressed already.

He snags her fork to steal a bite from her plate. She's eating leftover pashka from yesterday, and he closes his eyes as he chews, clearly savoring it. "God, I missed dairy. I think I could eat this every meal for a week and still not get tired of it."

Nikolai mentioned weeks ago that during the Triodion Season, he follows strict monastic fasting traditions, and she was shocked. During the Season, he's supposed to abstain from all animal products, fish with backbones, oil, wine, and sexual contact, with a few exceptions. There are days of complete fasting, especially during Holy Week, and he's otherwise allowed one meal on weekdays and two on weekends. It's no wonder the Easter feast is so meaningful after weeks of such sacrifice.

Though, when she reminded him she'd seen him every single Sunday for the last six weeks, he just smirked and said,

"No one's perfect, pet. Why do you think I'm so strict about the rest?"

Now, she takes another bite of the pashka and grabs her phone to check the time. "Is it later than I realized?"

He snags his mug from the counter. "You *were* tough to wake this morning."

"Well." She crosses her legs and takes a sip of coffee. "My teacher took advantage of me last night, and that wears a girl out."

Nikolai smirks at her and finishes the last of his tea. "I'll take advantage anytime you'd like. Miss Russell seems like she could maybe use some more hands-on instruction." He shrugs on his jacket and puts his mug in the sink.

"Whatever you think is best, Mr. Zaitsev," she says sweetly. She raises her half-full mug for one last drink. "Give me a second, and I'll get ready to head out."

He tilts up her chin and gives her a gentle kiss. "Stay as long as you like. Hit the button above the handle when you leave, and it will lock behind you."

"Oh." She blinks, then leans in for another kiss, rubbing her fingertips against his stubble. "Have a good day at work, sir. And thank you for breakfast."

"Of course, pet." He brushes his thumb along her cheek. "Have a good day."

He disappears into the foyer, and the door clicks shut behind him. She glances around the apartment. She's not used to being in this space by herself. It feels empty without him.

Coffee in hand, she walks into the living room and stops in front of the floor-to-ceiling windows. It's a bright, cloudless day, and the sun is a sparkling reflection over the lake. She snags a cushion from the settee and places it on the floor, sitting down to enjoy the breathtaking sight while she finishes her cup.

Her mind wanders to Nikolai. Does he ever just sit here and enjoy the view? Does he ever take time for himself outside their visits? Even on Easter, a day that is clearly important to him, he went into the office before she came over. She hopes, if anything, their time together forces him to slow down, to rest, to recuperate before starting the week again.

Her thoughts shift to last night, to his proposition, to his face when she said yes—surprised and happy and hopeful. She takes out her phone to pull up her search engine. She's familiar with High Protocol as a concept but isn't well versed on the specifics. Nikolai promised to send her some information, but it's obviously important to him, and she wants to prepare herself as much as possible.

There are many videos and websites, some of which look like they haven't been updated in twenty years. The first few results quickly confirm what she already knows: a High Protocol party is a formal BDSM party where submissives serve their dominants. There is often a dress code and strict rules to adhere to.

Unfortunately, things get muddier from there. Every website lists different rules, and some are so focused on only women being the submissives that she closes them before she finishes. Others offer even more conflicting information until she finally decides to text Nikolai instead.

> The internet is confusing on High Protocol, sir. How many rules will there be at the party? Are they difficult to follow? What else should I know going in?

The three dots appear instantly.

Researching already? My, my, Miss Russell. It seems yesterday's correction did wonders for you.

She grins and tucks her legs closer.

Just want to be a good student for you, Mr. Zaitsev.

Well done. Don't worry, pet. I'll ease you into the rules at home over the next month.

Thank you.

I know we discussed sexual limits when we first started, but if we're going to dive further into things, then we should discuss kink limits as well. I still have the Calypso limits checklist filled out that I can email you. You should send me yours before Sunday. We'll discuss them in person when you come over.

Yes, sir. I can do that.

Good girl.

Corinne smiles. She'll never get tired of him saying that.

She puts her dishes in the dishwasher to make it easier for his housekeeper and packs her stuff to head out. Walking out the door, she gets another text. She assumes it's Nikolai, but it's actually Margot.

Do you have a few minutes to stop by the office this week? I'd like to discuss something with you.

Her brows arch in surprise. With Margot, that could mean anything. She checks her schedule and replies.

Sure, I'll come in on Wednesday.

* * *

The Calypso Escorts office is in a discreet location in West Loop. There's no sign on the door, and you would only know what's inside if you were a potential client who preferred an in-person consultation. The interior is elegant with warm colors and luscious textures, perfectly inviting for their clientele and the services they're requesting.

Corinne walks in on Wednesday afternoon, says hello to the receptionist, and heads back to Margot's office. Margot's on the phone but beckons Corinne with a crook of her finger.

"Of course, Mr. Thorne. I'll make sure that will never happen again," Margot says as Corinne sits across from her. "Yes, I'll talk to him about it myself." A pause. "Absolutely. Of course. Have a great day." She hangs up and then turns to Corinne. "Sometimes clients just..." She raises her fist with a grimace.

Corinne grins. "I know all too well."

"I know you do. Which is exactly why I asked if you could come in."

"Oh?"

Margot leans back in her chair. "You're great at what you do, Corinne. You consistently bring in business; your recurrence rate is higher than any other escort. And you've been here for nine years. I think it's safe to say you know this business almost as well as I do."

Huh. She wonders what brought this on. "Thank you, Margot. That means a lot coming from you."

"Calypso has done quite well the last few years. So much so that I've been thinking about expanding outside Chicago to

Philadelphia. I've done some research, and they don't have this caliber of service there. It's ripe for the taking, and since I can't be in two places at once, I am looking for someone to run the Philly branch." She smiles. "And you were the first person I thought of."

Corinne inhales deeply. "I'm—wow, I wasn't expecting this." She laughs, utterly floored. "I don't even know what to say."

"Say yes." Margot laughs. "I'm just kidding. I don't need an answer now. I won't get into heavy planning until early fall, so you have time. We'd pay for your moving expenses, and your salary would be almost double what it is now, and that will only increase the more the business grows."

Corinne's eyes widen. She already lives rather comfortably; double her pay would be life-changing. "I would like some time to think about it. Chicago's my home. We've always bonded over that."

"I know. It's a big decision, Corinne. Take your time, alright?"

Corinne nods.

"But," Margot grins mischievously, "if you want to hear what I have in the works, I can share what I've been planning."

Whether Corinne goes or not, she still wants to know all about it. "Yes, tell me everything."

They spend the next hour discussing Margot's plans. She's wanted to run her own business for years, and this would be a huge step toward making that dream a reality. Part of her thinks she'd be a fool to say no; part of her aches at the thought of leaving her beloved city. Her mom lives here, her friends.

Nikolai, her brain offers.

She shoves that thought to the side.

When Corinne's mom comes over for their biweekly arts and crafts night, Corinne tells her about her conundrum while she paints and Violet crochets. Her mom has always known what Corinne does for a living. She herself was an erotic dancer when Corinne was little, so it's never something she's had to hide from her.

"Oh, Coco," Violet says. "That's a wonderful opportunity." Her mom has the same dark hair and eyes as Corinne and an hourglass figure her daughter has always been a little jealous of. She's in an oversized Billie Eilish concert t-shirt from the show Nikolai paid for.

"I know! But leaving Chicago!" Corinne frowns. "Would you be upset if I left?"

"Would *you* be upset if you left?"

Corinne sighs. "I don't know."

"I want you to do whatever is best for your happiness. If advancing your career makes you happiest, then you should go. If home is where you're happiest, then you have your answer."

"It sounds so easy when you say it like that."

"You've got a few months, right?" she asks, and Corinne nods. "Then there's no need to decide tonight. Go back to your day-to-day life, go to work, make beautiful art, and maybe your answer will magically appear."

"Just like that?"

Violet nods and squeezes her hand. "Just like that."

the house protocol

AFTER A HECTIC WEEK, Sunday arrives before Corinne knows it. If she's honest with herself, she can admit it's become her favorite day of the week. But for the first time she's met with Nikolai, she's nervous.

Nervous about her job decision, though she can put that on her mind's back burner for now. Nervous about what's shifting between her and Nikolai, something exciting and titillating. But also scary.

It's not that she's never done power exchange in her job before; she's been on both sides of it, in fact. But they were just scenes, and the dynamic was over when the scene was finished. Plus, she's never had the same amount of... chemistry with those clients. But everything is different with Nikolai.

She's trying not to question it too much. Not when she's having so much fun.

Adrian picks her up right on time, which is a pleasant change of pace compared to the car service Calypso uses. He's friendly but quiet, so Corinne enjoys the silence and takes in the passing city until they arrive.

When she exits the car, she straightens her outfit, a light-weight sweater tucked into a button-up skirt. She thanks Adrian for fetching her bag and exhales deeply before heading to Nikolai's apartment.

Nikolai doesn't take long to answer, and his eyes rake over her before he kisses her cheek. "Hello, Corinne," he says, closing the door behind her. "How are you?"

"Lovely now that I'm here." She kisses him. "How are you? How was your week?"

"Oh, you know. Day after day of meetings and people trying my patience. The downside to being the boss." He places his hand on the small of her back and leads her toward the pair of armchairs in the living room. "Would you like a drink before we start?"

"Sure, boss," she says with a grin. "Just some water would be nice."

Grabbing her chin, he leans in and kisses her, then whispers in her ear. "That's not my name, Corinne. Unless you'd like to be my sexy secretary sometime." He straightens before she can react and saunters off to the kitchen.

She blinks a few times, a smile slowly forming on her face. When he returns, she looks up at him with wide, innocent eyes. "I'm sorry I called you the wrong name, sir. Though if you want me to stop by your office sometime, that could certainly be arranged."

His eyes go dark for a moment, like he's imagining exactly how that would play out, before he shakes it off and hands her the water. "Let's put a pin in that, shall we?" He settles into the chair across from her and opens a drawer in the table at his elbow. He pulls out a tablet and a small box. "So." He crosses an ankle over his opposite knee and opens his tablet. "Let's talk limits."

"Of course." She fishes her phone out of her bag. A message from another one of her regulars is on the screen, but Corinne will text her back in the morning. "Do you have any questions about my list, sir?"

"I noticed you marked yourself as *curious* about public and private humiliation." He looks up from his tablet. "Could you tell me more about that?"

Humiliation is usually a limit. She's marked it as such every time she fills one out. She's worried about clients taking it too far or it sounding too much like the things nasty men love to tell her because of what she does for a living. But she sat and thought about what it might be like with him and couldn't see it being like that at all.

"I don't have a lot of experience with it. Well, not in a negotiated or consensual framework." Nikolai's brow furrows at that. "I'm not sure if it's for me, but I'd like to try." The corner of her mouth turns upward, eyes darting to her phone. "I can see it's something you're really into."

The seriousness of his face lifts, and he smiles as though he's been caught out at something. "I am indeed, pet. I find it can be exciting when everyone enjoys it." He taps on his tablet. "What phrases or actions are off-limits for you as far as humiliation goes?"

"Anything with my profession." The answer is immediate. "I don't want to be called a whore. I don't want to be treated in a demeaning fashion about my work." She crosses her legs. "You know how we played with CNC last week. I'd never want that framed as you getting whatever you wanted because you paid for it." She pauses for a moment. "Nothing to do with being a woman."

A shaky breath escapes her as she realizes how much she's exposed herself by sharing these things. "I don't think you would do those things, sir," she says, "but just to have them out in the open."

He places a hand on hers, his eyes serious and intent. "Never. You have my word." He holds her gaze for a moment longer and squeezes her hand before sitting back. "Thank you for sharing those things with me, pet. Now"—and here he smiles gently—"anything you'd *like* me to say? Focus on?"

"Hm." She taps her hand against the arm of the chair. "Slut shaming?" She huffs a laugh. "Maybe you already do a bit. Telling me how desperate I am." She shrugs. "Maybe there's more, but I don't know what yet."

His smile turns darker. "Well, pet, you are a needy little thing. I just call it like I see it." He taps out a note on his tablet and looks back at her. "Anything on here that's okay in private, but you'd rather not do in public?"

"At the High Protocol party? Or in the general public?"

"Let's start with the party." He scrunches his nose. "Scenes in the general public are situational for me. A lot can go wrong."

"I agree. I just wanted to make sure." She ponders his question. "I'm guessing the party will have a lot of rules. I'm a little nervous about breaking them by accident. Very overt public punishment would feel humiliating, and I wouldn't like that." She shrugs. "I can't think of anything else right now, sir, but like I said. I'm new to the High Protocol aspect."

He makes another note and smiles at her. "You'll do wonderfully, I'm sure. We'll start easy." He sets the tablet aside and sits back leisurely in his chair. "Your turn, pet. Any questions for me?"

She looks down at his list and narrows her eyes playfully. "Hmm. You don't like *massages*?"

He laughs. "I enjoy them immensely, but I've never been particularly invested in getting them. I'd much rather give them." His gaze turns hungry. "So much skin, so many touches. A whole new way to practice your patience."

She sighs and rolls her eyes, a grin threatening to tug at her lips. "Of course that's how you view it. Just another way to make me suffer."

"I am an unabashed sadist, pet. I thought you knew this by now." He looks her over again. "Other questions? Comments? Concerns?"

She glances at his list and then gazes back at him intently, raising one eyebrow. "Curious about religious scenes?"

He raises his own brow in turn. "I was raised in the Eastern Orthodox Church, and I love power dynamics. I wouldn't mind playing the corrupt priest to your innocent parishioner."

"Oh. Okay, Father," she responds, voice dripping with honey. His grip tightens minutely on the arm of his chair.

"Be good, pet."

Her eyes widen at the roughness of his voice. "Yes, sir." She will definitely file that away for later.

She reviews his list again and then her own, reminding herself of some of the differences. "There are some things on here that are limits because of the job. Whether for marking reasons or safety reasons. So, for example, I have breath play as a limit, but I'm not necessarily opposed to it. It's just..." She smiles, her pulse ticking up. She's nervous. She wants him to know she likes the same things he does. She doesn't know why it matters, but she needs him to know. "A boundary I set early on."

He studies her for a moment. "Has this boundary... changed? Is it something you'd feel comfortable doing with me under the right circumstances?"

Corinne rubs her thumb against the leather of the chair. "Eventually, I think." She glances up at him. "I will let you know."

"Alright, pet. Whenever you feel comfortable." He smiles at her. "Anything else? Limits, things you'd like to try, other questions you have for me?"

"No, sir. I think that's it."

"Excellent." He pulls out a piece of paper from the drawer. "Now, we discussed easing you into the mindset for the party. So, let's talk about house rules."

"Alright." She takes a deep breath, her heart speeding up a fraction with sudden nervousness. She quickly scans the page before her, which reads:

House Protocol for Corinne
While together, Corinne will:
- Only call Nikolai by the honorific "sir" during
  scenes
- Wear lingerie gifted to her by Nikolai
- Sit in Nikolai's lap or kneel before him unless she
  has permission otherwise
- Thank Nikolai after each orgasm and after sex.

"Any thoughts?" he asks. "Changes? Additions? These are negotiable."

"I already assumed saying 'thank you' would be on the list after last time. And the lingerie is no surprise." She winks at him. "Calling you 'sir' will be easy when I do it so often anyway. Is the kneeling rule for when you're sitting? Do you want me to kneel when I first get here?"

"If we're going right into a scene, then yes, I'd like you to kneel when you first come in. Otherwise, it's just for when I'm sitting, and even then, sometimes I'll want you on my lap." He sips his water. "And when I put your collar on, of course."

Her eyes widen, and she huffs a pleased little laugh. "What?" He hadn't said anything about a collar. She eyes the box on the table before looking at him again. "Is that what that is, sir?"

He picks it up and watches her with a smirk. "It is indeed." Lifting the lid, he removes a slim oxblood leather collar and dangles it from one finger. A small gold O-ring is on the front, and a matching buckle is on the back. "What do you say, pet? Would you like to play?"

collared

CORINNE

CORINNE'S HEART POUNDS, and her stomach flutters in anticipation. Placing the house rules list on the table, she kneels in front of him, back straight, hands in her lap. She looks up, her gaze holding his, not wavering even once. "Yes, sir."

"Sweet little thing." He slips the collar around her neck and buckles it, his gaze locked on her throat as he pulls back. "Look at you. Look how lovely you are in my collar."

She smiles at the praise, reaching up to touch it. The leather is soft beneath her fingertips. "Thank you, sir."

He gently tugs on the clasp at the back. "How would you feel about a lock?"

Her gaze widens, and she nods, grinning.

"A little lock for my little pet." He plays with it more, then adds, "And if I said I wanted to buy you a pair of shoes with locks on the ankles?"

"Hm, like cuffs?"

"Exactly like. An ankle strap heel, but it's cuffs instead of straps." He toys with her collar again. "I know there is quite the difference between wearing something for me and wearing something that locks for me, so I wanted to check." He leans in and kisses the skin just above her collar. "But I will admit, the very idea of it is driving me to distraction."

She sighs and angles her head back, baring her throat to him. Just the thought of him locking her into things makes her body pulse with heat. "Yes, I'd love that."

He presses a few more kisses to her throat before slipping his finger into the ring and pulling on the collar. "You're just desperate for everything, aren't you? Desperate to be owned like that, locked into my collar?"

Owned, her mind repeats, and she moans, her eyes falling shut. "You make me like this, sir."

"Oh, poor thing. Let's calm you down, hm?" She opens her eyes. He's rising from his chair. "I still have a few reports to look over before I properly enjoy my pretty pet, so wait here for me. When I return, you can kneel beside me while I work through them. Be good, and you'll get a treat." He smooths a hand over her hair and leaves, heading toward the office.

She brushes her hand over the collar again. She wishes she could go see it in the mirror, but she heeds his command and stays until he returns.

It's only a few minutes, but it feels much longer, with anticipation and desire heightening every second.

"So good, pet," he says when he returns. "Thank you for waiting." He's got folders in one arm and a thick cushion tucked under the other. He resumes his seat and places the pillow by his feet. "Come. Kneel for me for a while, and then I promise we can play."

"Yes, sir," she says, kneeling before him. "The cushion is nice. Thank you." She rests her head on his knee and looks up at him.

"I take very good care of my pets, didn't you know?" he says with a wink. He strokes her head for a moment, just smiling, like he's savoring the moment, before he sighs and grabs one of the folders. "I need to work for a while. Let me know if you need anything, okay?"

She nods and settles in, moving her head a little higher to rest against his thigh where it's more comfortable. "You work too much," she mumbles against his trousers. She always tells him that, but it's always true.

He tugs her hair and laughs. "Noted. Now, let me work."

Nikolai works for a little while, and she gets comfortable, tucking her hands between her legs. She's not sure how long they're like that, exactly. She just closes her eyes and lets herself drift along in this space they've created. Everything feels soft and dreamy, each sigh or turn of his page lulling her into a place of comfort.

Sometime later, he shifts, and she hears him stretching with a groan. Then his fingers thread through her hair, and she hums in response.

"Alright?"

"Yes, sir," she mumbles, her voice slurring subtly.

He brushes his hand over her hair for a few more moments before saying, "Pet?"

"Hm?"

"If I had a business trip coming up, would you still be interested in going with me?"

She looks up, her brow furrowing before her mind catches up to what he asks. She wasn't expecting something like this, at least not so soon after they discussed it last week. "Of course. When is it?"

"Mid-June," he tells her, gently winding a piece of hair around his finger. That's a couple of months away, and not so far off that her decision about Philadelphia would affect it. "I'll have concrete dates by Wednesday. I know we just talked about it, and considering where it is, I thought you might like to come with me."

She gasps, all thoughts about the job opportunity fleeing her mind. "France?"

He taps a finger on her nose. "Indeed. The stars seem to be doing their best to align."

She grins up at him and presses a kiss to his knee. "Thank you, sir. How long?"

"I'd need a week for work. Plus a day on either end for travel, so ten days or so?"

She purses her lips and takes a deep breath. "Sir." She wraps one hand around his socked ankle, caressing it lightly. "When was the last time you took a vacation?"

He looks off to the side as though trying to remember. "Well... I'm not exactly sure now that I think about it."

"What if you added another week? Took some time off work." Her palm slides up his calf as she kisses his knee again. "Took some time to rest for once."

Cupping her face, he strokes his thumb along her cheekbone. "A week in France just relaxing with my pet?" he murmurs. "You drive a hard bargain, sweet little thing."

The endearment stirs something within her, something small she's unable to name. But she looks up at him and gives him a bright, sunny smile. "Is that a yes?"

"That's a yes." He smiles back at her, warm and fond. "How could I say no to spending time in France with you?"

She leans into his palm and kisses it. "We're going to have so much fun together."

"Mmm, yes, we will. I'm looking forward to it."

He rubs his thumb over her bottom lip before continuing. "Now, you've been such a good girl for me on your knees. You deserve your treat, don't you?"

Looking up at him through her lashes, she nods. "Please, sir."

"Stand up, sweet pet. Let me see what you're hiding under those clothes, and then come sit on my lap."

Corinne stands, her legs feeling slightly like Jell-O from kneeling for so long. Undressing without hurry, she reveals her strappy bra with delicate, sheer lace in his favorite deep red and a matching thong.

"Damn," he breathes, and she lets him look his fill before she straddles his lap and presses her lips to his. He pulls back to look her over again. "Fuck." He skims his fingers over the edges of the lace, the teeny, tiny sides of her thong. "I am very lucky to have you for my own, pet."

She groans, that one statement shuddering through her. *Yours*, some little voice says inside her, but she dare not say it aloud, not when she's already a little spacey and mellowed from kneeling at his feet.

Grinding against his lap, his dick hardens against her. "Sir," she gasps as his hands brush along the lace, her skin, lighting every inch of her body on fire.

Nikolai snags the ring on her collar and pulls, eliciting a groan as she relishes the tug of it. His other hand cups one of her breasts before trailing down and slipping into her underwear to brush against her clit. Her mouth parts with a gasp.

"I'm going to make you come now. What's the rule?"

"Say 'thank you' when I come, sir," she says breathlessly, rolling her hips against his hand.

"Perfect. We're going to practice, okay? Make sure you remember every time."

She nods. "Yes, sir."

He grins wickedly. "Let me know if it becomes too much, pretty girl, though I don't suspect it will be for such a needy little thing like you."

She's already slick and wet for him, and it's easy for him to slip inside her, pressing the heel of his hand against her clit. Her own hand curls under the collar of his shirt. "God," she moans, rubbing herself against his palm before pressing her lips to his. She licks into his mouth, kissing him fiercely as he fingers her.

He growls and slips a second finger in, pushing hard with the heel of his hand. "That's it, just like that." He grabs her hip, helping her move harder, faster. "Come on, greedy pet, there you go."

She moans, fully fucking herself on his fingers by this point, grinding against the palm of his hand. Pleasure builds within her, and she moves faster, chasing it, every whimper and pant from her mouth getting louder as she does so. "Will you pull on my collar, sir?"

A sound that's more snarl than anything else rips out of him as he obliges. His grin is feral, teeth bared. "You like your collar? Like knowing you're mine?" He presses harder against her clit as he tugs at her collar.

"*Fuck.*" Hearing him say that heats her core, and she bucks against him. "Y-Yes, sir." She'll explode if she doesn't say it, if she doesn't give in to what her body and soul so desperately want, even if her mind wants to fight it.

"Yours," she finally breathes, and Nikolai groans deeply.

the pet store

CORINNE

"YES, MINE," Nikolai growls.

She gasps, grinding against the palm of his hand until it hurts, until she's coming, head thrown back, her whole body shaking with it. Her cries soften, and she whispers, "Thank you," against his cheek.

"So beautiful, darling girl." He lets go of her collar and strokes her back. "So lovely." He shallowly moves his fingers in and out a few times as she comes down. "Ready?"

Corinne nods. "Mm, yes, sir." She kisses down his throat. "Can we take your shirt off? Want to feel you."

"My my, what an eager pet I have. Go ahead and unbutton it for me."

As she unbuttons his shirt, he fingers her again, pulling her collar and pinching her nipples over the lace with his other hand.

Corinne hisses, still sensitive from her first climax. But this is her job; she's damn good at multitasking. She continues with the buttons, rubbing herself on his fingers, on the palm of his hand, as she teases the shirt from his trousers. Her hands find his skin, his broad chest and shoulders, and she shifts closer to him, not bothering to remove the shirt so he doesn't have to stop touching her. But she does yank down the cup of her bra and bring his mouth to her nipple. "Please, sir."

"So polite," he murmurs, latching on and licking, sucking, nipping at the sensitive skin. He flicks his tongue over the barbell, tugging with his teeth, making her gasp. While his fingers continue their thrusting, he uses his other hand to drag down the other cup, and he licks across her chest to the other side. "You have the prettiest tits. Would you let me fuck them?"

She comes, already worked up by his talented fingers and his mouth on her nipples. Her hips hitch on a moan, her fingers digging into his shoulder. "Fuck yes thank you sir please I want it," falls out of her mouth, all strung together as she's lost in the pleasure of it all. She's still shivering as she lowers her mouth to his ear. "Will you come all over me? Make me all messy?" Everything's still syrupy, all soft and hazy at the edges.

"My darling little pet, of course I will." His fingers gentle. "You're hungry for it, aren't you? Being used and wrecked. It's lucky I like making a mess of you." He leans in close and whispers, "You'll look so pretty, too, covered in my come." His hand speeds up again, a smirk curling one side of his mouth.

"Sir," she whines but still arches against him. She doesn't shy away, even if it's starting to overwhelm her. Reaching between them, she rubs his cock through his trousers. Part of her wants him to fuck her, but she'll wait, the idea of him coming all over her winning out. "May I—" She stops with a groan, his fingers already working her toward another climax, and fuck, he's so good. She keeps rubbing his dick, but she wants to feel the hot length of him in her hand. "May I touch you, sir?" Her eyes squeeze shut because she's about to come all over again.

"You're gagging for it, aren't you? Such an insatiable little pet, with such a drippy little cunt." She opens her eyes. He's watching her, mouth parted, eyes wide. "One more, for me, okay? You're so beautiful when you come. Just one more for me, then you can touch me, and then I'll fuck those pretty tits and come all over them."

Corinne comes again, just a soft ripple, like her body can barely take another wave of pleasure, even though she's always been able to come over and over again when the opportunity presents itself. She falls into him, like all her strings have been cut, and she buries her face in his neck.

She is... gone. The collar, the kneeling, the rules, the many orgasms. Hearing him call her *beautiful* and *darling little pet*. She is fuck-drunk, deep in subspace, and entirely under his thumb.

"Thank you," she mumbles against his skin. "Sir. Thank you."

"You are so very welcome." He smooths a hand over her back, easing his fingers from her body, before she hears him sucking them into his mouth. He hums in pleasure like he's greedy for the taste of her, and her cunt clenches, even after all that. "Still want to touch me? Still want me to fuck your pretty, pretty tits?"

"Yes, sir. Please." She scooches back to open his pants and pull out his cock. Sighing in appreciation, she wraps her hand around the length and slides her fist up and down. "You're so gorgeous," she whispers.

He groans and tucks a strand of hair behind her ear. "Thank you. What a sweet little pet I have." He tugs on her collar again and nudges under her chin so he can kiss her, his other hand unhooking her bra. "Wish I could fuck your tits while you wear this," he says against her lips. "Get my come all over this pretty lace *and* your pretty tits."

"You buy me pretty things just to mess them all up." She keeps stroking his cock, only letting go long enough for him to take off her bra. She sweeps her thumb over that spot under the head that always makes him react, and he shudders, breath rushing out of him.

"You are entirely correct. I love to see you in things I bought for you." He bites her lip, pulling it between his teeth. "And there is nothing sexier than the way you look after I wreck you, still dressed in all those lovely things."

She scoots forward and rubs her cunt, still covered in his lace, against his cock while she holds it in the palm of her hand. She's gentle with it so the lace isn't abrasive. "I could wear silk sometime," she says softly. "And I could grind against you until you come all over them."

He yanks on her collar, tilting up her chin, damn near snarling as he thrusts against her. "With that kind of promise I'll have some delivered to you tomorrow."

She drags her soaked cunt over him for a few more moments until he groans and reaches between them to fasten his pants. She's about to whine in response, but then he gets his hands under her thighs and stands, walking them toward his bedroom.

"I want to fuck these lovely tits now. Want to feel them around my cock before I come all over them."

Corinne hums, floating happily in his arms. Maybe she should say something sexy, but instead, she says, "I love when you carry me, sir." She tucks herself against his neck. "I feel small. And safe."

Was that a silly thing to admit? It's too late to take it back.

But Nikolai doesn't laugh it off. No, he inhales sharply and tightens his grip on her. She smiles against his throat—he likes her admission.

He makes his way to the bed and lays her down gently, pressing a kiss to her lace-covered cunt before moving his way up her body, nibbling her collarbones and kissing her mouth. He pulls back, sheds his clothes, and grabs lube from his nightstand. Dragging his hand up her leg, he eases onto the bed. He cups her cunt briefly before continuing up between her tits until he can run his finger under her collar. She loves that he keeps touching it, and she bares her neck for him.

His eyes darken. "That's a good girl." He finally raises the lube and drizzles it onto her chest before rubbing it into her skin and then onto his cock. "Push them together for me, pet."

Corinne looks up at him as she pinches her nipples and plays with the barbells, but only for a moment before pressing her breasts together. She doesn't have the largest chest, but it's more than enough for this. And if the weight of his gaze means anything, he's more than pleased. She can't help but writhe on the bed in response.

"What a beautiful sight," he breathes. Bracing one hand on the headboard above her, he holds his dick steady with the other. Then he slides the head of his cock between her tits, slow and steady, moaning as he does. "Fuck, you feel so good like this."

A sigh falls from her lips. His face is soft and relaxed as he strokes, rubbing against her. It's torture, the best kind of torture, to feel him fucking her but only for his own pleasure. It only takes a couple of minutes for her cunt to start aching and throbbing. She clamps her thighs together and whimpers, her skin slick despite the fabric. "I'm so wet, sir."

"Oh, is that so? Is my needy little thing's messy cunt feeling empty?" Sweat's beading at his hairline, and he breathes harshly as he slips into a new rhythm. "Still want to be filled, even after you rode my fingers? Always such a greedy little thing, aren't you, pet?"

Corinne moans, squeezing her tits together even more tightly. "Yes, sir. For you, always." She thinks about him fucking her all the time, thinks about how perfect his cock feels inside her, how his grip tightens whenever he comes—in her hair, on her hip, around her breast. Like he has to ground himself. She loves it. She wants it always.

She wants to wreck him as much as he always wrecks her.

Looking up at him, her face shifts to wide-eyed innocence. "Didn't realize how greedy I'd be when you brought me home from the pet store, huh, sir?"

His hips stutter, and his hand slips from the headboard and grips her face roughly. "Is that what you want?" he growls. "To be something I brought home, to spoil and care for?" His hips pick up speed again, hand leaving her face and lacing his fingers with hers, making little divots in her flesh as he pushes her breasts together even tighter. It's so rough that it aches, and she moans, arching into it. "Just my darling little pet, wearing my collar, well fucked at all times."

"*Please*," she begs. Nikolai using her like this is keeping her in that lovely, floaty space, and she leans into it. She lets it happen. She rubs her thighs together again, so turned on she can't stand it. "I'll be a good girl for you." She licks her lips. "You can get a tag for my collar so everyone knows I'm yours."

"Fuck!" His breath hitches, and then he jerks back. "Tongue out, pretty pet," he says in a rush. "Hands off."

It looks like it pains him to wait as she does as he says. He strokes firmly until he's coming, thick ribbons painting her tits, her chin, one on the very tip of her tongue. She's barely finished tucking her tongue back into her mouth before he's slipping down her body and shoving his way between her thighs. He pulls her underwear to the side and latches his mouth on her clit, his clean hand thrusting three fingers deep, working her quick and fast for one more orgasm.

"God." She's so far gone that she comes in seconds, her hips rising off the bed to grind against his mouth. "Oh my god," she breathes, shivering.

He's watching her as he flicks little kitten licks against her slit. She wipes his spend off her chin and licks it off her thumb with a smile. "Mm, thank you, sir."

Rolling off to the side, Nikolai grins and wipes his mouth on the back of his hand. He wraps an arm around her leg. He rests his head on her thigh, looking up at her with affection in his gaze.

Her chest aches at the sight.

"You're very welcome, darling pet. Thank you."

Her head is still swimming. "Fuck, I'm…" She huffs a laugh. "I don't usually let myself get this far into subspace." She gestures to herself, pliant and sated, with a soft smile and hooded eyes. He's made her like this twice now. "I hope it's okay."

He hauls himself higher up the bed, gathering her close and holding her tightly. "It's always okay. I'm honored you let yourself go there with me."

She's giving him big adoring eyes, but she absolutely can't bring herself to care. "Okay, I'm glad." Her hand traces the leather at her neck. "This was a surprise, and I love it so much. Thank you for getting it for me."

He reaches for the ring on her collar and rubs it as he presses his forehead to hers. "You look wonderful in it, pet. I'm glad you like it." He goes quiet before saying, "Did you mean it? That you want a tag for it? I know sometimes things get said in the heat of the moment, especially if it's an intense scene, but —" He clears his throat. "I just… wanted to check."

"I did. Mean it." She brushes his jaw, his beard scratchy against her skin. "I'm…" She takes a deep breath. She let herself get carried away, even though she meant every word. She's silent as she figures out the best way to phrase what she needs to say. "When we're here. Or even out there," she says, gesturing to the world outside, "together, I'm all yours. I would love a token of that, sir." She kisses him, long and deep, her heart stirring in her chest.

"I'd like that very much, sweet. Do you have anything in particular you'd like it to say?"

Humming, she thinks for a minute before shaking her head. "That's the pet owner's decision, isn't it?" She winks.

He tickles her sides, scrunching his nose at her. "And here my pet was being so sweet for me. Whatever will I do with you?"

She laughs. "Mm, I'm sure you'll think of something." Suddenly, an idea comes to her. "Sir, may I ask for something?"

His brows pinch together, his face growing serious. "Of course. Always."

She traces her fingers along his collarbone. "When we go to your party, can I have a leash?"

His lips part, and he stares at her, wonder evident in his eyes, before he kisses her fiercely. He breaks away to pepper light kisses all over her face. "You absolutely can, my darling little pet." He tugs on her collar, dragging her close, and whispers in her ear, "You'll look so pretty at the end of my leash."

Shivering from his breath in her ear and the promise in his voice, she pulls back to find him still absolutely dumbfounded. She laughs fondly and kisses him. "I can't wait, sir."

g.r.w.m. part i

NIKOLAI

THE MONTH after introducing rules to prepare for the High Protocol party is the most fun Nikolai has had with a partner in a long time. She's a quick study, his pet, though he's not surprised. She seems the type; dedicated and committed.

Not a thing like Miss Russell, he thinks to himself, smirking.

Corinne kneels for him most evenings together, and he never feels more settled than when she's there, leaning against his leg, his hand stroking her hair. She's done so well slipping into this new role, and sometimes, he can't believe how well-matched they are.

Two weeks before the party, he gets a call from Indali to confirm his attendance. "You're coming?" she asks. "Really? And you're bringing your little cat-girl?"

He sighs in fond exasperation as he opens the door to his apartment, phone clamped between his shoulder and ear. "For the last time, Corinne is not a cat-girl. She's just... a pampered pet." He sets his bag on the floor next to the entry table, drops his keys in the dish, and hangs his coat in the closet. "But, yes, I'm bringing her."

"Oooh!" Indali exclaims like a schoolgirl. "You never

brought the mayor's son to these, is all, and anytime I ran into him at one of the insufferable charity events you and I inevitably end up attending, he seemed like the brattiest little thing. Perfect for a good public punishment scene, if you ask me."

Indali has always liked them brattier than Nikolai. Elijah was fun and exciting, but Nikolai's brand of sadism doesn't align with bottoms just out to get punished. Indali, however, enjoys being mean for fun and pleasure in an entirely different way.

"Getting Eli to follow rules like that… It would take a more serious type of training and dynamic than the one I prefer, you know that." He walks farther into the apartment, turning on lights as he heads for the kitchen to make himself some stir-fry and come down from the day.

Indali snorts from the other end of the line. "Yes, Kolya, I *do* know. You like them more obedient. Whereas I"—Her silverware drawer rattles, and he smirks. Did she call him when she did so they would both do something other than work as soon as they got home?—"I enjoy a little more fight in my partners."

He hums in agreement, heating oil in his pan. "*Bez muki net nauki,*" he mutters, his mother's voice in his ears. It's what she said every time he and Indali got themselves into trouble—literally, "without torture, no science." Adversity being a good teacher had been the refrain of their adolescence, and it apparently made two very different impressions on them.

"*Da, tochno,*" she agrees. "I just want to be the adversity, that's all."

He snorts a laugh. "Just like always, eh, Dali?"

"Always, darling."

They chat for a few more minutes until Nikolai's stir-fry is finished, and they say their goodbyes, confirming lunch for Tuesday and, once again, his intent to come to the party.

"With your little Corinne," Indali croons before hanging up abruptly, cackling as she does.

* * *

The morning of the party dawns bright and clear on Saturday. Nikolai is downright jittery in the best way, the way one is before an exam or a presentation they know they will ace. They're good nerves, and he'll welcome them later, but right now? Right now he hauls himself down to the building's gym to run a few miles on the treadmill to try to calm his body down.

It works for a while, allowing him to do some work in the early afternoon. Work he won't be doing tomorrow while Corinne is here, recovering from what is sure to be an intense and prolonged headspace for them both.

When she finally arrives that evening, excitement courses through him with a vengeance after being suppressed for so long. She stands on the doorstep in a light raincoat, with her hair up as he requested, and he smiles and kisses her cheek. "Hello, pet. You're already looking even lovelier than usual. Come in." He takes her garment bag and ushers her inside.

"Thank you, sir," she says, giving him a quick kiss as he shuts the door. She slips off her shoes and hangs her coat in the closet while he hooks her garment bag over the door. When he faces her again, she gets on her knees, back straight, hands on her thighs, looking up at him expectantly.

He grabs her collar out of his pants pocket. "Are you ready?" He dangles the collar from his fingers, eyebrows raised in question.

She nods. "Very nervous, but very ready." She looks down, allowing him to fasten the collar around her neck.

"You're going to do wonderfully." He buckles it, relishing the experience. He will never tire of this exchange, no matter how often they have it. He helps her to her feet and kisses her throat where collar meets skin. "And you look delightful in my collar, as always."

She flushes, pink blooming across her cheeks. "Thank you, sir. I brought all my stuff to finish getting ready, but also..." She wraps her hand around the back of his neck to meet her in a slow, languid kiss. When she finally pulls away, her eyes rake over him. "I'm not used to coming over without us having sex within thirty minutes of my arrival." She winks.

Hooking her by the collar, he yanks it right up under her chin to tilt her head back. Corinne gasps. He's already starting to feel... sharper. God, he's missed this. He hasn't had a partner he's meshed with so well in a long time.

"Well, nothing says we *can't*." He leans in and bites at her bottom lip, then straightens with a smirk. "I planned on making you wait till later, but you know I'll never turn down an opportunity to fuck my pretty little pet." He releases his hold on her and steps back. "Your choice."

She takes her time answering, her eyes roaming his face as she considers. "I... I think I'd like to make myself wait, sir. So it's even better later." She grabs his hand and slips it under her dress. "But I've been wet all day thinking about tonight."

He takes half a step closer. "Show me. Let me see." He mockingly frowns at her and slides his fingers under the waistband of her panties. "My poor pet, wet and empty all day." Leaning in, he whispers as though he has a secret. "I've been in a similar state today, thinking about you at the end of my leash."

"Fuck," she whispers, and pushes his hand farther down until his fingers find where she's hot and slick. "See, sir? Just thinking about it has me so worked up."

Keeping his eyes on hers, he brushes along her center and circles her entrance before returning, pressing on her clit roughly. As he steps back, he examines his fingers in the hallway light, admiring the way they glisten. He looks back at her, a sharp smile on his face. "Oh, you are absolutely *dripping*." He brings his fingers to his mouth and sucks them clean as she watches, her eyes dazed and mouth parted. Then he tucks his hands in his pockets and nods toward the bedroom door as though nothing has happened. "After you. I'll bring your bags."

"Perhaps I made a mistake earlier," she says shakily as she passes him.

"Oh, really? Regrets already?" Dropping her bags on the bed, he smirks. He's going to have so much fun with her tonight.

He can't wait.

"Ugh." She unzips one bag and grabs her makeup. "Not nice when you know what you do to me, sir."

He follows her into the bathroom and crowds her against the counter, caging her with his arms, making eye contact in the mirror. "Pet, if you'd like to see me be not so nice, all you have to do is ask. No need to act out." He kisses the spot on her neck right above the buckle of her collar.

"I would never act out, sir," she says. "I was the best-behaved pet at the store."

"And now that I've brought you home?"

Corinne spins in his arms. "Are you saying I'm not a good girl?"

"Well, we'll see tonight, won't we?" he asks, all promise and heat.

She tilts her head before kissing him. "I guess we will."

Nikolai steps to the side to brush his teeth. Eyes bright as he watches her from the corner of his eye, a warmth in his chest grows with every moment shared in this space with her. It's comfortable. Intimate.

Domestic.

Which is something he hasn't experienced in a long time.

Filing that thought away for later, he finishes up and places a kiss on the back of her neck before walking into the bedroom to get dressed. He slips into his trousers and a crisp white shirt, which he leaves open at the throat, and secures his sleeves with a pair of monogrammed cuff links. Then he shifts his attention to the stack of boxes on his dresser and opens the one on top.

Excitement zips along his spine like electricity as he lifts the leather from the box. It's been a long time since he's worn this, and he'd be lying if he said he hadn't been excited about it all week.

He takes it into the bathroom and stands before the mirror to slip into the straps.

Corinne catches his eye as she's putting on mascara. "Oh, you didn't tell me you'd be in a harness, sir." She puts down the tube and sidles over to him, her hand coming to the strap at his shoulder. "Would you like some help?"

"Thank you." He fully faces her, his hands falling to his sides. "And maybe I wanted to surprise you, hm?"

"You're always surprising me," she says, face breaking into a grin as she buckles the shoulder straps. Then she takes the crossed straps in the back and brings them around the front, securing them to his trousers. "I never know what I'll find when I come over." She kisses his chest, right above the buckle. "Or when the courier arrives."

He smirks, tipping up her chin. "Finish your makeup, pet, and I'll give you some more surprises."

"Yes, sir. I'm almost done." She finishes her mascara and turns back toward him. "See? I'll put on my lipstick after I get dressed."

He presses a kiss to her lips. "Beautiful." Her hand in his, he tows her into the bedroom and guides her in front of the mirror. "Stand here." Then he grabs the stack of boxes from the dresser and places them on the bed. "I'd like to dress you tonight."

g.r.w.m. part ii

NIKOLAI

NIKOLAI CIRCLES her once before slowly undressing her, kissing and touching her skin as he goes. He returns to the bed with all three boxes, setting the top lid aside and kneeling in front of her. Caressing her calves and thighs, he takes off her underwear and places a kiss right above her clit, making her whimper.

Fuck, if that sound doesn't drive him wild.

He fastens the deep red garter belt around her waist before helping her into the matching silk panties, his mind already buzzing from dressing her in the lingerie he's bought her. The straps of the belt hang over her thighs, and he caresses one of them, staring up at her as he nibbles at her skin.

"Sir," she gasps, this close to a whine. "I'm never going to make it like this."

"Shh," he gentles, and opens the second box. He brings her foot to rest on his knee and pulls out a silk stocking, sheer except for the black contrast seam and the band at the top.

He takes his time, enjoying every second as he gathers the finely woven silk and slips it over her foot. Holding her gaze, he rolls the stocking up her leg and secures the garters, repeating the process with the other stocking and leg. When he finishes, he snaps the last garter, smiling wolfishly when she gasps.

He's still grinning as he stands and opens the final box. The bra he removes is a harness style with crisscrossing straps in black and deep red. Once he fastens it behind her back, he looks over her shoulder, and *God*, but she looks stunning, dressed in his color and wearing his collar.

Mine.

There it is: the headspace he knew would come tonight. But it feels different this time, and it's because of this delicious little thing standing in front of him. He can't wait to find out what the rest of the night holds.

Pulling himself away, Nikolai grabs the black tulle circle skirt she brought. He helps her into it and steps back to look at the masterpiece before him. "Hmm, there's something missing."

"Oh?" she asks with a raised brow.

"I promised you very special shoes, didn't I, pet?" He walks to the closet and returns with a beige box, complete with familiar white script printed on the top. He holds it out. "Open it."

She smiles up at him, excitement dancing in her gaze as she flips it open. Inside lies a pair of black patent leather Louboutin heels, five inches in height. In place of an ankle strap is a two-inch cuff fastened with a gold lock. "*Jesus,*" she says, lifting one from the box, her eyes the biggest he's ever seen them. "These are gorgeous."

Warmth floods him just from her reaction. Dressing her and having her enjoy what he chooses is one of the best feelings in the world.

"On the bed, sweet thing." He kneels again and slides the

shoe onto her foot, then fastens the cuff and closes the little lock with a *click* before doing the other. He takes out a necklace from the collar of his shirt and shows her the keys before helping her stand.

When he pulls back to take her in, his breath catches at the sight of her. "Oh, pet." Everything on her body was put there by *him*. Satisfaction and possessive pride settle in his bones, and he revels in it, in her. She is *his*, and she is beautiful. "You're breathtaking."

Corinne turns toward the mirror, her face lighting up as she takes it all in. The way he feels fulfilled knowing she likes what she sees, what he gave to her, is all-encompassing, sparking a flame inside him.

Swiveling to her left, she lifts one foot to get a good look at the locked cuffs. Her gaze finds his in the mirror, and she's wearing the warmest smile. "Sir, I feel so beautiful. Thank you for all of this. Everything is gorgeous." She walks back to him. "And it was sweet of you to dress me."

He snags her by her collar and pulls her close. "You're very welcome. You look ravishing. I'll be the envy of everyone with you at the end of my leash." He digs something out of his pocket. "I believe I owe you another lock, and then I've got a couple surprises for you."

"More surprises?" she asks, her arms snaking around his waist. "You're going to spoil me absolutely rotten."

He kisses her deeply before dangling a heart-shaped gold lock between them. "And? You're mine to do with as I like. Part of bringing you home from the pet store, remember?"

She looks up at him with a sweet little smile and nods as her gaze falls to the lock. "Yes, sir."

"Turn around for me." He slips the lock through the clasp on her collar before clicking it into place. *Mine*, he thinks again, tugging on the lock. He whispers in her ear, "What a sight you are."

She shivers. "Thank you, sir."

"Go get your lipstick. Then it's time for surprises."

She spins and kisses his cheek before heading into the bathroom. When she returns, her lips are painted a lovely shade that complements her oxblood collar and lingerie.

"Lovely as always. Now be good and come here for me, hm?"

"Aren't I always good, sir?" she asks, sauntering over as he pulls a box from his pocket.

He hums skeptically, the corners of his eyes creasing as he hides his laugh. He hands her the box. "Open it."

When she does, a pair of gold chandelier earrings awaits her. A ruby stud adorns the top, followed by cascading branches of diamonds, and ending with a teardrop ruby. "Oh," she breathes. "Sir, these are lovely."

"They're a family heirloom," he murmurs, running his fingertips over the earrings, watching as they gleam in the low light. "Zaitsev rubies. My grandmother's favorite."

"Sir." He looks up and catches the warmth of her gaze before she leans in and kisses him tenderly. "I love them. Thank you for lending me something so important."

Nikolai clears his throat. "They're a gift, pet. For you to keep."

"No." She shakes her head. "They're your family's. I couldn't."

"You can and you will," he says, his eyebrow arched sternly.

She presses her lips together before they curve into a soft smile. "Thank you, sir."

He puts the earrings on her, and possession swells fiercely within him at seeing her in Zaitsev jewels. With a step back, he takes her all in, walking a slow circle around her. "You are the most stunning creature, pet." He trails his fingers along her arms, her chest, toying with the edges of her harness before reaching up and flicking the ring on her collar. "You know, this is looking a little bare. Should we fix that?"

Her eyes widen. "Really?"

He pulls out the tag, heart-shaped like the lock. On the side that will face everyone, *Pet* is engraved in an elegant script. On the side that will face her, his initials, *NZ*, are engraved in his handwriting. He twirls it at eye level, making sure she can see. "What do you say, pet? Do you want it?"

She rubs her thumb over his initials. "Of course, sir," she says softly before falling to her knees and looking up at him expectantly.

"Darling little pet," he breathes, pulse hammering. "How perfect you are." Seeing his marks of ownership—the earrings, the tag—is exhilarating. Knowing she's allowed it, chosen it. "When you wear these..." his thumb brushes the tag before tracing her jaw and stroking the earrings, "...everyone will know you're mine."

He helps her to her feet, smoothing her skirt and tugging her harness to settle it. Then he walks to the foyer to put on his black suit jacket and grab her raincoat. It's May, but she needs something to cover her ensemble, especially since her skirt is sheer. "Ready?" he asks, holding the coat out for her as she joins him.

"Wait," she says, taking his arm and pulling him to the mirror in the entryway until they're side by side. "We make quite the picture, don't you think?"

Eyes roaming over her, he grins wickedly, the knowledge she's his tonight in a new way, more fully than she has been before, settling in him and tightening his focus, his thoughts clear and precise as he stares at the picture they make.

"We're devastating, pet. You'll bring the room to its knees."

He leans in and whispers, "And then I'll put you on yours," before delicately licking at the shell of her ear, delighting in her shiver. He takes his leather gloves out of his jacket pocket and pulls them on, watching her in the mirror as he leisurely tugs them into place.

"Oh!" he says, reaching into the closet. "Can't forget this." He reveals her leash, the gold chain and oxblood leather a perfect match for her harness and collar. He winks as he coils it up and tucks it in his coat pocket. "Now we can go."

"You got it for me after all," she responds as they walk out the door. "Thank you, sir."

"Anything you want, all you have to do is ask." He takes her hand, placing it in the crook of his elbow as he leads her to the elevator. "I can't wait to put it on you. You will look so lovely."

"I can't wait either. Even if I am ridiculously nervous, I'm still excited." She laughs anxiously. "I just don't want to mess up."

He kisses her again sweetly. "You'll be wonderful. And if you mess up, well, I'll just have to discipline you for the broken rules when we get back, won't I?" The elevator arrives, and they step inside. "And if you do well, then I'll show you just how much I reward little pets who obey the rules."

Corinne's breath hitches. "Are you going to tease me all night, sir?"

His smile is just this side of cruel. "Of course I am, sweet thing. You really should have factored that in when you chose to wait." He tugs on her collar, her new tag jingling. "I'll have you begging and crying before tonight is through."

She takes a shaky breath but then looks up at him through her lashes. "Do you like my new tag, sir?" she asks coyly, and takes a step closer, pressing them together. "Do you like your name at my throat?"

Nikolai lets go of the ring and wraps his hand around her

throat, gently, softly, not squeezing at all but just resting there, entirely possessive. His eyes are dark, a hunger hiding in them that he hasn't felt in a long time. When he speaks, his voice darkens.

"There is nothing I love more than my name being at your throat, pretty pet. Tonight, I own you, and this way, neither you nor anyone else can forget it."

leashed

NIKOLAI

NIKOLAI LEADS her to the car and opens the door for her before following after. The car takes off as soon as the door shuts, Adrian unseen behind the privacy screen already rolled up between them.

Corinne grabs Nikolai's hand. "It's been a while since you've done this, right? What are you looking forward to?"

He mulls over the question. "I'm very much looking forward to leading you around on your leash. Watching you carefully follow all the rules and kneel at my feet." He takes a deep breath. "Knowing you're submitting so wholly to me, giving so much to me... It's a thrill I haven't felt in a long time. There's no better feeling. Knowing you're mine to look after, to take care of completely. To reward and punish as I see fit. I have been looking forward to this for weeks."

"So have I. So much."

He sweeps his hand down her cheek and rests his thumb against her chin to hold it gently. Warmth swells against his rib cage as he kisses her. He could kiss her all night, but there are things to discuss first. "Let's go over the rules, shall we?"

"Alright." Corinne ticks each one off with her fingers as she recalls. "Submissives should serve their dominant first, kneel or sit at their dominant's feet and wait for permission to do so, wait to speak to other dominants until they receive permission from their own, and call dominants by their titles." She pauses. "Submissives should *not* eat or drink without their dominant's permission or sit while their dominant is standing, unless told to do so."

His smile is amused and proud—he wasn't quite expecting her to have them memorized word for word, but perhaps he should have. "Studious little thing, aren't you?"

"Hush," she says with a laugh, squeezing his knee gently.

There's a distinct pause as he raises his brows at her, and she smiles up at him like she didn't just tell him what to do tonight of all nights.

"I'll remember that later, sweet thing."

She nods, her face sobering. "Yes, sir. I'm sorry."

He waits a moment before he continues. "Are your public sex limits still the same? Anything we'd do in private is alright in public?"

"Yes, I'm up for everything."

Lately, he's begun to notice the specifics of Corinne's humiliation kink. She just wants to be a pretty thing, a lovely little object, that doesn't have to be anything other than taken care of. She takes care of the needs of so many different people, and he takes care of her. Because that's what you do with things you value and cherish.

So his expression is patronizing at best when he says, "Of course you are. You're the neediest little thing." His gaze rakes over her body. "Such a greedy cunt you have, only satisfied when full."

"Sir," she half admonishes, half whines, and he looks down his nose at her, disbelief in the set of his brow.

"Am I wrong?"

"No, sir." A small smile tugs at the corner of her mouth.

"Then I have one more rule, pet, and this one is mine," he says. "You must ask permission to come, understood?"

"Yes, but"—she pouts—"that means you're going to tease me, sir."

Nikolai thumbs at her bottom lip, mockingly pouting back at her. "Of course I am. You're just too exquisite when you're frustrated. I can't help myself."

She starts to protest, but he shushes her with a kiss, slow and teasing, tugging on her collar, satisfaction rolling through him.

Mine, he thinks, letting it settle over him, letting it push him even further into that headspace.

The kiss is heated enough for them both to lose track of time. Before he knows it, the car is pulling off to the side.

"I didn't realize we'd be here so soon," Corinne says. "Or is your mouth just that distracting, sir?"

"Oh, my mouth is assuredly that distracting." He unbuckles himself and takes her hand to help her out of the car. Straightening her coat, he waves to Adrian in thanks and ushers her toward the door of a large brick building. It's a general-use event space Indali has rented for the evening. He presents their invitations at the door before heading inside to coat check. "It's time. Are you ready?"

She takes a deep breath. "Yes, sir." She slides her coat off her shoulders, and he gives it to the attendant along with his jacket.

"Corinne." Nikolai's holding up the leash now, and he crowds in so close she's forced to look up at him. "Who do you belong to, pet?"

She looks him directly in the eye. "You, sir."

The rumble that comes out of him is deep and dark, all pleasure and triumph, and she whimpers in response. He clips the leash to her collar, tugging gently on the chain, a sinful smile twisting his mouth. "Come along," he commands, and turns to walk into the event hall.

Nikolai is never more acutely aware of his surroundings than when he is in this headspace. He knows precisely where Corinne is as he leads her toward the wide double doors. As he enters the room, he slows, taking his time, surveying the open space.

There are couches, chairs, and kneeling cushions everywhere, interspersed with alcoves full of finger food perfect for hand-feeding, and spaces designated for play. He makes his way deeper into the room, soaking it all in, reveling in the palpable energy of people who love the same things as him.

Many people are already here. Some eye them as they enter, while others are wrapped up in their partners or conversation with others. They see him, but more importantly, they see her —the leash, the collar, the tag with his name on it, even if they can't read it... Each item clearly portrays who she is in this space and who she is to him.

His beautiful little possession.

He pauses a few times to greet people he knows, toying idly with the chain of Corinne's leash, all the while looking around for— "Dali!"

Indali looks up and grins as she glides over. She's in a forest green lace bustier with a pencil skirt slit so high on the side it's a wonder you can't see whether her lingerie matches the outfit. Her heeled sandals lace up the tops of her feet and around her ankles, and they look as mean as he knows Indali likes to be. Several gold chain chokers adorn her throat, and a shockingly large cross nestles against her cleavage.

He smirks at the double-banded leather wrapping around her upper thigh. She's wearing an entirely different kind of harness than his own, and by the end of the night, some cute little thing will end up writhing and stuffed full of whatever Indali decides to use with it.

"Kolya!" She kisses each of his cheeks when she reaches them, tucking a paddle under her arm and briefly flicking her eyes to Corinne. "It's been a long time since we've seen you at one of these."

Twitching the leash in his hand, the chain jingling, he otherwise ignores Corinne, deliberately not introducing her. And if he doesn't, then Indali won't ask either. Possessions aren't included in conversations, after all, even the prettiest ones. "It's been a long time since I had someone to bring. You know I'm not usually one for random play with people I hardly know."

Indali hums in acknowledgment, then idly slaps her hand with the paddle. Nikolai chuckles, earning a raised brow from his friend.

"No need to raise an eyebrow at me, Dali," Nikolai continues. "We both know you've always been more eager for a varied list of playthings than I have. And you look like you want to be mean to some poor little creature tonight."

"We can't all be as lucky as you, Kolya," she drawls, giving him a sidelong glance. "With a pretty girl at the end of your leash."

Nikolai smiles, possessive pride swelling in his chest at Indali's acknowledgment of his pet. He pulls on the leash until Corinne steps in close, and he tilts his head, examining her dispassionately. "She is rather pretty, isn't she?"

He uses the handle to raise her chin before he licks delicately at her lips, humming to himself at the yearning in her eyes, her body arching toward him. Watching her give in to this, to him? Nothing beats it. He has her wholly, and he will let her want for nothing. "Yes, such a lovely thing, my darling little pet."

"I'll let you have fun with your pet, Kolya," Indali says as she makes her exit, probably recognizing two people who've become so entranced with each other it'll be lucky if anything pulls them away.

He kisses Corinne in reward, a sweet gesture for being so good. "Are you hungry?"

She nods. "Yes, sir."

She's doing well with the rules, and he's delighted with her. With his picture-perfect pet.

He leads her to a nearby table and leans down to slide a velvet cushion in front. "Kneel," he says, waiting until she sinks onto the cushion and looks up at him.

Nikolai loops the handle of her leash around one of the table legs, tying it off as though he needs to because she'll wander, as though she's not going to stay exactly where he's put her, because he put her there. It's a heady feeling, and it has been far too long since he felt it.

He walks to one of the hor d'oeuvres tables and gathers a drink and a plateful of snacks, bite-sized pieces of everything, and makes his way back. She's exactly where he left her, and he smooths her hair as he passes, before sitting in a nearby chair with his legs spread wide.

"Pet," he says, getting her attention. "I want to feed you and make sure you have plenty of energy for later." He stretches to unloop the leash and grasps it in his hand again. "You can choose, pretty. Would you like to sit on my lap while I feed you or stay at my feet?"

She smiles at him softly with hooded eyes. "Your lap, please, sir."

He crooks his finger at her. "Up."

She stands, walks the few feet between them, and sits in his lap. Wrapping her arm around his shoulder, she leans into him and nuzzles his jaw.

He gets a hand on her collar and holds tight, halting her wonderful nuzzling. He turns his head just enough so his lips brush her ear. "Next time…" his voice is deep and rough now. "Next time, my darling pet, I expect you to crawl." He holds her collar for another split second and then releases it, smoothing his hand over her shoulder.

She whimpers and wriggles against him. "Yes, sir," she whispers.

Such a good little girl, he thinks. *Obedient and mindful and responsive.* He couldn't have asked for better, especially for her first High Protocol event.

He is so proud of her for being so quiet for him. He knows it must be difficult since she usually distracts his unwelcome acquaintances at parties, but the way she's following the rules tonight delights him.

He rearranges her until she's straddling his lap, knees tight to his hips. Setting his plate on the small table, he leisurely removes his gloves and tucks them under the shoulder strap of her bra. Her leash is still looped around his wrist as he holds a grape to her lips. "Open up."

Confusion flitters over her face momentarily before she opens her mouth and takes the grape, keeping his gaze as she bites into it.

"At dinner, we'll stick to the rule about who goes first. But right now…" He places another grape between her teeth. "Hold this, please," he says, satisfied as she obeys him. "Here, we do what I want." He gently walks his fingers up her leg, under the hem of her skirt, and over the silk of her stockings as she keeps the grape right where he put it.

"And what I want," he continues, "is to feed you first. And then…" He leans in and opens his own mouth, kissing the grape from her lips to eat it before sitting back. "Then I'll eat."

Nikolai can *see* her submersion into subspace in real time, her posture slackening, her eyes going glassy. "Oh, pet," he whispers, smoothing circles into the silk over her knees. "You're perfect. Look how beautiful you are. Such a pretty little thing." His hands travel farther up her thighs, his thumbs dragging along the insides. The slide of silk over her skin is driving him wild, and his cock twitches in his pants. "Do you feel good?"

Corinne smiles and rolls her hips. "Yes. So good, sir." She touches her forehead against his. "Do you?" she asks, her voice so sweet.

"Oh, better than I have in a long while, pretty thing." His hands reach the tops of her stockings, and he snaps the straps of her garter belt against her skin before running his thumb along the crease of her hip. "Would you like me to make you feel even better?"

greedy girl

NIKOLAI

CORINNE WHINES, her brows drawing together. "Please, sir."

"Yeah? Needy little thing, aren't you?" His fingers travel toward her center, and he brushes the back of his hand between her thighs. "Oh, pet, you're dripping." He slips a fingertip under the fabric of her panties, sliding it through the slickness he finds there. "What a messy little cunt you have. Just for me, aren't you?" He drags upward to her clit, gently circling. It's hot and swollen against his finger. "How do you suggest I help with this drippy little thing? Do you want my fingers?" He slips one smoothly inside her and pauses. "Or do you still want to wait?"

She moans. "May I have your fingers? Please, sir." She clenches around him. "I'm aching."

"Poor empty thing." Nikolai watches her for a moment. "How many? One?" He crooks the finger inside her slowly. "Two?" He slips a second finger in with the first, twisting his wrist, hitting all the spots she likes.

She cries out *loudly* as he moves inside her, rolling her hips against his hand, her eyes slipping closed. She seems completely unaware of the spectators around them, their eyes drawn to the sounds of her pleasure. Corinne may be unaware, but he certainly isn't. And their lustful gazes send his pulse into overdrive.

"May I have three, please, sir?"

"Three? What a greedy girl you are." He slips a third finger inside her, pushing down with his grip on her hip, pressing his fingers as deep as he can manage in this position.

Corinne moans again as she rocks against him, using his shoulders for leverage, over and over until— "Sir? Sir, please may I come?"

"Hmm, no, I don't think you can. Not yet." He grabs her collar and holds her still. "But if you want to sit like this, pet, I could allow that. No coming, but at least this greedy little cunt won't feel so empty, will it?"

A choked gasp falls from her lips, and she whimpers, gasping like she's crying, even though no tears fall to her cheeks. "N-No, it won't, sir." She opens her eyes. "Thank you for filling me up, sir."

"Oh, you're so very welcome. Now, since one of my hands is occupied"—he gives his fingers the barest of wiggles—"you'll need to hold the plate so we can finish our snacks. Okay?"

She's beautiful. Perfect. Stunning.

He wants to ruin her.

Nikolai snags the plate off the table with his free hand and passes it to her. "Hold this, darling, there's a good pet." He feeds her another piece of fruit, his fingers lingering near her mouth until she licks them clean, too.

But then his little temptress sucks one of his fingers into her mouth. Her gaze, soft and relaxed, never leaves his as she does so. She slowly fellates his finger for a moment before she pulls off with a wet, noisy sound, kissing his fingertip.

"If you're hungry for something else, I'd be happy to oblige you." He tugs his finger from her mouth and eats his own piece of fruit, chewing slowly. "Is that what you want?" His eyes dart around the room. "For everyone to see how good you look with your mouth full of cock?"

She doesn't answer, but her cunt clenches around his fingers in response. "In that case." He removes his fingers and holds them out to her while he moves their plate. "On your knees once you've finished cleaning up your mess."

Corinne's eyes lock with his, and she takes his hand and licks his fingers clean, wrapping her mouth around each one and sucking the taste of herself off them. When she finishes, she slides onto the floor, crouching to put the pillow in place before she kneels.

Nikolai teases his gloves from the strap of her bra. He never breaks eye contact as he puts them back on, settling them snugly before lazily undoing his belt and trousers to pull himself out. His cock is thick and hard, precome beading at the tip as he strokes himself. "Tongue out," he says roughly.

She opens her mouth wide and sticks out her tongue.

Using the leash around his wrist to yank her forward, he grabs her collar and places the head of his cock on her tongue. "Show me," he tells her. "I want to see how badly you want it, pet. Show me."

She moans, and it's such a wanton, needy sound. Wrapping her mouth around his dick, she watches him and presses the flat of her tongue against the head before hollowing her cheeks. She slicks up the length and then lowers her mouth until she's pressed to the hilt.

Fuck, she feels incredible.

Corinne swallows around him, then pulls off, taking a noisy breath, before sucking him off in earnest. She wraps her fist around the base, working in tandem with her mouth, doing all the things he loves. The sight of her at the end of his leash while she sucks his cock like she'll die if she doesn't is damn near overwhelming.

His fingers tangle in her updo, helping her take him deeper, setting a pace without pushing too hard yet. "Look at you. Gagging for it, weren't you, sweet thing? You need it so badly." He jerks his hips up, fucking the warm, wet heat of her mouth. "Do you want me to come down your pretty throat? One last treat before dinner?"

Corinne nods, mouth still firmly wrapped around his dick, her eyes pleading.

He starts up a rhythm, thoroughly fucking her mouth. "What a good girl you are," he pants, quickly losing himself in the pleasure of her mouth. "Take it so well, pretty pet. You're made to take it like this, fuck." People are watching, but that makes it better. They know she's his, know she's owned and cared for, his pretty little pet.

"Come on," he continues, his mouth running away from him, "show me how bad you want it. Come get it, just like that." He's chasing his release now, holding her leash tight, reveling in the knowledge that he's got her right where he wants her: her mouth around his cock, his collar around her throat, deep in subspace. Willing and eager and desperate for him, and he wants to see her as he ruins her. "Look at me."

Her eyes are full of tears from the force of his thrusts, and she pushes her shoulders back and looks up at him through her lashes, her gaze full of heat and longing as he ravages her mouth. She blinks, and tears fall down her cheeks.

"Fuck." He wipes his gloved thumb across her cheek. "Oh, darling, look how beautiful you are, crying for me. You perfect little thing." He's right on the edge, and he's never felt like this in his life. It's so good; they're so in sync, he's losing his mind.

She's perfect, fuck. She's everything.

It takes two, three thrusts before he pushes in deep as he

comes, his entire body tensing from the force. "Oh, fuck," he groans, long and loud, head thrown back but his eyes still on her, her leash clamped tightly in his grip. She swallows each pulse, mouthing around the head once he finishes, lapping up any stray drops before pulling off.

Her head falls to his thigh, and she looks at him softly. "Thank you, sir."

He's panting hard, still twitching all over. "Fuck, you are welcome. You earned it, darling, damn."

Nikolai takes a moment to come down, and Corinne rests against his thigh before tapping it three times with her index finger to get his attention.

"Yes, pet?" He pulls her up, settling her on his lap.

She kisses his ear before whispering. "May I come, sir?"

He taps his lips with the handle of her leash, smiling lazily at her. "Are you sure?" He looks her over—tear tracks on her face, lips swollen and slick. Beautiful. "You don't want to wait?"

She shakes her head. "No, sir, I want you. Please."

With a groan, he presses the handle of the leash to her mouth. "Hold this, would you?" Corinne grips the leather between her teeth, and the sight alone makes his cock twitch like he didn't just come down her throat seconds ago.

He takes off his gloves and rearranges her until she's straddling his lap so he can get his mouth on her pretty tits. "Ask before you come, darling," he says. Then he slips three fingers back inside her.

She cries out around the leash in her mouth and grinds against his hand, her own hands threading through his hair as he tugs down her bra and wraps his mouth around her nipples. She's riding him like she's desperate, her brow furrowed, her pace furious. And it takes no time at all until she's pleading around the leash between her teeth. "Please may I come, sir? I need it so badly."

He can't take his eyes off her, the way she keeps the leash in her mouth, her pretty tits shiny with his spit, cheeks flushed and makeup a mess. She is beautiful. "Yes, such a good girl. Go ahead and come."

A sob slips past the leash. Her body shudders, and when she finishes, she's *shaking*. Enthralled with his perfect little pet, he gentles her through it, keeping his fingers inside her as she comes down. Falling against him, she tucks her nose into his throat. "Thank you, sir. Thank you so much."

"You're so welcome. You earned it, and you were so good at asking. What a good girl you are for me."

Sighing, she pulls back, her languid gaze meeting his as she brushes back the hair falling in his face.

He takes the leash from her mouth and kisses her, affection welling inside him fast and strong. "Hello, darling," he says, easing his fingers out of her body and licking them clean.

"Hello, sir."

He settles her on his lap, holding her close for a few minutes while they both bask in the afterglow. Finally, he asks, "Are you ready for dinner, pet?" He gently flicks her nipple before righting her bra. "You need to eat something to keep your energy up. We have even more in store this evening."

She pulls back and nods, eyes hooded, still deep in subspace.

Fucking beautiful.

what are the rules, pet?

NIKOLAI HELPS CORINNE STAND, straightening her skirt and putting her back together, even though there's no hiding how well fucked and spacey she looks after a rather forceful face-fucking. Which, if his smug grin is any indication, he's delighted by.

He grabs her leash and gives her a kiss. "Come along, pet."

He takes his time leading her to dinner, passing several people in varying levels of fetishwear. They move toward three long tables set in a *U* shape, and Nikolai whispers to her, pointing out the tables of food, each lined with chafing dishes, and the stacks of cushions available for submissives.

"Give me your hand," he says when they get to the table, and he slips the strap of her leash over her wrist. "Go get a cushion, a thick one, and then come back and kneel for me."

Corinne does as she's told, wobbly on her heels, but she returns and settles on the cushion. Nikolai is talking to someone, but she can barely pay attention. She's floating so intensely while kneeling before him that she has to grab his calf to keep from slumping.

He smooths a hand over her hair before tipping her face toward him. "Alright, pet?"

She nods slowly. "Yes, sir. Just feel very... high?" She takes a breath. "It's a lot."

He studies her more closely, brushing his thumb along her cheekbone. "Too much?"

Her brow furrows, and she takes a moment before responding. "No? I don't think so. I don't want to leave, sir." She's had so much fun and doesn't want to disappoint him.

"Shh, shh, we won't. I just want to make sure I'm taking care of you, darling. You've been so good for me." He scoots his chair back and pats his lap. "Come up here for a bit, pet."

Corinne nods and stands before curling up in his lap. She rests her head against his shoulder.

"What's your favorite movie snack?" he asks, stroking her back.

Her brows knit in confusion. "What?"

The corners of his eyes crinkle. "Humor me."

"Um. Peanut M&M's."

Nikolai hums deep in his chest. "Always a good choice. I like black licorice, myself." He strokes a bit more firmly before asking another question. "Comfort movie?"

"Wait." It takes a few seconds for her brain to catch up. She pulls back, blinking up at him. "Black licorice? Who likes black licorice?"

Quirking a brow, he chuckles. "I do, pet. Don't act too shocked. It's what licorice is *supposed* to taste like."

She wrinkles her nose. "Agree to disagree, sir."

"Alright." He tweaks her nose, and she laughs.

"Hmmm, favorite comfort movie. I have to go with *Kiki's Delivery Service*."

"A classic, though I'm partial to *Castle in the Sky*, myself."

"You know." She tucks back against him. "I don't think I've seen it."

He rubs his hands over her arms. "We'll have to remedy that. I have all those movies. We'll watch it sometime." He looks her over again. "How are you feeling now?"

She hums, checking in on herself. She feels relaxed but no longer like she'll drift away like a lost balloon. "Better, sir." Her eyes narrow. Did he ask his arbitrary questions to pull her out of subspace? "Oh, you're clever."

His smirk is smug as he reaches for his glass of water and takes a sip. "Almost like I know what I'm doing, hm?"

Her gaze narrows even further. "You do, sir." She kisses him. "Thank you."

"You're very welcome." He raises the glass to her lips. "Now drink up, pet."

Nikolai's care not to spill and the gentle way he holds the back of her neck touch her deeply. He's so good to her. Her smile of thanks when she finishes is genuine and soft and full of affection.

He cradles her in his arms, chatting with the people sitting near them and giving her sips of water. Eventually, he taps her cheek with the handle of her leash. "I'm hungry." He loops the leash around her wrist again before saying, "Go fetch us dinner, sweet thing. Make sure you get enough for both of us." He tugs at the ring on her collar and kisses her roughly. "Go on."

"Yes, sir." She gets up and walks to the table. With a plate in hand, she fills it with enough chicken scallopini, penne, and green beans for them to share. She can see now why he pulled her out of the intense headspace she was in. She's unsure how well she would've stayed upright, let alone successfully fetched food for them.

She comes back and kneels at his feet before offering the plate.

"Good girl," he says, accepting it from her before cutting the food into smaller pieces. He eats a bite before offering a piece of chicken at the end of his fork. "Here, sweet thing."

She takes it, and her stomach suddenly makes it known that she is, in fact, ravenous. She taps his knee and waits for his permission to speak before she whispers, "I'm very hungry, sir."

Nikolai chuckles and feeds her some pasta. "I figured. There's a reason dinner is always in the middle of these things. Water?"

She nods and lets him carefully pour it into her mouth. "Thank you, sir." She rests her head against his thigh, curling her arm around his leg.

"You're welcome, pet."

He ensures they're both well fed, feeding her bite after bite, but not so much that she feels too full.

Once they've cleared the plate, he asks, "Have you had enough? Do you need anything else?"

"No, sir." She grabs his hand and kisses it. "Thank you."

After a few more minutes of chatting with the woman beside him, he stands and helps her to her feet. "Should we go see what others are up to? Maybe you'll see something you like, hm?"

"Yes, please." She looks up with a playful grin. "I'll be taking mental notes, sir."

"Wonderful. Come along." He leads her into the main space, passing through various play spaces. "Stop me if you see something you'd like to watch."

Corinne wants to watch everything, even if she's done much of it before. There's palpable energy in this room, especially from each scene they come across, and she wants to enjoy every aspect she can.

They first happen upon two men with dark skin and short

hair playing with rope. Corinne enjoys being tied up but doesn't let most clients do it, as it puts her in too vulnerable a position.

He's still watching the scene when Corinne spots his friend from earlier over to the right. She takes a few steps in that direction, the leash pulling taut between them, and she tugs on it to get his attention.

"What is it?"

"There's your friend," she says, pointing. "Unless it bothers you to see her... occupied."

The woman—Dali, she thinks as she suddenly remembers her name—is seated on a chair before a kneeling redhead wearing cat ears and a tail. Dali's skirt is pulled up to her hips, and her hand is fisted in the woman's hair while she eats Dali out.

Nikolai walks up to her and huffs a laugh. "A cat-girl, of course," he mutters to himself. "And no, I don't mind."

As Corinne gazes at them, it suddenly hits her that people must've watched everything she and Nikolai did. She doesn't care, of course; she told him she was comfortable with it. But she didn't even think about it in the moment, too caught up in the intimate space they had made for themselves for other people to enter her mind.

"Come along. I'll properly introduce you to Indali some other time," he says, pulling on her leash.

A few minutes later, they come to a woman whipping a man tied to a Saint Andrew's cross. They both have fair skin, and the woman, with her blond hair in a tight bun, is significantly smaller than the man with marks across his back.

Corinne has never tried whips. She's thought about it, but it's risky when the top isn't skilled. A question pops into her head. "Am I remembering correctly that whipping is a limit for you, sir?"

Nikolai's gaze turns steely. "What are the rules, pet?" he asks, every ounce of warmth missing from his voice.

Oh. Here is the sharpness Elijah has mentioned so many times, which she has yet to see for herself. She's done so well, and now her mouth has run away from her. Corinne isn't used to having to be quiet around him, especially at a public event. "To not speak without permission from my dominant. I'm so sorry, sir. Truly."

"We'll deal with it when we get home," he says, his timbre so deep that she swears she can feel it scraping her belly. "Understood?"

She nods, anticipation and fear battling within her. She hates his disappointment, but maybe she'll somewhat enjoy what's coming for her. "Yes, sir."

"To answer your question," Nikolai continues, his voice softening, "you are correct. However, it's more because it's not a skill I've ever had occasion to learn. It's a bit... intense for most people." Turning her around to watch, he whispers in her ear as he pulls her close. "Look at all those pretty marks on his skin. He seems to be enjoying himself, doesn't he?"

The thing about whips: they're noisy. The man jumps when he hears each crack a split second before the leather hits his skin. But the way his body bends and arches against each hit, like he's savoring every blow? It's unmistakable how much he's enjoying it.

"Yes, sir." She turns in his arms and faces him, taking his lead and trying to forget her misstep. "We'll be gone two whole weeks in France." She rubs her fingers against his harness. "You can mark me up there, you know. The first week." She trails the back of her hand along his jaw, his stubble scratching her skin. "Mouth. Hands. Implements." Brushing her thumb along his lips allows her to feel his sharp intake of breath.

Nikolai somehow gets even closer, gets right in her space,

and uses the handle of her leash to tilt her head back so she has to crane her neck to look at him. "Would you like that?" he asks, quiet and serious. "My marks all over you?"

"Yes." She looks him directly in the eye. "Bruises and bites. Welts, maybe?" She bites her lip. "I can look at them and press on them as little reminders when you're working."

"Anything." He hooks his finger through the ring of her collar. "Any kind of mark you want, you'll have it. Perhaps with something quite mean... I have a crop I think you'd like." His eyes flit back to the scene. "A challenge for my pretty pet."

The crack of the whip echoes in her ears like a heartbeat. "Is that so?"

"Oh, yes. I will hurt you till you cry..." He tugs on her collar. "And then fuck you till you're screaming for me..." He presses a slow kiss to her mouth. "And then pamper you like you deserve."

Her breath catches at his promise. When she pulls back from the kiss, her eyes roam over his dark gaze, his stubble, his gorgeous mouth. "I can't wait, sir." She kisses him again, and maybe she's sharing too much when she says, "I look forward to everything we do together."

He brushes his thumb along her cheekbone. "That makes two of us."

like you were made for it

"ANYTHING else you'd like to do tonight, pet?" Nikolai asks. "Any more secret desires in that pretty head of yours?"

Corinne grins up at him. "Oh, I have many, many, many desires, sir. I'll keep you apprised of them from now on since you like to hear them." She leans forward to whisper in his ear. "There are so many things I want to do with you. Bruises, bondage, lots of naughty little roles to play." She pulls back. "But for tonight, I don't have anything else on my party to-do list unless you do."

"It's not very nice to keep such delightful desires to yourself." He tuts at her, flicking one nipple through her bra and then the other. "How can I take care of you if you're keeping secrets? Naughty pet." He slowly steers her away from the Saint Andrew's cross and toward the seating area. "I'd like you to kneel for me a little bit longer. Put that hot mouth of yours to good use before we leave, and then I'll take you back to my apartment and show you just what naughty little pets get for keeping things to themselves. And for breaking the rules."

She nods, embers sparking to flame in her belly. "Yes, sir."

"Good girl." He walks toward a chair, her leash hanging

between them until he sits. "Come here. Show me you can keep being good for me, hm?"

"Yes, sir." She gets on her knees and crawls the few feet between them, reaching for a nearby pillow to put between his feet. She kneels on top and slides her hands up the inside of his thighs. "Would you like me to warm your cock, sir?"

His smile turns dark and a little wild around the edges. "I would like that very much. You look so pretty with your mouth around my cock. Even more so kneeling at the end of my leash, with my collar at your throat."

Lip caught between her teeth, she unfastens his belt and trousers, then pulls out his cock. Her eyes never leave his as she gives it a kiss, lowering her mouth around his length. She lets out a little sigh and closes her eyes.

"See?" He strokes her hair. "Isn't that better? Isn't it nice when you don't need to do anything but this?" Corinne whimpers in response because yes, it is. "You're a very good pet, letting me use you like this."

She hums around his cock, appreciative of his praise. Her hands nestle between her knees, and she rests her forehead against his abdomen. It takes a moment, but she relaxes into it. Nikolai using her while she kneels before him, not even for pleasure, but just for the sake of it, is more than enough to make her soft and floaty all over again. Her shoulders slump forward, and a trail of spit slips from the corner of her mouth.

"There we are," he says. "Perfect, just like that. Look at you, waiting so patiently. You look so pretty like this, darling." He thumbs around her mouth, cleaning up the saliva. "Like you were made for it. Meant for just this, just a lovely, warm place for my cock."

The softest whimper escapes her mouth. It does so much for her, being his little pet to use as he sees fit—a warm mouth, a wet cunt. A way to shut off her mind and let him take control of everything for a while. She's never trusted a client like this; she's always on guard. But with Nikolai...

With Nikolai, she can let go.

She nuzzles his torso in appreciation.

"Sweet little thing, aren't you? My sweet pet. I'm so lucky to have you, lovely." He continues in that vein as she sinks deeper and deeper. She's unsure how long they stay like this, but after a while, he taps her cheek with the end of her leash until she glances up. "Time for us to go."

Eyes hooded and gaze unfocused, she slides off of his cock, her chin covered in drool.

"Messy little thing." He pulls a handkerchief out of his pants pocket and hands it to her. "Clean up your mess, and then we'll leave."

The handkerchief is embroidered with *NZ* like her tag, and a grin graces her face. She wipes the spit off her face and hands the cloth back to him. "Thank you, sir."

Watching her, he accepts it and returns it to his pocket. He glances pointedly down to his cock twitching on his lower belly. "Well?" he asks sharply.

She nods and tucks his cock back into his underwear as best she can in its current state before fastening his pants and belt. He studies her when she finishes, his gaze *hungry*. "I'm going to wreck you, darling little pet," he tells her, dark sincerity in his voice. "Entirely and completely." He smiles and tilts his head the other way. "And you're going to thank me for it."

Aching desire pulses through her, and she moans. "Please, sir."

He strokes her face before putting his gloves back on, then stands and helps her up. Wrapping her leash around his fist to shorten the length, he pulls her to walk closer to him, keeping just a little tension on the collar. "Come along."

She's so deep in subspace again that she has to concentrate

on keeping herself upright in her heels, but she follows along, enjoying each and every tug at her collar.

He gets her into her coat, walks her outside, and helps her into the backseat. He knocks on the roof, letting Adrian know they're ready. "Corinne," he says as the car starts to move. "Look at me, pet."

She looks at him and tilts her head, resting it against the seat.

"I am very proud of you. Even with the mistake, you did very well at the party tonight." He brushes his mouth against hers. "You were made for this, darling."

Her chest fills with warmth, something loosening and unfurling within her at his praise, at having made him proud. "Thank you, sir. I loved it. And you were so lovely to me."

"You did exceptionally well." With another kiss, he reaches into her coat and under her bra and gently pinches her nipple, smiling against her mouth as she gasps. He rolls the barbell between his fingers. "You have the prettiest tits. The things I want to do to them." He bites at her earlobe before whispering, "When we go to France, I'm going to make them all pretty with my marks."

"Fuck," she gasps, her cunt aching at the thought. Spreading her coat open, she crawls into his lap, managing not to hit her head on the roof, even while buzzing from the party. She pulls down the cups of her bra and brings his gloved hands to her breasts. "You can be rough now, sir."

He bites at her nipple, digging in with the points of his teeth, drawing forth a hiss from her lips. Pulling back, he slaps her other breast. It bounces from the hit, and he slaps it again that much harder. "I always enjoy being rough with you. Do you have a favorite way to be roughed up?"

Corinne whines at his question. "I'm limited because of marks," she sighs in frustration, resting her forehead against his and closing her eyes. "I wish I didn't have to worry about it, but it's bad for business." She straightens. "But you can fuck me hard. You can spank me and slap me. Just… not my face. I had a couple of bad experiences." She winces. "I'm talking too much." Of course her clients know she sees and fucks other people, but they don't always want to hear or think about it when she's half-naked in their laps.

"You're not," he says. "I know what you do for work, pet. I don't mind, and you don't have to pretend with me." He slaps both of her tits hard, the leather making it hurt even more, and she groans. "I'm still going to take you home and spank you till you're tender and then fuck your desperate little cunt till you come so hard you're crying." Nikolai keeps his eyes locked with hers, smiling ferally as he pinches her nipples hard. Corinne gasps. "I want to ruin you, pet. Would you like that?"

"*Yes.*" She scoots forward and grinds against him. He's still hard beneath his trousers, and she means to tease him, but she can't help but moan as she does. Tugging him closer by his harness, she kisses him. His lips are rough against hers, and she melts into it, unable to get enough of his mouth, his hands, his body beneath hers. "Fuck, you make me crazy."

He grins wolfishly. "That is entirely the point. I want you undone for me, *because* of me." He kisses her again, holding her hips tight, pulling them down to keep the pressure of his cock against her cunt. "You need to be fucked, don't you? You need something in this poor empty little cunt, don't you?"

"Y-Yes," she whines. She threads her fingers through his hair and grinds against his dick, gasping as he helps her along. "Please, sir. Need your cock."

Suddenly, the car pulls off to the side. "Stop," Nikolai commands, voice deep and dark as he halts the movement of her hips. She gasps, her cunt aching from the loss of friction. "I need to get you to my apartment now so I can fuck you properly. Leash on or off? I can make it so no one can see it if you want it on." He tugs on it gently. "I'll put it right back on if you want to take it off. Your choice."

Corinne presses her forehead against his. "On, please, sir. I don't want you to take it off yet. Want you to hold it while you fuck me, please."

"Fuck," he groans out, pressing his forehead into hers even harder. "I absolutely will, don't worry. You belong to me tonight."

He kisses her again, softer than they have been, but still rough. "Alright, hold still for me," he says. He gingerly pushes her back to give himself room to work. He threads the handle of her leash down the arm of her coat until it's resting in her palm. "See?" He slips the handle around his wrist and holds her hand. "Still mine, pretty pet. Even when we look respectable."

She looks at their entwined hands, at the leash around his wrist, and smiles at him lazily. "You think of everything. Thank you."

Nikolai sets her to rights again, though there's only so much he can do at this point. He makes sure her coat is fastened and her hair is smooth, and he uses a handkerchief to try and tidy some of her makeup. He smiles ruefully at her. "I'd keep your head down if I were you, sweet thing. If anyone is curious about what we've been up to, your makeup would tell them." He brushes his thumb along her cheekbone. "You cried such pretty tears for me tonight."

"Mmm." She leans into his touch and kisses the palm of his hand. "They'd know what *you* did to me, sir."

He snags her by the collar, his dark eyes shining brightly. "That's right. Because I own you, don't I? My sweet little pet. You're mine."

Her breath catches in her chest. He'd said he owned her before they left for the party, but it feels different now, after everything they've done. She knows it's true, feels it deep within herself. She'd do anything he wants right now, even if that's a dangerous thing to think. Because she's his, and he'd take care of her like he always does. She can let go and not worry for once in her fucking life.

"Yes, sir, I am," she responds after a beat, barely recognizing her voice.

The smile that slowly breaks over his face is dark and hungry, like he's *thrilled* she's trusted him enough to let him bring her here. "Beautiful. Absolutely beautiful." With that, he smooths a final stray lock of hair behind her ear before he opens the door, his hand with her leash clasped firmly with hers.

i love to hear you beg

CORINNE

HIS HAND IS her sole anchor to keep her wits about her enough to get up to his apartment. Nikolai takes her coat when they get inside, and then he smirks as he grabs the handle of her leash again.

"On your hands and knees, pet," he says, stepping back as she complies. "Come along, needy little thing." He backs toward his bedroom as he watches her.

She starts to crawl forward, but her skirt gets in the way. "Wait, please, sir," she says and stops to slip it down her hips. Then she continues immediately, crawling out of the skirt and keeping her eyes on his as she follows him to his bedroom. Every movement forward, every tug and pull on her leash, makes her cunt wetter and achier. He isn't even touching her, but a moan escapes her all the same—a whiny, frustrated thing. She's so turned on it feels like she might cry all over again.

He pouts at her, an exaggerated mockery. "Something wrong? Is that greedy little cunt feeling empty?"

"Yes, sir. I need you."

"Poor pretty thing," he croons, walking into the bedroom.

"Tell me, is it dripping for me? Have you made a mess of yourself already?"

"Yes," she chokes out. "I'm so wet. It's all over my thighs."

"What a filthy girl you are." He stops her progress and loops her leash around the short post on his footboard. "A moment, pet. I'm feeling a bit overdressed." Nikolai watches her with a smirk as he takes off his suit jacket and cuff links, eyes on hers as he rolls up his sleeves, his gloves still on. He's moving so slowly and methodically, she's losing her mind. "That's better, don't you think?" He keeps the harness as well, and it pulls tightly against his chest muscles as he squares his shoulders.

"Yes, sir," she says, breathless and pained, rising on her knees. She squeezes her thighs harshly to try and distract herself from the ache between her legs.

"I'm sorry, I've left you waiting, haven't I? You poor neglected thing." He comes back to her and takes her leash, pulling upward to bring her to her feet. "I'd like to undress you now," he whispers in her ear, biting at the lobe, making her gasp. "I want you in nothing but my collar and leash." He slips a strap off her shoulder before he pauses with a cruel laugh. "I almost forgot. I have to spank you before I fuck you." He licks at the delicate rim of her ear, then bites gently at her jaw. "My little pet needs to be punished, doesn't she?"

She sobs but answers his question. He's in such a mood tonight that she doesn't think it would go well for her if she didn't. "Yes, sir."

Nikolai grins as he pulls off her underwear, tucking it in his pocket as always. He doesn't remove the rest of her lingerie, though. Or her heels. Instead, he walks a slow half-circle around her, snapping the strap of her garter belt against her thigh before stepping close and grabbing her ass with both hands. "You're going to make such pretty sounds for me, aren't you?"

She gasps. His fingers are so close, *so close* to where she wants them, and she presses back, arching her ass into his hands. He's so hard against her, and fuck, she wants him so badly. "Sir," she moans.

He smacks her ass lightly. "Be good." He sits on the bed. "Over my knee, sweet thing."

She climbs onto the bed and nestles over his lap.

He smooths one gloved hand over her ass and up the groove of her spine before fitting it around the lock on her collar and pulling the collar against her throat. He kneads his fingers, pressing divots into the skin of her ass as he warms her up so slowly.

Corinne groans in frustration. "Sir, I'm aching. *Please.*"

Nikolai shushes her gently, not changing the firmness of his touch until a few moments later when he slaps her ass. "Better? Just that eager for your punishment, huh?"

She bites her lip because that's not at all true. "I just want your cock inside me, sir," she murmurs.

"And you'll get it. Once we're done here." Then he slaps her ass properly. The leather makes the sting even worse, and she moans. There's a second hit to her other cheek. Then a third. "Feel free to keep begging, though," he says, starting a rhythm. "You know I love to hear you beg."

"Please. Please fuck me." He smacks her even harder, and she cries out. "Please, sir!"

He continues spanking her, hit after hit, making Corinne moan and writhe under him.

"Your ass is the most stunning shade of pink, pet," he groans a few minutes later. "Fucking perfect."

"Don't you—*fuck*—don't you want to feel it against you while you fuck me?"

"Desperate little thing," he says, fondness in his voice as he seizes her ass with both hands, pulling the cheeks apart. "Of course I do." When he hits her this time, he uses both hands, smacking and pulling, leaning down to lick the tender skin. "So beg me, little thing, one last time. Beg me for it."

"Please, sir," she asks shakily. "Please fuck me. Want you inside me. Can't stop thinking about it all fucking night. All week." She cries out after a particularly hard hit. "Haven't you missed my cunt? Missed it tight and hot around your cock? Please, *please*."

Nikolai growls and helps her stand, kissing her roughly. "I'll never get tired of hearing you beg. Never." He steps back, eyes raking over her. "I meant it when I said I wanted you in just my collar and leash."

He undresses her—removing her bra, unlocking the cuffs of her shoes, slipping off her stockings, now snagged and torn from crawling. "Beautiful," he murmurs. He's on his knees, kissing and nipping at her exposed skin, every touch setting her on fire.

She's a gasping mess by the time he finishes. "Sir, please." Fuck, she's shaking. "Please. I can't take it anymore. I need you inside me." Her voice is foreign to her ears, rough and wrecked. "I need you, please. I'll do anything."

He takes off her garter belt and throws it behind him. "Those are dangerous words, pet. You're very lucky I'm not one to take advantage." His tongue trails along the slick on her thighs, and he drags his fingers through it, his gloves shiny and wet. He licks at them, humming in satisfaction. "Delicious as always, darling."

But a kernel of nervous displeasure buries itself in her gut about her *dangerous words*. She's only half paying attention when he finally stands and flips her over, positioning her so she's braced against the mattress while he takes out his cock and rips open a condom. He grabs the leash and holds it tightly as he lines himself up, the head of his length bumping against her swollen cunt. "Ready?"

He's right there, ready to fill her like she desperately wants, but she needs him to know first. She doesn't want him to think she's being careless. "No," she says softly. "I know. I know it's dangerous." She can't stand the thought of him thinking less of her, thinking she can't handle herself. A sob builds in her chest, and she tries to push it down, but her voice is watery when she continues. "I wouldn't have said that to anyone else."

He brushes a gloved hand down her back, gentling her. "Shh, pet, I know. I know that. I was only teasing." He leans over her and kisses her cheek. "You can say those things to me, sweet thing. Because you're mine, and I take care of what's mine." He strokes the head of his cock along her slick center, teasing her just a bit more before he positions himself at her entrance again. "Alright?"

Corinne takes two deep breaths, letting his words reassure her, focusing on the pull of the leash, of his cock right up against her. The third breath comes out trembling, but from want instead of anxiousness.

She nods.

"That's it, sweet thing. What a good girl you are." His hips press forward, a growl tearing from his mouth. "Fuck, pet. Perfect. So fucking perfect."

"Oh, god." Finally, *finally*. "You feel so good, oh my god." She grinds back against him, meeting each slow thrust, and it feels so perfect to finally be filled that she doesn't even care that he's still teasing her with a languid pace. She twists her hands in the bedding and bends her neck forward to create more tension from her collar and leash.

Catching on, he pulls harder on the leash, smacking her ass as he picks up the pace. "You make the loveliest sounds. I'd like to hear you even louder." He puts more power behind his thrusts, and now the obscene clap of his flesh meeting hers echoes in the room.

"Fuck!" It's all so intense, the harshness of his thrusts, his gloved hand hitting her sensitive ass, the tight pull of the leash. She has to tilt her head back to keep from choking, and her body is so tense that her muscles are starting to burn. "Sir," she moans, completely overwhelmed, not holding back because he wants her to be loud. "Sir, I want..." It's hard to contextualize what she wants, what her body and mind are aching for. "Can we—I want to feel you closer to me."

He pulls out and flips her over, her tits bouncing as he enters her again, his thrusts quick and sharp. Tugging on her leash, he licks up her throat. "Better?"

"Yes, sir." She wraps her arms and legs around him, baring her neck to him. Nikolai completely surrounding her is precisely what she needed. She feels... protected when he's on top of her, like he could keep every single bad thing away from her. She moans shakily, overcome and trembling, as she rolls her hips against his. Her moans get louder as she chases her climax. "May I come, sir?" she asks breathlessly, not sure if his rule from the party still applies. "Please."

"Not quite yet. Be good."

She whines, biting her lip and squeezing her eyes shut as she tries to pull it back. Then she feels him lean in even closer.

"Who do you belong to, pet?"

"Y-You, sir," she says when she finally gains control, tears slipping down her cheeks. "I'm yours."

"Yes, you fucking are," he growls, hips speeding up. "You're mine. All of you."

Corinne gasps, affected every time he says it, every time he verbally claims her.

He wraps her leash around his hand until his skin is pressed ever so lightly against her throat, tilting her head back. "Would you like to come now?"

She arches into him, giving herself to him. "Yeah, I want to come. Please, sir. Want it. Fuck, please."

"Go on, sweet thing, you deserve it."

His permission pushes her over the edge, and she sobs, her fingers digging into his shoulders as pleasure washes over her. "Oh my god," she gasps, her chest heaving. "Sir." Her hands tremble as they move to cradle his face. "Thank you." It's barely a mumble; she's so fucked out of her mind that she can hardly keep it together.

"Damn, the feel of you when you come around my cock."

She can tell from the harshness of his rhythm that he's about to follow her. "Yeah?" She looks up at him with hooded eyes and whispers, "I wish I could feel you come inside me."

The choked-off sound he makes is one she's certainly never heard before. "Oh, fuck!" His climax overtakes him as he buries himself to the hilt. The muscles in his arms are corded with tension, even through his shirt, and his hips grind against hers as he finishes.

Corinne hums as she watches him, a pleased grin gracing her lips at his reaction, at the noise she wrestled from him with just one little sentence. As he comes down, she caresses his face and kisses him gently. "Thank you, sir."

With a chuckle, he buries his face in her throat and presses soft kisses to her leather collar. "My god. I've never meant 'you're welcome' more in my life." He nuzzles at her, loosening his hold on her leash. "How lucky I am, darling, to have a pet such as you."

Warmth blooms in her chest. "I think I'm the lucky one, sir." She brushes her thumbs over his cheekbones. "You give me so much when you have no obligation to do so." She kisses him again. "I just... I love every moment we spend together."

"The thing I want most is just to spoil you and show you how much I appreciate what you give me. You are the bright spot in my week and what keeps me going." Nikolai takes a deep breath. "Corinne, you... you are so precious to me."

drop

CORINNE

TEARS WELL IN HER EYES. She's never felt as hazy after sex as she does right now, but it's more than that.

Corinne cares for him. A lot. She's known that for a while but didn't realize the intensity until tonight.

Wrapping her arms around his neck, she buries her face in the collar of his shirt. "Thank you, sir."

He pulls out and holds her, gentling her as they come down from both the sex and their eventful evening. After a while, he stands and scoops her into his arms. "Come along, pet. Let me spoil you a bit." He walks them to the bathroom, where he sets her on the short cushioned stool that magically appeared a few weeks ago. He drapes her leash over the towel rack and turns on the tub faucet.

It's chilly in the bathroom, so she brings her knees to her chest and hugs them close while Nikolai readies their bath. The stool is close enough that he can keep a hand on her for the most part, and she's glad of his touch. She's slowly started to come back to herself, and now she can feel every ache in her body from the kneeling and crawling and everything else they've done. And she's tired. So tired.

But his touch is soothing, and she leans into it gratefully.

Stripping off, Nikolai tosses his harness and the remnants of his suit in the corner and lays his gloves on the counter. He crouches in front of Corinne, taking her leash in his hand. "Time for this to come off, pet. The collar, too. It's not waterproof. But, if you'd like, we can put your collar back on after our bath."

"Please," she says with a frown. "I wish you didn't have to take it off."

"I know. I'll figure out something you can wear in the water, if you'd like." He kisses the top of her head before opening the lock and unbuckling the collar, then setting it reverently on the counter. He takes her earrings next and places them next to the collar.

Then he scoops her up and lowers her into the warm water before joining her, the scent of lavender wafting around them.

"Thank you for tonight, pet." He settles her against his chest. "It was beyond wonderful."

Corinne closes her eyes as he wraps his arms around her. "And what did you enjoy, sir?" she asks as they always do after a scene. Her mind is clearing now, even if she still feels wrecked.

"All of it. Everything." He tilts a handful of water along her arm. "I liked you on your knees for me. I liked having you in my lap. I thoroughly enjoyed feeding you—that may become more regular." He moves her hair and kisses the spot on her neck where the clasp of her collar rested just a minute ago, making her shiver. "But what I loved most was how you seemed to enjoy it, too."

"I did." She huffs a laugh. "God, Nikolai, I really did. I loved you feeding me. I cannot express how much I love being led around on your leash. How..." She takes a deep breath, trying to get her thoughts together. She'd never experienced it this way before, so she's never had to put it into words. "How you talked about me to your friend like I really was your pet. Your... possession."

"Someone certainly has a thing for objectification, hm?" he asks, a smile in his voice. "Don't think I didn't notice. I loved owning you tonight. My perfect pet." He leans in and gently bites her shoulder, trailing up toward her ear. "The best accessory a man could have, huh?" He nips at her earlobe. "Meant to be pretty and wet for me always, and nothing more."

She takes a shaky breath, surprised by how much she's affected by what he says. "I don't even know why I like it so much. Not when more male clients than I can count have treated me like that over the years." She traces a pattern of water over his knee. "But it was so nice to just... shut off."

Nikolai caresses her arms. "It might be because you know, at least I hope you know, that you aren't just a thing that exists for my pleasure. You're a businesswoman; you're smart, clever, and talented. You're so many things. But it's nice to pretend, to give in to those thoughts that just want you to relax for a while, to let someone else handle things. The second you want to stop, we stop, and you can be in charge again." He nuzzles her temple.

"You take care of others for a living, pet. Is it any wonder you'd like someone to take care of *you* sometimes?"

Oh.

Before she knows it, tears are slipping down her cheeks. "No, sir." She sniffles. "When you put it that way, it does make sense."

"The very best part is," he whispers, kissing her cheek, "my favorite thing in the world is to take care of you. And if taking care of you means baths and delicious foods and pretty clothes, then wonderful. But if it's also letting you have freedom from making choices, then even better."

"Sir," she says softly. He is being so sweet to her that her chest aches. And she wants to say something lovely in return; she wants him to know how much she likes and appreciates him. But that ache morphs into a heavy weight, suffocating her until everything turns dark and gloomy.

And, suddenly, a deep, wretched sob escapes her mouth.

"Oh, pet," Nikolai breathes, pulling her close. "Hold on, we're standing up now, okay?" He gets her out of the tub and grabs a towel off the warming rack, then dries her throat quickly before wrapping her in the towel. And all the while she can't stop crying, tears streaming down her face. "Here," he murmurs, putting her collar back on. "Come on, precious. Up we go." He carries her back to his bedroom and settles her in the bed.

Everything has been so lovely, and she doesn't know why she can't stop. "I'm so sorry," she gasps as he crawls in with her. "I don't know what's wrong with me."

He tuts gently as he rocks her and holds her close. "Hush now with those apologies. You have nothing to be sorry for. It's subdrop, precious, nothing else. I should have prepared you better, should have warned you."

"Oh," she breathes, hiccuping. She knows about subdrop, of course, but she's never experienced it. But she's also never had a scene or experience this intense.

"It's okay, darling, let it out. It's alright, I've got you."

Knowing is half the battle, and after a few minutes, her sobs calm until they're just quiet little gasps.

"It happened so suddenly," she mumbles when she's finally collected enough. Her chest is hollow with sadness, and her mind and body are exhausted. "I don't want to feel like this right now."

"I need you to do a few things for me, and then we can sleep." He reaches for his nightstand drawer and pulls out a bag of protein granola bites and a bottle of water. "I need you to eat and drink at least this much, okay?"

Corinne nods. "Okay." She sits up, accepting the food as she crosses her legs. She rips open the bag and puts one of the bites in her mouth, bringing her other hand up to her collar while she eats. "Thank you for putting it back on, sir."

He smiles and opens the bottle of water. "Of course."

She sniffles and leans in for a quick kiss, eyeing the open bottle in his hands as she pulls back. She thinks back to him giving her water at the party and then glances at the bag in her lap. "Did you want to feed me, sir? I'm sorry, I'm not... I'm a little out of it right now."

With a shrug, his eyes dart to her lap. And, honest to god, an embarrassed smile forms on his lips. "It's alright, darling. All I want is to take care of you, however you need."

She bites her lip, grinning at his blush. God, she... Okay.

Corinne... has feelings for him.

It's stupid of her, and it's breaking every rule in the sex worker handbook, but here she is. She's just going to admit it and move on.

As best she can.

She scoots closer so she's practically in his lap and opens her mouth.

His smile brightens, his eyes crinkling at the corners. He takes the bites from her and pops a little granola ball into her open mouth. "Thank you, pet." He's fiddling with the bag like he's nervous.

"You're the one feeding *me*, sir," she says. "May I have some water?"

"Of course, darling." He holds the water for her and helps her drink. "I know I'm feeding you, but I'm thanking you anyway because I know how special it is to be the one who takes care of you."

Her eyes roam over his face, and she strokes his jaw. "You're so sweet, sir." She drops her hand to his knee and squeezes it. "I know you're a very busy man, but if you ever did find the time to have a relationship, whoever you chose would be so lucky to have you."

"Well, thank you, pet." He clears his throat. "You've taken the words right out of my mouth." He helps her finish her snack and water. Then he takes her hair down and sits back. "Would you like something to sleep in? I could get something of mine."

She nods enthusiastically. If she sleeps in anything while she's here, it's always silky and beautiful. But something that belongs to him sounds lovely. "Yes, please."

He eases out of bed and goes for his dresser, then returns with a worn-out Oxford shirt and a pair of boxer briefs. "They'll be big," he cautions, holding them out. "But likely more comfortable for it."

Of course he went to Oxford. Not like she didn't go to Northwestern herself, though her art degree never brought her the kind of money sex work has. She crawls to the edge of the bed before standing. "Will you put them on me, sir?"

"Of course, darling pet. Arms up for me." Nikolai helps her into the clothes and then kisses her gently. "There. Better?"

She nods. Both pieces are soft and comfortable, even if the underwear is loose on her hips. "Yes, sir, thank you." She gets back in the bed and pulls him in with her, tangling her legs with his and closing the distance between them with a kiss.

A fog of sadness still lurks at the edges of her mind, but crying and eating and talking have helped a lot. "I feel like I could sleep for twelve hours," she says.

Nikolai runs his fingers through her hair. "Nothing to say you can't. You're mine all day tomorrow, too, remember?"

"Mm, yeah." She snuggles into him, pressing her face

against his collarbone as she closes her eyes. "You never sleep, though, so you'd be lonely."

He chuckles and rubs soothing strokes down her back. "I sleep plenty, sweetness. Don't worry about me. I'm here to take care of you, alright?"

"Someone needs to take care of *you*, sir," she mumbles, the softness of his hand already lulling her to sleep.

He hums in response, deep in his chest, his hand never stopping its slow, sweeping strokes down her back. Corinne is asleep moments later, drifting off to the thought of how nice it would be to fall asleep in his arms all the time.

She's certainly too tired and too far gone to scold herself for it. She can do that in the morning.

work

NIKOLAI

WHEN NIKOLAI WAKES the following morning, he and Corinne are wrapped around each other. Pressing a kiss to the top of her head, he slowly extricates himself from their tangle of limbs. Afterward, he stands and watches her for a few minutes, chest tight at the sight of her in his clothes, sound asleep in his bed.

He finally shakes himself and heads to the bathroom before returning to snag a pair of black joggers and a white V-neck.

"Right," he says to himself, closing the door behind him before walking toward the kitchen. "Breakfast."

It's been a long time since he's handled a drop, either his own or a partner's, and because it's Corinne, he wants to go all in on the comfort. He starts with kasha, toasting the buckwheat with butter, salt, and an egg before adding it to boiling water and turning it down to simmer. He buys the kasha at a deli in Ukrainian Village that imports it from Russia. He refuses to buy it from the health food store. It's not the same, no matter what people claim.

Nikolai gets coffee going for Corinne, and, for himself, he makes tea in the electric samovar Indali got him for Christmas last year. He's grabbing more ingredients from the fridge when the bedroom door opens with a click. He heads toward the hallway, smiling softly when she approaches, all sleep-rumpled and bleary-eyed.

"Good morning, darling pet." He engulfs her in a hug before grabbing the backs of her thighs and hauling her up in his arms.

Corinne presses her face to his neck and tightly wraps her limbs around him. "Good morning," she says groggily. He's not surprised; Corinne is always slow to wake. "Do I get to be carried everywhere today?"

"Would you like to be?"

"Mm, yes, please."

"Then so be it." Carrying her into the living room, he grabs a blanket from the back of the couch before heading to the kitchen. He lays it on the counter and sits her on top of it.

Glancing around the kitchen, she grabs his waist and pulls him closer. "You've already been busy."

"I had to get up early and start breakfast for my pet." He leans back so he can see her face, eyes crinkling as he smiles. "She's a hungry little thing, you know."

"She is," she says with an adorable little pout. She sniffs at the air before looking at him. "What are you making?"

"Kasha. Buckwheat porridge, essentially. Russian comfort food."

"It smells lovely." He couldn't agree more. It's warm and earthy, and the scent alone can instantly calm him.

Nikolai kisses her. "Would my pet like some coffee?"

She smiles up at him. "Yes, please."

He grabs a mug for her and pours the coffee, adding a healthy dose of half-and-half—just how she likes it—and crosses back to her, handing it over with a kiss. "Now, I can prepare your kasha a few different ways." He prepares his tea as he speaks, mixing in a spoonful of raspberry jam to the zavarka concentrate before diluting it with hot water. "My mother used to put dried fruit in sometimes, and my father eats his with milk, and I've been known to add onions and mushrooms with a fried egg on top."

"Ooh, the last one." She takes a sip of her coffee. "Everything is better with a fried egg on top."

"Breakfast bowl it is, then." He kisses her temple, then crooks a finger through the ring of her collar, using it to raise her chin. He studies her, checking for any outward signs of distress. "How are you today, pet?"

She tilts her head and hums while she thinks. "I feel tired. A little lower energy than normal? But I'm not sad like last night." She smiles softly. "I feel content, actually."

Relief floods him—he was more concerned than he realized. "I'm glad to hear it." He brushes his thumb just under her bottom lip. "We'll still take it easy today just to make sure, okay?"

"Okay. That's probably for the best." Corinne nuzzles into his hand. "And how are you, sir? I know it can affect you, too."

Nikolai briefly takes stock of himself. "I'm feeling a little more tactile than usual, but otherwise, I'm alright." His stomach growls, and he looks down at it, affronted. "Hungry, too, it seems."

"Have I been too much of a distraction?" she asks with a mischievous grin.

He narrows his eyes playfully, happiness blooming in his chest. "You *are* rather distracting, sweet thing." The timer dings on his phone, and he quickly kisses her cheek. "Let me check the kasha, and I'll get our breakfast bowls started."

Corinne drinks her coffee while he cooks—frying up mushrooms and onions after he takes the kasha off the heat. "Tell me about your friend from last night. Indali."

Nikolai smiles, shaking his head as he remembers Indali's

cat-girl from the party. "Indali and I have known each other our whole lives." He grabs bowls while the onions and the mushrooms caramelize. The kasha is ready, so he spoons generous helpings into both dishes. "Our families have been friends for hundreds of years, and my parents and her father decided to come to America together."

"Oh, wow." She peers into the bowls, probably looking for something to steal. "And did one of you introduce the other to BDSM, or did you both just happen to fall into it?"

He passes over a small bowl of dried apricots he got out in case she wants it on her kasha. "Indali convinced me to go to a meetup at a bar our first year in college. She was interested and didn't want to go alone." He looks over at Corinne, lips quirked in a smile. "We were both intrigued enough to go to the next newbie night, and the rest is history."

She crosses her legs and nestles the bowl of apricots on her lap. "Thank you, sir." She grabs one and takes a bite. "And have the two of you ever..." She trails off, wiggling her eyebrows with a shimmy of her shoulders.

Nikolai barks a laugh as he divvies up the mushrooms and onions, turning to grab a couple of eggs from the fridge. "We tried, but only once," he says, cracking them over the hot pan and seasoning them with salt and fresh-ground pepper. "But we both expected to be the top in the encounter, so." He shakes his head, chuckling. "Her mama is still sad about it."

"No switching amongst you, huh?" She laughs. "Poor Mama."

"She has reminded us many times how easy her life would be if we would"—and here he raises the pitch of his voice—"'Just *be together*, Nikolai, then I don't have to get to know anyone else, huh? I know you're a nice boy who goes to church and can take care of my girl.'" He deposits the eggs into their bowls of kasha with another shake of his head. "If I tried, Indali would throw me in the lake."

"A nice boy," Corinne repeats with one raised brow, then takes the bowl. "Thank you, sir."

He exaggerates an affronted look. "Are you implying I'm not?"

She reaches for her collar and looks at him pointedly. "Do I need to remind you what we did last night, sir?" She flicks the tag. "What would her mother think?"

He grabs the collar by the ring and crowds into her space. "What she doesn't know won't hurt her," he whispers, and kisses her lightly. "Also, are you implying I wasn't nice to you last night?"

"You made me beg for an awfully long time, sir." She pouts.

God, she's cute. The sunlight is streaming in through the big windows behind her, gilding her dark hair, and he wants nothing more than to kiss every freckle dotted across the bridge of her nose.

Corinne takes a bite. "Damn," she sighs, her shoulders loosening. "You're making up for it now, though."

He loves cooking for her, loves feeding her, and warmth blossoms in his chest at her obvious enjoyment. "There are many ways to be nice, sweet pet." He grabs his own kasha to dig in.

"Okay, I take it back. You're a very nice boy." She sips her coffee. "Does that mean you're missing church this morning for my sake?"

"I'll go to Typika tomorrow before work," he says. "You are my priority today, pet."

Her gaze softens, and she sets down her mug before she pulls him closer. "Thank you, sir. It's awfully sweet, the way you take care of me. I feel so cared for when I'm with you." She smiles almost sadly. "I was trying to tell you that last night in the bath, but then..." She huffs. "You know what happened."

He puts his bowl on the counter, shushing her as he cups her face in his hands. "Pet," he says, brows drawn together as he strokes her cheekbones with his thumbs. "Dropping is normal. It happens. Last night was *incredibly* intense." He studies her face, hoping she believes him. "Am I right in remembering you've never done something that intense before?"

"No, I haven't. Nothing like that." Her eyes roam his face. "I know it's normal." Her mouth turns up at the corner, but the half smile isn't reflected in her eyes. "I promise I'm not berating myself. Just. It doesn't mean I liked that it happened."

He hums disbelievingly at her. "It sounds like you're upset it happened. Even if you're not berating yourself."

Her hand slides up to his chest, her gaze falling to track the movement. She's silent for several beats before she speaks. "Do you like the idea of sobbing uncontrollably at work, sir?" she asks quietly, hesitantly.

Work.

Hearing that word is like being plunged into the Arctic Ocean. For a moment, he let himself forget that, for her, this is work, even if she enjoyed last night and seems to be enjoying this morning.

He clears his throat. "When you put it that way," he says with a rueful chuckle, his chest tightening, "I suppose I'd feel the same in your shoes."

"It's funny because I trust you. I trust myself with you. So I wasn't scared that it was happening. Just... disappointed." Her smile this time is genuine and warm, a ray of sunshine through the gloom. "Thank you for helping me through it."

He pushes his own sadness aside. Today is an aftercare day, and that means good things only. He returns her smile, his own just as warm. "You're welcome, pet. Remember, I take very good care of what's mine."

After breakfast, they spend the rest of the day wrapped up in each other, watching Studio Ghibli movies on the couch as promised, teasing each other with light caresses. Until Corinne breaks and climbs over him, riding him slowly in his old college t-shirt, the sight alone almost enough to make him lose control.

When their day is finished, he helps her gather her things, feeling grounded and centered.

"Do you feel good enough to go home?" he asks.

"Yes. I feel lovely, sir. Thank you." She gives him a kiss. "I'm sorry I can't join you this Tuesday. I'd been booked for that day for months."

He's attending an awards ceremony and asked her last week if she was free. "That's alright, pet. It happens. I'll see you Sunday, as always."

She nods. "Sunday, then."

It can't come soon enough.

seeing red

NIKOLAI

TWO DAYS LATER, Nikolai's milling at the Castillo Awards, a prestigious ceremony held annually in Chicago to honor immigrant authors and poets. He's been a donor for many years and is always invited to the event because of it.

He's flying solo tonight since Corinne was already booked, but that's alright. He can handle one night by himself, can't he?

Everyone in attendance is dressed to the nines, in long gowns, sharp suits, and traditional garments from a number of cultures. He's stationed himself at the back of the room before the ceremony starts, people-watching and mostly keeping to himself. As his eyes scan the room, his mind can't help but drift to Corinne.

Does she like poetry? She's an artist, but what other types of art might she enjoy? Maybe next year she can come with him.

"Always looks good at the end of the year, eh, Zaitsev?" an older man asks before introducing himself as Jackson Something-or-Another and pulling Nikolai out of his thoughts.

"I don't follow," he says, accepting the handshake.

"These events." Jackson gestures toward the other guests and spills his drink in the process. Nikolai steps back.

"Donating makes the board happy, makes the nattering do-gooders shut up when you wave your yearly donations in their faces. And above all"—he takes a sip—"tax deductible. Good for the company, good for us." He laughs, and it takes a considerable amount of control for Nikolai not to lay into him here and now. Control that comes easier when Corinne is here to steer the conversation elsewhere.

A flash of red catches his eye through the throng. Did he dream her into existence just by thinking about her?

No, Corinne is here.

And she's here with someone else. An Asian man who is tall, broad-shouldered, and, frankly, devastatingly attractive. Nikolai's so focused on how small her hand looks tucked in the crook of her date's elbow that it takes him a moment to fully see her gorgeous sleeveless gown in deep red. The bodice hugs her deliciously and flares into a full skirt at the waist.

"And the ball-and-chain, too," the man next to Nikolai continues. "She loves 'literature,' so, heh, here we are."

Nikolai is barely paying attention to him, too busy staring at Corinne and noticing the glimmer of light reflecting off her ear.

Because she's wearing the earrings, the Zaitsev rubies, he gave her the night he owned her so completely. And as she walks across the room, the slit in her deep red dress reveals the shoes he bought her two months ago, the gold-studded Valentino pumps.

Corinne is dressed like she's *his*, like it's *his* arm she's clinging to, *his* peers and business connections she's charming.

"She was nagging me the other day—"

"Johnson, I'm not interested in talking to anyone who would compare marriage to imprisonment," Nikolai says, not even looking at him as he walks away, eyes still glued to her.

He shouldn't be staring, but he can't help himself. Not with her. And as he looks at her companion again, he recognizes him from the list of honorees they were given: Oscar Wei, winner of this year's Castillo Award in poetry. He can't help but notice the kindness of Wei's face, how his mouth curls into a gentle smile as he watches Corinne.

Do I look at her like that, too? Of course I do. Everyone Corinne spends time with must look at her like that because how could they not?

And she doesn't stop touching him—grabbing Wei's hand, kissing his cheek, whispering in his ear until he laughs. Sure, she is physically affectionate with Nikolai when they're together at events, but this feels different. Wei is mostly silent, letting Corinne do most of the talking as they mingle, shyness evident in his posture and demeanor. It's reminiscent of what Corinne does for Nikolai but on a more intense scale. And all the while, the light glitters off the rubies in her ears.

Nikolai breathes deeply, unclenching his jaw to try to compose himself. Would it be this hard to see her with someone else if she didn't look like she was *his*? It's fucking with his head, the way he can see himself next to her in all the things he's picked out for her.

Get it the fuck together. This is her job. He's never had a problem with it before. Sharing isn't something he worries about, generally. He doesn't have the time or energy to do so. But he's never had a dynamic as intense as the one they share, and Corinne is dressed like she belongs to him, even though she had no idea he'd be here.

He doesn't understand. Why would she wear those things?

Why is his heart twisting in his chest?

Just then, as Corinne and Wei head toward the tables to find their seat, she turns her head and sees him.

He nods, face impassive, as his heart pounds in his ears.

She nods back, a surprised smile on her lips.

As Wei pulls out a seat for her, Corinne leans in, says something, and heads toward the exit closest to Nikolai. She catches his eye and subtly nods toward the door before walking out.

He takes a moment, breathing deeply, before following her at a distance, eyes glued to her back. She has to know he's right behind her.

When has he ever been able to deny her?

She continues down the hallway until the crowd thins, until there's no one around but service staff preparing to bring in whatever they're having for the first course. Then she turns a corner, which reveals an alcove to a smaller meeting room, and she spins to face him, hitting him with that warm smile that's dazzled him since their first night together.

"Well, well, well," she says, "fancy meeting you here."

Up close, Nikolai takes the opportunity to drink her in, and she's even more stunning. The earrings are perfect with this dress, as are the shoes.

He wishes it were for him.

"Hello, p—" He cuts himself off. That's not who they are right now. "Good evening, Corinne. You look stunning."

"Oh. Good evening to you, too," she singsongs, making a show of her formality, her brows raised in amusement. "You look very handsome yourself, though you seemed so serious in there."

He doesn't like being this... professional with her. It's not even professional, but it's not *them*, and he hates it. "This is a serious event. Very"—he trails his finger along the chandelier earring—"fancy."

She licks her lips and steps closer. "I loved your earrings so much that I wanted to wear them again." She slowly parts the slit of her dress and kicks out her foot, glancing down for just a moment. "And the shoes you got me a couple of months ago."

"I noticed, pet," he says, and curses himself at the slip. "And dressed in my color to boot." He *shouldn't* say what's on the tip of his tongue. It's wrong and unfair, but his emotions are everywhere, and he can't help himself. "You look an awful lot like you're *owned*. And not by the person you're with."

Corinne tilts her head, her eyes narrowing as she studies him, like he's a puzzle she's trying to solve. "Does that bother you, Nikolai?"

His own eyes narrow at the use of his name; it's not something he's used to hearing from her nowadays. "I don't know that bother is the right word. Though it's not quite wrong, either."

"Hm." Her brows pinch, and she nods. "You don't like me in your things, in *your* color? Or"—her gaze locks with his—"you don't like seeing me with someone else?"

"I don't like you in my things, in my color, when you're with someone else, and I happen to witness it. It might be different if it were one thing or two." His eyes roam over her slowly, intentionally. "But you're head to toe there, Corinne," he says, correcting his slipup from earlier. "I won't lie and tell you it has no effect on me."

"Then what if I told you," she says, voice smooth as silk, stepping into his space, placing her hand on his chest, "I was in your lingerie too?"

It hits him like a punch to the gut, and he barely manages to keep it off his face. He wants to pull on her collar, drag her to him, and lift her chin, just this side of uncomfortable, to make her see him. He wants—God, it doesn't matter what he wants. She's not his right now, not wearing his collar, even if it looks like she should be.

He settles for tipping her chin with his finger, which he trails back down to rest lightly against her throat, just where her collar would sit if tonight were different.

"Should you be sharing that with me, pet?" Fuck it, he doesn't care. She *is* his pet. He leans in a little closer, using his height to tower over her. "Or are you being a wicked little thing right now, telling me this?"

She tilts her head back to look at him. "Maybe," she whispers, all wide-eyed and soft-smiled. "But..." She rubs at his chest over his suit. "It can be our little secret, sir."

"Our little secret," he agrees. He waits a moment longer, staring into her eyes before dropping his hand and stepping back. He arches a single brow. "Now, it's about time you get back to your date, isn't it?"

"Yes, sir." She leans in and kisses his cheek.

He isn't expecting it, not tonight, and he inhales sharply, like electricity has burned through him. His hand comes to her waist and squeezes. If he doesn't put some distance between them right now, he'll have her up against the wall and damn the consequences. He clears his throat. "I'll see you on Sunday, pet."

She nods. "Yes, Sunday." Then she reaches up and rubs his cheek. "You had a little lipstick. Don't want to ruin your"—she mockingly frowns—"serious billionaire persona." She winks and then saunters off toward the ballroom with a laugh.

"*Fuck.*"

temptation incarnate

CORINNE

CORINNE CAN'T SLEEP. It's Saturday night, and she can't stop thinking about the man she's supposed to see tomorrow.

About the way she gave herself to him so easily at the High Protocol party. The way he took care of her afterward.

The way he looked at her the night of the awards ceremony.

Covetous. Possessive. Outside the bounds of their allotted time together where he has zero say in what she wears or who she sees.

She's seen this before, and it has never ended well. There was her childhood love, Will, of course, and a few other lovers and clients throughout the years. If Corinne were smart, she'd nip it in the bud right now. She'd tell the agency she can't see him anymore and send his gifts back to him.

But as she tosses and turns in bed, a little voice in her mind just won't be quiet.

You liked it, it says. *You liked wearing his things, and you liked him seeing you in them. You'd be his all the time if things were different, if you weren't client and escort.*

"It doesn't matter," she says aloud. Things *aren't* different

195

and never will be. Not only is he her client, but he has made it apparent he has no time or inclination for more than what he pays her for. And even if he did, his behavior at the award ceremony suggests her job would, once again, be an issue.

And that's not even bringing the Philadelphia offer into the equation.

If she were smart...

Ugh. She doesn't want to give him up. She can at least admit that to herself. Maybe she just... needs to reset their boundaries. She'd told him weeks ago she is his when they're together. She just has to remind him it can't extend beyond that.

But when they're together? She'll let herself have that. As much as she wants.

* * *

Nikolai answers his door the next day with a kitchen towel over his shoulder.

"Hello, pet," he murmurs, and her mind flashes to Tuesday when he struggled not to call her that. Struggled and failed.

"Hello, sir." She kisses his jaw before setting down her bags. "How are you?"

"I'm alright." He clears his throat and averts his gaze. "It's been quite the week." With a hand on her back, he leads her toward the kitchen. "How was yours?"

"Same." *I couldn't stop thinking about you.*

They enter the kitchen, where her collar lies on the island near the ingredients he's laid out for dinner.

"I cleaned and conditioned it earlier." He grabs it and turns to her. "Kneel for me, sweet pet?"

It's a question. It's never been a question before.

He's as uncertain as she is.

She takes his free hand and squeezes it gently. "Would you

mind if we talked first? About what happened the other night?" She needs to settle this before he puts that collar on her throat, before she lets herself sink into that headspace with him.

His brows pull together, but then he nods. "Of course." He gestures behind her. "I was working on dinner, but we can go to the living room if you'd like."

"Here is okay." She hops onto the counter, hoping the familiarity of talking in the kitchen together might make things easier.

"Alright." He moves to the chopping board next to her, bringing a colander of veggies with him. He takes a moment and then says, "Did you have a nice evening?"

"Yes, I did. I was surprised to see you there."

"I enjoy literature." He gazes at her again. "You looked beautiful. I can't remember if I told you."

"You did, thank you." She reaches for a cherry tomato from the bowl and pops it into her mouth, more to give herself something to do than from hunger. Then she takes a deep breath. "Listen—"

"Corinne—" he says simultaneously, and they both chuckle, the awkward tension diffusing the smallest amount.

"Go ahead." If he goes first, maybe it will be easier to respond.

He puts the knife down and looks at her, his dark eyes as piercing as ever. "Tuesday was... difficult for me, pet."

She knows that, of course, but she still nods and waits for him to continue.

He steps in front of her. "It's not—you're not mine, not all the time, and I know that. I promise you I am fine with it." He huffs a laugh and shakes his head. "I wouldn't have been with Calypso as long as I have if I had trouble sharing. It's more..." He trails off, gently tucking a piece of hair behind her ear. "I wasn't prepared to see you dressed like you were mine while you were with someone else, especially when you had no idea I would be there." His eyes study her before he places his hands outside her knees on the counter.

"It was outside the time you're mine," he continues, "and yet there you were, not only in my favorite color but in things I'd bought you, things that laid *my* claim specifically." He thumbs at her ear as though she's still wearing his beautiful rubies. "And then you came to me, dressed like you belong to me, and I was *tempted*."

His eyes are hot and heavy as they rake down her body, his thumb dragging to the hollow of her throat, his tongue darting out to swipe over his bottom lip. This man never ceases to stoke the embers of desire in her belly, even while apologizing.

"I don't like that I felt like that," Nikolai says. "And it's on me that I did because you did nothing wrong. All those items are yours to do with what you want, when you want. I feel like I failed. I am trying hard not to be jealous because I do not own you." He leans in, pressing his forehead to hers. "But in that moment, I wanted to. I wanted to remind you who you belong to, and that's not alright. I almost gave in, sweet thing. I would've done almost anything you'd asked if I hadn't sent you away when I did. And it has been a very long time since I allowed myself to be tempted so badly."

Her eyes roam over his face, over the dark circles beneath his pained eyes. This has been weighing on him; guilt has been gnawing at him like a hungry, desperate animal all week. And yet, his desire for her still lingers in the weight of his gaze.

"Almost anything?" she murmurs. She strokes his beard with the back of her hand. "Would you have... gotten on your knees if I'd asked you to?" She tilts her head and licks her lips. "Slipped under my dress and taken me apart?"

He shifts his hands to her knees and slides up until his

fingertips are just under the hem of her sundress. "I would have," he breathes. "If you had asked, I would have."

"And what about now?" Corinne's gaze is steadfast, even as her chest rises and falls with quickened breath. "Would you kneel now? Or is that only a temptation when I'm with someone else?"

He slides his hands a little higher, eyes still locked with hers. "You're temptation incarnate, pet." He slowly drops to one knee, and then the other, eyes never leaving her face. "I've never been good at resisting temptation, and I used up all my resolve already."

She widens her legs to make room for him. "What else would you have done?"

He reverently noses at her thighs. "I would have left you wet and dripping, your thighs smeared with it." He noses higher, scraping his teeth and grazing his short beard over her sensitive skin, drawing a gasp from her. "You would've had to have been so quiet."

She spreads her legs even more and rakes her fingers through his hair. Even here, like this, she wants him so badly. "Would you have teased me like you always do? Or would you have needed me too badly?"

He shakes his head, moving into the space she's made for him, her skirt riding upward. "No time for teasing. You would've come as many times as I could manage." He presses forward, almost under her skirt now. "To remind you," he rasps, like he's forcing the words out.

"To remind me of what?"

"That you're mine, pet." He buries his face in her thigh and heaves a deep sigh. "And that isn't something I have the right to do."

She is quiet for a long stretch as her heart pounds against her sternum. "Nikolai," she says gently. "Look at me."

He does as she asks, his eyes now rimmed with red.

"Your honesty about this really means a lot to me. Thank you for telling me." She looks down at him, running her hands through his hair, brushing her fingers against the buzz of his undercut. "I *love* being yours. But you're correct. It's not a right." She pauses. "It's a gift." Corinne leans down and presses their foreheads together. "I am yours when I give myself to you." She brushes her lips against his. "I am yours when I am with you."

I want to be yours always. But she can't share that aloud, not if she wants to keep him in her life. Instead, she pulls back and steels herself for the difficult line she has to draw. "But I was not yours that night."

"I know, pet. That's what made it so dangerous."

"I was so surprised to see you that I wanted to say hello. And then when I saw your reaction to me... I will admit I pushed." She smiles sadly. "Some defense mechanisms are hard to shake."

"You shouldn't have to shake them." He cups her face in his hands. "I was an ass, and I'm sorry."

"Thank you."

"You were beautiful, Corinne. And once I calmed down during the ceremony, I could appreciate my pet in all her pretty things, dazzling everyone who saw her."

Corinne laughs gently, her eyes softening. "Dazzling, huh?"

"That's the way people see you. Smart, charming, funny. *And* you're gorgeous on top of it all?" He shakes his head, smiling. "I always know people envy me when we're out together. This was the first time I understood it through experience."

"You are sweet, sir," she says, heat creeping along her cheeks. "Though, maybe you are a little biased." She grins. "I'm not everyone's pet, after all."

"No, you are not. But that just means I'm better equipped to know these things. I have firsthand experience."

"Thank you, sir." She brushes her nose against his. "I would love my collar now."

"Of course." She expects him to stand and pull her off the counter to kneel before him, but no. He stays on his knees and reaches for the collar. "Bend down for me, sweet pet."

Warmth blooms in her chest like a field of wildflowers in the spring. This beautiful man is kneeling for *her*, even when collaring her. She lowers her head, and Nikolai fastens the leather around her neck.

"Perfect," he says when he finishes and tugs at the ring of her collar. "My perfect pet." Standing, he kisses her slowly but deeply, and she lets herself slip into that wonderful place she only knows with him.

A few minutes later, she pulls back. Heat is pulsing between her thighs, and if he keeps going, they may not eat. "Are you having me for dinner, or should I let you get back to cooking?"

He groans. "Don't tempt me again. Didn't we just go over this?"

She laughs. He moves back to his vegetables, but not before handing her a bowl of them already chopped for her to snack on.

She crosses her legs on the counter, perching her bowl between her thighs. "You know." She grabs a carrot. "We only have a month left until you whisk me away to France."

He digs into his pocket and hands her a note in his handwriting. "Details about a High Protocol party happening at a chateau outside Paris at the end of our business week. You seemed to enjoy the last one. I thought you might want to go to another one."

"Ooh, a chateau. That sounds very fancy." She reads over the paper and looks up at him with one brow raised. "Submissives must be naked, huh?"

He drags his eyes hotly over her body before a smirk tugs at the corner of his mouth. "Rules are rules, little thing."

"What a sacrifice that must be for you, sir," she says, a mockery of concern falling over her face.

He sighs dramatically. "Someone has to make sacrifices around here. Thank you for recognizing my struggle." A genuine smile threatens to break his smirk, and she pokes at his side until he laughs. God, she has so much fun with him. Even if this is the only thing they'll ever have, it's still such a wonderful part of her life.

"And what will we be up to after your night of sacrifice? You haven't told me much beyond Paris."

He hums and lays the vegetable slices in an oval baking dish. "Well, I figure we can sightsee and be proper tourists in Paris, and then we head to Bordeaux." He slides her a sly look. "Maybe I'll let you into my trunk full of goodies to pick some out for the party."

She raises one brow. "Is there a whip?"

"Guess you'll find out, won't you?"

Nikolai finishes preparing dinner, and then they move to the dining room to eat the steaks, potatoes, and roasted vegetables. They talk more about France, about the place he's rented outside Bordeaux for their second week, and what they might get up to in the countryside.

"And more than anything," he says, "I'm looking forward to two whole weeks with you all to myself."

Corinne sets down her wineglass. "Why do I have a feeling that by the time we reach Bordeaux, I'll be covered in bites and bruises?"

Eyes trailing over her body, he smirks at her. "Because you are very smart. I've wanted to bite you and bruise you ever since the day I met you."

She watches him for a moment before getting out of her

chair and straddling his lap. "Is that so?" Wrapping her arms around his neck, she nuzzles at his throat. "The very first day?"

He grabs her hips and settles her before letting one hand drift upward, tracing the path his eyes took moments ago. Her breath catches in her chest. "Your skin gets so pretty and pink from my beard." He looks up at her, a lazy smile spreading along his lips. "I couldn't help imagining how lovely you'd look covered in bite marks." He skims his other hand around to her ass and grabs roughly. "And I've wanted to mark up your ass since the day you let me fuck it."

"Fuck." She grinds against his lap, the thought of being marked as his for so long driving her wild with want. "Want you to. Want all of it."

Delicately, he drags his teeth over her throat and collarbone. Then he picks up her wrist, eyes finding hers again, and drags the points of his incisors down her arm, before ending with a little nip right at her elbow. "My pretty pet. All covered in my pretty marks."

"Sir," she gasps, her hips shifting as she presses her body against his. "You're teasing me."

He nips along her inner arm, over her shoulder, scraping his way to her throat. "Oh, pet," he croons, just a little patronizing, "did you expect any less?"

"That's not fair. Not when I have to wait so long."

"Impatient little thing," he breathes in her ear. "Whatever am I going to do with you?"

She whimpers. "I just..." Her hands tighten in his hair. "I want—"

An idea sparks to life in her mind. There *is* a way for him to leave his mark upon her now that doesn't break her rules. It's so damn simple, actually.

She stands and hurries toward the foyer.

"Pet?" he calls after her.

Corinne rummages around in her bag until she finds what she wants. He's only a few feet behind her when she turns around. Crossing the distance between them, she holds up a black felt-tip pen.

He arches an eyebrow. "And what have you got there?"

"A pen," she replies, voice light and sweet. "To mark me with, sir."

labeled

NIKOLAI

HIS BREATH STUTTERS, and his eyes widen before he reins it in, gathering himself. He just barely manages a cocky smirk. "Needy little thing," he says affectionately, pulling her close and grabbing her wrist instead of the pen. "Just can't wait to be all marked up."

"If you don't want to, I suppose we can wait." She shrugs and turns around to put the pen back.

Or at least she tries to. His hand snakes out and catches her around the waist. "Who said I didn't want to?" He takes the marker and opens it, pulling down the neckline of her sundress and hovering the pen over the lacy edge of her bra. Suddenly, an idea comes to him. It might be risky to say after what they've just discussed. But it's her idea, isn't it, letting him mark her all over? "I owe you an apology."

Corinne's brows pinch in confusion. "Oh?"

He thumbs at her bottom lip. "Yes, I was quite neglectful, you see." He looks down at the marker, millimeters from her skin. "What do you do with things that belong to you when you know they will be away from you?" He watches her closely to ensure she's on board. He'll abandon it if she doesn't want to play along, if it's too soon.

But a hint of a smile tugs at her mouth before she schools her face again. "You label them, sir."

"Exactly right. I see now that you had to go and do it yourself, huh? That's not very good pet ownership, is it?"

Corinne shakes her head. "No, sir. And I didn't have my collar. What if I'd gotten lost?" She frowns, like just the thought of it scares his little pet.

"I should fix that now, shouldn't I?" He takes her hand and pulls her toward his bedroom. "Come along. I need room to work, to make sure I label you properly." He pauses, pulling her close for a kiss. "I couldn't bear it if you got lost, little thing."

She whimpers against his mouth. "I'd be so sad and scared."

He tuts, nibbling her lip, and threads his finger through the ring in her collar to tug her along. "Poor little pet. We can't have that." When they reach the room, he tucks the marker behind his ear and crowds against her. He slides his hands down over her waist, her hips, gathering the skirt of her dress to pull it overhead.

His eyes are hungry as he takes her in, standing in his bedroom in nothing but her lingerie, the deep red complementing her beautifully. "Pretty little thing." He drags his fingertip along the lace resting against the swell of her breasts. Reaching behind her, he smoothly unhooks her bra with one hand and lets it fall to the floor. He ghosts his hands over her ribs to her underwear and pushes slowly until it slips down her hips and thighs to join her bra below. "On the bed," he breathes, tucking his nose just beneath her ear, inhaling her scent. "I need room to work."

Corinne nods and lies down in the middle of the bed, amusement and fondness written all over her face.

"Perfect." He walks closer, then kneels next to her. "Where

to start, where to start," he muses to himself, eyes raking over her. "Ah." He scrawls *NZ* on each of her beautiful tits and sits back to admire his work. "That's better already."

Glancing down to see what he wrote, she cups her breasts in her hands, showing care not to cover the letters. "It does, sir."

This time, the marker touches right above her pretty little cunt and continues up the midline of her body to the hollow of her throat. *"Property of Nikolai Zaitsev"* is scrawled over the length of her when he finishes, the letters large and clear.

Elbows propping her up, she lifts her head to peer down again. "Fuck," she whispers, trailing her index finger over the letters covering her body. She glances at him, her mouth parted, breath shallow, eyes glazed with desire.

She wants this just as much as he does.

He moves across her body, tagging his initials wherever he pleases, from her thighs to her hands to her shoulders. He marks her as his, the initials on her skin mirroring the ones on her collar.

Slipping his hand between her legs, he groans at her slick wetness. "Does my little pet like this? Like being marked as mine? Does she like being owned?"

She moans and rubs against his hand. "Yes, sir. So much." Her eyes roam over her own body, all the places he's marked her, before returning his gaze. "And you? Do you like me like this?"

"Oh, pet. You've never looked more perfect." He kisses her hard, biting at her lips, his mouth letting her know exactly how much he loves her like this. When he pulls back, he grins darkly at her. "Turn over for me. One last thing, and then I'll show you how else I take care of my things."

She rolls onto her stomach and writhes against the bed. "Like this?"

He hums at the sight, spreading her legs so he can settle

between them. "Stay still," he commands with a slap to her ass. He settles his hand on her lower back, right in the arch, and signs his name from one side to the other, twice, the letters large and flowing, bending with the curve of her back. "There. Perfect." Then he pulls her hips up, watching as her back dips and his signatures shift. "Stay just like this, alright?"

"Yes, sir." She settles into place. "What did you write?"

"Oh, I've signed you, darling, in English and Cyrillic. The way one signs their name on ownership papers, you know." He's sinking further into his headspace, details sharpening, everything around him coming into clearer focus. And if her resulting whimper is anything to go by, she's in the same state.

He unfastens his trousers and takes off his shirt before throwing it… somewhere. His cock is hard and aching, and there's a large dark spot on the front of his underwear. He pulls the condom out of his pocket and rests it on her back, making sure she hears the crackle of the wrapper, feels the pricking edges against her skin. "Oh, pet, you do look perfect like this."

She half moans, half sighs in, he assumes, relief. Relief that, for once, he's not going to drag it out and make her suffer before finally slipping inside her. "Thank you, sir. Want you so badly. Please."

He slaps her ass again, still wishing he could mark her like that, too. *Soon.* "Well, I did say I take good care of my things." He tears open the condom, rolls it on, and lines himself up. "I liked you asking for permission to come at the party. So, consider that the newest house rule." He drags his hands down her back and settles them at her waist before pushing forward, groaning at the tight grip of her cunt.

"Sir," she moans.

He fucks her quick and rough, grunting and groaning, running his hands across his signature. God, he wants her like this always, wants her marked as his, so it's obvious, so it's unquestionable. It goes against everything they just discussed, but he pushes that thought aside to be dealt with later. Not now, while his pretty pet lets him use her like this. "Is this what you wanted? To be owned? To be used how I like, since you're mine? Is this what you were after?"

"Yes, sir," she gasps, each word punctuated by his thrusts. "Please. Want to be good for you. However you want. I'm yours."

He snarls—that's the only word for the animalistic noise that rips from his mouth—before he bends forward and cages her in with his body. "Say it again."

Corinne reaches back and wraps her hand around his neck, pulling him closer. "I'm yours."

Growling in her ear, he envelops her with his body, and oh, he can hear how close she's getting.

"Please may I come please?" It's all strung together in a rush like she's losing control of her pleasure.

He chuckles. While his original plan was to make her wait like usual, he supposes he can be nice for once. "Go ahead, there's a good girl."

She lets go with a sob, her cunt clenching around his cock, and she shudders beneath him. "Sir," she breathes, and he never stops, never slows. "Fuck. Thank you." She leans over and nips at his arm gently.

"You're very welcome, sweet pet." He picks up the pace. "I wonder if you'll still be thankful later." He gets a hand under her and rubs at her clit, fast little circles gliding effortlessly with how very wet she is. "Another."

She gasps, and she spreads her legs a little wider. "Do I —*fuck*—do I need to ask?"

"Every time, darling. Don't forget." He sits up, taking her with him, one arm around her torso and the other still toying with her clit. "I've found positive reinforcement works best with wayward things. So, I'm going to make you feel so good you'll never, ever forget who you belong to." He punctuates the last few words with especially hard thrusts.

Corinne's head falls to his shoulder. "I promise I won't forget. I think about it all the time."

Goose bumps erupt all over him as a shiver races down his spine. *God. Does she really?* "About being mine?"

She bares her throat as her thighs begin to shake. "Yes, sir."

Perfect, perfect, perfect. He can't believe he has her, this mesmerizing, dazzling woman. He takes the invitation, nipping and licking at her throat, wishing he could set his teeth and bite. "Oh, I like the sound of that." He leans back, putting some distance between their bodies so he can change the angle of his hips. "My poor pet," he croons, hand still toying with her clit. "Hung up on how very owned she is."

She cries out when he changes angles, as his thrusts roughen. She grips the hand at her waist, lacing their fingers. "Sir. Sir, please. May I come?"

"So soon? Well..." He thrusts harder, faster, his breaths harsh now. "I suppose. Greedy thing. Go ahead."

She comes again, even harder than the first time, arching against him as she moans. His fingers don't let up from her clit, and she hisses. "Thank you," she whines, but he can tell she's oversensitive from how she's writhing against him.

Sweat drips down the groove of his spine, his brain lighting up in the best possible ways. "You're welcome. Fuck. You look so lovely coming on my cock like that, did you know?"

She's a whimpering mess by this point, already sounding like she's close again. "Fuck," she gasps, moaning, so obviously overwhelmed. "Sir. Please. It's too much. Please let me come."

He won't be able to hold off much longer; his orgasm is building in that way that means it's going to be damn near overpowering. "Yes, come on, there's my good girl."

She comes once more, trembling as she falls slack against his restraining arm, barely mumbling her thanks as he takes her weight and chases his own release.

"So good, pet, fuck, you're perfect." It's coming at him like a runaway train, and he doesn't fight it. He lets it hit him square in the chest at a thousand miles an hour. In a last-second decision, almost more impulse than thought, he pulls out, ripping the condom off and pressing her to the bed. "And you're *mine*."

He roughly fists his cock once, twice, before he's coming all over her skin and his declarations of ownership. Every muscle in his body locks, and he cries out, twitching and grunting as he comes so hard his vision whites out. With a groan, he rubs the sticky, slick ropes of his spend into her skin, claiming her in the most primal way possible.

Her breath hitches. "God," she breathes. "Damn."

He presses gentle kisses along her shoulder, nuzzling at her as he comes back to earth. "I couldn't have said it better myself."

With a laugh, she turns to face him as he rolls onto his side.

"Hello," he says, caressing her face with his fingertips. "Beautiful, precious pet."

"Hello, Nikolai, sir." They stay like that for a few minutes, just gazing and touching, his heart so full he can scarcely breathe. Corinne traces her fingers along the letters all over her skin as he drinks her in. "Do you feel better?"

His hands join hers, his gaze soft and fond. "I absolutely do." He outlines the initials inked on her hip. "How do you feel?"

She bites her lip and grins. "Claimed." She tilts her head. "Would you like to take a picture of your handiwork?"

He thinks before answering. "You know, I think I would." Standing, he grabs his phone from his charging station and arranges her how he wants her. He snaps a picture of her sitting on the bed before telling her to roll over to show off the smeared signatures covered in his spend.

Once he's finished, she turns to her side. "Will you send them to me too, sir?"

He taps around on his phone before setting it down and walking back to her. "Done. Now, important question. Could I interest you in a bath?"

She opens her mouth to answer, then it falls into a pout. "I know I should, but then I'd lose my markings."

He tilts his head, studying her, gaze lingering at her throat. He slides a finger under her collar before toying with the tag. "Pet." He's treading on delicate ground. "Would you want something more... discreet? For France? You could wear it whenever you wanted that way if you'd like."

Her eyes widen before her face settles into something pleased and hopeful. "A day collar?"

"A day collar," he confirms with a nod, exhaling with relief. "Is that something you'd want?"

She studies him for a moment before climbing into his lap and kissing him. "Yes," she whispers. "I would love that."

He continues kissing her, hands delicately touching the places he's marked, keeping the ink as intact as possible. "Do you want me to choose it? Or would you like to give some input?"

"Mm, that seems like another pet-owner decision, doesn't it?" She laughs. "In all seriousness, sir, you have an uncanny ability to pick out things I love. I trust you completely."

A smirk, proud and pleased, tugs at his lips, and he trails his fingers along her collarbones, pausing in the hollow of her throat. "I can't wait to see you wearing it, pet."

wrapped around your little finger

CORINNE

"I THINK WE NEED ANOTHER DRINK," Elijah says, frowning at his empty glass. "What say you?"

"After today? What do you think?"

Corinne had met with a new client that afternoon who'd been so rude and aggressive that she left thirty minutes in. He proceeded to harass her by calling and texting her work phone until she blocked his number. Then he switched to bombarding the poor receptionist at Calypso until Margot herself had to get involved to inform him he would *not* be getting a refund since he'd violated their terms of service.

Corinne needs every drink she can get, really.

Elijah kisses her cheek. "Then I'll bring you two." He slides out of their booth and heads toward the bar.

She takes a deep breath, grateful that Elijah was up for going out to take her mind off things. She resolutely doesn't think about how Nikolai was the first person who entered her mind when she wanted to call someone.

But then she pulls her work phone out of her purse to see if there's an update from Margot. The screen lights up with a text from Nikolai instead.

I hope it's not overstepping, but Adrian mentioned you were upset when he picked you up today. Are you alright?

Corinne smiles softly and unlocks her phone to respond.

You're not overstepping. I had a run-in with an awful client. But I left, and thankfully Adrian was nearby to pick me up right away. He was a lifesaver honestly.

I'm glad he could get you, pet. How are you feeling now?

I'm... okay. Or I will be. I hate it when this happens. It makes me gun-shy with new clients for a while.

That makes sense, pet. Margot banned this one, I assume?

Yes, of course. Though he certainly didn't make it easy.

She bites her lip. Should she tell him? Would he mind when he messaged her to begin with? She starts typing, deletes it, and then types it all over again. She hits *send* before she can chicken out.

I wanted to call you when it happened.

The dots appear and disappear a few times, her gut churning anxiously as she waits for his response. Finally, his message appears.

You can always call me if you need me, pet.

Her heart flutters against her rib cage.

You really wouldn't have minded?

I'll always answer for you. I'd never mind.

Okay. Thank you, sir.

"And what is that smile for, Corinne?"

She looks up from her phone as Elijah sets three drinks on the table, including two gin and tonics, which he slides over to her.

"Nothing." A guilty blush paints her cheeks as she slips her phone back into her bag.

"That's not nothing. *And* that's your work phone." He takes a pointed sip of his whiskey ginger and then cocks his head with a smug curl of his lips. "It's Nikolai."

She sighs and grabs her glass. "And what if it is?"

"Oh my god, Corinne."

"What?"

"You like him."

Corinne takes a drink, ears burning. "I like a lot of my clients."

He narrows his eyes. "You know what I mean."

She groans and scrubs her hand over her face. "Okay, yes. I like him. Are you happy now?"

"Yes, I am, actually." Elijah leans in with his chin resting on his hand, glee dancing in his eyes. "You are always Little Miss Professional, but you've been breaking the rules for him since day one."

She hums noncommittally and takes another sip. Elijah doesn't even know that she didn't charge Nikolai extra for prep the one time they had anal sex, or about the photos she let

Nikolai take last week. And he'll certainly never know what she's been thinking about for the France trip.

He grabs her hand across the table. "You deserve something nice, Corinne."

Her face scrunches unpleasantly. "Is it nice? He's my client. And you know he has no interest or time for a relationship. Which is why he uses the service in the first place."

Elijah shrugs. "Maybe he'd make time for you. You ever think about that?"

Sure she does. In moments of weakness when she lets herself dream about what this could be if their situation were different. "Maybe. But I also don't want to ruin what we have by trying to make it something it isn't. So." She downs the rest of her G&T and grabs the second. "I'm going to enjoy our Sundays and have a wonderful time in France, and that's that."

"So you don't think he has any feelings outside the perimeters of the services you provide?"

Corinne thinks about Nikolai's confession last week, about his reaction to seeing her with Oscar—*I do not own you. But in that moment, I wanted to.* She thinks about how he dotes on her, how he just messaged her to check in and told her she can call whenever she needs. How he knew in the first place because he'd offered his driver to her.

"I don't know, Elijah." She worries her bottom lip. "He was always generous with you, too."

"Yeah, but he sure as hell didn't take me to France for two weeks. I wanted to go to Amalfi with him one time, and he told me he would be too busy working and didn't trust me enough to behave myself."

She laughs despite herself. "That's because you're a brat."

"You are right, darling. But I'd say Mr. Zaitsev is happily wrapped around your little finger."

And Corinne hates how much she wishes that were true.

* * *

The next three weeks pass both too quickly and not quickly enough as the date of their trip inches closer. There are several moments during her Sundays with Nikolai when he is exceptionally sweet or playful or affectionate after absolutely ruining her, and Elijah's voice nags incessantly in her ear.

As if her own traitorous thoughts aren't enough.

A couple of days before her trip, she stops by the Calypso office to get her paperwork for her health screening. Margot is in her office, and Corinne leans in the doorway to say hi.

"Ready for Paris?"

"Well, I still have errands and packing to do, but am I spiritually and mentally ready for two weeks in France? I absolutely am."

Margot regards her for a moment before arching her brows. "And Philadelphia?"

Corinne takes a deep breath. "I still haven't decided."

"I have someone who wants it. An old friend who lives in New York who's ready to start right away. But I came to you first, so I want to honor that." She tilts her head. "Could you let me know when you get back?"

She wasn't expecting to have to make such an important decision while playing tourist with Nikolai, but she supposes there's nothing to be done. One way or another, Corinne has to make up her mind.

"My first day back," she says, her smile not quite reaching her eyes. "I promise."

* * *

On Friday night, Corinne is running through her packing list a final time when the buzzer rings. She grins and crosses to the panel to let Nikolai in. "You can come on up," she says over the intercom, then opens her door and waits for him.

She's nervous; she hasn't had anyone new over in... well, she can't remember how long. And, of course, she's never had a client over. Last names and addresses are hush-hush for safety and security, but it's hard to travel with a client, especially overseas, and keep your identity to yourself. He knows she's Corinne Ryan now; an address isn't going to hurt.

A minute later, Nikolai arrives at her landing, dressed more casually than the tuxedos and suits he often wears when they're not at his place—dark jeans, a black henley, and brown Chelsea boots that match his leather jacket. And god, does he look good.

She's in leggings and a lightweight blush-pink sweater, her hair pulled up into a high bun and his diamond studs in her ears. She grins at him from the doorway. "Hello, sir."

"Hello, pet." He kisses her on the cheek before tucking his hands in his pockets and leaning against the doorframe. "About ready?"

"Yes, I'm just doing a final packing list run-through." She gestures for him to come inside.

He spends a minute looking around, head falling back to take in the high ceilings and large windows. His eyes scan her studio space, which is divided from the living room by a folding screen. The drafting table and easel stand near the windows, supplies tucked neatly into every corner of the space. Canvases in various stages of completion are stacked against the wall, and a nearly finished portrait is still up on her easel.

"Who is this?" he asks.

"My mom."

He studies it. Worry and hope fight within her as they always do when someone she cares about looks at her art. What does he think of it? Of her stark lines and vibrant colors? Of the way she brings her subjects to life?

"She's beautiful," he says, and her heart swells. "Your *art* is beautiful, Corinne. I've only seen what you've shown me on your phone." He looks away and turns to her. "Experiencing it in person is something else."

Color rises to her cheeks. "Thank you, sir."

"Maybe I should commission you to create something for the apartment."

"I'd be happy to. Though..." She trails off with a nervous chuckle.

"What?"

"I'm not sure my style is your style."

He arches a brow. "And why is that?"

Corinne bends down and flips through a few canvases to show him. "My art is colorful. Your apartment is... more muted."

Nikolai barks out a laugh, grabbing her hand and pulling her up. "You're not wrong, pet." He wraps his arms around her waist. "Maybe I need a little more color in my life."

"Do you?" she asks, the weight of his gaze stealing her breath.

"I think so." He presses a gentle kiss to her lips. "Is there anything I can help with?"

She momentarily forgot that he was picking her up to take her to the airport. "Oh, just carrying my giant suitcase down the stairs when we're ready? You'll learn I cannot pack lightly, sir."

He chuckles. "I can do that. You know," he says, his eyes sparkling with amusement, "you could have packed nothing, and I'd have bought you an entire wardrobe, right?"

"That leaves too many things to chance, but if you still want to buy me a new wardrobe, we can just buy a new suitcase in Paris."

"Oh, can we?"

She laughs. "If you want to, sir." She kisses his cheek. "Okay, okay. Let me finish my list. Make yourself at home." She grabs her phone and goes upstairs to her bedroom to ensure she has everything.

Corinne comes back down a few minutes later with her charger. "I did, indeed, forget something. Even though I already packed the plug adapter." Nikolai's sitting on her couch, eyes far off, like melancholy has tugged him somewhere far away. "You alright, sir?"

Nikolai huffs, eyebrows drawn together as he finally looks at her. "I'm alright, pet. Just a bit envious of your darling little apartment. I've never lived in a place like this. It feels like a nice place to live."

She puts her charger into her travel bag and hops into his lap. It feels weird, but nice, to have him here, and she's pleased he likes it. "Well, I'd love some more room, but I still love it. And the neighborhood." She kisses his cheek. "Nothing to stop you from moving, sir."

He wraps his arms around her waist, holding her close. "I'm afraid I'm used to all the space now. I need room to wander." He scrunches his nose at her and lightly tickles her sides. "Besides, I know you've gotten awfully used to my bathtub, *rybka moya*."

Giggling, Corinne squirms away from his fingers. "It seems you've discovered my weakness, which I'm sure you won't exploit whatsoever." She plays with the buttons on his henley. "And what does that mean?"

"Oh." He tucks a loose strand of hair behind her ear. "It means *my little fish*." He clears his throat. "It's a term of endearment. A fitting one for you."

"Does that mean you find me endearing?"

Tilting his head, he strokes her cheek with his thumb. "That should be obvious by now."

Her belly flip-flops, and she kisses him gently. "Sir, I know we don't have long before we have to leave, but—" She pulls back. "You can officially mark me however you'd like now."

"Oh." He tugs at her hips until she's laid out on the couch, Corinne gasping at the sudden shift. He pushes her sweater up and pulls her leggings down just enough to expose her hip bone. When his gaze meets her, it's so heavy that it makes her breath catch in her chest.

"Tell me, pet," he rasps. He licks his lips. "Do you want it?"

three hundred thousand

CORINNE

HER BODY IGNITES with anticipation and the promise of things to come, her hips arching toward him. "Yes, sir. Please."

For the first time in their six months together, Nikolai latches his mouth to her body, digs in his teeth, and sucks at the tender skin of her hip.

Her eyes flutter shut as a moan parts her lips. It's been so long since anyone has done this that it sets her nerve endings on fire, as though she might combust from this alone. "Harder, please," she whimpers. Because she can. Because she wants it.

Groaning against her skin, Nikolai bites more deeply, and his lips seal even tighter against her hip bone, sucking and pulling, tongue coaxing the bruise along.

"*Fuck!*" It hurts, sharp and achy at the same time, and she's so instantly turned on she's almost dizzy from it. She rakes her fingers through his hair, watching his jaw work as he sucks at her hip. He keeps at it until she's gasping and moaning, her chest heaving from the tender pain.

He tucks his fingers under the waistband of her leggings and tugs them down her body.

"Oh my god," she whispers, lifting her hips to help him.

He doesn't get them far, one leg off all the way and the other only right under her knee, but it doesn't matter. He moves to her thighs, biting and sucking, fingers digging in and making their own bruises on her skin. "Fuck, pet." Pulling back, he takes in his handiwork so far. "You look perfect. So goddamn perfect."

She's a writhing, soaking mess by this point, and he has to know how badly she wants him. "Fuck me. Please, sir. Do we have time?" She tugs the lace of her underwear to the side so he can see how wet she is. "Please."

He groans and drops his head to her thigh. "We don't have time, pet, but I won't leave you hanging. I'll take care of you." He licks his lips and fiercely latches on to her clit, sucking hard while his fingers come up to join his mouth. He slips two inside her, another moan leaving him.

Crying out, Corinne twists and tightens her fingers in his hair as he brings her closer to the edge. She's so worked up and sensitive from the bruises he's sucked into her skin that she's already shaking, already almost there. She snatches his free hand and presses his thumb into the bruise at her hip, and fuck —"Please, sir. May I come?"

He pulls off just long enough to say, "Give it to me, that's it, my pretty little thing, come on," before putting his mouth back on her and pressing just a bit harder on her new bruise.

Her body curls inward with a cry when she comes, the combination of pain and pleasure overwhelming her until she's trembling beneath him. She stays like that as he licks her through it, until she's twitching from sensitivity. She whimpers. "Holy fuck. Thank you." She laughs softly. "That was unexpected."

Sitting back, he wipes his face with the back of his hand and smiles wolfishly. "You're very welcome. I thoroughly enjoyed it as well."

She nods toward a door to the right before reaching down to get back into her leggings. "The bathroom is there if you want to properly clean up."

He returns a couple of minutes later while she's slipping into a pair of loafers. "Ready now?"

She throws her travel bag over her shoulder. "If I can't get fucked before we leave, then yes, I'm ready," she says with a wink and a purposeful glance at his jeans.

He narrows his eyes and blatantly adjusts himself before walking over and grabbing her suitcase. "Trust me, pet, if we had time, you'd be properly fucked. But we don't, so that'll have to do."

She laughs and gives him a kiss. "I suppose." She opens the door, and he follows her into the hall. She locks it and leads him downstairs. "Thank you for coming to pick me up. It was sweet of you. And it was also nice to see you outside our usual haunt."

"It was no trouble. You have a lovely home." He holds the door for her as they walk outside, heading toward the car idling at the curb. "I liked seeing you in your own space."

"Yeah?" She grins. "Is it what you expected?"

He hands her into the car as Adrian gets out to put her luggage in the trunk. "I don't know that I had expectations, now that I think about it. But it feels very *you* either way."

"I'll take that," she says after she tells Adrian hello. Once they're settled in the car, she clasps Nikolai's hand. "I can't believe we're finally going to France. It's been so long since I've been."

He slips on his sunglasses and strokes the back of her hand with his thumb. "It's been a long time since I've been to France and done anything but work. I'm looking forward to it."

"I am so proud of you for taking time off, sir." She kisses his cheek with a loud smack.

He snags her chin and pulls on her bottom lip with his thumb. "Early in the trip for such cheek, isn't it, pet?"

"What?" She blinks at him slowly, feigning confusion. "Weren't you singing the praises of positive reinforcement recently?" She tilts her head and smiles sweetly.

Nikolai laughs out loud and leans in to kiss her. "Touché." He sits back and props his ankle on his knee. "Would my sweet pet like a present?"

Anticipation and hope bubble within her, and she bites her lip. "Is it what I think it is?"

He chuckles. "Let's find out." He looks forward. "Adrian?"

Adrian reaches for a box on the seat beside him and hands it to Nikolai. "Here ya go, boss."

Holding it out to her, Nikolai says, "For you, pet."

Her hand comes to her chest. She knows that box—bright red leather embossed and trimmed with gold. *Cartier.* It feels so special, and the package is so iconically lovely that she almost hates the idea of opening it. But her day collar is in there, to mark her as his wherever they go the next two weeks. And that's even more enticing than the pretty box.

She opens it. Inside lies an exquisite diamond line necklace set in what she assumes is platinum, the stones sparkling brightly in the light.

Of all the many, many things he's bought her over these last several months, he's never gotten her anything that compares to this. It's stunning. She can't even imagine how much it cost. "Sir, this is breathtaking." Her voice is thick and her gaze watery as she looks up at him. "This is certainly more than I expected."

"Turn the clasp over."

She picks up the necklace and flips it over. His very familiar initials are engraved on the back of the clasp. "Like my collar," she says reverently, her hand once again coming to her chest.

"A day collar. I did promise."

Corinne knows her face must betray every forbidden feeling she has for him. She should mask it before he realizes just how far gone she is, but she couldn't if she tried, too moved by what he's given her. "This is beautiful. You are so wonderful, Nikolai. Sir. Thank you."

He smiles and motions for her to turn around. "Let me put it on for you."

She nods and unfastens her seat belt before following his command. Taking advantage of the fact he can't see her face, she breathes deeply and gets herself at least somewhat in check. But that's difficult when he's marking her as his, that declaration clear for all to see over these next two weeks, even when they're not together.

Taking the necklace from its case, he unclasps it and lowers it over her head. He latches it before kissing the spot where the clasp lies against her skin. "Beautiful, pet. It suits you."

She touches the chain at her throat as she faces him. "You always know what suits me and what I like. You're exceptionally and unnaturally good at it, actually."

He brushes a thumb against her cheek. "I'm an observant man," he whispers. He strokes the necklace with delicate fingers. "And our tastes align. My very, very pretty pet." He kisses her, softer than usual, and she sighs against his mouth.

Her heart is about to float out of her chest. She gently slips her tongue against his, keeping the languid intensity he's started. She pulls back and nuzzles him. "I have a present for you, too."

He arches a brow. "A present? For me?"

"Mmhmm." She kisses him again. "But I can't give it to you until we arrive."

He sighs exaggeratedly, all chest and shoulders. "Cruel pet, making me wait so long."

An evil grin tugs at her mouth. "Mm, a taste of your own medicine."

His eyes narrow as his legs spread and his shoulders straighten, taking up a bit more room than before. "Have you changed your mind?" He studies her. "You want to be a naughty little thing now? I could have sworn you'd much rather be my sweet pet, but I guess I was mistaken."

"I never said that." She scoots closer so she can curl into him. "I love being your pet, sir." And she does, more than anything. She's never felt like this with anyone. She tries her best to keep it tucked away; a hidden alcove behind a bookshelf in her heart. Tries her best to remember that she's working, that he's not her boyfriend or, or husband, whisking her off to France for a romantic getaway.

Her thoughts are leading to a dangerous place, a field of land mines threatening to betray her heart or her wits with one wrong step. She takes a deep breath to clear her mind and then slides her hand into his. "You have me for two whole weeks." She kisses his palm. "What are you even going to do with me?"

Grinning wickedly, he toys with her hair. "Don't you worry. I have many plans. But I can't tell you until we get there."

Her brow furrows, and she pouts at him, thankful for the playful distraction. "Now *I'm* getting the medicine."

He pouts back at her, flicking her necklace. "Poor little pet. Your suffering must be awful."

She frowns even more. "It is. You tease me and edge me all the time."

His frown matches hers again, though he's fighting a smile as he does it. "Oh, I am so neglectful of you. It's disgraceful, really."

She laughs. "It is both cute and entirely wrong for you to pout, Nikolai Zaitsev."

He lets it drop, laughing with her. "Whereas you, pet, look absolutely adorable when you do." He links their fingers and rests their hands on his knee.

They spend a few minutes discussing what they want to see in Paris: the tourist spots, museums, restaurants.

"I haven't been since studying abroad," she says, "so it'll be fun to see if anything has changed." She shrugs. "Or maybe cities that old always stay the same in some ways."

Nikolai hums in agreement. "Old cities are ageless, in a way. Athens feels like there's never been a time it didn't exist, almost like it exists outside the bounds of time." He meets her gaze. "You never told me you'd studied in Paris, pet. What else did you get up to at university?"

"Ah." She shrugs. "The usual things, I'm sure. But it's also how I started doing this. I had a full ride, but not enough to pay for expenses. And, well, I grew up around sex workers. My mom was an erotic dancer when she was younger, had lots of friends in various aspects of the business. I knew I'd make money, so I decided, why not? I thought I'd stop escorting when I got out. And I did, for a bit. But the money is so much better than anything I was making from my art. So"—she grins up at him—"here I am."

"I, for one, am not sorry you chose this career path." He idly brushes his fingers along her new collar, staring straight ahead momentarily. "Is that what you'd do, then? If you weren't doing this? Art, full time?"

Should she tell him? Should she share that she has a job offer to explore this work in a new way? In Philadelphia. Her mind quickly slams that thought away. It might ruin their trip, and they haven't even gotten to Paris yet. No, she'll tell him after, however she chooses.

"In a world where it would make me as much money? Maybe. But I also like what I do. I like sex. I like making people feel good. I like forming connections with people in this very niche way. But, you know... am I going to do this forever?" She catches her bottom lip in her teeth. "There will come a time when I won't be young and won't be as desired. And then... well, I'll have to find something new, won't I?"

He huffs. "You will always be desired. But I'm sure you'll have a plan. You're smart and talented." He pulls her close and kisses her hair. "You'll succeed in ways you can't imagine. I'm certain."

She didn't mean for the conversation to turn so heavy, but she's grateful for the comfort his arms always bring her. "Thank you, sir." She thinks for a moment and then laughs. "Of course, my mom is still beautiful, and she's nearing sixty. So I guess I have quite a few years left in me."

"Pet, I have very little doubt you will be one of those women who are stunning their entire lives." He sits up and kisses the back of her hand before lacing their fingers together. "You will be successful however you choose to proceed. I know it."

She squeezes his hand in thanks, and then her mind flashes to what she might look like at sixty, perched in his lap, his hair turned silver, still so gorgeous she can't stand it. There's a collar at her neck, and they look so happy and— "Okay, okay," she says, trying to clear her mind. "No more serious existential discussions for the rest of the day. Why am I thinking about whether I'll still be fucking people for money when I'm fifty when my sir is taking me to *France*?"

"Why, indeed, pet?" He kisses her and toys with her necklace, his other hand on her hip, pressing gently against her bruise. She gasps against his mouth, and god, she's looking forward to more of this in the next couple of weeks.

The car comes to a stop at the airport, and he breaks away. "Are you ready?"

"Of course I am," she responds with a bright smile, letting him lead her out of the car.

* * *

Message from Elijah:

> Holy shit. Do you even know how much that necklace costs?

> THREE HUNDRED THOUSAND, CORINNE

> There are 32 carats around your little neck. THIRTY-TWO.

Oh.

> Yeah. OH. Are you still not convinced?

bare

CORINNE

THE NINE-HOUR FLIGHT to Paris is infinitely more pleasant on a private plane.

She's stretched out on the couch (the *couch!*) under a cashmere blanket, drinking champagne from a crystal flute. Nikolai finishes his call with his assistant and smiles at her from his seat across the plane.

"You look comfortable."

"My entire body is *reclined* on an airplane. I can stretch my arms as much as I want." She raises her arms and snuggles further into the couch as he gives her a barely concealed smirk. "What?"

"You're just being very cute."

"Well, excuse me, Mr. Private Jet. Not all of us are used to such luxury."

"I know," he says, voice and gaze softening, though she's unsure why. "I just..." He clears his throat. "... like seeing you happy, pet."

Her belly flutters, and her voice gentles. "I'm always happy with you, sir."

* * *

"What do you think?"

They just had dinner and were lazily strolling back to the hotel when she found a beret at a little tourist stall near the Champs Élysées. She tilts the angle slightly before turning away from the mirror to face him as he pays for it.

He smiles at her. "You look lovely, pet." He holds his hand out to her and laces their fingers together as they walk back onto the street.

"Thank you, sir." It's nice out, not chilly at all, but she still snuggles close to him as they walk. "How often do you come here?"

"A couple times a year, usually. I wouldn't mind coming more often, though. I always enjoy it."

"And what shall I do to entertain myself while you're working, sir? Any rules to follow?"

"Any rules you had in mind? I figured we could keep things low-key when we're not together so you can enjoy Paris to the fullest."

"Hmm, no, not really." With her free hand, she grabs her day collar and thumbs along the row of diamonds. Then she looks up at him mischievously. "Can I send you naughty texts?"

His eyes narrow. "You can. If you make them too distracting, I make no promises about the consequences."

She gives him a look, sweet and wide-eyed. "Define 'too distracting,' sir."

"You know, I don't think I will." His smile is somehow serene and calculating all at once. "Use your best judgment. You're a good girl; I'm sure you'll be fine."

She pouts. "That hardly seems fair. How can I get in trouble if I didn't know I was being bad, sir?"

"Oh, but isn't that half the fun? And who said your consequences would be bad? I'm sure I'll enjoy them immensely."

She huffs, and Nikolai laughs and kisses her cheek, tucking her hand into the crook of his elbow to bring her even closer. Her face softens at the closeness, and she melts against him. Though, her mind is already churning with ideas of sexts and photos to send him. How much can she say and do before she crosses that line?

They walk the rest of the way back to their hotel on Avenue Montaigne, taking in the scenery and the bustle of fellow tourists. They stroll past boutique after boutique for the major fashion houses, while chatter and laughter from restaurants meet them as they pass.

When they arrive and step inside the elevator, she crowds up against him and slips her hands into his back pockets. "It's almost time for your gift."

He raises a single eyebrow and wraps his arms around her waist. "Oh, is it? Any hints for me, pet? Or should I just bide my little bit of remaining time?"

"No hints, but I'll give it to you as soon as we get to our room." She rises on her tiptoes and kisses him.

"Making me wait again, I see," he says with a chuckle, returning her kiss with a playful nip at her lips.

As soon as they enter their suite, she pulls him into the bedroom and pushes him toward the bed. "Sit down, please, sir." She grabs her phone from her bag and then straddles his lap.

His face is all curious amusement, but a small part of her worries that maybe she miscalculated and he won't want to do it.

But she's here now, and she'll regret it if she doesn't give it to him. "So." She pulls up the email. "I pushed up my regular testing since I'd be here for my usual appointment. I did it three days ago and haven't been with anyone else." She hands him her phone to show him the results. "Would you like to go without condoms while we're here?" she asks, nervousness peeking through her voice.

The second his eyes scan over the screen, he's pulling her close and kissing her fiercely, and she gasps at the over-whelming quickness of it. "The whole time?" he asks, breaking away from her mouth and breathing harshly.

"Yeah." She kisses him again and then pulls back. "If you want."

Nikolai's hands are in her hair, holding her still as he kisses down her throat, biting along her necklace, sucking kisses into her collarbones. "Pet," he says, still nipping at every inch of skin he can see. "What makes you think I wouldn't want that?"

She arches against him, his mouth alone making her breathless. "I... I don't know. I just wanted to make sure you knew it was available, but I didn't want you to feel pressured."

"Into what? Marking you as mine in yet another way?" He bites at her wrist, bringing it to his mouth and sucking on the thin skin there, another bruise in the shape of his mouth left in his wake. "How could I ever say no to that?"

She takes his chin with her other hand and tilts his face until his eyes meet hers. "I haven't done this in a long time," she whispers.

"How long?" His eyes are intent on hers. "A pretty pet like you deserves to be properly owned and claimed always."

Her answer is heavy on her tongue. Because then he'll know... he'll know she hasn't done this for anyone else since Will. There was Natalie a few years ago, but it's not like she had a dick to worry about. And she never even thought about doing it with a client, not when it would break the rules. Both hers and the agency's.

"Eight years," she says, her voice nearly breaking.

He inhales sharply, but it's only a moment before his lips curve into a smile, soft and pleased. "Well, then, my darling little pet is giving me something special, isn't she?" His head falls to her collarbone as he holds her even tighter. "Because you want nothing more than to be owned, don't you, sweet thing?" He kisses along her necklace again. "I can give you that, pet. I'd like nothing more."

Relief washes over her like a balm. "Please, sir." She pulls him up for a kiss. "I want... I want to do everything we can't do at home. Or can't fully do." Another kiss. "Be rough with me. Mark me." She presses her forehead to his and rolls her hips against his lap. "Come inside me." Her mouth meets his once more. "Choke me."

His hand is at her throat the moment she says it. There's no pressure, not yet, but the promise is there in the way his long fingers delicately wrap around her throat, the way his thumb is positioned ever so gently below her jaw. "Really?"

"Yes. Whatever you want to do to me, sir."

"Carte blanche, hm? My little pet likes to live dangerously, I see." He leans in, dragging his nose along her neck. His mouth is pressed to her skin as he speaks, lips brushing against her. "Are you sure?"

She presses into his restraining hand and nods. "You know my limits, sir."

He bites at her throat before leaning back. "On your knees, then." When she follows his command, he stands and grabs something from his bag, then returns with her oxblood collar dangling from his finger. "Do you want it, pet?"

Something within her clenches at the sight; a want, no, a *need*. Like she's dying of thirst, and he's offering her a cold glass of water. "Please," she begs.

He smirks darkly. "Then strip for me. Let me see everything that's mine."

Nikolai always looks at her like she's the most beautiful woman he's ever seen, and now is no different. She takes her time stripping down to her underwear, discarding her beret and clothes on the floor. Her legs spread open, letting him see the bruises he left on her thighs. Pulling at the side of her panties, she fully reveals the largest bruise on her hip, and she presses into it until it draws a hiss from her lips.

"Can't stop touching it, can you?"

She shakes her head. "No, sir." Rising onto her knees, she takes off her underwear and tucks it into his pocket. She always likes it when he does that.

He chuckles before crouching and securing the collar around her throat, just above her new day collar. As he fastens it, he looks into her eyes, one finger curling around the ring and yanking, tugging her body along with it.

Something within her instantly settles, like a cat curling up for a nap in the afternoon sun, even while her skin buzzes with want. Everything feels right now with his collar around her neck.

"Want you, sir," she whispers.

Nikolai grabs her face and kisses her roughly. "Pretty pet." He stands and unfastens his belt. "I want to use your mouth, sweet thing. Open wide for me." His hands make quick work of his button fly, then he reaches into his jeans, pulls out his cock, and strokes it while watching her.

She whimpers softly, the thought of it bare inside her cunt hitting her so strongly that she aches between her thighs. But she opens her mouth and looks up at him expectantly.

Tapping the head on her lips, he smears sticky precome all over them. "You want to be a messy little thing, don't you? Ridden hard and put away wet, hm?" He slips the tip past her parted lips and holds it there, devouring her with his gaze.

"Makeup a mess, covered in spit and come. A messy, filthy little pet."

She groans, nodding around him. She closes her lips around the head and sucks on the tip.

Suddenly, he's grabbing her by her hair and tugging at the root. "Hold still," he growls. "I'll take what I want from you." And with that, he thrusts into her mouth.

Damn, she loves it, the tugs at her skull, the fullness in her mouth. He's pushing deeper now, slowly increasing the depth and the force of his movements, inching closer to the back of her throat. "That's it, pretty pet, just take it. Watch me fuck your throat, sweet thing. That's what it's for, isn't it?"

Fuck. She moans hoarsely in response, unable to do anything more to agree with him. She's so turned on already, wet and sticky between her thighs as he uses her. She wants to touch herself so badly, but she can't, not when she's here to be used by him, to please him. His dick brushes her throat, tears spring to her eyes, wet and glossy.

"I'll have you choking on it soon, pet." He pushes a little further, a little harder, ever closer to making his words a reality. "I want to wreck you. So I'll choke you on my cock, and then I'll choke you while I fuck that pretty little cunt, and you'll be so happy, won't you?"

Corinne blinks up at him, her whimper muffled around his cock. She focuses on breathing, on relaxing her throat, on letting him take whatever he wants. She's wanted so many things with him for so long, and now she finally gets to have them. No worries about what she can or can't do because of other clients. It's just Nikolai for the next two weeks, and it's freeing to give herself to him in a way she never could before.

"You feel so good. What a perfect little mouth you have. Made for it, weren't you? Yeah, you were made for this." He's picking up speed now, grunting as he fucks her face before he pulls out roughly. He holds her mouth open, and saliva trails from her lips and falls down her chin. "Such a messy little thing," he says condescendingly. "What should I do with such a messy thing?"

"Please fuck me." Her voice is scratchy as she tries to catch her breath. "I'm aching for you, sir. Please!"

"Up on the bed," he orders, pulling his shirt over his head. "On your knees, but I want your hands braced on the headboard." He swats her ass as she crawls past him.

She does as she's told, looking back to watch him undress. She makes her appreciation obvious, her gaze heavy, her back arching in anticipation.

"Look at my delicious little pet." He gets a knee up on the mattress, pausing to grab a handful of her ass. His fingers dig in so roughly they'll leave a mark. "I bet you're dripping for me." Crowding behind her, he reaches between her legs, slipping against her slick center. "Oh, what a drippy little cunt you have. Poor little thing." He pushes two fingers inside her, twisting and scissoring slowly.

"Oh, fuck," she gasps, her cunt squeezing around him. It's so good, but still not enough. Not when she's so close to getting what she wants so badly.

"And so empty. That's no way for a pet to be, is it?"

"Sir, please." She widens her legs and presses her ass back against him. "Need your cock inside me, please."

"So demanding," he tuts at her. "Lucky for you, I want the same thing." His fingers slip out, and she watches over her shoulder as he rubs her wetness all over his cock. He grabs her hip with his other hand, nowhere near gentle, and steadies her as he lines himself up. "Hold still, pet."

Turning back to the headboard, Corinne stills and takes a deep breath—inhale, exhale. She lets her eyes drift shut, wanting to focus entirely on what it will feel like when he finally sinks into her. It's quiet, nothing but the rasps of their breathing. It's like she's on the edge of the precipice, like everything will change after this. Maybe it will, or maybe it's just lust making her think that, but every nerve ending within her is alight with anticipation all the same.

"Sir," she says softly, affectionately. Not hurrying him, just... sharing the moment with him.

"I know, pet," he murmurs, gently kissing her shoulder before he finally presses forward.

choked

NOTHING HAS EVER FELT MORE perfect, more right, than Nikolai pushing into her cunt, completely bare.

Her cry meets his groan, which is long and loud as he bottoms out.

"Oh, fuck," he gasps, his hips flush to her ass. "Oh, pet." He kisses and bites at her shoulders.

"Sir." Maybe she's not supposed to since he told her to place her hands on the headboard, but she has to touch him. She drops one hand and laces their fingers together at her hip.

"So fucking wet," he breathes, like he's in awe, and she clenches around his cock in response. His other hand drags up her body and tugs on the leather collar before wrapping around her throat. "Ready, sweet thing?"

Just his hand, large and possessive, around her throat is enough to make her gasp. She melts against him, moaning at the slick friction with nothing between them. "Yes, sir."

He starts a punishing pace right off the bat, but the hand at her throat stays light, only the barest hint of pressure as he fucks into her brutally. He sets his teeth at the joint of her shoulder and neck and bites down, worrying at the skin between his teeth.

With his body surrounding her, filling her, she feels wholly possessed. She keens, her fingers tightening around his at her hip to ground herself. "Wanted this for so long," she gasps.

Nikolai's mouth lets go of her shoulder and trails upward, sucking at her earlobe, scraping his teeth along the shell. "I didn't let myself think how amazing you would feel like this because I knew it'd drive me crazy." His voice is harsh in her ear. "You're perfect like this, fuck."

The pressure of his hand at her throat increases, fingers tightening against her pulse. Her body instinctively tries to inhale sharply but can't, not when the breath is smaller and shallower than she's used to. *There's a reason you don't do this,* a small voice tells her as her heart pounds in response. It's too dangerous a game to play with a client.

But it's Nikolai, it's her *sir*. It's the fear of falling backward but with the absolute knowledge that the strongest, most protective arms will catch her. She whimpers, her hand on the headboard coming to his raised wrist, squeezing it to ask for more.

"Tap my wrist twice if you need me to let go," he says, then his grip tightens. He picks up the force of his thrusts, teeth returning to make a bruised mess of her shoulders.

A strangled moan is trapped in her throat, her ears ringing as blood rushes to her head. Every pulse of her heart echoes in her ears, every thrust of his cock drives her higher, her entire world narrowing to those two things until it overwhelms her, until the *pleasurepainfear* combination becomes too much.

I'm going to come. She panics, reaching for his arm, trying to ask for permission but unsure if it comes out with everything so narrowed and dim.

Nikolai lets go, and she comes instantly, everything rushing toward her at once. She's gasping for breath, her senses over-loading with wave after wave of pleasure, barely noticing how he pulls her closer, how he whispers in her ear.

"Perfect, pet, you're so fucking perfect," he praises, kissing her throat.

She's shaking, whimpering. She's never come so hard in her life. "Thank you," she moans, her voice hoarse, dazed in a way she's not used to.

"Fuck, you're welcome. You're fucking stunning when you come for me, sweet thing." The rhythm of his hips is falling out of sync, his control slipping like it always does when he's close. "Do you want another?"

She hums, pleasure already building and spiking. "Yes, sir. Please?" She reaches and cups the back of his neck, baring her own to him.

He slowly squeezes again. His hips speed up just enough to make a difference. "You're so beautiful like this, my darling little pet."

She caresses his neck and shoulder as a silent thank you. His grip is still light enough to talk, just a promise of what's coming. "Can I ask to come now? That's why I panicked, sir."

"A new rule, pet: when we engage in breath play of any kind, permission is granted ahead of time." His hand tightens gently. "Ready, little thing?"

She takes a deep breath and nods, small whimpers falling from her lips as he continues to fuck her roughly.

He wastes no time and tightens his grip.

It's even better now, knowing she doesn't have to ask to come, doesn't have to keep a check on her orgasm in case he says no. She just... lets go. She surrenders herself to his hand, his cock, to the burn in her lungs and the blood pounding in her head.

It's submission like she's never felt before, not even the

night she spent at the end of his leash. Her life is quite literally in his hands, and letting go at such a basic, fundamental level pushes her under the depths, weighed down by a simple hand at her throat.

She doesn't even realize she's going to come again until it's happening. A hoarse whine slips through his chokehold, and she shudders against him, tears falling down her cheeks as he lets go, oxygen flooding her with a rush.

He licks at the tears on her cheeks, whispering, "Perfect, pet, that was perfect. Look how beautiful you are when you cry for me."

She doesn't stop coming, wave after wave hitting her as she gasps for air. Unable to keep herself up, she falls forward, arms braced against the headboard. "Sir," she moans, needy and desperate, not even sure what she's asking for.

Both of his hands are gripping her hips now, imprinting them with finger-shaped bruises as he pulls her onto his cock and chases his climax. "You want it, pet?"

It takes her a moment to realize what he means, to remember what started all this. His come inside her, filling her up. She groans, her cunt clenching around him again. "Please. Please come inside me."

"Love it when you beg, little thing. So fucking good for me." It takes one, two thrusts until he's coming with a low groan, his hips grinding against her ass.

Corinne gasps as his cock pulses and twitches inside her, filling her with his release. Some primal part of her feels claimed and sated by it, marked as his in an entirely new way. "God." She presses back against him. "Thank you. Holy fuck."

"I should be thanking *you* for this wonderful gift. Thank you, my sweet little thing." He caresses her skin, up her stomach, over her breasts before he pulls out. "On your back, pet, there's a good girl." After helping her roll over, he kisses his way down her body until he's between her thighs. Mesmerized as his come leaks out, he catches it with his finger and pushes it back in, drawing a whimper from her lips. "Beautiful," he murmurs.

His gentleness and attention overcome her. She caresses his face. "You're so sweet to me, sir." Her cunt aches and bruises litter her body, but still. He's so sweet.

With a soft hum, Nikolai smiles up at her. "Of course, I'm sweet to you. You are precious, didn't you know?" He kisses the bruises on her thighs, her hips. "My precious little pet."

Warmth washes over her. She's gone so deep for him she'll never be able to walk it back.

She rakes her fingers through his hair as he kisses his markings. "I like you calling me 'little thing.'"

The corners of his eyes crinkle, and he grabs her hand and kisses the inside of her wrist. Then he moves up to lie next to her. "I thought you might," he says, tweaking her nose. "Your objectification kink is one I'm enjoying discovering."

"It's sort of new to me, too." She curls up against him, tangling their legs. "So we're discovering it together."

They lie there for a long time, hands wandering slowly, lazily. There's no need to rush when they have two whole weeks together. Tonight was even better than she imagined. She still can't believe they get so much time here. It will be difficult to return to normal when they get home.

Eventually, she asks, "Should we try to get some sleep, sir? If I can, anyway." Corinne is a night owl by nature of her job, and while it's late in Paris, it certainly isn't in Chicago. Hopefully, the jet lag won't be too atrocious.

"I suppose." With a groan, Nikolai rolls away, stands, and scoops her into his arms. "Come along, *rybka moya*," he says, and she grins at her new nickname. "A hot bath will help, I'm sure."

you are good

THE BATHROOM IS JUST as beautiful as the rest of the suite, with white marble and silver and glass accents, modern and yet undeniably French. The tub is almost as big as the one at home, with the bonus of the Eiffel Tower twinkling outside the French windows.

He sets her on the counter and starts the bath.

"Are you ready for this week, sir?"

"As in workwise or spending time with you?" he replies with a quirk of his mouth.

She grins right back. "Both."

"Well, I am always ready to spend time with you, pet. And I'm mostly ready for work. I might spend a little time tomorrow preparing. But you can keep me company." Usually, he dreads work-week prep, but the thought of doing it with Corinne in his lap, or maybe kneeling at his feet, has him looking forward to it.

"Alright. For the work dinner on Tuesday, should I play my usual part for you? I wasn't sure since you said you know this client well, and it's a much smaller group."

"We can be more casual about it, more intimate." He glances at her over his shoulder. "It will be a leisurely dinner, and if I've brought you all the way to France with me, they're going to assume it's more serious than not."

After he pours some bath oil into the water, a gentle scent of almonds wafts in the air. He lifts her and sets her in the tub before taking off her leather collar and climbing in behind her. Her day collar is still on, and he brushes his fingers along the row of diamonds. Does the collar settle her as much as the sight of her wearing it does for him? Something about the perpetual symbol of her belonging to him sends a warm rush of affection through his blood, and he can't resist bending to kiss the spot just above the clasp.

Twisting some rogue hairs at her nape around his finger, he continues. "You'll do wonderfully on Tuesday, pet. You always do. I'm always happy to have you with me at these things. You make them not just bearable, but pleasurable."

She wraps his arms around her. "You just need someone there who isn't trying to impress you or the other way around, is all. Someone who's there for you and not there to play the games of business. A little retreat in the chaos of quid pro quo negotiations." She laughs softly. "I suppose we have our own quid pro quo, but... I'd like to think we both enjoy it."

He chuckles along with her. "We very much do, darling. This is a much more fun quid pro quo than the ones I usually deal with." He nibbles the side of her neck. "I'm thrilled with this particular arrangement," he whispers into her skin. "There's none of the uncertainty or worries that come with a relationship. Everything is agreed and decided upon. No surprises, except the good kind. It's perfect." He places a kiss on the other side of her throat. "It's everything I could want."

"Right," she whispers. "Perfect." She clears her throat. "And where are we having dinner?"

"A charming place called *Chez Louise*. You'll love it."

"I'm sure I will. It's hard to find bad food in Paris. Even

McDonald's tastes better here." She tilts her neck, allowing him full access. "I should take you to some of the cheap little holes-in-the-wall I frequented in school. It wasn't a touristy arrondissement, so I doubt you've been. When you're a student, you learn to stretch a euro but still eat good food."

The offering of her delicious skin is more than he can resist, and he bites a little more fiercely at the edge of her collarbone. Then he pours some bath oil into his hands and starts a gentle, cleansing massage of her shoulders. She groans, no doubt stiff from travel, and grows more pliant as he works.

"I'd love to see your school-day haunts. I'll admit, I'm curious about international student Corinne."

"Well, what do you want to know? I'm an open book." She spreads her arms and thighs as far as possible within the confines of his arms and the tub. She's being playful, but he can't help but glance down at her water-flecked breasts and stomach, his cock twitching at the sight of her cunt. Will this hunger for her ever be satisfied?

He blinks to clear his mind. "I don't have anything specific. Mostly, I'm just curious about you at that age. I imagine *that* Corinne is different from the Corinne I know now, but maybe not as much as most would suspect." With gentle hands, he turns her around to rub her legs. She closes her eyes and hums while he works at the muscles of her calves, and he smiles to himself, pleased.

"I was less sure of myself then. Most of my peers were wealthy. They could afford tuition and a study abroad program on top of it. Some girls invited me shopping once, and I couldn't afford anything in any of the stores they went to. There were moments like that the whole semester. I felt embarrassed and alone sometimes because of it. Not the whole time; I made friends from other programs, and I had a great time overall. Just... the poor kid routine hit hard sometimes."

Uncomfortable awareness of how wealthy he's been his whole life flares within him. Their interests are so similar that sometimes he forgets how different their lives are.

"When I started doing this," she continues, "when I stopped counting every penny and was able to relax? To have fun, to splurge, to not worry?" She blows out a breath. "It's nice to be here and enjoy myself in a whole new way." When she opens her eyes, she catches him staring intently at her.

He squeezes both of her calves and takes a deep breath. "I'm not sure what to say that won't make me sound like a privileged jerk." He shakes his head. "I've been wealthy my whole life. My father threw money at me instead of any kind of emotion or interest, but my mother somehow managed to be humble and grounded even with all the opulence she married into. Maybe it's because she grew up without; maybe it was just her nature. Who knows?"

He slides his hands over her hips and grips her waist, helping her rise on her knees so he can wash her chest and stomach. "I'm glad I could provide an opportunity to get you back here, at least. We can make it the trip you always wanted."

He wants that. He wants nothing more than to be the one who can give that to her.

"It already is," she says gently before kissing him. "Just tonight alone has been absolutely perfect." She closes her eyes as he washes her. "Thank you, sir."

"You're welcome, pet."

"Do you see your parents often?"

He's glad her eyes are closed; otherwise, she'd see the pain that crosses his face. "My mother died right after I graduated college," he murmurs. It still aches, and he's sure it always will. "My father and I haven't spoken in years. His assistant sends holiday cards and pretends they're not the same generic thing he sends everyone."

She opens her eyes with a tilt of her head. "Oh, sir. I'm so sorry." Suds covering her chest, she wraps her arms around him and rests her cheek against his collarbone. "I can't imagine losing my mom. I'm sorry you had to."

A wave of gratitude for this darling woman washes over him. He takes a slow and steady breath. Sadness always overcomes him every time he thinks of his mother and how she never got to see the person he became, how different he is from his father.

"Thank you, pet," he says, smoothing his hand over her hair and back, taking comfort from her presence. "It remains the worst thing I've ever been through. I miss her dearly." He clears his throat and then smiles to himself. "She would have liked you, you know."

Her eyes are misty as she straightens, but she's smiling that warm, gorgeous smile. "Yeah?"

He nods, lips curving at the corners. "Oh, yes. She loved nothing more than subtly outsmarting my father's business associates at events, and she was charming and educated enough to do it beautifully. She would take me to museums and bookshops." He chuckles. "And she taught me about fashion and jewelry, too, you know. Though I'm sure I've exceeded her expectations on those fronts."

Corinne grins cheekily and pokes his chest. "So I have *her* to thank for all the lovely things you pick out for me. She sounds so lovely, Nikolai. I wish I could've known her. She really did a fantastic job turning you into the person I know now." She curls against him again. "And I don't just mean the gifts. Just..." Her hand comes to rest right over his heart. "You are good. And I'm glad you're in my life."

Her statement sucker punches him, the surprise and poignancy knocking him off-kilter. Rarely has he thought of himself as *good*. He does good works when he can and lets his money facilitate others more often. But Nikolai himself? He's just a person who works too much and doesn't have enough people in his life who care about him. Outside Indali, he can't remember the last time someone said they were glad he was in their life, and even she doesn't say it often because that's never been how they are with each other.

With a kiss to her forehead, he places his hand over hers and squeezes it gently. "Thank you, sweet pet. I try very hard to be someone my mother would be proud of." He cups her face with his other hand. "I am glad you're in my life, too. You are exceptionally dear to me, my darling girl."

Her gaze softens, and when she leans in to kiss him, her hand is shaking beneath his.

foolish

CORINNE

THE NEXT MORNING, Corinne wakes up in Nikolai's embrace. It took her a while to fall asleep with the time difference, but the sleep she did get was deep and restful.

As usual, he is already awake, and he kisses her neck when she shifts.

"Good morning, pet," he murmurs, voice still gruff from sleep.

"Good morning, sir." She snuggles back against him. "It's Sunday."

"Mmhm." The sound is muffled, his lips pressed against her throat.

"It's our day," she whispers, her mouth tugging into a grin.

He kisses her neck once more. "It is."

Her smile turns mischievous, and she clears her throat. "It's the Lord's Day, as well. Will you be forgiven for missing service while gallivanting around Paris this week?"

Nikolai chuckles. "I might have plans to go, you know. The Cathedrale Saint Alexandre Nevsky isn't that far from here."

She huffs fondly, but then she bites her lip. "Do you want me to go with you?"

His breath hitches. "Do you want to go?"

"If you want me to." She brings his hand to her mouth and kisses his palm. "I know how much it means to you."

"I'd love to take you. But morning service starts at 8:45, and honestly"—he nips at her throat with a chuckle—"I'm not sure you have any skirts or dresses in your luggage that cover your knees."

With a gasp, she looks at him over her shoulder. "Are you suggesting I dress like a slut?"

He arches an eyebrow, a smirk hiding in the corners of his mouth. "In the eyes of the Russian Orthodox Church, pet, everyone who's not dressed like a nun is dressed like a slut."

"I'll start dressing more appropriately just for you, Father," she says, and turns back around with a wriggle of her hips.

He groans and nips at her shoulder. "Behave, you."

Corinne hums smugly. "Yes, sir." Her voice is dripping with honey.

"For such a good girl, you certainly do like to push the boundary sometimes," he mumbles. But the smile in his voice tells her he's delighted by her sass.

* * *

After a round of sex and a leisurely breakfast at a café near their hotel, they spend most of their Sunday at the Louvre. They only planned to be there for a few hours, but they both should've known Corinne would lose track of time in arguably the best museum on earth. And Nikolai certainly didn't remind her.

"Oh my god," she says when she pulls out her phone. "It's already five; you should've said something."

"And interrupt my pet gazing misty-eyed at Cézanne and Benoist all afternoon? Absolutely not."

Her cheeks heat, and she playfully pushes at his shoulder. "Hush."

"Never." He pulls her flush against him. "I could watch you walk around a museum all week and be perfectly content."

That evening, they order room service, and Nikolai spends an hour preparing for the week while Corinne kneels at his feet. He strokes her hair, plays with the clasp of her collar, and idly kneads her neck and shoulders. She's so relaxed by the end that he has to scoop her up and put her to bed.

They play tourist for a few hours Monday morning and visit the Eiffel Tower. The view of the city is breathtaking from the top, and they take turns pointing out Sacré-Cœur and L'Arc de Triomphe and Les Invalides. Afterward, Nikolai leaves for work, and she spends a couple of hours shopping as her sir demanded —and paid for.

When she comes across a schoolgirl blazer and skirt in Louis Vuitton, she smirks and asks to try it on. She slips into it —shirt and tie included—and makes a sweetly seductive pose in the mirror, then takes a picture to send to Nikolai.

> Bonjour, Mr. Zaitsev.

> Little miss, that'd better be leaving the store with you.

She grins, mind already flaring with ideas of what they could do with her outfit tonight.

> Oh? Is Mr. Zaitsev finally going to take my virginity tonight?

> And steal it from your future husband, Miss Ryan? I'd like nothing better.

The night ends with her bent over the hotel desk with her

plaid skirt hiked up, riding high from Nikolai licking his spend from her cunt, and she can't imagine finding this perfect of a connection with anyone else.

* * *

It's an unusually stormy Tuesday night in Paris when they meet with Nikolai's client for dinner. Even with a car service picking them up and Nikolai shielding her with an umbrella, her shoes are waterlogged by the time they make it inside the restaurant, *Chez Louise.*

The atmosphere is elegant but more relaxed than she was expecting, with dark wood pillars glowing in the sconce light. Mirrors are set into every wall, surrounded by textured wallpaper and punctuated by tile mosaics of birds of paradise, lilies, and lupine. Scattered stained glass windows face the street, backlit by the streetlamps that dot the sidewalk outside. The overall effect is comfortable and sophisticated in a way only the French seem to manage as effortlessly as this.

"I assumed a client dinner meant somewhere stuffy," Corinne says as they wait for the host to seat them.

Nikolai smiles, though his posture is stiffer than usual in her company. "Have I ever taken you somewhere like that?"

"No, you haven't."

He nods. "Stuffy places are overly pretentious." He scans the room. "And Joséphine has never been the type to be impressed by anything outside of good quality and excellent service."

The host returns and gestures for Corinne and Nikolai to follow him. "Madame Silvain is already waiting for you."

When they make their way to the table, two women stand to greet them. One is pale, slender, and dressed in a smart pantsuit, with her gray hair pulled back in a simple chignon.

The other has curves for days, with tan skin and a wavy dark bob. She's wearing high-waisted jeans and a crisp white shirt.

"Nikolai," the older woman says, leaning over to kiss his cheeks. "It's been so long since I've seen you, I was worried you'd forgotten about us."

He returns the greeting, his smile small and bordering on impersonal, save for the crinkling near his eyes. "Someone like you, Joséphine? Impossible. I apologize for my absence. You know I don't like to interfere with the overseas offices too much when they run smoothly. I trust the people I hire to do their jobs and treat our clients well. Or should I have ignored that bit of advice from you?"

Joséphine huffs and then looks over at Corinne. "And who is this?" Her gaze is somehow both amused and appraising. "Is Nikolai Zaitsev no longer a bachelor?"

Stepping back to Corinne's side, Nikolai slides one hand to her lower back and ushers her forward. "Joséphine, allow me to introduce my girlfriend, Corinne Ryan. Corinne"—and here he gives Corinne his usual warm smile—"this is Joséphine Silvain, president of *Banque Paris* and one of my most long-standing international clients."

"A pleasure to meet you," Corinne says, extending her hand. "Nikolai was sweet enough to bring me along on his business trip." She grins up at him. "And to extend it for a proper vacation."

"Nikolai? Sweet? Ha!" Joséphine gestures toward the other woman. "This is my wife, Liv. Another *Américaine*."

"She always says that like it's a bad thing," Liv replies with a laugh. "And yet Jo proposed to *me*."

Nikolai barely conceals a smirk. "We all know Joséphine loves a challenge."

As soon as they sit, it's evident Joséphine is a frequent patron of this restaurant. Even though the waiter is not wearing a name tag, she knows him by name and orders two bottles of wine and several hors d'œuvres without looking at the menu.

After the waiter brings wine to the table, Josephine leans back with a glass. "I hear rumors of a new system, Nikolai. Your account manager played coy when the team asked him about increasing prices. I hope you're not about to make me look elsewhere after so many years working together."

Nikolai crosses his legs and lazily drapes his arm over the back of Corinne's chair. "Have we ever raised prices without exemplary new services to justify the increase? Surely, you trust me more than that by now."

Corinne jots down mental notes as she watches two business masterminds—the president of the largest bank in France and the CEO of the largest cybersecurity company in the world—go head-to-head. If Philadelphia is in the cards for her, she has her very own business course playing out in front of her.

"Are they always like this?" Corinne whispers to Liv as the waiter takes Nikolai's order.

"Just wait until they're drunk. It's like business negotiations are a competitive sport for both of them." Liv glances at her wife before continuing. "We've got to steer the conversation whenever there's a pause unless we want to listen to this all night."

It takes about twenty minutes for poor Liv to get a word in edgewise finally. "Oh, look, the main course is here. What a perfect time for a segue." She turns to Nikolai as the waiter delivers their plates. "Now, how did you two meet?"

They've been asked this question at least a dozen times by this point, and Corinne waits for his usual canned answer.

"A mutual friend. Actually, a few mutual friends." His hand drifts from the back of the chair to Corinne's shoulder. "I'd be annoyed at how well these friends know me, but"—he shrugs

—"how could I be, when it's turned out so wonderfully for me?"

Well, that... isn't his canned answer at all. It's real. As real as it can be without saying he pays for her company. And maybe it's the amount of wine she's had, but her belly flutters in response.

"It's been wonderful," Corinne says.

"And how did Mr. No-Nonsense win you over, huh?" Joséphine asks, cheeks now painted red from wine. "With his bearish reputation?"

Corinne laughs. "Nikolai? No. Well, okay, I've heard that from one of our friends, but he's always been really lovely to me."

"That's so sweet," Liv says, with a hand to her chest.

"*Merde!*" Joséphine exclaims. "What has she done to you, Zaitsev?"

Nikolai narrows his eyes and lifts one finger from his glass to point at Joséphine. "Nothing you'll benefit from, Jo, so don't even try."

Liv leans forward. "Jo, on the other hand, *was* a complete bear. She was so hot but such a pain in the ass." She giggles with a waggle of her brows. "I had to grind her down."

"Oh, did you now?" Corinne says.

"Mmhmm! It's amazing what some good love can do." Liv takes another drink. "Right? When did you two know it was love?"

Corinne's breath catches in her chest. They've never had to answer that. They've never *prepared* to answer that. Her heart pounding, she turns to Nikolai with a nervous laugh.

"There wasn't a single moment." He shrugs. "More like... the making of a quilt." He chuckles. "I helped my grandmother make one once. It starts with mere pieces of fabric, but then pieces become squares, squares become sections, and then, where all you had before was a collection of bits and ends, suddenly, you have a blanket. Warm and comforting, with care and intent in every stitch." He shakes his head and reaches for his wine. "But isn't that always the way?"

He says it so comfortably and casually, as though he *had* prepared a response for that. Or maybe it's because it's another easy lie to keep up their charade, like how they met or how long they've been together. Those have always been easy things for her to say, like it's another fact of her life.

But she can't do that this time. Because right now, in the middle of a restaurant in Paris, surrounded by people she doesn't know, she realizes the man who is paying her for companionship and sex is the man she has somehow fallen deeply in love with.

She has broken the number-one rule in her line of work, after a string of other broken rules, when he has been clear from the beginning that he is not interested in romance.

And she is foolish if she thinks she can keep doing this like it won't eventually rip her apart.

deep breaths

CORINNE

LIV IS NOW WAXING poetic about how she fell in love with Joséphine, but Corinne can hardly concentrate.

"Excuse me," Corinne says with what she hopes is a convincing enough smile, "I'm just going to run to the restroom."

Nikolai turns and reaches for her hand. "Everything alright?"

"A little too much wine, I think. I'll be right back."

Thankfully, the bathroom is a single, and she doesn't have to worry about someone barging in as she tries to pull herself together. She retrieves the extra concealer and mascara she always keeps in her bag since they often come in handy in her line of work.

She gives herself a scant minute to cry, to berate herself for how foolish it was to let herself get into this situation, to let herself fall for an unavailable man, to accept the fact this has to end, sooner or later.

And the longer she lets this go on, the harder it will be to say goodbye.

When her minute is over, she inhales, then exhales, then

looks in the mirror. Her eyes are smeared with black, and her knuckles are white as they grip the basin. Sniffling, she dries her tears and fixes her makeup. As she's finishing up her mascara, the sparkle of diamonds at her throat catches her eye as it reflects the dim light of the bathroom.

His collar. His sign of ownership.

When we're together, I'm all yours, she told him all those months ago.

But that's just it, Corinne. You're not actually together.

Refusing to cry again, she shoves that thought away, squares her shoulders, and walks back into the restaurant. "I'm back!" she exclaims, and sits next to Nikolai, willing her heart to return to its normal pace.

"Are you okay?" Nikolai asks, his gaze soft from worry and a healthy dose of wine. He has no idea the realization she's just had. He has no idea she's in love with him.

"Right as rain." She gulps from her own glass before somehow giving their companions a dazzling smile. "Did I miss anything juicy?"

* * *

By the time they return to the hotel that night, Nikolai is drunk. She's never seen him have more than a couple of drinks before, but maybe Joséphine brings it out in him.

Shoving down the agony and guilt from tonight's revelation, she loops her arm around his waist to steady him as they walk inside. If she can just get him to sleep, she can hole up in the suite's living room and process what's happened. And what she's going to do about it.

"Come on." She guides him toward the elevator. "Let's get you upstairs."

A loose, languid smile spreads across his mouth, and he

wraps his arm around her shoulders, pulling her close and nuzzling her hair. "Did you have a nice time, pet?"

"Mm." She hits the button for their floor, and the doors close before them. "Dinner was delicious."

"*You're* delicious," he slurs with a chuckle, before pressing kisses to her face.

Corinne smiles despite herself, even if it doesn't quite reach her eyes. She's in love with him; of course she's going to find him charming.

They arrive at their floor, and she tugs him down the hallway to their room, each of his steps too careful as he attempts to follow her in his intoxicated state.

When they get to the door, he closes in behind her and snakes his arms around her waist with a loud sigh against her throat. She's fumbling for the key card, and he's kissing under her ear.

"I'm glad you were there tonight. S'much better when I'm not alone."

She squeezes her eyes shut. Why does that make her heart ache?

Deep breaths.

"I'm glad, too, sir," she whispers before opening the door. As it shuts behind them, she pulls away, needing some distance. "Let's get you into something comfortable. And get some water in you before you sleep. Otherwise, you'll regret all that wine in the morning."

"Pfft. It's French wine. They would never let their wine cause regrets." But he allows her to help with his shirt buttons.

"Whatever you say, sir." It's strange, undressing him without a plan for it to lead somewhere. Without kissing him. Without being driven by lust. Once he's down to his boxer briefs, she pushes at his shoulders to sit him on the bed and fetches a t-shirt and a glass of water. "Here." She slips the shirt over his head. "Now, drink up for me, sir."

He drinks obediently, then rests his head against her chest with a content sigh. "I thought I was the one who did all this for you." He huffs a muffled laugh against her skin.

Her fingers find their way into his hair of their own accord. She clears her throat. "I told you that you need to be taken care of sometimes, too."

Humming in acknowledgment, he holds her closely.

Her jaw trembles at his nearness. She should push him away but can't bring herself to do so.

What is wrong with her?

Nikolai lifts his head, his eyes bleary and unfocused. "Bed?"

"Yes, sir." She pulls away to change into a night slip she purchased on her shopping trip yesterday. When she climbs in with him, the urge to cry is so strong she can barely hold it together.

"Mm, c'mere," he murmurs, and flings an arm over her as soon as she turns out the lights. It only takes a minute before his breathing deepens and his arm goes slack, but it seems like a lifetime.

The five minutes she waits before crawling out from under his embrace is an eternity.

Deep breaths.

Slipping into her robe, she leaves the bedroom and closes the door behind her. The view of the Eiffel Tower, shimmering in the darkness, draws her onto the balcony. Here she is, in one of the most beautiful cities in the world, in the *City of Love*, with the one person she can never be with.

She falls onto the nearby chaise with a sob. Every bit of anguish and despair she's caged in these last few hours breaks free, and she couldn't stop crying if she tried. She sends a silent thank-you to whoever is listening that Nikolai is likely too drunk to wake up and come looking for her anytime soon.

Nikolai, who has told her more than once he wants nothing more than what they have—a business arrangement, a transaction. *Quid pro quo,* her mind supplies from their conversation in the bath. But over the last few months, Corinne has taken his affection and touch and praise and gifts and twisted them into something they're not.

What hurts the most isn't even the fact he will never want her the way she so desperately desires. It's the fact she has to do the right thing and end this for good.

Fuck, how can she tell him goodbye? What will fill her Sundays without his laugh and his cooking and his strong arms around her? What will Monday mornings be like without waking to the smell of eggs and kasha and coffee, without his teasing about her bedhead, without his goodbye kiss?

A church bell rings, yanking her from her thoughts and informing her of the hour. It's late, and if she wants any chance of getting some sleep, she needs a plan in place before she gets back in bed.

Deep breaths, Corinne.

She tugs her phone from her robe pocket and opens her calendar. She has to figure out when to tell him and whether she will need to recommend another escort to accompany him to any events outside their usual Sundays. It's the least she can do after calling things off with him for, seemingly, no reason.

But her eyes are immediately drawn to her most recent entry on the day after they return from France, marked in red so it's hard to miss.

Margot deadline: Philadelphia decision.

Oh.

Of course. Her *reason* is right there. A chance to get away, to start anew, to dive into an exciting project and keep her mind off a certain Russian billionaire obliviously sleeping in the next room.

Biting her lip, she does the time zone math, pulls up her contacts, and hits *call* before she can change her mind.

It takes a few rings before there's an answer.

"Hey, it's Corinne." She clears her throat and plasters on a smile, if only to convince herself. "Is now a good time to talk?"

philadelphia

NIKOLAI

NIKOLAI WAKES to the soft ring of his alarm the following day, his body heavy and languid, his brain sluggish and off-kilter from an excess of wine. He groans, pressing the heels of his hands harshly against his eyes, trying to force his good sense to return quickly. He should know better than to drink like that with Joséphine.

He shuts off the alarm and allows himself a moment to gaze at Corinne before kissing her forehead and getting out of bed.

As he readies the shower, he remembers her taking care of him last night, and an unexpected warmth washes over him from the change in their usual roles. It's not something he usually allows, or puts himself in the position to need, and he can't help but think if it'd been anyone but her, he wouldn't have let his guard down so much, wouldn't have indulged in the good wine and better company until he stumbled back to their room.

Of course, Liv threw him by asking when they'd known it was love. For all the preplanned answers he and Corinne have, that never crossed their minds. Maybe it should have since that would be the assumption if he brought her to client dinners overseas. And perhaps he should have panicked at the idea of answering with nothing to fall back on, but it had been as easy as breathing to tell Liv what she needed to hear.

It wasn't untrue, exactly. Their relationship isn't a romantic one, but it wasn't difficult to describe just how easily Corinne has fit into the spaces in his life that have been empty and shut for so long, the parts of himself that revel in high protocol and power exchange. The bits and pieces that have always liked taking care of people and cooking and providing for those he is close to.

Yes, he had some of that with Elijah, but not nearly to the same extent. They didn't get up to things that needed quite as much aftercare, and Nikolai would be lying if he said he didn't miss it during his time with Elijah. But he has all those things with Corinne now. Her presence *has* become a warm quilt— something to keep the chill of his usually isolated existence at bay.

She is still asleep when he steps back into the bedroom, dressed and ready to leave. He smooths her hair from her face and kisses her temple before leaving. Then he stops at the front desk and arranges for breakfast to be sent up in an hour so his sleepy little pet has one less thing to deal with when she wakes.

* * *

When he returns to the hotel that evening, he can't help but smile to himself in the elevator at the prospect of spending the evening with Corinne. She's been quiet today, only sending a few texts, but he's sure she's been busy playing tourist again.

He walks into the suite and drops his bag on the entry table, loosening his tie as he steps further into the room.

"Pet?" he calls.

"In here." Corinne is sitting on the bed with her hair in a bun and her laptop open in front of her. Her empty breakfast tray is still on the bed. "Hey, how was your day?"

"Hello." He bends down for a kiss and places the tray on the nearby table. "It was good, though it's improved significantly in the last few seconds." He hangs his jacket and tie in the closet and slips out of his shoes before joining her on the bed. He lies next to her and props himself on an elbow. "How was yours? Any sightseeing today?"

"No, I..." She closes her laptop. "... had some stuff to take care of today."

He sits up, studying her. "Everything alright?" Something is... off, but he can't put his finger on what.

"Yes!" she says quickly. "I got a, um, a very exciting job offer. From Margot, actually." She pulls her knees up to her chest. "She's wanting to expand Calypso to Philadelphia." Corinne smiles, but it's no smile he's ever seen. "And she's asked me to run it."

It hits him like a fist to the gut. But between business and kink scenes, he's spent enough time perfecting his poker face that he manages not to show it. Instead, he kisses her cheek. "That's amazing, Corinne! And it speaks volumes of how Margot trusts you. Congratulations, pet."

"Thank you."

He *is* happy for her, but in the back of his mind is bellowing a haunting mantra of *Philadelphia, Philadelphia, Philadelphia*. He should ask if she's made a decision yet, but fuck if he wants to.

"Wow, Philly, huh?" For the first time in years, he worries he can't fake his smile like he needs to. "Have you ever been?"

"Yes, but just for a school trip years ago. You know, the Liberty Bell, Independence Hall, the Rocky statue." She laughs. "The three pillars of American democracy."

His smile is maybe a little smaller than it would typically be, but it's still there.

Philadelphia.

"For what it's worth, you'd be amazing at running a branch of the agency. You're driven and passionate and smart as a whip. You know the business like the back of your hand. Margot couldn't have chosen a better person to ask." Nikolai means it, every word. But he doesn't want her to go.

He hopes she doesn't ask what he thinks she should do because he's unsure if he can tell her to take it. Suddenly, something fierce and loud is banging from the other side of a wall deep inside him, something he can't examine closely right now or he might break down right in front of her. Something that's been there for a while, but *Philadelphia* has activated it like a sleeper agent trigger word.

No, he can't fucking deal with that now. Not here, not with her. He shoves it away to deal with when they get back to Chicago.

Corinne grabs his hand, tugging him from his thoughts. "Thank you, sir." She takes a deep breath. "That means a lot to me. Especially now that I've seen your business prowess at the dinner table." This time, her smile is tinged with sadness. "Maybe I can call you for pointers?"

Squeezing her hand tightly, he brings it to his lips for a kiss. "Of course, pet. You can call me for anything, always. Whatever you need." His eyes roam her face. He doesn't want to ask, but fuck, he has to know.

"You've decided, then?"

She nods, her gaze falling to their joined hands. "Yes."

He takes a slow, deep breath. He's already dreading the yawning chasm of weeks ahead when Sundays return to their dull existence, with hours spent in the office if only so they aren't spent in his too-big apartment, where he would no doubt see her everywhere.

Nikolai shoves that thought behind the wall with the other banging thing he can't face right now.

"When—" He closes his eyes to center himself before opening them, hungry for every second now that they're numbered. "When would you go?"

"We're still figuring out specifics, but probably October. A lot of things to figure out between now and then."

Four months. He has four months to try and eke out as much time with her as he can. Maybe he can stock up, maybe he can build up enough moments with her to last him... as long as he needs them to last.

He doesn't think about how it's only sixteen Sundays. That feels like significantly less time than four months does.

He clears his throat. "I'll help however I can. Business advice or otherwise. Whatever I can do to make it easier for you, alright?"

Corinne sets her laptop aside and lies beside him, her arms wrapping tightly around his body. "Thank you, sir. I appreciate it so much."

He pulls her close and buries his face in her hair, letting her familiar scent soothe the ache that's formed behind his sternum, small and persistent and shaped like her eventual absence.

What the hell is he supposed to do without her?

* * *

They have dinner at a small café near the hotel. Their walk is quiet and easy, his arm wrapped securely around her shoulders, keeping her tucked close as they traverse the streets of Paris. Their conversation veers anywhere and everywhere except the one place it shouldn't, the specter of Philadelphia looming large between them, the uninvited third guest to an otherwise intimate meal.

By the time they're back in the hotel elevator, Nikolai has her pressed against the wall, with his fingers wound in her hair as he kisses her hungrily, needing to touch her and forget everything else.

"Mm." She nips at his mouth, and her hands slip into his pockets. "You know. We've never met an elevator we didn't love to fool around in."

He chuckles against her lips, the hand in her hair tilting her head back, moving down to her jaw as he sucks light kisses along her throat. "Nothing wrong with having habits, pet."

The elevator stops. "As long as we're not getting boring and predictable."

He kisses back up to her ear and nibbles the lobe. "Us? Never." The scent of her perfume has faded over the course of the day, but it's still strong this close to her skin. He inhales deeply, taking it in and burying it deep in the recesses of his memory.

Four months. Philadelphia.

"Shall we get out now, sir?"

He hauls her up and wraps her thighs around his waist before walking to their room and allowing her to unlock the door. He presses her against the wall just inside and kisses her again, memorizing the feel of her mouth, the taste of her tongue, and the way her chest expands when she sighs against him.

Eventually, he carries her to their bed and gently deposits her on top, eager hands wrinkling the linen of her pants as he grips her thighs, sliding up and up until he's pushing at her shirt, bending to kiss the skin he reveals. His hands wrap around the curve of her ribs, fingers spread wide, kinesthetically tracking every sigh, every gasp, every variation in her breathing.

"Sweet little pet," he breathes against her skin, "I can't get enough of you."

Her hands tighten at his shoulders, her breath hitching as he nibbles at her skin. "I can't get enough of you either, sir," she whispers so softly he can barely hear it.

He makes quick work of her shirt and bra, needing his skin on hers immediately, needing to feel every part of her pressed against him. His shirt joins hers on the floor, and he slides off the bed and kneels, pushing her pant leg up and kissing her ankle, tracing the delicate bone with his tongue while tugging off her shoes, before his hands reach for the waist of her pants and pull everything off.

His eyes drink in the sight of her body, her skin almost glowing from the twinkling tower and city lights through the window.

"You look like a saint," he breathes, eyes tracing every edge and curve, admiring how her diamond collar sparkles in the low light. "My gilded girl, illuminated in gold."

A slow smile lifts the corners of her mouth. "And what am I the patron saint of, Father?"

"Workaholics, perhaps." He kisses her calf, bites at her shin. "High Protocol sadists with no one to cook for, possibly." He breathes in the smell of her skin, dragging his nose up her thigh. "And me for certain."

The heady scent of her arousal rolls off her in waves as he inches closer to her center, and he sways forward, eyes falling shut as he chases it. "Tell me, Saint Corinne, if I said my prayers to you, would you answer?" He opens his eyes and looks up at her before he makes contact, damp heat radiating from her center, and he ghosts the tip of his nose mere millimeters from where he wants to be. "If I asked for your blessing, would you give it?"

She hums and tilts her head in thought. Her thumb strokes his cheekbone. "Have you done good deeds?" She smooths it over his mouth. "Have you learned to work a little less and enjoy life a little more?"

"I've tried." His voice is soft and reverent in the hush of this new intimacy. "I am *trying*." He rests his head on her thigh, sighing into her touch. "For you, Saint Corinne, I am trying."

Corinne sits up. Cupping the back of his neck with a trembling hand, she pulls him forward until his forehead touches hers, her brown eyes tender and warm. "Then, yes, Nikolai, I give you my blessing."

His mind and soul ease as though he's just confessed, as though her blessing has absolved him, his spirit at peace in the sure presence of divine grace. It should feel blasphemous, and yet surely God would understand. What else is a man to do when presented with someone so clearly meant to be worshiped?

His hands skim down her sides to her thighs, and his thumbs dip inward and brush against her at last. He gasps at the feel of her, heat and slickness on the pads of his thumbs as they slide up and down, teasing them both.

"God," she moans, rolling her hips against his hands. "See? You've got me all worked up already. Like you always do."

He drags one thumb down the seam of her and presses the tip of his finger inside. "Just want you to feel good, pet. You're so good for me, sweet thing, you deserve it."

Her brows pinch, and she closes her eyes. "Sir, please."

Readjusting, he presses two fingers in instead, eyes drawn to her face as she takes them. She's beautiful, and he can't help but breathe, "Perfect, so fucking perfect," against her mouth.

Her head falls back, revealing the long line of her throat,

already mottled with bites and bruises and begging for more. He takes what's on offer and sucks hard at her neck, her collarbones, more bruises blossoming under his lips.

Nikolai's so hard he can barely think, but he wants to see her fall apart first, *needs* to see it. He presses his thumb against her clit just how she likes. Then he grips her hip and pulls, encouraging her to move. "Come on, there's a good girl."

"Oh, fuck." Corinne leans back on her elbows and grinds against his hand, her moans and sighs getting louder as she gets closer. "Sir, please," she gasps, eyes opening and finding his gaze. "May I come?"

"Yes, pet, whenever you want. Let me see you, such a pretty little thing like this." Her cheeks are flushed, and her hair is curling right at her temples from summer humidity. She's never looked more stunning.

Finally, she comes with a groan, her back arching as pleasure overtakes her.

He gentles her through it, whispering praise and sweet nothings. He eases his fingers from her, kissing away her gasp. "Just for a second, pet. I won't leave you empty, promise."

He gets undressed before sitting against the pillows and picking her up to straddle his lap. "Wanna watch you, little thing. You look so good when you're riding me."

"Do I?" She rubs her slick cunt along his length. "Do you want me to put on a show for you, then?"

He doesn't want a show, doesn't want something falsified for the sake of it, doesn't want anything less than the real thing. Yes, at the end of the day, her job is to give him what he wants and make sure *his* desires are fulfilled, but with the honesty of a man confessing, all he wants at this moment is *her*.

He wants to see Corinne as she is, taking exactly what she needs from him. *Four months* and *sixteen Sundays* and fucking *Philadelphia* are running through his mind, the cruelest ticker tape looping endlessly within his brain. He needs to remember what it's like when she's not anyone but herself with him, when there's nothing between them but desire and pleasure.

"No. I want to see you fall apart. I want to see just how good I make you feel." The last part comes out on a groan, his head tipping back as she rubs along his length. "Come on, pretty pet," he grits out, gripping her hips. "Show me."

unfiltered

NIKOLAI

"YES, SIR," she whispers. Corinne takes his cock in her hand and sinks down slowly with a moan. "This what you want?" Her voice is already breathless as her hips move in a sultry, languid rhythm. "For me to take my own pleasure?"

He groans, fingers digging deep into her thighs. God above, her cunt is incredible. "Yeah, pet, just like that. I want to watch you make yourself feel good. You make me feel fucking amazing all the time; you deserve it. Fucking perfect girl for me, always."

Corinne's hips quicken, drawing forth the most gorgeous sighs and moans from her mouth. By this point, her hair is a mess, and a flush is spreading from her cheeks to her throat. Sweat is gathering at her collarbones, and her breasts are swaying with each thrust. Every inch of her is begging to be touched, kissed, licked, and bitten.

His palms roam up and down the span of her ribs, the arch of her shoulders. His fingers are slick with sweat as they glide over the hollows of her collarbones to her breasts, as they circle her nipples in time with her circling hips.

"Beautiful," he groans, bracing his feet and flexing his thighs to push his hips up, giving her a better angle. "Fucking gorgeous, how perfect you look riding my cock, taking what you want. So good for me, pet, so good."

Corinne cries out, but it's not from pleasure. No, he knows the ways she moans and sighs and begs for more. This is the sound she makes when he edges her, when he withholds pleasure, when he makes her wait.

It's frustration.

His hands slide down her body, answering her cries like a sailor lured to a siren. "You need more, pet? Need me to touch you here?" His thumb drops to her clit and gives her the pressure she needs. "Better, sweet thing?"

"Yes," she groans, leaning into his hand. "Oh my God, yes." Her thighs tremble around his hips. "*Sir.*"

Nikolai smiles, affection blooming in his chest at the sight of her—undone and high on pleasure, absolutely radiant with it. His good girl, his saint, his sweet pet.

His.

"That's it, pet, go on. Let me see you."

Her eyes flutter shut, her gasps more desperate as she rides him harder and faster. "May I come? *Please?*"

Nikolai aches to kiss her through it, but he doesn't want to ruin this moment. His eyes are locked on her face, taking in every breath, every bead of sweat as it trails down her temple, her lips bitten red and lashes fanned over her cheeks. He wants to tattoo this image on his eyelids, wants it burned so deep into his brain it's all he'll ever be able to think about.

"Yes, sweet thing, go ahead. You earned it; go on."

He's as deep inside her as he can be when she comes, her body stilling before she slows her pace to a grind, wringing out every ounce of pleasure. "Damn." She leans in for a kiss. "Thank you." She sighs. "I forgot to say thank you earlier. I'm sorry."

Wrapping his arms around her waist, he pulls her even closer and presses kisses to her chest. "You're welcome, pet. You looked so incredible earlier that it was thanks enough." His thighs are trembling, both from held-back desire and the way he dug his toes into the mattress to keep steady while she took what she needed from him. "So fucking gorgeous, darling pet."

Corinne holds on to him tightly, fingers gripping his shoulders as she finds her rhythm again. "You feel so good like this," she whispers.

His hands trail down to her hips and help her along. He wants to keep her like this always, right here in his lap, flying high and feeling good. "You want another?"

She nods. "Yes, sir."

He draws her down for a kiss. "Go on, then." He nips at her mouth. "Show me how badly you want it."

Her laugh melts into a moan. "I thought you didn't want me to put on a show."

"I don't. I just want to see *you* want it... unfiltered. I can feel how wet you are. I can see the flush on your pretty skin and how your body is trembling. You want it. And I want to see that. Don't hold back."

"Unfiltered?" She stills. "I don't think I can come right now unless you're touching me."

His hand slips between their bodies. "Like this?"

"Yes." Clinging to him, she finds her rhythm again. She sobs, her voice a desperate, wretched thing. "I—I need you."

"You've got me," he says, an assurance, a *promise*. Because it's true. She's got him, however she wants him. He matches the rhythm she's set, fingertips swirling around her clit. "I'm right here; you've got me."

Corinne finally comes, head thrown back and lips parted as she trembles in his arms.

Nikolai's body is vibrating with unreleased tension, but his mind is focused on her pleasure, his own orgasm nothing but an eventuality in the back of his mind.

He wants to give this to her, to allow her to satisfy herself on her own terms, in a way outside their usual dynamic. He wants to be who *she* needs for once, if only to prove he can be. He wants it as much as he usually wants to be Sir to her Pet.

"I've never seen anyone so beautiful," he whispers, hands caressing her body as she comes down. "You're so lovely, especially when you fall apart like that for me. Perfect, perfect, perfect girl."

She kisses his forehead, and when she pulls back, she's blinking back tears. But she smiles and kisses his mouth. "Let me make you feel good, sir."

"No." He shakes his head. "Later. I want to focus on what you want right now."

"But that is what I want."

Oh.

He presses gentle kisses to her lips, her cheeks, the tip of her nose. "Okay." He cradles her against him and rests his forehead against hers. "Okay, pretty pet, help me feel good."

Her cunt squeezes around his cock each time his hips rock with hers, driving him higher and higher. "Do you want to come inside me?" she whispers. "Or all over me?"

Nikolai groans and presses as much of their bare skin together as he can. What a choice to be offered. While usually it'd be more of a struggle, he can't imagine being anywhere other than where he is right now. His long-ignored climax is barreling toward him now that it's been let off the leash, and pulling out is the last thing he wants. "Like this," he pants and bites down on her shoulder. "Just like this."

They take their time, Corinne riding him with the most beautiful, sensual movement of her hips and Nikolai meeting every thrust. He loses himself in her, the closeness of her body, the softness of her skin, the intoxicating grip of her cunt.

He's not sure he's ever clung to her so tightly. They might

merge any second, their bodies giving up the fight to keep their atoms separate and allowing them to meld into one, even just this once. Finally, he's crying out, every single muscle clenching, from his head to his toes, fingertips dimpling her skin, and his nose tucked into the base of her throat. He sees stars, the vastness of the universe pumping in his blood, and he's buoyed by the certainty no one will ever hold a candle to the woman in his arms.

In all his days, he will never find someone like her again, but he refuses to be sad while his pet is sated and pliant in his arms, won't let thoughts of *sixteen Sundays* or fucking *Philadelphia* steal this joy from him, this completeness.

When he comes back to himself, when he pushes that relentless mantra from his mind, the welcome weight of her is in his lap, the solid, physical evidence that she's here with him, still. It releases him as though his strings have been cut. His body goes lax and conforms itself to her. Then he pulls her backward against the bed, still connected in the most intimate of ways, as he learns to breathe again.

After a few minutes of shared caresses, Corinne asks, "Should we go get cleaned up, sir?" She kisses his chest. "I know you have an early morning."

He sighs at the reminder, wanting nothing more than to stay in this moment forever. He kisses her forehead and squeezes her tight. "Yes, I suppose we should, though I'm comfortable enough to fall asleep right here."

They opt for a quick shower instead of their usual bath, if only in deference to the late hour. When they're both clean, he takes his time toweling her off, luxuriating in this ability to care for her, to pamper her in the simplest ways.

For as long as he has her.

When they go to bed, Corinne drops off before he does, her breathing evening out and mixing with the soft whoosh of the air conditioner. Nikolai lies awake, fingertips sketching idle patterns against her skin as the time limit he suddenly finds himself in repeats over and over and over on a loop.

He needs to make a list of things he wants them to do together before she leaves, places he wants to take her or events he'd like her to accompany him. He needs to call his realtor's office and see if they have anyone they can recommend in Philadelphia. He needs to ask Margot for her business plan for the expansion and offer any advice. He needs to find a free weekend when they can go away together, just him and his pet and an uninterrupted number of hours, so he can soak up every possible minute of her presence.

A glance at the clock informs him it's been two hours since they climbed into bed. If he needs anything right now, it's some damn sleep.

He comfortably spoons up to Corinne from behind, his larger frame wrapping around her as tightly as it can, like if he just holds her close enough, he can keep her with him for longer than four too-short months.

The moment he tries to let himself sleep, pain builds behind his ribs, a sharp push that frightens him. Because when it decides to make itself fully known, it could shatter him. It could alter his entire life, and he's not sure he's ready for that.

He doesn't look at it closely; experience has shown him that if he pushes himself before his feelings have fully worked themselves out, it will only end in unmitigated amounts of anxiety.

So instead, he kisses Corinne's neck, right above the clasp of her diamond collar, and lets himself drift, cocooned in the scent of her skin, the soft sounds of her breathing, and thoughts of Philadelphia firmly pushed from his mind.

please don't do this

NIKOLAI

THE NEXT FEW days fly by in a whirl of meetings and evening walks along the Seine, with nights spent tangled up in each other. Every moment is covered in a thin layer of existential crisis as whatever revelation he had that night works itself out. At the same time, he impatiently waits, holding the inevitable anxiety at bay by force of will alone.

What he does know is the dwindling time with Corinne makes his chest ache with grief, his heart rate spiking each time he thinks of that first Sunday without her. What is he meant to do with himself in the face of her absence? Wander around his too-big apartment? Cook himself dinner whenever he manages to leave the office at a decent hour? Sit alone at the counter where she used to sit and steal food with a sly grin while wearing his old Oxford shirt?

Would she find it weird if he tucked that shirt amongst the things he bought and keeps for her in his apartment so she doesn't have to bring them over every week? Shampoo and toothpaste and face creams and slippers. Trivial, everyday things that unknowingly settled his soul to see them in his apartment, and now...

He doesn't want to think about those things right now, not when it would rob him of enjoying every moment he *does* have with her, so instead, he holds her hand, walks through the Parisian twilight with her, and kisses her every chance he gets.

* * *

On Saturday afternoon, they leave Paris and drive an hour outside the city to the Chateau d'Aboville. The hills and vineyards are green and verdant in the summer sun as they cruise through the Loire Valley, their rented Aston Martin Vantage handling the curves with ease.

"Oh," Corinne breathes when Nikolai turns down the path of the venue. "I know you said 'chateau,' but I didn't realize how... grand it'd be."

Smiling, he glances at her from behind his sunglasses. "A chateau is, by definition, fairly grand, pet. I don't know if they make them any other way."

She smacks his arm playfully. "Haven't you ever been to a kink club that takes itself a little too seriously? They give it some grand name and isn't that grand at all?"

He laughs, slowing as they get closer to the entrance. "Of course I have. That's most of them. But this is France. It's usually the other way around. A mundane name for a grand building."

"*Touché, monsieur.*"

He maneuvers the car to the small line of vehicles in front of the stately entrance. "Any last-minute questions? Or requests?"

She thinks for a moment. "I just want to be your little possession tonight, sir. That's all."

For the last time is unspoken.

He ignores the pang in his chest. "Just a pretty little thing for me to show off, hm?"

She nods with a smile, but it's not as bright as usual.

The valet takes the car, and Nikolai grabs Corinne's hand as he leads them inside to check in. The chateau was built as the Belle Époque dream home of a famous perfumer 150 years ago. The interior is bright and sunny, with high ceilings and numerous doors thrown open to the summer sun, the grandiose nature of the building mellowed by the simple elegance of its more modern French decor.

Someone takes care of their bags as he checks them in, and they're already waiting in the room by the time he and Corinne make their way upstairs. The front desk also slipped him a note that his packages are waiting in the safe.

He follows Corinne into the suite, pleased the accommodations are as elegant as advertised. A cheese platter and a bottle of wine are laid out with a welcome note. A basket with blankets, snacks, and water bottles is also on the desk.

"An aftercare kit. That's thoughtful." She snags a couple of grapes from the cheese platter and pops them into her mouth.

"Mmm, yes, one of the perks of this type of event. You'll see most of your favorites in there, or you should, anyway." He walks over to her and takes a piece of cheese for himself before tilting her chin with his finger. "That's the last time you feed yourself until I say otherwise, alright?"

Nodding, she presses her lips together. "Yes, sir. I'm sorry." She wrinkles her nose. "I really do have a habit of doing that."

He tweaks her nose, then heads toward the bedroom. "I guess we'll need to come up with a consequence for you, hm?"

She steps behind him and wraps her arms around his waist. "Like what, sir?"

Nikolai hums in thought, reaching for his garment bag and dopp kit. "I'm not sure yet." He turns his head to look at her mischievously. "Be a good girl, and you won't have to worry about it, hm?" He turns in her arms and kisses her gently.

"Very well." Her eyes flit over the room, taking in the crown molding and intricate plaster ceilings. "We need something like this back home." She laughs nervously before stepping out of their embrace. "In Chicago, I mean."

Right. Chicago won't be her home much longer.

He clears his throat. "Oh?"

"A luxury BDSM experience." Her hand ghosts over the aftercare basket. "Catered to your every want. A place you can stay on-site for a full weekend event. Private suites available for monthly rent for sex workers or regulars." Her gaze is wistful when she turns back to him, but then she blinks, and it's gone. "Chicago doesn't have anything like this."

"Pet, I don't think the *United States* has anything like this."

She takes his hand. "Thank you for bringing me to such a special place."

Nikolai's heart constricts. "There's no one else I'd rather bring here."

Corinne looks away, and she clears her throat. "I'm going to freshen up."

"Okay. But first, would you like to see what you'll be wearing tonight?" He had everything made here in France. He stopped by the shop days ago to approve and pay and have them delivered straight to the chateau.

She laughs. "I thought I wasn't supposed to be wearing anything tonight."

"No *clothes*. But there's nothing in the rules about accessories."

"Well, alright, then." She sits in one of the armchairs and crosses her legs. "What *accessories* will I be wearing?"

He flashes her an excited grin and walks to the safe. He pulls out the boxes and sets them on the table beside her chair. Then he hands her the first one.

"These first, sweet thing."

"Sir," she says, and he gives her an encouraging nod. She opens it to find two matching tennis bracelets, the diamonds gleaming in the afternoon sunlight. She reaches out to touch them. "Oh, these are beautiful." A small smile tugs at her mouth. "And they match my day collar."

He smiles, quietly pleased. When he told her all those months ago that he enjoyed spoiling her, he may have downplayed how fulfilling it is to give gifts to the people in his life. It's less about flaunting his wealth and more about using his money to make the people he cares about happy.

If the last few days have taught him anything, it's that he cares for Corinne deeply.

"Of course," he murmurs, studying her face, committing every detail to memory before the clock runs out. He grabs the next two boxes, each slightly bigger than the first. "Now these."

One box holds a diamond hip harness that circles each thigh and trails up to meet another row of diamonds at the hips. The other encases a diamond bralette with crisscrossing straps to frame her bare breasts, and in the middle sits a large teardrop ruby to nestle between them.

"Indali mentioned a jeweler years ago, an artisan in Paris who does bespoke work." His heart is pounding. "I had them made just for you."

Corinne takes a deep breath, and her hand shakes as she traces the jewelry. "Sir," she whispers, her eyes never leaving the gifts. "Are these..." She clears her throat. "What stones are these?"

"Diamonds, sweet thing." He kisses her temple. "And a ruby, of course. Only the best for you."

Her eyes squeeze shut, and her face crumples. When she finally looks up at him, her gaze is shiny with unshed tears. "Why would you give me something like this?"

Nikolai's brows knit in surprise and confusion. "Why?

Because I want to." Kneeling before her, he traces his finger up her arm and stops when he reaches her day collar. "Because you deserve them." He splays his hand over her diamond collar before he cups her face in his hand, thumb brushing her full bottom lip. "Most importantly, though…" He presses a kiss to her mouth, gentle and sweet. "Because you're mine. My lovely, precious pet."

Now the tears fall. "But I'm not." She shakes her head. "I'm not yours, Nikolai."

His heart plummets to his stomach.

Corinne gestures around the room. "You pay me for my companionship, and we… play these games"—her hand falls to her collar—"where I belong to you. For a night." She smiles sadly. "For a trip. And then you go about your life, and I go about mine. Because that's the nature of this business. Because that's what we agreed to. 'Protocols and parameters.'" A shaky breath escapes her, pain still etched all over her face as her gaze falls to the jewelry. "Please don't do this to me when I'm not actually yours."

Sweat beads along his hairline, and his breath comes in short, sharp inhales as her words sink in.

The idea that she's not his, that she's never been his, is something he can no longer accept.

His lips part with a trembling breath, and he can't stop himself from asking the question he shouldn't ask. Not when she is moving on to a bigger and better life. Not when it breaks every fucking rule he's ever had.

But Nikolai Zaitsev is more of a selfish man than he'd like to admit.

"What if you were?"

the number one rule

CORINNE

CORINNE'S EYES widen with a gasp.

Surely he doesn't mean... No. No, he just told her this week that he's grateful he doesn't have to deal with a relationship.

"You don't want me the way I want you," she says, shaking her head.

"You'd be surprised."

She sniffles and huffs a laugh. "Would I?"

Sitting back on his heels, Nikolai stares at her, eyes roaming her face. "Yes, I think you might be. It's been an enlightening week."

Her heart pounds against her rib cage like a drum. "Are you going to make me guess?" she whispers.

Nikolai breathes deeply and closes his eyes, his shoulders trembling as he exhales. "No, I won't make you guess." He opens his eyes. "You know my reasons for choosing *this* type of relationship"—he squeezes her hands—"over the more... standard type of romantic partnership. And for a very long time, it was enough. No one could make me rethink my choice." He smiles at her, a little shaky around the edges.

"And then I met you," he continues, "and I think from the

very first night, all those reasons have slowly been melting away, all my worries have been settled and assuaged, just by you being exactly who you are. And I'm a fucking idiot without an ounce of emotional intelligence or self-awareness because it took until just now to realize how hard I'm falling for you."

Corinne should be happy. She should be. This is what she wants, isn't it?

But Nikolai Zaitsev is a passionate man, and this... this isn't passionate. This is... intellectualized. This is a billionaire CEO pivoting at a board meeting.

Is he just upset she's moving? Is it her reaction to his gift? Is he trying to placate her? Obviously, he cares for her, but this isn't anywhere near what she feels for him. And that's... fine. He can't help how he feels.

But it isn't enough.

"You don't have to pretend." She tries her best to smile as she stands. "I would rather you didn't, actually."

He falls back, and his mouth opens, then shuts again. "I'm not pretending," he says, his voice quiet and soft, as he stares up at her from the plush carpet. "I wouldn't. Not about something like this."

He has never lied to her. Not once. She has no reason to believe he's lying now. But all she can think about is how she's loved too hard in the past, only to be met with a mediocre facsimile of love in return. And she won't do that to herself again.

"Nikolai, I—" She takes a shaky breath. "There are rules I adhere to whenever I am with you. We negotiated and agreed to them, and I follow them like I'm supposed to. But there is one rule. An unspoken one. A rigid and necessary boundary in place to keep a dynamic like this in its professional box." She grips the sides of her dress to stop her hands from trembling. "Do you know what that is?"

He nods emphatically. "No feelings. It's the number one rule." He laughs ruefully. "I've never broken it before. Never even come close."

"Me either. Not once." She lets go of her dress and touches his cheek. "But I've been breaking that rule for you." Her voice turns to a whisper. "For longer than I should admit. And that is... a terrifying thing to share. And if I hadn't broken down over what I'm guessing is millions of dollars worth of diamonds..." She shrugs. "I probably never would have. I would've gone to Philly, and you would've eventually moved on with your life."

His brow furrows. "I don't know about all that, p—" The title catches on his tongue.

"You don't?"

The corner of his mouth crooks into a half smile. "You're not the kind of woman one gets over, Corinne. Not as easily as you're making it sound."

She wants to believe that, but how can she when he told her less than a week ago that what they have is all he wanted?

Corinne bends down and kisses his forehead. "It's been quite a week for me." Everything she's been bottling up these last few days is threatening to explode, and she needs space to let it out. "I haven't been sleeping well. So I could use some time to come down. Maybe take a shower and have a nap. And maybe you could use some time to think about these new feelings. And what they mean for both of us."

The last word is heavy on her tongue—it holds new meaning now.

He searches her face for a long moment, eyes roving over every inch until at last, he nods and stands. "Of course. Take your time." He pulls one of the room keys from his pocket and lays it on the desk. "I'll be back in a little while." He hesitates before he gently presses a kiss to her forehead.

Then he crosses the room and leaves her alone in the suite.

Her gaze falls to the diamonds resting against periwinkle velvet, and her hand trembles as she touches the dazzling jewels. It's no secret Nikolai is a billionaire, and he's spent hundreds of thousands of dollars on her in the last six months (and on her day collar alone). But these are... another level. Why would he give such a thing to a woman he pays for companionship and sex?

If she called up Elijah and told him what she's done, he'd chew her out for turning down *bespoke diamonds, Corinne, what is wrong with you?!*

And as much as she loves her darling friend, that's not what she needs right now.

Instead, Corinne takes a long hot shower. As soon as the scorching water touches her skin, a sob wrenches from her chest. Instead of pushing it down, she allows herself the big cry she's been holding in since she told him about Philadelphia. And once there's not a single tear left to shed, she gets out and dries off.

When she opens her suitcase, she reaches for something to sleep in and brushes one of his t-shirts that somehow made it in with her things. Taking a deep breath, she slips it on before shimmying into a pair of underwear and crawling into bed.

He hasn't worn it yet, but it still smells like his detergent, like his apartment, like *him*. No matter what he decides or how his heart lands, she just wants to enjoy this nearness to him.

She tries her hardest to sleep, but it's a slippery, elusive thing. After forty minutes of tossing and turning, she grabs her phone. There is a message from her mom.

> Hope you have fun in the countryside this week, Coco. Love you!

She smiles, tears stinging her eyes. It's late morning in Chicago, and without a moment's hesitation, she calls her.

"Hey, Coco," Violet says. "You didn't have to call; I'm sure you're busy."

"Mom." Damn, she's already crying again. "I fucked up."

"Baby, what happened? Are you in trouble? Do I need to call the embassy?"

It's such a *mom* question that she laughs. "No, I'm not in trouble with foreign officials. Nor have I been taken, before you go all Liam Neeson on me."

"Okay, because I did renew my passport just in case."

Corinne laughs again. "I am almost thirty years old."

"And I would still come and get you! Do I need to come get you?"

"No." She fiddles with the edge of the sheet. "I'm in love with Nikolai."

"Oh, honey. Don't beat yourself up over it. It happens in this type of work. How are you doing? Does he know?"

"Kind of? He knows I have feelings for him. And he said he has feelings for me, too, but just this week he told me he's happy with our client-escort relationship. That it's so much better than romance. And it was obvious today that he either just now realized his feelings or was just saying it to make me feel better. Or because he's upset about Philadelphia. And I don't know which way is up."

"Is that why you decided to move to Philly in the middle of your trip? Because of this?"

"Yes?" It's embarrassing to admit. She should've said yes beforehand. She should've made the bold move for her career instead of letting a man force her hand. "It seemed like the best way to end this thing and get away."

"Running away almost always feels easy, honey. It's pure survival instinct."

Fuck.

"Are you happy with your decision?" Violet asks.

She muffles a sob. "No. I don't want to leave you or Elijah or…" She exhales loudly. "Him. But I feel like I should be happy with it. I should be jumping for joy at such an amazing opportunity. To put my own mark on this field."

"I'm sure there are ways to do that that don't involve moving away from everyone you love."

"Yeah?"

Her mom laughs. "Yes, Coco. You've got your whole life ahead of you." She's quiet for a moment. "Where is he now?"

"I asked him to leave to think about things and to give me space because I'm exhausted from realizing I'm in love and then, you know, running away from it, as you so aptly put it."

"In my experience, even the brainy ones have thick skulls. I bet time to think is exactly what he needs. You rocked his little world, and now he needs time to come to terms with it."

Corinne huffs a laugh. "Okay, Mama."

"I'll keep the phone close by in case you need me."

"Okay, love you."

"I love you, too."

Corinne snuggles deeper into bed and tries to take her mom's encouragement to heart. Maybe her ridiculous and beloved Sir just needs some time to figure himself out.

It doesn't fully soothe the anxiety in her belly, but it is, thankfully, enough to help her fall asleep.

f***ing woo her

NIKOLAI GOES DOWNSTAIRS. The party will start soon, and there's a line of naked submissives in the lobby, waiting for their training to begin before the formal dinner. This event is more formal than Indali's parties back home and requires the submissives to train to learn the chateau's protocols.

He should be dropping Corinne off to join them. He should be enjoying their double takes at her diamonds, at how beautiful she looks at the end of his leash. Instead, she's upstairs crying, and he's...

Well, he's an idiot.

He roams the chateau until he comes across a quiet parlor tucked away on the western side, lined with French windows providing a gorgeous golden-hour view. The room is thankfully empty, and he settles in one of the plush club chairs arranged throughout, his gaze falling to the sprawling gardens.

He inhales. He exhales.

It's been eight years since his relationship with Olivia. It's been eight years and twice as many escorts, and it worked so well for him that he never considered anything more. It was pleasurable and easy, and most of all, safe.

He can admit now how traumatized he was after he came home and found Olivia had left him without a word. He'd fallen hard and fast, put his entire heart on the line, but that's just who he is. Nikolai has never done anything by half measures, and if he's going to fall for someone, of course it will be with his entire being.

Which is precisely why he hasn't let himself. Or at least that's what he thought. But then Corinne came along.

Corinne, who is as fascinating as she is stunning. Charming and elegant, with a sharp mind and a gorgeous heart. A precious pet who submits so wholly, so beautifully. A business-woman who loves what she does and is damn good at it, and he respects her for it immensely. Clearly, Margot sees it, too, or she wouldn't have offered Corinne the position in Philadelphia.

Nikolai will support and encourage Corinne however he can, but the thought of losing his pet... And the way she looked at him in that hotel room, like she couldn't possibly believe his realization was true. It's clawing at his heart, and he doesn't know what he's supposed to do to fix any of it.

He taps his thigh. Before panic overwhelms him, he does what he always does when everything feels impossible.

He calls Indali.

The phone rings several times, and he mentally counts the hours to make sure he isn't calling her at a terrible time.

Damn it, Indali, pick up.

"If my math is right, Kolyenka, you should be at your chateau of sin right now, so I can't think of a single, solitary reason you'd be calling me."

He laughs at her imperious tone. "Dali, your math is right, but my timing is all wrong, and I'm about to have an anxiety spiral in a chateau parlor room. Do you have some time?"

"Well, fuck, darling." The rustling of papers comes through the line. "Of course I do."

He sighs and stands before pacing the room, needing to ease the nervous energy in his body. "I have feelings for Corinne. Romantic ones."

"Kolya!"

"And she feels the same. In fact, she told me first, and I sort of... confessed in response."

"Oh boy. Okay. What happened?"

He tells Indali about how perfect everything has been with Corinne, at least until she told him about Philadelphia, and how the sudden possibility of not having her in his life gutted him. How it was even harder after being together for days in France. How it took her getting upset over endless strings of diamonds for him to fully recognize that maybe there is a reason everything has been so perfect with this particular woman.

"Dali, it's the *one* rule. No feelings. It's a business arrangement. And you know I don't *do* romance anymore. But when I think of her leaving, of not seeing her again..." His hand comes to rest over the heart squeezing painfully in his chest. "It's like I can't breathe."

"Mm, I see." Ice clinks in a glass. Is he driving her to drink? "Tell me. How many business associates do you shower in millions of dollars' worth of diamonds?"

"Is that fair?" He huffs. "You know the only other *business associate* I've had like this for a significant length of time is Elijah, and we didn't have nearly the same level of..." Of what? Feelings? He rolls his eyes at himself, catching the defensive deflection for what it is. "None, okay. I've never bought any associate, of any kind, gifts like that."

"So you thought, 'let me spend all this money on a frivolous gift'—because, Kolyenka, darling, your pet has never seen money like that in her life, and if she won that amount in the lottery, she'd probably buy a nice apartment and pay off her student loans like a normal person. But you thought, 'let me spend all this money on a woman who is nothing more than a business associate to me.'" She laughs. "A totally normal, professional, nonromantic thing to do."

Nikolai groans and drags his hand down his face. "I *know*. I get it. It's fucking absurd from the outside, but it made complete sense at the time. She's precious to me, Indali." His voice is quiet now, raspy. "I really did think it was the dynamic that made me feel that way because it's always been so easy with Corinne. It's not like I've got great experience to measure against, after all. And I wanted to give her something beautiful made especially for her. I wanted to show her off tonight, I—" He sighs and hangs his head. "If I lead with the wealth, they're not using me for it."

"Has she ever made you think she's like that?"

He scoffs at the very idea. "Of course not. She *isn't*." He knows that like he knows his own name. "But it's not like I made the decision after I met her. I've been this way since Olivia. I think they call it a trauma response."

"Ooh, I love it when a man talks therapy to me."

He chuckles despite himself, almost reluctant to let her pull him out of his spiral. "Dali, what am I going to do? How the fuck do romantic relationships work when they're healthy? It's been so long, I can't trust myself to know."

"Well, I'm hardly the model of happy, healthy relationships, but maybe this will help you listen to your own damn gut. Why do you think you can't breathe at the thought of not seeing her again? And before you answer me immediately, stop and take a second to actually think about it."

His mouth is already open to respond, but he closes it. That unnamed feeling that's been banging against the walls of his heart since she told him she's leaving roars to life. His immediate instinct is to panic, to shove it away, but for once, he just lets it happen.

He lets himself feel it.

Nikolai grips the back of the nearest chair and lowers himself gently. "Oh, fuck." He blinks. "I'm in love with her, aren't I?"

"Mmhmm," Indali singsongs, positively gleeful, and he wants to both kill her and kiss her. "And how does that revelation affect everything you've just told me? How does it affect *her*?"

"Well, the diamonds are certainly not the little I-think-I'll-spoil-her gesture I thought they were. Christ." He closes his eyes and slumps in his chair, voices of the party starting elsewhere filtering back in as his brain refocuses. "I need to tell her. She deserves to know."

"She sure does. But—and I'm only saying this because obviously you haven't been thinking things through where your new love is concerned—you need a plan. About your future, about Philadelphia. Don't just tell her you love her and expect it to just all work out. If you're committed to her, show her."

"Okay. Okay, yes, a plan." His confidence is growing; he's good at plans. "*Spasibo*," he says, thanking her, inordinately grateful for her in this moment. "I'll let you go. *Ya tebya obozhayu.*"

"*Da*, I love you, too. Oh, and Kolyenka? Do something nice, yeah? Something for *her*. Fucking woo her."

Nikolai hangs up with a chuckle, his mind already working.

First, a plan. Then, wooing.

He pulls up his notes app to get started. His realtor gave him a contact in Philadelphia. He'll need to call them to find a few places and set up a time for them to speak with Corinne. She should at least pick out her own place, even if he's buying it for her. And he can have his assistant look into moving companies to take that stress off her plate.

He'll need to speak with the board of trustees about lessening his presence in Chicago. Working remotely would allow him to see her as much as possible while continuing his duties. Maybe they can open a small office in Philadelphia; having a presence on the East Coast wouldn't hurt. And of course, he can fly her back to Chicago as much as she wants.

The thing he's most excited about is just the ability to talk to her whenever he wants. Texts throughout the day, phone calls after work. They could cook dinner on the phone and watch movies and text through them. Send silly videos and memes to each other and vent about demanding clients when they get home, shoes clunking by the door and coats rustling over the line. He could call her on Sundays, always Sundays, maybe after church, and they could set up their week together, make sure to schedule time with each other, even as far apart as they are.

Fuck, he wants it. He's never wanted anything more. They'll figure out the long-distance thing, and who knows? Maybe someday she'll come back to Chicago, or he'll move to Philadelphia and travel back to Chicago only when necessary.

But maybe they should figure it out *together* before he gets too ahead of himself.

Corinne didn't believe him earlier, and why would she? His declaration was less fireworks and skywriting than something like that should be, and it was certainly less than she *deserves*.

With a deep, fortifying breath, Nikolai leaves the parlor and heads to the concierge desk. The party has started now; the lights have been lowered, and sultry music with heavy bass plays throughout the first floor. And as much as Nikolai wishes he and Corinne could enjoy tonight's event, there's something much more important he must do.

"Good evening," he says to the woman behind the desk. "I'm wondering if you could help me with something."

yours

CORINNE

CORINNE ISN'T sure how long she sleeps, but by the time a door latching wakes her up, the room is bathed in purples and oranges from the setting summer sun.

Nikolai walks over to his suitcase, movements slow and careful, clearly trying not to wake her. He grabs a pair of jeans and a short-sleeved button-down before heading toward the bathroom.

"Hi," she murmurs.

He stops and faces her. "Hello. I, uh." He rubs at his jaw, and his beard rasps audibly against his palm. "If you're feeling up to it, or want to, I have something I'd like to do for you."

She turns on the light and blinks until her eyes adjust. She gestures toward herself—messy hair, puffy eyes, his t-shirt, which has slipped off one shoulder—with a self-deprecating grin. "I'm a bit of a mess."

He looks at her like she's the eighth wonder of the world. "You're lovely. I don't get to see you sleepy and rumpled as often as I'd like. But you have time if you want to change. I need to shower."

As often as I'd like.

Oh, the way the tightly coiled worry in her gut loosens with one single statement, with one spark of hope.

She nods. "I can change."

"Okay, great. I'm going to—" He gestures toward the bathroom. "I'll be out in a few."

"Okay." She dislikes how stiff and awkward things are, but she hopes whatever they're about to do will break the ice.

She puts on a sundress, not even worrying about a bra, not while they're in this place. The dinner must be happening now, and while she's sorry to be missing it, she wouldn't be up for such a thing tonight.

After brushing her hair, she sits on the bed and waits for him to finish so she can brush her teeth. Usually, she'd just go inside while he's in the shower, but maybe that would be too intimate now.

Fuck, she hates this so much.

He comes out a few minutes later, wisps of steam trailing behind him. His skin is still damp, and the thin cotton of his sky-blue shirt sticks to his defined chest.

His gaze roams over her. "You're so beautiful, Corinne," he says, stopping a few feet away. He doesn't crowd into her space like he usually would. "Are you ready? Or do you need a few?"

"Just a few."

When she returns, he's already in his shoes and waiting for her by the door. She slips into a pair of sandals and joins him. "Ready."

He holds out his hand.

Her eyes dart between his face and his hand, hope blossoming in her heart before she takes it.

Nikolai smiles at her and leads her into the hall and toward the stairs. Music is playing now, and voices carry from somewhere in the chateau. She'd be serving him if things hadn't gone awry, bringing him food and kneeling at his feet, her leash held loosely in his gloved hand.

"Do you mind walking for a few minutes?" he asks, pulling her from her thoughts. "I promise it won't be long."

"No, I don't mind."

A warm breeze greets them when they step outside. They walk around the chateau as the sun continues its descent, past the tidy strip of lawn onto a winding footpath nestled between the trees. The farther they continue, the quieter things become, the chateau party fading and leaving them with nothing but rustling leaves and the patter of their footsteps.

Nikolai stops and faces her once they spot a clearing ahead. "Will you close your eyes? Just for a few steps, I promise."

She tilts her head but nods. "Okay." She grips his hand tighter, allowing him to guide her the rest of the way.

"Alright, beautiful," he murmurs. "Go ahead and open."

They're standing in a meadow of wildflowers, a sea of blues and pinks and purples and whites surrounding them. In the center sits a large blanket, a wicker basket, and a bottle of champagne in a bucket of ice. Lanterns with candles encircle the blanket, flames dancing in the dimming sunlight.

She'd jokingly mentioned this months ago, soaking with him in his bathtub after one of their first intense scenes. "You remembered," she says, her hand coming to her chest and tears springing to her eyes.

"I remembered," he echoes, and helps her sit on the blanket.

"This is... incredible. You were busy while I was napping."

His grin is almost boyish as he settles next to her, and it's the cutest thing she's ever seen. "Yes, well. I'm nothing if not well equipped to execute a plan."

"It's that CEO prowess," she says, trying to lighten the tension.

He fiddles with his watchband, nerves evident in every rotation and click of the finely wrought links. "I didn't just set up a picnic while you napped." He stares at his knees and takes a deep, slow breath before looking up. "The picnic was actually the thing I spent the least time on. Most of it I spent thinking, as you asked."

She nods, waiting for him to continue.

"What you said before, about pretending. I have never pretended with you. Corinne, I've never felt this way about anyone. I think about you all the time, wishing I could see you or talk to you. I want to call you and hear about your day, hear about work, hear about your fucking grocery run. I want to hear the sound of you kicking your heels off by the door. I want to know which cabinet you're opening by the groan of the hinges and think, 'Oh, that's the cupboard with the stemware; it was that kind of day.'"

He kneels, his head bowed as he reaches for her hands. "I want to help you find a place in Philadelphia. And I want to figure out long distance and how to build something when we're far apart. I want to come visit and end up with too many bottles of cologne because I never remember to grab it from either house before I leave. I want us to figure out how often we can see each other and make this work regardless of who lives where."

He looks up, eyes bright with tears. "I want to share your Sundays, but also your Mondays and your Tuesdays and all the rest of them, too. I want to learn how to love you like you need and spend every second of every day practicing until I perfect it." He squeezes her hands. "Because, Corinne, I have clearly been loving you badly if you thought I was pretending."

Happiness and relief overwhelm her, blooming like the field of wildflowers around them. She inhales shakily. "You love me?"

Chuckling, Nikolai cups her face in his hands. "As if it is

possible to know you and not love you, pet. Yes, I love you, and I will keep loving you as long as you let me."

A larger smile has never crossed her face as she throws her arms around his neck and squeezes him tightly. "I love you so much, Nikolai." She pulls back to look him over, so full of joy she can scarcely breathe. "So much."

"Kolya," he whispers. "When it's just us, outside of Sir and Pet, you can call me Kolya, if you'd like."

"Kolya," she exhales, testing it on her tongue, cherishing this new intimacy. "Looks like we both broke the rules, huh? I fell in love with my client, and you fell in love, period." She laughs and shoves him playfully. "I can't believe you love me!"

He snags her around the waist and pulls her into his lap. "Of course I do! Have you met yourself?"

"Yes, but I've also met you, Mr. I-Don't-Want-a-Relation-ship. Which, I will remind you"—she wags her finger—"you just told me this week."

"I was blind and perhaps a little stupid, as Indali was happy to reveal when I called her, panicking." He rolls his eyes dramatically. "I'm out of practice! It took me a little while to catch up to my own feelings."

She strokes his beard with the back of her hand. "I could only go by what you told me, Kolya."

He hums in acknowledgment. "I know, and I'm sorry." He brushes his thumb over her bottom lip. "I was following the rules so hard I almost missed the signs."

She presses her forehead against his. "Where do we go from here?"

"Well, there's something I need to do first, and then we can figure all that out." He sets her back on the blanket and snags the picnic basket. When he opens it, he pulls out a pomegranate and a paring knife.

Using the blade, he slices a circle around the top of the fruit.

"Do you remember the night I asked you to go to the first High Protocol party?"

She catches her lip between her teeth. "Yes, sir." It was the same night they talked about coming to France. There was pomegranate chicken and jokes about Hades ensnaring Persephone.

"What we do"—he nods toward the chateau—"is its own sort of underworld, don't you think?"

"Yes, sir."

He puts down the knife and pries off the top of the fruit. "And like our king of the underworld, I want nothing more than the dazzling, warm goddess before me..." He looks up with a soft smile before cutting the pomegranate along each ridge. "To choose to be by my side." He gently pulls the fruit open, and four sections, ripe with bloodred seeds, splay in the palm of his hand. "Not just as my pet. Not just for a night." He takes a couple of seeds and holds them to her lips. "But as my partner and my love, every night."

Corinne nibbles the seeds from his fingertips before setting the rest of the fruit aside and kissing him soundly. "Yours," she whispers. "Really and truly."

"Really and truly, rybka moya."

She doesn't want to break this spell. But there's one more thing to ask, one more worry to squash. "Kolya, when we get back to Chicago, I will still be having sex for a living..." She's scared as hell, but not knowing would be worse. She can't relive Will all over again. "I need to know you will be okay with that. I need you to think about what it was like the night you saw me with Oscar and imagine what that reality will look like."

Nikolai traces gentle patterns on her arms. "Do you remember what my biggest problem was that night? What bothered me the most?"

"I was in your color." Which she did because she was three

days into her realization of her feelings toward him, and she wanted to feel like she belonged to him. Even just for one night.

"You deliberately went out looking like mine when you weren't." He taps her nose. "What will the difference be if we're actually together?"

She can't help but smile. "I will be yours."

"Exactly," he murmurs, a single finger running beneath the diamonds of her day collar. "You'll be mine, and that makes all the difference. And as far as Philadelphia goes, even if you weren't stopping that side of the business, it wouldn't bother me. I may not be the *most* emotionally aware person, but I know that for certain."

God, Corinne loves him so much.

She takes a deep breath, both in relief and in preparation. Because if they're being honest, there's one last thing to say.

"What if I don't want to go to Philadelphia?"

mine

NIKOLAI

NIKOLAI'S EYES GO WIDE. "But I thought… it's such a huge opportunity? I thought you were excited?"

"I've known about it for months," she says. "I kept going back and forth. It's a *fantastic* opportunity, but I wasn't sure I wanted to leave Chicago. And… and I hated the thought of leaving *you*." She shakes her head. "And I would tell myself, 'That doesn't matter; he's just my client. I can't think like that.' And I'd push it away to deal with later."

She sighs before continuing. "Then Margot asked for an answer by the time I got back from France. And Tuesday night, in the middle of dinner with Joséphine, I realized I was in love with you, and I knew, well, at least I *thought,* you didn't feel the same. And I had to get *out.* I had to get away from you."

"Oh, pet," he breathes, grabbing her hands and kissing her cheeks. "If you want to go to Philadelphia, go. Please don't let me stop you. We'll navigate the long-distance thing. I'll buy you an apartment. Fuck, Corinne, I'll even follow if you want. But if you still want to stay in Chicago, then stay."

"You would buy me an apartment?"

He scoffs. "Of course, I would. My realtor put me in contact with someone in Philadelphia. I called her tonight to get information for you, and she said we can meet with her when we get back to Chicago."

Her gaze softens. "The fact you would follow me, Kolya. That you'd buy me an apartment... I can't tell you how much that means to me. I am so lucky."

"I'm the lucky one," he says with a shake of his head. "I just want you to follow your dreams without anything holding you back."

"Philadelphia was never my *dream*. You know, I talked to my mom when you left, and she told me I was running away. And she was right. But she also told me months ago that I should be where I'm happiest. And, sir, that's with you."

Nikolai gives her the sweetest, most loving kiss. Looking back, he can't believe he didn't see the signs, that he didn't realize this incredible woman is the love of his life. "And do you have a dream, sweet pet? Or will you let me spoil you so rotten you'll never work another day in your life?"

She laughs. "I think you and I both know I would get bored. Even if I was heartbroken, the job in Philly did excite me. Something new, something meaty to sink my teeth into. I've wanted to start my own business for a long time and make something of my own." She looks toward the chateau hidden behind the trees. "If I'm going to dream big... you know, Chicago doesn't have any place like this."

The corners of his mouth hook into a knowing smile. "We don't. And I might know of an investor or two. There's a man in cybersecurity who, rumor has it, is into that sort of stuff."

Her brows arch. "Is that so?"

"Mmhmm. And his friend, Indali? Her family owns about a dozen boutique hotels in Chicago. She might know a thing or two about the hospitality side of things."

Corinne launches herself into his arms. "You are wonderful, and I love you so much."

"I love you." And he wants nothing more than to show her just how much.

So Nikolai kisses her. He kisses her and kisses her, taking his time to worship her beautiful body. He presses his lips to her mouth, her eyes, her nose, the long column of her throat, the delicate sweeps of her collarbones, and the points of her shoulders. He kisses down her arm, the bend of her elbow, and pauses to breathe in the comforting scent of her bodywash. He kisses the inside of her wrist, the center of her palm, and the tip of every finger, pressing his love into her skin, pledging his devotion.

"God, pet," he breathes, pushing his hands up under her dress and gripping her waist tightly. He doesn't have anything else to say, nothing beyond expressing gratitude and amazement for the gift that is the incredible woman in his lap, loving him.

When she pulls her dress overhead, she's only in her lacy underwear, and her bare breasts make him groan. He sucks each nipple into his mouth, tugging on the barbells with his teeth, letting his confined cock grind against her as she moans in pleasure.

"Sir, I need you."

"Eager little thing," he croons sweetly. He lays her on the blanket and undresses himself before slipping off her panties and getting on top of her. His fingers skim her chest, her abdomen, dipping to where she's already wet for him. "Always so eager for me." He is awed, enraptured; he's under her spell, and he'll stay here forever, happily.

"How could I not be?"

He slides his cock along the seam of her, getting it nice and slick, his girl whimpering and whining as he rubs against her clit.

"*Please.*"

He chuckles. "How gorgeous you are when you need me this badly, pet." She's entrancing like this—moonlight on her skin, her hair; her body quivering with want.

"Sir," she gasps breathlessly. "Don't tease me."

"Okay, love, I won't. I'll be sweet tonight, darling, don't worry." Then he finally slips inside her.

"Oh," she groans, her brow furrowing as he bottoms out and then pulls back to thrust inside her. Corinne wraps around him, her hips meeting his in a slow, syrupy rhythm.

They've done this countless times, but it's different now. She's *his*, always, and he wants to get lost in her forever—the flutter of her eyes when he pushes in deep, her sweet taste when he kisses her, how she looks at him, so full of love his chest aches.

Her desperate little gasps when she's close.

"Can I come, please?" Her voice is breathless.

"Yeah, sweet thing, go ahead. I want to watch you."

Pleasure overtakes her, and her eyes squeeze shut, her mouth falling open on a moan. He's never seen a more beautiful sight.

"Sir," she whimpers, nuzzling her face to his neck.

"I know, baby, I know." Whenever she comes with his cock buried inside her, it's a battle not to come immediately, her cunt wet and slick and tight, making him hold on for dear life every time.

"Thank you." Her gaze is soft and hooded, and as she kisses him, she grinds against him, slow and dirty.

"Fuck." Will it always feel like this? Like he'll die without her in his arms, without being inside her? "How can I say no to you, huh? Impossible."

She grins. "God, I want you inside me all the time."

"Maybe I can work from home sometimes, hm? You can sit on my lap and keep my cock warm all day. This sweet little cunt wrapped around me tight." He grabs her hip and gives a hard thrust. "A perfect fit."

Corinne groans, bucking against him. "Please, sir. Want to be full, want to feel good."

"Made for it, aren't you, baby?" Sweat is pooling in the hollow of her throat, and he can't help but lick it up. "My pretty pet, made to be right here on my cock, all day, nothing else to do."

"Yeah, yeah, fuck. Oh my God."

He's winding her up, bringing her with him on the steady climb to climax. His rhythm is almost compromised, though— her clenching and grinding melting his damn brain. Her moans turn so frantic that he knows what she's about to ask before she opens her mouth.

"Sir, please let me come," she begs quickly, her brows pinching as she tries to hold herself together.

"Yeah? Again?" His own orgasm is building in the pit of his stomach, the base of his spine. "Go ahead; be a good girl and come for me."

Her body shudders, holding on to him as she rides it out, and God, the grip of her is enough to send him over.

"You want it?" he grits out. "I'm so close, baby. You feel so good."

"Yes," she moans, her hair splayed beneath her, her breasts bouncing with each thrust. "Please come inside me. Want it so bad."

"Oh, *fuck*." His climax is yanked out of him, every nerve in his body lighting up all at once. All he can see is her—her beloved face, his beautiful pet. "I love you," he breathes, over and over and over.

When he finally comes down, he kisses her lips softly. "Hello, my love."

"Hi." God, her smile is breathtaking. "I will never tire of hearing that."

He nuzzles her. "Then I'll never stop saying it."

"Better than your first time?"

He laughs, satisfied and breathless. "There's no competition, love. Not even a little." He strokes his finger along her cheek. "French countryside live up to your expectations?"

"Even better since it came with a very lovely surprise."

Then her stomach gurgles loudly.

They both laugh, and Nikolai sits up. "Why am I not surprised my pet is hungry?"

"To be fair, we haven't really eaten since breakfast."

He gets back into his underwear and gives her her pair before he grabs the basket. "Well, thankfully, I brought sustenance." He nods toward the bucket. "Open that champagne for us, sweet thing."

Corinne shimmies into her panties and snags the bucket. She pops the bottle with ease as he takes out sandwiches and the pomegranate from earlier, as well as berries and a mini chocolate tart.

"Wow, look at all this," she says, pouring a glass and handing it to him. "For us to share so you can feed me, sir."

"Good girl." He lets her sip some of the champagne before taking a drink himself. "The chateau was very accommodating when I told them I needed help setting up a romantic picnic for my pet."

"I'm sorry we missed the party tonight. I know we were both looking forward to it."

He shrugs. "It's just a party, pet. Your happiness is a thousand times more important than that." He kisses her forehead.

"There will be others, and we'll go all out. And you can wear your diamonds, if you want them."

"Of course I want them, Kolya." She sighs and crawls into his lap. "I've never received something so beautiful. It was just... too much when—"

"I know. I know, Indali set me straight." He chuckles. "Not my brightest moment."

"I look forward to my sir showing me off while I'm bejeweled in the gorgeous diamonds he gave me. With both my collars. And my leash." She smiles sweetly. "Marked as yours in every way."

He grumbles, deep in his chest, so full of love for this woman that he's fit to burst. "Yes," he says. "*Mine.*"

And he'll be the luckiest man alive to be able to prove that to her every single day.

TWO YEARS LATER

"I'M SORRY TO INTERRUPT, but Nikolai's looking for you."

Corinne is speaking with a guest in the front lobby, and when she turns, Margot is standing behind her in a sexy gold pantsuit with a forest green bustier.

"We'll chat more tomorrow," Corinne tells the man with a smile.

She approaches Margot. "Did he send you to fetch me, or are you heading out?"

"I'm heading out, but Elijah and Indali are arguing, and your fiancé looks like he's about to murder someone."

Corinne laughs. "I'm sure he's just fine." She gives her friend a big hug. "Thank you for coming."

"Honey, you killed it. I've never seen a place like this. You're changing the damn game."

Corinne has spent the last two years working to open *L'Ani-malerie.* It took months just to find the perfect location, but they finally stumbled across an old Gilded Age mansion at the edge of the Prairie Avenue district that needed a lot of work and was priced to match. And with Kolya's money, Indali's hospitality expertise, Margot's extensive client list, and Corinne's vision, they turned a battered old house into a luxurious BDSM resort and club that's booked for the next six months.

"I couldn't have done it without you. Even if it meant not going to Philly."

Margot shrugs. "We're doing just fine in that regard. My friend is killing it over there." She squeezes Corinne's shoulder. "Good night, Corinne. I hope your grand opening weekend is a success."

"Thank you, Margot. Good night!"

The grand opening is an entire weekend affair. Guests arrived this evening for a formal party where play is allowed, but the emphasis is on socializing. Tomorrow, things will really heat up, with various activities during the day, ending with a strict High Protocol dinner and play party. And they'll say farewell with a grand brunch on Sunday.

The weekend is sold out, so she's been running around all night—playing hostess, making small talk with guests, directing staff to handle the minor problems that arise.

She waltzes through L'Animalerie in a sheer, heavily beaded dark red sheath gown, with layers of tulle falling from the hips in an open overskirt. Her diamond and leather collars are fastened around her neck, her hair is up in an elegant chignon, and she's wearing the Zaitsev ruby earrings. She enters the grand ballroom, nodding to the bouncer, and scans the crowd for Kolya.

The ballroom is the main event area, with play spaces set along two walls. When they renovated, she wanted to keep the magic of the original house; they restored as much of the beautiful woodwork and plaster as they could but filled the space with chic, luxe furnishings in rich colors and modern decor that works seamlessly with the history around them. And, of course, each room has an animal motif or focal point, making it the grandest, most luxurious *pet store* you've ever seen.

It's getting late, just another hour left of the party, and she's starting to feel every hour of the busy week and even busier day. She's stifling a yawn behind her hand when she catches Kolya crossing the room to find her, looking as gorgeous as ever in his perfectly fitted tuxedo.

Relief is written all over his face.

She grins. "Needed to escape the children?"

"Indali and Elijah are worse than an old married couple," he says with a sigh.

"Maybe they should just get married already." Elijah and his gentleman broke things off last year, and Indali and Elijah have always had some... strange tension between them. Corinne has hoped their two best friends might hit it off, but they're too busy bickering for that to happen anytime soon.

"I can't decide if it'd be better or worse."

"I vote better because they can put that energy into something productive, if you know what I mean."

"I know what you mean." Kolya settles her hand in the crook of his elbow and walks her toward the office. "How are you, pet?"

"Well, you already caught me midyawn, but..." Her eyes sweep the room, taking in the space, the music, the guests. "It turned out so well." She looks at him. "Better than I imagined."

He beams at her, pride shining in his gaze. "You did all this, pet. You worked so hard, and I am so proud of you." He gives her a deep, heady kiss that makes her lightheaded. "With that said, I think it's time to enjoy a little relaxation." He pulls her into her office, where her leash and diamond harnesses are lying on her desk.

"Oh. You don't think it's too early to quit? It's the first night."

The leash holds more meaning now than when he first put it on her two years ago. Corinne is in boss mode when they're here, which means being available to staff who need assistance. But they all know a leashed Corinne is an off-duty Corinne, and she's to be left undisturbed unless they want to catch Nikolai's ire.

"You have been working nonstop for months on this, my love." He cups her face with his other hand. "You have an hour left. Enjoy your own party and take a well-needed break. You can start again at dawn if you absolutely must." He kisses her forehead, and his voice gentles. "Let me take care of you, little thing."

"Alright." She sighs in surrender. "If you say so."

Kolya nuzzles her nose, a very quiet "*thank you*" passing his lips. Then he helps her out of her gown and underwear and into all her shimmering diamonds. When he finishes, he clasps the leash to her leather collar. He looks her over, appreciation evident in his eyes. "Have I told you yet tonight just how stunning you are?"

"Mm, once or twice, sir. You look pretty handsome yourself, you know." She rakes her fingers through his hair. It's streaked with a bit of gray these days, making him even more distinguished.

He shakes his head. "You have me beat by miles. Now"—he steps back—"come along, pet." He starts toward the main room, letting her leash hang loosely between them.

As Corinne follows him back into the ballroom, guests turn to watch their entrance. She loves walking through this space as his spoiled girl, his pampered pet, naked except for the diamonds draped along her body. Her staff jokingly call her the ringleader, and she is most of the time, but now, she is just his. And she loves it so much.

Kolya snags a thick cushion and leads her to an oversized chair facing the room. He sits and places the pillow on the floor. "Kneel for me, little pet?"

She gets on her knees. "You're asking tonight, sir?"

He spreads his thighs wide and pulls her closer by her leash. "Sometimes I can be polite," he teases. "And sometimes I like watching you choose to listen, to do as I ask. Knowing you choose this... it's a heady thing, pet. Always."

Corinne slips off her heels, her feet aching. She settles against him, her head on his thigh, her hands resting in her lap. She looks up at him with a soft smile. "Well, I wouldn't want to disappoint my sir." Her gaze turns mischievous. "Though maybe you also like to see how well you've trained your pet."

He hums, toying with her leash, smoothing his hand along her hair. "I always enjoy that. You know I love to watch you be so good for me."

She kisses his palm before closing her eyes and relaxing into their sacred space. "Talk to me? Don't let me fall asleep."

"Should I tell you what a triumph you are? How wonderfully you've done with the opening?" He pets her languidly. "Or should I tell you how often you were coveted tonight? How many people eyed you with longing, with desire, with thwarted ideas of possession?"

He toys with the lock on her collar before continuing. "You are entrancing, pet. I'd be lying if I said I wasn't pleased by how their faces fell when they noticed your collar, noticed you were owned."

She smiles despite herself, lulled by his hands and voice. "My darling, possessive sir," she says fondly. "Maybe they just wished they could be a pampered little pet, too."

"Mmm, maybe you're right."

They're quiet for several minutes, Kolya petting her, Corinne finally unwinding after a long week. "You're amazing, you know that?" he asks. "Look at what you've done. This is an unparalleled undertaking, and you managed it perfectly."

She opens her eyes and looks up at him. "I never would've done it without you, sir."

"Oh, I don't know about all that, pet. You would have gotten there eventually." He delicately traces the outline of her lips. "Sometimes it's easier to take such a leap when you know someone will be there to catch you."

She thinks of all the times he's been there to support her, to give her space to try things, to push her limits, to find her fullest self. Corinne can't even imagine what her life would be like without him in it, and she certainly never wants to find out.

"You're always there to catch me, Kolya." She grazes his thumb with a kiss. "That makes everything easier."

He cups her face and bends over to kiss her mouth sweetly. "I will always take care of you, rybka moya," he murmurs. "Always."

And as Corinne rests, kneeling at her sir's feet, she takes comfort in the fact there's not a single doubt in her mind that he means it. That he loves—and will love—her forever.

bonus scene!

Oh? Is Mr. Zaitsev finally going to take my virginity tonight?

And steal it from your future husband, Miss Ryan? I'd like nothing better.

Want to finish the schoolgirl scene mentioned in chapter 35? Go to darcyromaine.com/newsletter-signup or scan the QR code below and sign up to receive "School of Pleasure" for free!

acknowledgments

Darcy and Kat would like to thank everyone who made this book possible:

- Our editor, Nia Quinn. Thank you for always being concerned about the state of Corinne's stockings after crawling on the floor. You're the realest one.
- Megan Barker for creating our beautiful cover and being patient with our many adjustments.
- Cindy, who gave this a heartfelt beta read.
- The friends who graciously answered sensitivity questions.

Thanks to the other half of our Crüe, Em and Cindy (yes, a second mention!). We love you dearly.

Thanks to our friends who have read, shared, and supported our debut story on Kindle Vella and in novel form, especially Suzie, Liz, Jordan, and Lori.

Thanks to our number one fan on Kindle Vella, Jinxie Ekstrom.

Chicago—we spent the most delightful weekend of our friendship in your windy city. We hope we did you proud.

To the unrestricted and unsupervised time we had on the weird and wild corners of the internet: you raised us and led us to many Personal Discoveries, and for that, we offer our eternal gratitude. We wouldn't be the freaks (affectionate) we are today without you.

And thanks to you, dear reader, for giving our Little Debut Novel That Could a chance.

Darcy would like to thank her husband for bugging her for years to be a writer (I love you so much!), her mom for supporting her even though Darcy will never let her read this, and her dog, Hercules, for being the cutest anxiety muppet who has ever lived. She'd also like to thank Kat for being the bestest friend and briancell (no, that's not a typo) mate a girl could ever hope for. I want to share cupcakes with you for always [two hearts emoji].

Kat would like to thank her husband and son for being the best hype-men a girl could ask for as she embarked on this new adventure and her co-workers for being excited for her in the way only fellow Book People can be (even if this book is far too spicy for some of them). Lastly, she'd like to thank Darcy for being the most wonderful twin flame briancell mate (still not a typo) on the planet, someone who understands the devastating effect of a single, "Hey," who loves to add to our cadre of Joint Boyfriends even as we lament our predictability (we love them dark haired and earnest, and that's okay), and the best forever museum date in the whole world. In all the AUs, and AUs of AUs, we will always find each other [two hearts emoji].

Darcy Romaine writes forbidden romance with bisexual characters and enough heat to top the Scoville scale. When she's not penning her latest novel, she enjoys playing D&D, catching Broadway shows, and watching questionable movies with Kat Alexander because a hot actor forced them. She lives in Philadelphia-ish with her darling but devilish husband, a muppet of a dog, and too many cats. Keep up to date with new releases and receive spicy bonus content by signing up for her newsletter at darcyromaine.com.

Kat Alexander is an author of spicy contemporary romance. A West Coast expat, she enjoys music with loud guitars, books with questionable love interests, and time spent with family and friends.

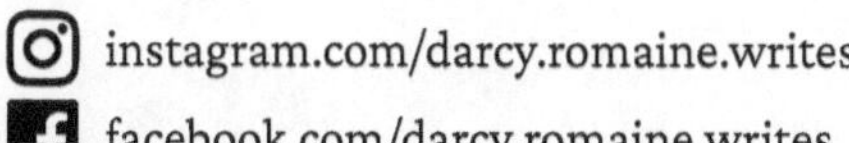

instagram.com/darcy.romaine.writes
facebook.com/darcy.romaine.writes